THE FIVE ARCHES

THE FIVE ARCHES

by

GEORGE BLAKE

COLLINS

14 ST. JAMES'S PLACE LONDON

1947

PRINTED AND MADE IN GREAT BRITAIN BY
WM. COLLINS SONS AND CO. LTD.
LONDON AND GLASGOW

CONTENTS

5

CONTENTS

CHAPTER ONE

THE SUPERINTENDENT ENGINEER

I

TWILIGHT FELL over the Mediterranean, a swift and ominous darkling. What had been but half-an-hour before the lighted stretch of tawny sandhills, green tufts of palms and an occasional white villa along the Egyptian seaboard were now a smear of purple-brown, a vague, blurred line of division between the starred sky over the Delta and the foam-broken turbulence of the Middle Sea.

The ship *Matamoka Maru* of the Nippon Yusen Kaisha was barely an hour out of Alexandria, heading through the Great Pass westward-bound. The hour was just past eight of a night in August, 1937. The Mediterranean, black in the gathering darkness, was stirring to the whip of an offshore wind, and the little vessel had started to pitch into the short waves that rise with surprising ferocity in that landgirt and nearly tideless sea.

It was cold on deck, the night wind treacherous after the heat which, palpable as a ceiling, had lain over Alexandria city and harbour all afternoon. The human population carried by the *Matamoka Maru*, as it might be that of a country townlet or large village, was remotely below decks, secure and heedless within the shell of iron that rode the waves or dashed them aside in crashing curves of spray. The visible ship was but a small constellation of navigation lights, a white upper wilderness of deckhouses, lifeboats and ventilators, wanly lit by caged electric bulbs. Against the crashing of the seas only the hum of fans, sucking air into the oily heat of engine-room and stokehold, suggested the warmth of interior life. Now and again a small and muffled figure crossed the bridge before the black funnel from one side to the other.

Otherwise, the only human figure to be seen in the darkness gathering over the Japanese ship was one which, muffled to the

ears in frieze overcoat, scarf and tweed cap, leaned over the rail
of the boat deck on the port side.

Neither cold nor noise of wind and sea nor his own remoteness
had any place in the consciousness of this individual at that
moment. He was, in fact, regarding the disappearance of Egypt
into the darkness with profound satisfaction. His view of the
blurred coastline and the tufts of palms, now mere wraiths against
the sullen aftermath of sunset, was the reverse of romantic. There,
he was saying to himself, there goes the East for the last time.

Thirty-odd years in the East ; eight times backwards and
forwards from China to Scotland on leave ; and he had had
enough of it. He had now only a soldier's farewell (as he would
have phrased it to the boys in the Club) for the colour and wealth
and smells of it. That stretch of Egyptian coast over there was a
despised symbol, the last extension of the dominion wherein he
had been so long a slave. Man ! it was grand to think that Gib
would be the next landfall, the gateway to the Western Ocean
and the old proper ways of life. You're going home, son, he
addressed himself, though he could hardly utter the words for the
choke of happiness in his throat ; you're going home to Scotland,
for good.

Egypt disappeared, lost in darkness and distance from his
sight. He took to pacing the short and tortuous passage among
lifeboats, scuttles and cowls that was the only promenade possible
on this cluttered upperdeck of the *Matamoka Maru*. This was not,
he reflected with a grin, anything like one of the old Blue Funnel
ships that had carried him on most of his leaves ; nothing at all
like the big P. & O. in which once, on the strength of a thumping
bonus from the Dockyard, he had swanked it with the nobs,
sitting down to dinner every evening in a boiled shirt. But a
retired chap had to watch the pennies, and the Japs, give them
their due, knew how to choose and run a tidy wee ship. Just
4,400 tons, 3,975 horse power on triple expansion, and a mean
speed of fourteen knots—a tidy, economical job, if in a now
outmoded order of shipbuilding.

A tidy job—there it was. The figure of this passenger halted
under a lamp that, below the bridge, shone on the ship's bell and
a brass plate beneath it. The man was thus revealed to be a
stocky person of less than middle height and rather more than
middle age. Such hair as showed below the line of the tweed

cap was white. The face was broad and short as to the nose, with brown eyes that now considered the legend engraved on the plaque. It had for him the validity of a perfect poem, thus :

No. 379
BUILT AND ENGINED
by
TOD & BANNERMAN, LTD.
GARVEL
1908.

Clyde-built. The *Matamoka Maru* was no chicken, but the stuff was in her ; material and workmanship alike were of the best. Those reciprocating engines below still turned as sweetly as ever they did, like a sewing-machine, only mellowing in perfection with use and age. The thought gratified the lonely passenger, and with his aesthetic pleasure there mingled a pride, so profound that the brown eyes flooded with emotion to see that homely title in print—Tod & Bannerman.

He belonged there ; he was out of the same stable as the good little ship. It was in Tod & Bannerman's fitting-shop that he had started apprentice engineer, a wee laddie of barely fourteen, away back in the Nineties, and from there that he had passed, fourth engineer in the old *Erica*, to the eastern adventure now nearing an end. It was a real bit of Home.

He turned away, and the butt of his Manila cigar went over-side in a parabola of fire. The increasing cold of the night was palpable now ; beyond the small, heaving island of the ship was only a noisy, dark welter of seas. He turned down a hooded companionway abaft the slowly swaying funnel and re-entered the warm world of the ship's interior, clotted with Japanese smells. Only a few of his fellow-travellers were seated round the tables in the bar, and he ignored them, his only concession to form being an unbuttoning of his frieze overcoat and the loosening of the knot in his scarf. The tweed cap remained on his head, as if it were the defiant symbol of British indifference to the East and its denizens.

Behind the bar proper, under a bright light, stood the white-jacketed Japanese steward, the flat, grinning face like the creation in old ivory of a comic artist. It gave you the idea that the black hair and the white teeth had been stuck on as afterthoughts or improvements on a toy-maker's dream.

"Vlisky-soda, Mis' Clam, pliss?" the steward greeted him in falsetto.

"Water," said the passenger gruffly. "I've told you before."

That was these Japs all over. They got hold of an idea, like the whisky-and-soda business, and made it into a rule, governing all their Occidental contacts. They never got round to the back of a problem. He had no use for the Japanese. Not like the Chinese, who were wise, humorous and straight. You never knew what the Nips were getting at behind those grinning teeth of theirs; he'd wipe the grin off their flat faces if he had his way. John Chinaman was about right when he called them monkeys. They would make a lot of trouble in the East before they were finished, that lot. They were making enough already in Manchuria and China, if it came to that.

The man in the tweed cap rehearsed these views in his mind without passion but with profound conviction. That was why he kept his cap on in the bar, asserting his independence as the only Briton, among just a few low-caste Europeans, on this bit of Japanese territory. That was why he turned his back on the eager grin of the barman and, still standing, sipped his nightcap with deliberation. If he had been forced by prudence to travel nearly native in a third-class ship, he was still going to keep the Old Country's end up against the Nips, who would insult you with their very grin if you gave them an inch of rope. He had said his soldier's farewell to the East, Far, Middle and Near, but he would still maintain the independence of the West. He was the man who was going Home, not this teethy baboon who knew or thought so little of Scotch whisky that he would drown its goodness in a bubble of chemicals. It was the English in India who had started this confounded fashion.

The passenger finished his peg, replaced the glass on the bar, nodded curtly to the obsequious oval of ivory behind it, and went below to his stateroom, well forward under the bridge on B deck.

As he closed and locked the door behind him he enjoyed a complete change of mood. This was his bit of Home, his Home from Home. Here he was shut of the little Yellow Men, for he had long ago put the fear of God into his steward, an elderly near-Eskimo from the Kuriles in any case and not one of those grinning Police narks the Army was insinuating into every department of Japanese life. With conscious enjoyment he stripped to shirt and trousers and slipped on a dressing-gown in heavy blue silk ; he exchanged his black shoes for a pair of heel-less red slippers with swansdown lining.

The cabin, though one of the best in the ship, was small by big liner standards. With an engineer's interest in these matters its occupant had carefully measured it with the two-foot boxwood rule he carried in a special pocket on his hip.

Fourteen feet by twelve he made it, with a slight taper forward near the bulkhead, where the wash-basin was, conforming nicely to the moudling of the ship towards the bows. (Trust Tod & Bannerman for a knacky job !) That wash-basin, the cot with its gilt rails, and a sort of wardrobe-cum-writing desk built against the after-bulkhead would have given any woman the feeling of overcrowding in her sleeping apartment, but this lone traveller had further cut down the available space by filling every corner, even under the cot and the wash-basin, with a remarkable collection of trunks, packing cases, cartons, cylindrical containers in zinc, and mere parcels wrapped in sacking. He was not the man to entrust his treasures to the Baggage Master of a Japanese ship. The little devils would have them opened and examined and, maybe, rifled while, only an hour out of harbour, the Captain was nodding and grinning and directing complimentary hisses at you over the dinner table.

The impedimenta in this cabin confessed at once the identity of the lonely British passenger. A great brown trunk in wood, clearly the repository of its owner's reserve wardrobe and smelling powerfully of eastern sandalwood, bore on its lid in white lettering the legend :

JOHN R. CRAM

SUPERINTENDENT ENGINEER

Kwanghai & Shangchuan Dockyard Co., Ltd.

If he had chosen to open a yale-locked cash-box within a padlocked strong-box, it would have been seen from his passport that the Foreign Office knew him as Mr. John Rolland Cram, born at Garvel, Scotland, on the 28th of October, 1877 ; height

5 ft. 7 in. ; colour of eyes, brown ; colour of hair, black. If he had cared to display certain personal papers in a pigskin folder under the cash-box it would have been revealed that he was used to sign himself in the old-fashioned way, in round, bold, old-fashioned handwriting, as " Jno. R. Cram."

Now in his slippers in his own stateroom, Mr. Cram considered his belongings and his own condition with lively pleasure. He had uprooted himself from the East, and a large proportion of his worldly goods were here in his own cabin with him, going Home. With the liveliest pleasure he anticipated the distribution among his relatives of the gifts he had carefully chosen, each marked off on a list—fine tea-sets from Osaka for the married womenfolk, boxes of cigars for the men, bolts of stiff Canton silk for the likely brides within his family circle, a big bottle of green Kajaput oil to be divided as occasion might arise, whether as an embrocation or a hair lotion ; watches, cigarette cases in antimony and the like for the young men. If he had forgotten any of the younger folk, and he could not be sure, there was in reserve a rare store of those engaging trinkets to be picked up dirt-cheap anywhere East of Suez. And he had always a cheque-book.

That was the queer thing, as Mr. Cram saw it ; that his knowledge of the family circle he was about to re-enter was only on paper, so to speak. The fixed points within it were few surviving adults of his own generation, and he could not for the life of him be quite sure about the names, ages and identities of the children they had fathered or mothered. Even the personalities of some of the in-laws were apt to get mixed in his memory.

That was the way of it when you were past fifty. When he was home last, in '27, he had spent half his leave in hospital with recurrent malaria, and the boys and girls of the next generation were to him thereafter just a rabble of noisy brats, most of them needing a good box on the side of the head or their backsides well skelped. But the womenfolk had been industrious in writing him, and a fairly exact picture of the spreading family tree had developed in his mind ; he believed himself to have a reasonably firm grasp of the social situation he was about to meet. Anyhow, he was going Home, and the heart of a rather lonely and ageing man swelled to envisage the pleasure his gifts would bring.

Aye, it was an awful thing age ! It had its recompenses of wisdom and tolerance and patience, but it was frightening sometimes to think of so much time spent, so much time wasted, time always passing. There was nothing to be done about it, but, man ! even a sensible, engineering sort of chap could feel a bit sad, with that feeling of things slipping away when your spirit wanted to believe that they were only beginning to come into clear prospect.

Mr. Cram filled his last pipe of the day ; he favoured a powerful and distinctly-flavoured flake tobacco, named for occult commercial purposes St. Dominic. (The same small tobacconist back home in Garvel had been sending him his regular monthly consignment for more than thirty years on end, and never a parcel missing. St. Dominic was not a brand to be got in the East through the usual commercial channels. The fact had always conferred on Mr. Cram an agreeable small air of eccentric distinction among the chaps in the Club.) He sauntered across to the little writing-desk set against the after-wall of his cabin and picked up a little picture, an ornament, with a flat and tarnished gilt frame and a hinge at the back to prop it up like a cabinet photograph.

This was a proof of the engraved note of a bank that had been somebody's commercial dream and had, somehow, failed to come into existence. The gothic lettering expressed the promise of the Garvel Ship and Linen Bank to pay to the bearer One Pound sterling on demand. This undertaking was surmounted by a head of the young Queen Victoria within a floral medallion ; below was the conventional figure of Britannia.

The student of economic history would have seen in the thing an interesting and somewhat touching emanation of an age of hopeful expansion, probably the mid-Forties of the Nineteenth Century, but for John Cram the sheet of thick paper, now the colour of coffee with age and exposure to eastern climes, had both an æsthetic and a profound symbolic value. The head of the young Queen was flanked by two miniature drawings, which were indeed exquisite examples of the engraver's art. One, on the left, depicted the classical frontage of the great Customhouse at Garvel as seen from the River, a full-rigged ship and a primitive steamboat with an enormously high smokestack intervening, but nicely separated to display the building in a bright sun at the right angle. The other was of a railway bridge in solid stone spanning a broad thoroughfare, with the shapes of warehouses, masts, a factory chimney, a stretch of estuarine water and the hills on the farther shore faintly limned in the background.

It was this latter picture that specially endeared his odd little possession to John Rolland Cram and had made it the companion of all his travels and sojourns ever since, many years before, he had come on it in a drawer in his Grannie's house when he was clearing up after her death. It displayed to him the essential elements of the scene at Home as he had known it in his childhood and youth ; it depicted a corner of the northern world which— as he was fond of saying when explaining his strange desk ornament to a new acquaintance—he knew like the back of his hand.

His Grannie's cottage had been at the top of the steep street that, in the picture, ran down to the five-arched bridge. The Five Arches, as the townsfolk had come to call that passage under the railway towards the harbours, formed the architectural feature which had first greeted his eyes on stepping over the threshold every morning for many years on end. Schoolboy or apprentice, he had passed through one or other of the Five Arches almost every day, and several times a day at that, until he had swallowed the anchor. He never forgot how surprisingly painful, like the deadening of a shock, had been his emotions when, returning from a voyage in 1900 or thereabouts, he had gone exploring up through the Five Arches to discover that his Grannie's cottage and the byre behind it and the big vegetable garden, out of which his Grannie contrived to make a living as dairywoman and green-grocer combined—with a little home-baking of oatcakes and soda scones when she had time—had been flattened and cleared to take the foundations of the new electric power station.

They were a go-ahead lot, the Town Council, and electricity was the big thing of the future, but it was a pity somehow that the old, kindly things had to go. It was on the same trip that he had seen Daft Sandy Quinn's moulding-shop being all dressed up as a creamery for the Co-op. Everything had to be big . . .

The *Matamoka Maru* lurched to the smash of a seventh wave on her port bow, and Mr. Cram was obliged to subside into the swivel chair bolted to the deck before the desk. From this, his elbows on the flat top, he picked up the valueless pound note in its gilt frame and stared with quite a curious intensity of concentration at the little engraving of the Five Arches.

This was a habit he had found growing on him as age, and

perhaps loneliness, overtook him. He had come to see in that picture of a railway bridge over a shabby enough street in a northern seaport a symbol of the phases of his own life. The indulgence of this fancy gave him a great deal of pleasure and satisfaction, ministering at once to his engineering senses of order and progression and to the romantic instincts that lay beneath these imposed qualities. He had built up on his little curio in its dull gilt frame both a satisfactory synthesis of life as he had known it, and expected it to end, and something like a fairy story. The varying sizes of the arches, and the manner in which the engraver had depicted the fall of sunlight and deep shadow within them, had greatly stimulated Mr. Cram in his imaginative exercises.

For him each arch had come to represent a phase of his mortal voyagings.

Thus the first narrow one on the left, too close against the embankment for traffic to pass—though it had made a champion pirate's den or ship's lazarette when you were a boy—stood for his childhood. In the picture it was flooded by sunlight, with only a hint of darkness under one of its curves ; and that was as it should be. His boyhood had been happy except for certain baffling lags and gaps : such as that he and his sister Beth did not seem to possess a father in the flesh like other children and could count as Mother only a fleeting, distracted, sometimes tearful visitant to his Grannie's cottage. Now the frustrations had ceased to matter, even if their causes were sordid enough. At nearly sixty, Mr. Cram could be easily sentimental over a happy childhood, remembering summer afternoons on the heights of the Broomhill, the nannygoat tethered to the apple tree in his Grannie's garden, and all manner of things rendered mellow and delightful by the years.

The fifth and last arch, on the extreme right of the engraving, hardly interested him. It was almost wholly dark, and he remembered how in the eyes of childhood the actual passage was remote and high, near the top of a steep bank above a retaining wall, and how he had been told by his Grannie that he would surely go to jail or be killed if he dared to venture up there. Wee Johnnie Bell the grocer's bairn had fallen down the slope and over the supporting wall to his death ; so there, let that be a warning.

Now John Cram saw the fifth arch as symbolizing old age and

death, and he took the inevitable prospect calmly. By a careful measurement of the width of the various arches as depicted on the bank note, in relation to the number of years represented by those he had already passed through, he had long ago satisfied himself that he was destined to live to be seventy. A year or two either way did not matter.

The ship was pitching steadily now, with an occasional cork-screw roll thrown in for variety, and John's stocky person reeled as he crossed the stateroom, unlocked a suitcase and from his private bottle poured himself a noggin into the tooth-glass. This was a rare indulgence, confessing the rapt enjoyment with which he was now considering the mystery of life.

His symbolical system, this strange, quasi-mathematical analysis of one man's existence, was working out perfectly to his way of thinking. From the wash-basin he turned to look again at his talisman and concentrated on the features of the second arch, the first to the left of the three wide central arches. Its width represented a longer space of years than the first and fifth ; the brightness of sunlight and blackness of shadow reflected his own conception of the joys, ardours and sorrows of the period.

This was the arch of youth and young manhood.

It wouldn't be just right, John demurred into himself, to call it youth from the beginning. He was only a wee chap of fourteen when he was sent to the engineering ; far too young, as he saw now, to be wakened by his Grannie at five every working day and sent off down the hill in the dark of a winter's morning, as often as not with the winds and rains of the West battering and drenching and chilling him before he got to Tod & Bannerman's gates before the horn went at six o'clock. It was a long day in the hot, oily atmosphere of the fitting-shop for a growing laddie. The meal-hours were too short and too competitive for a child among the journeymen and labourers, decent chaps as they were, in Brannigan's celebrated Eating House for Working Men. In the winter months there was little enough time for a good tea when he got home to his Grannie's in the evening after the horn had gone at half-past five again. It took twenty minutes in the washhouse with soap and soda and Monkey Brand to get the oil and red lead out of his hands, face and neck ; and his Grannie had to make a special boiling of water in the copper.

There was the night school after that, a lot of haflin boys

yawning and dozing over their close mechanical drawings with T-square and protractor on the propped drawing-boards, half of them hardly able to see what they were doing. No wonder a lad dropped into his bed at ten, after a cup of cocoa, as if he had been shot. His old Grannie had always called it co-*co*a in the antique way.

No : it was not good enough, Mr. Cram allowed to himself in his maturity. He would have no truck with all this Socialist nonsense, but the new hours for a working lad, eight to five, were about right in his considered estimation. The dashed thing was that the hard, old system did produce the finest craftsmen in the world. Clyde-built in shipbuilding and engineering ; great work perfectly executed. You couldn't get away from it.

He could not himself regret an hour of that hard time spent. It had taken him places, as the Yankee chaps in the Club used to say. It had helped him to see a good bit of the world, especially in eastern waters. He had sailed with many an interesting skipper, made friends with many a first mate whose least tale of personal experience would make your hair stand on end, messed with a lot of grand lads out of the engineering shops of Clyde, Tyne, Wear, Tees, Mersey and Belfast Lough. He had been close, over ten years of sea-going, to decency, meanness, painful death, heroism, jealousy, joviality—all the things the experience of travel conjures up out of the personality of the plain man. If it had not been for those dragging hours of boyhood in the shops, if it had not been for the stamp of Tod & Bannerman's on him (or so he modestly reckoned) the Dockyard's resident Super at Rangoon would never have offered a chap temporarily on the beach the post of First in the new S.S. *Scarab*, latest and biggest of the Line, 400 feet overall, twin screw, 6,250 gross tonnage, nearly 7000 horse power to his hand.

All that made up the sunlight which flooded the second arch in the picture. That was a grand bit of a man's life when, competent and well-trained, mature but still young, he advanced steadily in his profession, increasing influence nicely offset by increasing responsibility. That was the time when a wise man, having held his horses and taken his fun as he found it by the wayside, looked about him for the right girl and married her.

Anybody who could at that moment have invaded his stateroom unobserved would have seen John Rolland Cram off his

guard, a man enduring once more the emotions of an old but
unforgotten failure. Now he sat on the edge of his cot, his mouth
open, his eyes clouded and unseeing. He was the man who had
failed to choose the right girl.

Lora was the daughter of an American dentist in Victoria,
Hongkong. Pretty as a picture, she was in her early 'twenties,
with all the tricks of innocence and trustfulness her sort could put
on as he might open a valve in the engine-room when the bridge
called for a few more revolutions. Not a man of his own sort in
Victoria or over at Taikoo Bay had dared to hint to him that she
was a bitch, though most of them must have known it. A delirious
fortnight of honeymoon in Japan, a fortnight of settling down in
the nice little house in the Dockyard compound at Kwanghai,
then off on a trip up the Coast ; and when he came back it
was to find that Lora was gone, leaving only a scented, pencilled
note in her large florid handwriting. " Best of luck, Jock ! " she
had written airily ; but she was gone to Singapore with that
Irish doctor who, obliged to resign his R.A.M.C. commission,
had become the almost official abortionist of all the European
communities from Rangoon round to Amoy.

Mr. Cram did not in his maturity condemn Lora. He
blamed himself for having failed to see the sort of girl she was,
utterly unsuited to settle down with a quiet, home-loving sort
of chap like himself. He should have gone Home and chosen a
sensible lass out of a Garvel tenement house or off a Lowland
farm. The failure was his own : one of his few failures in the
normal enterprises of a man's life ; and he had never had the
heart to repair it. No children of his own, no son, only a brood
of dimly-envisaged nephews and nieces.

That accounted for the segment of shadow within the second
arch in the picture on his bank note, but it was all done with now.

John rose from the cot and started to undress. The flow of
his thoughts carried him comfortably into a contemplation of his
middle years. In the engraving this third arch was the widest of
all and the least shadowed, as the artist had seen it. It had been,
in his reasonably modest but not absolutely humble estimation,
the phase of maturity and success. Only inside himself did the
memory of Lora rankle. To his world he was the Superintendent
Engineer of the K. & S., master of six square miles of dockyards,
of the machinery, supplies and staff of a fleet of thirty sea-going

ships, not to mention six tug-boats and an armada of barges and sampans. He was the man with the big salary, all manner of perquisites, and a pensionable future : chairman of the Finance Committee of the Club, a dab hand at the clay-pigeon shooting, and a shrewd and frequent adviser on mainland affairs to the Governor on the Island.

This was the person who now passed, at the age of nearly sixty, from the third to the fourth and second last arch ; this was the man who was going Home for good, now a slightly tubby human being, standing insignificantly in his shirt-tails in a stateroom of an elderly and far from luxurious small liner of the Nippon Yusen Kaisha.

Taking even Lora into account, however, he was not at all displeased with his situation. After all, he had started as the boy from his Grannie's dairy, running up tenement closes with his noisy cans before most folk were awake. He had been the apprentice laddie, pushing in the dark through the gusty rain-storms of West Scotland to get to his work at six in the morning. It was something, surely, to be coming Home as a chap who had done fairly well for himself—and for the Old Country, if you liked to look at it that way.

John Rolland Cram was going Home for good, passing from the third arch to the fourth. In the artist's vision of this phase there was ample sunlight under the keystone, and if the far end was dark, then John accepted it innocently as signifying the inevitable onset of the fatal illness that must come to every man. That promise of sufficient sunlight in his veteran years of leisure was enough. It was to be sunlight on the Firth, with white yachts heeling to the breeze out in the fairway and little waves plashing on the shore at the foot of his garden. How clearly he remembered.

This was the dream he had cherished and elaborated over three decades of time, the necessary comfort of an exile's heart. It had sustained him in grief, loneliness and fear, as when, caught up in the Shanghai troubles and after a beating by the Japanese soldiery, he had waited, locked up with the scum of the Bund, for death at dawn. It had now the clarity of one of those blue-prints that were his professional delight. He was going to buy a seaside cottage with whitewashed walls and a roof of blue slates, a cottage on the shores of the Firth.

There would be a tidy kitchen garden and a high hedge of hawthorn between its back door and the main road and, before its front windows, a rough lawn falling at a gentle slope to the sea wall. There would be steps set into this wall, leading down to a stony beach and a concrete jetty, off which would ride on an endless line a 12-foot rowing-boat, varnished and clinker-built by Smith's of Tighnabruaich, and, beyond that utility craft, an 18- or 21-foot motor-boat, also varnished but carvel-built this time, with a 7-9 horse power Kelvin engine and a speed of, say, seven knots. The rowing-boat would be for pottering about, for offshore fishing and, now and again, a bit of fun at the flounder-spearing over the sandy shallows at the head of the loch. The motor-boat would be for larger adventures on the Firth and, John piously believed, the proper entertainment in picnics and similar outings of his friends and relatives.

A lonely man's fancy had played happily on this theme. To be sure, the cottage would be in one of those wee coastwise hamlets under the Strone. He was confident that he would find in such a place the company of lots of old retired chaps like himself, not necessarily from the East, but of his own sort : veteran master mariners, chief engineers and heads of departments from the up-river shipyards and engineering shops. He saw them all waiting at the pierhead of a morning for the paddler from Garvel to bring the mail and the *Glasgow Herald*.

He had wondered if he should cut rose-plots in the rough lawn running down to the sea, but had gravely decided to wait and see the lie of the land and the set of the prevailing winds. One of his happiest thoughts was that he would buy a sheep to graze and fertilize the lawn : one of those thick-coated blackface ewes with luminously-flecked grey eyes. Who was to keep house for him was a bit of a facer, of course, but John had envisaged a decent, middle-aged widow woman, preferably of the Highlands, and had vastly enjoyed himself, planning a backward extension of the cottage that would give this respectable body a nice room to herself and a decent kitchen to work in. And there would have to be a modern bathroom thrown out at his own end of the house.

The dream could be elaborated endlessly, but at the core of all John's thinking and planning were the ideas of sunlight and peace : sunlight on the waters of home, peace in his heart. In his dream he wrote a poem (a notion that would have vastly amused him) and the theme of it, as of so many lyrics, was love, that love he had borne to his native land through the many years of adventure, trial and success. Now it was about to come true, and his heart was high, so that he hummed a tune as he went about the last offices of the night.

He slipped his upper dental plate into a brass bowl kept for that special purpose, adding a dash of disinfectant fluid from a blue bottle among the several bottles on the shelf above the wash-basin. Then, without any apparent trace of self-consciousness, a wholly commonplace figure in his pyjamas, the pot-belly of advanced middle-age contributing indeed a touch of the ludicrous to his contours, he stood with his eyes closed and the fingers of his left hand resting on the bedside table, and in a clear voice recited the evening prayer he had learned from his Grannie long ago and had never once in many years, in the best times and the worst, failed to say, in an unmistakable West Scottish accent, at the moment of bedding :

> *Now I lay me down to sleep.*
> *I pray Thee, Lord, my soul to keep :*
> *And if I die before I wake*
> *I pray Thee, Lord, my soul to take.*

This ritual observed, Mr. Cram donned a pair of pink, hand-knitted bedsocks, heaved himself between the sheets, switched out the light and fell sound asleep within the minute.

The *Matamoka Maru* lurched onwards through the night. Wary brown eyes in the yellow faces on the bridge conned her progress with the zeal of the imitative.

She was by no means alone on the Middle Sea. Up from behind, an arrogant and high-riding galaxy of lights, came the great P. & O. *Ranee*, the whisky-sodas sparkling in the first-class lounge and hollow-cheeked brigadiers waltzing with hard-voiced *memsahibs* to the air from *The Maid of the Mountains* as provided by the ship's orchestra in the ballroom. Ten miles ahead, and always drawing away from the little Japanese liner, S.S. *Theodosius* of the Blue Funnel, homeward bound from Canton, brushed aside the Mediterranean seas from her slanting bows and, with her high, straight funnel, seemed austerely to suggest that, while all sorts

of foreign parties might make an amateur pass at the business of
seafaring, you had to leave the gist of the matter to a medium-
sized ship owned in Liverpool and built and engined on the
Clyde. Flashy little liners of the Messageries Maritimes crossed
from Marseilles to the North African ports. The narrow seas
between Sicily and Cape Bon were cluttered with slattern tramp
steamers, British, Italian and Greek ; and a C.P.R. liner of some
distinction was cruising from Tangiers to Tunis with a complement of gawping and vociferous nonentities from the suburban
extensions of most of the considerable towns of Britain and
Northern Ireland.

In none of these ships was a more reasonably happy man than
he who, going Home for good, was now sound asleep in the best
of the not-very-elegant staterooms of the *Matamoka Maru*.

2

The approach of Jno. R. Cram to the native shores was a
matter of deep, and in some cases almost agonized, interest to his
relatives at home. Even to young nephews and nieces who had
hardly known him in the flesh this Uncle John from China was
a legendary figure, capable of benefactions delightfully surprising.
He was returning to a people who, while they occupied a whole
range of subtly graduated situations in the order of provincial
society, were almost all and almost constantly aware of the
economic pressures. It was thoroughly believed among them,
although it was seldom even whispered, that Uncle John had
Money.

They were a folk in whom generations of traffic, first with the
West Indies and then with the East, had engendered the simple
faith that gold is to be picked up almost anywhere overseas. The
town, sprawling high and wide over the steep foothills where the
ship-channel merged with the Firth, had sent generation after
generation of sugar refiners, engineers, mariners and shipbuilders
on the business latterly known as Empire-building. The native
breed, with much of the restless Celt in it and an unstable economy
always urging it outwards, was of the kind about which such as
Rudyard Kipling were to make ballads and tales. Its scions were
to be found in the engine-rooms of small ships on African lakes,

among the dank tin-dredgings of Burma, and on the sugar-cane plantations of Queensland. Most of the great mansions of the West End were proudly known by all to have been built out of money made in West Indian sugar or in the building of ships for the famous steamship lines of the world, with just one or two founded on shrewd dealings in Scotch whisky. Almost every boy in that northern seaport, nestling against the wet hills, had the makings of a rare collection of stamps to his hand.

The notions of travel and exile thus circulated as an element in the very blood of the people or were worn as the badge of a regional pride. It was a sentimentality that could blind them to certain grim incidentals to the making of an Empire—to the thought of bleached bones on endless Patagonian plains or of shrunken but well-preserved corpses in snow-shelters up Great Bear Lake way ; to the vision of rows of white stones in military cemeteries all the way from the Khyber to the Deccan ; to the reality of an army of drunkards and wasters, boozing themselves to ignominious deaths in every second dive between San Francisco and Suez ; to the sorry spectacle of an untrained lad fighting a lonely, losing battle against the prairie so effulgently placed in the class of Paradise by the posters of the Canadian Government.

They did not estimate, these innocent people, the sheer loss to themselves of brains and muscle when, in one of the cyclical times of bad trade, a thousand skilled artisans would wait on the Queen's Quay on Saturday mornings for the tenders to take them out to the liners westward-bound across the Atlantic, everybody singing, with the desperate, tragic sentimentality of the Scot, the fine tunes of *Auld Lang Syne* and, still more ironic, *Will ye no' come back again ?* They were least of all educated to see that the Empire their brothers and uncles and cousins had done so much to create was but a ramshackle string of possessions across the surface of a jealous world.

So Uncle John, it was assumed by his kin, was coming home a wealthy man, the potential dynamo of vast and pleasing changes in several drab and all-too-familiar ways of living. It was accepted that a man who could afford to retire to his native land about the age of sixty must possess, not only a good pension, but also substantial savings. And had not Uncle John after all been for years the very pattern of monied generosity ?

If it was not a bolt of fine silk for every bride's wedding-gown, it was a full teaset of the most fragile china for her mother, all the principal pieces duplicated and each piece deliciously packed in bran in its own cardboard box. The small boys of the clan received regularly each year their consignments of Chinese kites, of ferocious colour and enchanting design. Their fathers could count on the Christmas box of 100 Manila cigars, their sisters on a prettily-painted fan, at the least, or a trinket-box in soft Chinese silver. It was known that Uncle John, without asking questions, had put up three hundred by return of post to get the Kilgallon twins, who were only orphan second-cousins at the best, set up in their general store-cum-post office in the remote Galloway village that had been their forgotten father's birthplace.

The range of possibilities was boundless ; and John Rolland Cram had, in fact, unconsciously imposed his personality and importance on several households in his native town of Garvel. He had sent home so many things of even the trivial decorative order that something of the very atmosphere of Kwanghai was reproduced in a number of Scottish homes from tenement flats to semi-detached villas. He had showered on his relatives so many fans, pictures of Fujiyama, ashtrays in antimony, daggers in ivory sheaths and so forth that the plain Scottishness of their abodes was apt to be lost in a welter of *chinoiserie*.

Even as John was turning into his cot in the *Matamoka Maru* on that night of August, 1937, one of his gifts looked down on a scene far beyond the experience of its Japanese originator.

This was a sizeable, framed picture of Fujiyama which, from above the mantelpiece of a tenement kitchen in Garvel and from behind an array of brass candlesticks, china dogs, matchboxes and a vase containing tapers, loomed above the bent back of a man who worked with a stub of pencil and slips of paper at one end of a well-scrubbed deal table. His back was to the fire in the burnished kitchen range, and it would have been seen by anybody entering the kitchen through the door beside the dresser, with its shining crockery and gleaming pot-lids, that the student was a lean person of middle age, the hair thinning on the top between untidy black growths on the side of his head. He was in his shirtsleeves and waistcoat, and though a stud still held the neckband of his khaki shirt together, he wore no collar. He was in his stocking soles, and the big toe of his right foot had burst through his heavy worsted socks in grey.

Close by this man's side a woman bent over the sink, her person occasionally obscured by the soapy steam that rose from the water in which she was kneading a garment with violent motions of her arms and shoulders. When at length she straightened her tired back and held the garment up for inspection it was to reveal a figure as slender as her husband's. When she had rung out the cloth and pulled out the plug and turned her face to the incandescent light above the table she would have been seen to be pretty in a faded, remote sort of way remarkable in the overworked wife of a working man. Her hands were red and glistening with suds, but the strong arms were white and shapely. The grey in her hair mingled sweetly with an original auburn.

"Are you never finished with that nonsense?" she asked.

"Just a tick, Beth," her man replied equably, adding with a twinkle: "Can you tell me will the Rangers beat the Hearts at Tynecastle, or will it be another of these dashed draws?"

"Don't ask me. I wonder you waste your time and your money on this silly gambling."

"A bob a week! And a chap up in the Port got four thousand quid out of Littlewood's the other week."

"I wonder how much you've spent on this rubbish in the last ten years and never got anything back but a silly wee postal order for fourteen shillings."

"Ach, it's a bit of sport!"

These marital exchanges were mild, conventional. They had the passionless quality of custom. Beth Bryden was secure in the knowledge that Davie, her husband, was a well-doing working chap, a foreman blacksmith with Tod & Bannerman's, and not one of those drinkers. If the man was daft on sport, men were like that. She knew exactly for what cherished purpose he dreamed of winning a small fortune through the weekly gamble on what he called his "coupoon"; and while she wholly disapproved the object of his dream she did not, being a sensible and modest woman in whom the doctrines of Calvin were deeply ingrained, believe that good money could ever come out of any wagering and therefore did not allow the possibility to trouble her.

She hung her washing on a pulley let down from the ceiling, wound the alarum clock on the mantelpiece, filled a black kettle and set it on the hob, drew the curtains of the big kitchen bed and turned down the covers.

"Time we were having a sleep," she observed. "I've a rare blanket washing to-morrow."

"Saturday's a daft-like day for a blanket washing," suggested Davie.

"It's the day I get you and Curly out the house and away to your silly football match and lets me and Addie get on with the work. Are you never finished yet?"

"Ach, we'll just let it go like that. I'll run out to the post wi't. Best of luck, ma bonnie wee coupoon!"

He kissed the form with a comically boyish gesture and folded it into its envelope. Then he tilted his chair back, his feet against the boot-rack, and stared across the room at the gleaming pot-lids.

"So John'll be home in a fortnight," he said.

"That's what his letter says," Beth agreed, releasing her body from the clasp of corsets of apparently formidable strength.

"I'll bet you he's made a rare packet of money outby," mused Davie fondly.

Beth's head came swiftly through the decorous, scalloped neck of her flannel nightdress, and her grey eyes rested firmly on her husband's handsome profile.

"If he has," she snapped, "he's worked for it, and he'll need it for his old age. My, Davie Bryden, if I ever hear you say a word to my brother about money I'll . . . !" Her accusing eye fell to his feet. "And see you and change these socks in the morning, or I'll know the reason why."

"All right, all right, lass! Keep your hair on," returned Davie easily, rising from his chair. "Where's ma slippers? I'll away down to the pillar-box. I'll no' be a jiffy."

But Beth was already in her first childlike sleep when he returned after a crack at the close-mouth with young Willie Blackadder, who had been at the Dogs out at the Potteries and had such a story of fallible fancies and successful hazards to tell as Davie Bryden could not for the life of him resist, not that he had ever tumbled to the Dogs himself. As he undressed with a delicate care for his wife's peace and screwed out the gas to slip into the great bed beside her his fancy played more happily with the Palmerston's chances against the Gaels in the First League to-morrow. He planned that he and Curly would make

for that high range of the terracing to the East of the stand
whence, he had firmly decided, the best over-all views of the
game were to be had.

3

Six miles away, in the kitchen of a small upland farmhouse
on the edge of the Bent Moor below the Scourie, a woman sat
alone, a letter in bold handwriting on her lap. It was signed
Jno. R. Cram and had reached her only an hour before, having
been thoughtfully picked up at the village Post Office a mile
away and handed in by the shepherd at Meikle Scourie on his
way home with a freshly-charged accumulator.

The woman, who was dark but looked tired and older than
her probable years, had wept over the epistle. A large tear had
fallen on the page to spread and smear the word " home " in one
of its flowing lines. There was nothing in the letter of personal
sentiment to justify the tears. The writer had addressed her as
" Dear Effie " and decently subscribed himself " Your sincere
friend " ; and that was precisely the point of bitterness for the
lonely woman. It had come to her, a more or less formal intimation of the writer's return home for good, in her capacity of
widow of his cousin, Sandy Rolland, tenant of this mountainy
farm of Corsewellhill.

But there had been the day, long ago, when John Cram had
been fell fond of Effie Templeton, the forester's daughter at Bent
House, and she, had she but realized the profundity of the fact,
had been fell fond of him. He had come to Corsewellhill from
Garvel each week-end to walk with her and woo her and give
her his quaintly simple devotion, and she had been turned in the
head by her own power over a serious boy who was only an
apprentice engineer ; and it had been almost in abuse of that
power that she had accepted the cruder, boisterous approaches
of his cousin, Sandy Rolland, tenant farmer in Corsewellhill. It
was queer how a girl, as flighty and foolish as they are made,
could be taken by the promise of a sure position and of a house
and fireside of her own. It had seemed so much to become the
mistress of Corsewellhill.

Ah ! she had been young and unwise ; and big Sandy Rolland

turned out to be not much more than a drunken brute, so that now she was lonely and sorry for a mistake made in vanity and pride by the silly, pretty girl she had been thirty years ago. Nor had she ever been able to forget John Cram and his simple devotion, his young seriousness ; and now John Cram was a big man coming Home from the East with a fortune, and she was now no more than his sincere friend, the recipient of a nearly formal letter from her deceased husband's cousin. That was why the tear had fallen on the single sheet of foreign notepaper. A sincere friend he might well be, but it was too late for love.

She started suddenly in her chair, her head up and turned towards the window, her mouth open a little in alarm. The night wind had risen in the always surprisingly cold ferocity with which late August can intimate the sure coming of the winter, and it might have been the whip of a gust under the blue slates in the roof. Tam, her only boy, was away on the other side of the hill at Tullybog and, if she knew his father's son, would lie deep and long in the hay in the shed with that hoyden of an orra lass over there. (It would be a bad day for Effie Templeton when he brought to Corsewellhill that trash with her powder and paint and hair she had got bleached in Garvel at dear knows what expense !) Her daughter Mary was to be at the W.R.I. in the village, and it would be an hour yet before she came up the loan from the Bent road in the oxter of young Shields from Penilee.

The woman relaxed a little as she thought of these things, then started again as she thought to hear a scattering of the gravel that surrounded the dwelling house on its little terrace above the Laigh Park, as the four-acre field before the steading had been immemorially called. It would be Him again, Him from the Quarry. God ! Would he never leave a weary, done woman alone ? Yet she was too proud to confide in her son, too timid to speak to Macdougall, the policeman, The dark, urgent, mad man from the Quarry held her in terror.

Swiftly she ran over in her mind the tale and order of her nightly precautions. Yes, every door was locked, every window on the ground floor snibbed. She had locked from the inside even the door of the room in which she sat alone, had drawn the curtains behind the blue linen blind, and lowered the wick in the lamp until the flickering of a dying fire was brighter at moments than the glow from within the bowl of opaque glass.

She heard the noise again ; it would be from round the corner outside the big door between the barn and the kitchen. The sudden screech of an owl brought her heart so near her mouth that she was nearly sick with fright. The momentary silence thereafter had the effect of somebody putting a heavy knee on her chest and lungs and pressing, pressing. Then came the turgid, brutal footsteps on the deep gravel, thumping it and scattering it at once. Round the corner of the house ; approaching the window ; stopping. Then, expected but terrifying, his knock on the window-pane, a peremptory rapping of his knuckles : the warning of one who means to be master.

She tried to shrink inside her body. She did in fact crouch back within the wings of the padded chair as if that might delude Him into believing that the household of Corsewellhill was in bed and asleep. But she knew that he knew exactly the movements of Tam and Mary, spying over miles of country-side from the lip of the Quarry as the sun set and the dusk came down. She tried to hold her breath.

The big knuckles knocked on the pane again and nearly forced her to proclaim in a high, wavering cry her defeat by fear. She was held to reason only by her familiarity with the man's ritual terrorism. Some night he might at last seek to break in on her, but his crazy wooing had for long gone according to a rhythm— the trying of the big door, the crunching on the gravel round the gable, the two separate knocks on the glass. The paralyzing moment was on her now, a long tension that suddenly relaxed as the feet moved away. Her breathing resumed its freedom in a flurry of gasps. The footsteps passed along the terrace by the kitchen garden and suddenly ceased. That was his invariable way : a leap over the low wall into the Laigh Park and away across the fields to the darkness of the Quarry Glen.

After a time she dared to screw up the wick in the lamp and fill the room with a brighter primrose glow ; she threw a last log on the fire. She thought of the farm tasks to be done and of the rising at five for the milking. But still she could not move from her chair or even pick up the *People's Friend*, so thoroughly was she held in an exhaustion of reaction from the alarm. She felt herself beaten, a prisoner.

For more than a year now the Man from the Quarry had haunted her. He was near mad, she knew, but men like

Macdougall the policeman and her own Tam, in their lazy country way, saw him only as a sort of comic character, a wee thing soft in the head ; and she had to carry alone the knowledge that he lusted darkly even after her ageing body and—perhaps, poor demented soul !—even more desperately the comfort and security he fancied to abide in Corsewellhill.

She saw no way of escape. It would be good if, when Tam brought that trash of a girl from Tullybog home as his wife and Effie Templeton's days at Corsewellhill were finished and done, she could slip away and find herself a wee room in Garvel. But who was to take her in and give her a roof over her head, for it would have to be an act of charity ? A hard-working woman was never anything but the bondslave of a poor hill farm.

Her unhappy, bewildered mind turned to John Rolland Cram and his letter. At the least, he had remembered her, telling her that he was coming home. Never mind that marriage of his ; it had given him little enough comfort. Perhaps, she allowed herself to think, conscious like a girl of the blush that heated her cheeks, two old sweethearts who had made little enough of their love affairs might in the autumn of life, without the storms of passion that afflict the young, even just for the sake of comfort and company and mutual service on the economic level, form a cordial and duly contented partnership.

The wistful train of thought was broken, but pleasantly, by the unlocking of the door of the boilerhouse behind, and the clatter of tackety boots on the concrete floor. That was Tam returning through the close and coming in by the back as the old custom of Corsewellhill ordained. The rule had been laid down soon after their marriage by her man, Sandy Rolland, so that she would know when he was safely home from a night with his friends at the Railway Tavern in the village. She was happy to hear the sounds of a bin being opened, of a barrow trundling into the stable. That was Tam taking a feed of mashlum to Daisy, the big Clydesdale mare in foal to Dunure Professor.

Effie Rolland passed through the cold outbuildings and stood at the boilerhouse door, looking across the close to the loom of dim light in the stable.

" Is that you, Tam ? " she called, her voice trembling a little.

" Who did ye think it was ? "

Her son slammed the stable door behind him and came across

the close, the lamp swinging in his hand and dramatizing the movement of his heavy farmer's body.

" Did you see Mary anywhere ? " she asked.

" I'm no' paid to look after Mary," he retorted roughly. " Could ye no' go to yer bed and stop botherin' ? "

She turned indoors away from him. He was a big, coarse contemptuous man like his father, but he was her first-born and it was her fate to love him. In the cold, stone-paved dairy she emptied out of a churn the opaque water with which it had been scalded. There would be time in the morning to wash it out properly. But she wished that Mary could come home and complete the triangle within which now lay her only illusion of security.

4

After eleven o'clock that evening the electric light was still burning in the upstairs and downstairs front rooms of a semi-detached villa in Garvel. This dwelling stood in a quiet road high up on the hill and nearly a mile to the westward of the canyon of tall tenement houses, in one of which Davie and Beth Bryden had now been for more than an hour asleep.

The soulless incandescent gas-light of a street lamp, its civic usefulness half-lost amid the branches of one of the limes that pleasantly bordered the roadway, gleamed on a tidy front garden, of which the little plots, oblong and circular, revealed in thin drilled arrays of lobelia, alyssum, echeveria and begonia the sure and typical touch of the suburban jobbing gardener. It also revealed beyond the ten yards or so of garden enough of a fabric in sandstone, with a high peaked roof and rather ambitious bow-windows, to suggest to any passer-by sufficiently knowledge-able in such matters that it contained some five or six rooms with the usual offices in a reasonable degree of adequacy ; that it was a sound speculative builder's job of 1904 or thereabouts, before everything had to be put up in brick and roughcast and tiles ; and that it would fetch some £850 at the prices prevailing in this year of grace, 1937.

This semi-detached villa, "The Neuk" according to the whimsically-lettered nameplate on the tall, iron gate, housed at

that moment a man who, its owner, was in fact speculating
morosely on the maximum market value of his property. His
estimates were so confused and so harried by other distracting
elements of his financial condition that, in one explosion of wish-
fulfilment, he reckoned that " The Neuk " might fetch as much
as £1100, especially if it was true that Imperial Chemical
Industries thought of setting up a factory on Nellie's Brae. Mr.
Daniel Rolland had for English money and the power thereof an
almost religious awe.

He was a man of an appearance that exactly matched his
eccentrically lugubrious personality. According to the custom of
small places he had been given the nickname of Dismal Dan, and
as with most nicknames, as with folk songs and ballads, it possessed
the deadly, curt quality of rightness. He was a man not yet old,
by any means, but as he sat in a completely lack-lustre state in
his chair, his face grey and sour, his eyes heavy and dully resentful,
his lower lip thrust out with the sullen truculence of a scolded
child, he appeared to bear a timeless burden. That face was long,
the hair above it cropped short though still freshly brown ; and
the illusion as of age, or as of one carrying an inherited and
intolerable responsibility, was oddly heightened by a ridge or
range of short, thick hairs which, escaping the normal sweep
of his razor, ran from above his ears to the ends of an indeterminate
moustache, there to mingle with long hairs growing out of the
nostrils of a deceptively bold nose.

Eleven hundred pounds, Daniel Rolland was saying to himself.
Subtract five-fifty for the bond held by that old skinflint, Fairrie
the builder, and that left another five-fifty. It was always something, reflected Dismal Dan, but it wouldn't do. It would take
a couple of thousand to get his business of ironmonger on its feet.
His slender faith in continuing solvency now resided in the
approaching return of his cousin, John Cram, from the East.
John would be rolling in money and had just the right sort of
experience, not to mention good connections ; and it would be
a nice thing, Daniel reflected charitably, for John to have something to keep him interested.

At this point a long and dismal whinnying of flatulence
sounded from within his person, and Mr. Rolland gasped a belch.
There it was again. He was a martyr to indigestion and cherished
the belief that his interior was riddled with gastric ulcers. His

health did not give him a chance to put his best into the business, and he would even allow to himself that the morose manner his chronic acidities had imposed on him made it all the more difficult to attract and retain customers. When John came home and took up a share, he would have a rest and try the cure at Harrogate. He even toyed with the idea of undergoing the X-ray examination and the inevitable subsequent Operation that were at once his dream and his secret fear. Papa's Operation was a legendary prospect in the household, ranking in dramatic promise with the day, endlessly postponed, when the Twins would set out on their first visit to London.

On the other side of the gas fire sat Dismal Dan's wife, busy with her needle on a garment of more intimate frivolity than the casual observer might have related to her apparent maturity. Lily Rolland was in fact a well-preserved woman with a bold and shapely face under dark hair. The exuberance of her torsal development was offset by the neatness of her ankles and legs, which she was apt to display at some length ; and a worldly man with a shrewd eye for such things would have rated her amorous possibilities rather high. Her manifest vitality and sanguine spirit, even in the silence that was diversified only by the hissing of the gas, were in quite fantastic contrast to the aura of enervated gloom which hung, like a mist, round the personality of her mate.

She heard the whine of his flatulence and the sad, self-pitiful puff of his eructation, and she threw a hostile glance at the dull grey face with the lines of hair across the cheeks. It was only a flash of hostility, for she had learned the uselessness of anger, even hysterics, against the monstrous strength of his egocentricity.

Miserable old brute ! Lily Rolland was saying into herself with ferocity. Contemptible, selfish, lazy lump of imaginary illness. No fun nor even tenderness, in bed or out of it ; so lost in the bleak bogs of his own fecklessness, so hostile to normality in human relations, that he was rapidly running a sound family business into bankruptcy and herself and her children out of all the comforts and hopes she had entertained for them. All this talk about his wonderful, rich cousin, John Cram ! Lily did not think, from what she remembered of him on his last visit when the children were babies, that John Cram would be such a fool as to bolster up in business, with good money, the monstrosity who gloomed in his miserable aloofness in the armchair opposite hers. The best chair, too.

At the same time, Lily Rolland's mind played intensely with the possibilities of John Cram's legendary fortune. She could not think precisely how it would operate in her own case. If she played her cards properly, being nice and friendly and hospitable and coy all at once, with a wee hint here and there, there might be a squirrel coat in it. Braunstein's had some lovely grey ones, and the price wouldn't really be much to a rich man from the East or terribly greedy on her own part.

To do her justice, however, Lily Rolland was much more concerned to think how John Cram's money might help Cha and the Twins, her children. If the Twins could only be sent to Willy Klein's School for Rhythm Pianism in London ; if somebody would take a real interest in Cha, and encourage him, and buy him a partnership in something—well, then, through the success of her children, a mother might be liberated from a tyranny of dullness. Get going up to London to see the Twins and perhaps make a romantic friendship with a man in one of those London hotels, and he asking the number of your room.

These agreeable dreams were suddenly shattered by an outburst of noise from the room above. It proceeded from a piano played with precision and a certain amount of violence by four hands. The air was that of a song from *Rose Marie*, and if the choice reflected a somewhat imperfect taste, it could be heard that the syncopated arrangement was clever and the technique of the players adequate, if a thought relentless. The attack was bold in the extreme, the tempo unflagging. Altogether, the racket with which the pianists filled that suburban street at ten past eleven of a late August evening was a surprising breach of provincial convention.

"O dear ! O dear !" groaned Dismal Dan Rolland, putting a tired hand to an agonized forehead.

"The Twins have got to do their practising, haven't they ?" retorted his wife sharply.

On a long stool before the piano in the upstairs drawingroom, which was rather confusedly but gaily furnished, with a salmoncoloured cretonne predominating, the nineteen-year-old Rolland Twins sat rigidly upright and pounded away in their earnest labours.

They were the authentic twins of tradition in being singularly alike in appearance and exactly alike in dress. They had inherited from their mother a certain dark and petulant prettiness, and now they were attired in a sort of uniform of blue serge skirt, white knitted jumper with polo collar, and green tie, knotted in the masculine way. A green matching ribbon on each dark head diversified the ringleted results of elaborate and no doubt expensive barbering. The difference of individuality was acknowledged only by a string of green glass beads round one slender neck and an amber string round the other.

The Twins jointly bore the air of deliberate arrangement, of careful production ; and so it was in fact. It had for two years now been accepted by themselves and their mother, with whom the glad idea had originated, that their talent for the precise playing of popular music should be professionally developed. They were to be the Rolland Rhythmic Twins, stars of the concert hall, the vaudeville stage or the wireless studio.

The name had been quite solemnly discussed and fixed. But for the gloomy penuriousness of their father, or so Mama had convinced them, they would now be studying under Willy Klein in fabulous London. As it was, Mama had squeezed just enough out of Papa to get them a fortnightly lesson from Skeets Macloy, band leader of the Bushrangers at the Ballroom in Kempock, and this master had assured them, in an idiom which sounded to them both apt and natural, that they were sure going places. Then, when Uncle John came home from China and heard them play, the dream of London and Willy Klein would almost certainly come true. That was why they now practised so assiduously, with indeed so much pathetic intensity. Mama said Uncle John had loads of money, and the Twins did not doubt their power to deserve its aid.

As Lily Rolland listened carefully, happily and with a completely sincere concern for the future of her daughters, there broke into their music a highly discordant note. The Twins had passed from their first piece, by a series of vehement modulations, to *The Blue Danube*, Beryl at the top end of the piano imposing some sparkling decorations of the melody enunciated lower down the keyboard by Sybil, her senior in age by exactly 43 minutes. Now, however, the tinkling charm of the Strauss waltz, like a happy play of windbells, was most grossly penetrated

and overborne by a bellowing from a wireless set turned on
to nearly its full strength. It gave out a melody with its own
enchantment but in utterly intolerable contrast to the stylized
charm of Nineteenth Century Vienna. That quiet suburban
street in West Scotland heard the negroid nostalgia of the
Southern States of North America assault Europe in *Begin the
Beguine*.

"Dear, dear, dear!" wailed Daniel Rolland. "That's too
much!"

"It's that rascal Cha," his wife agreed, bundling her sewing
on the table beside her. "I'll sort him."

The intrusion of the lugubrious but haunting air on the
Twins' brisker performance had meanwhile brought the latter
to a stop in a flurry of sharp, staccatto discords in the upper
registers of the piano. Beryl was always the snappier Twin—so
temperamental, her mother explained it to sympathetic friends—
and now she turned on the stool, her lips thin with anger, her
eyes hostile, and threw a shrill protest towards the backward part
of the room.

"You're just a dirty cad, Cha, and you were never anything
else."

"My tune's as good as yours, and a dashed sight better
played." The voice of their tormentor drawled and teased and
sneered all at once.

"If you don't put that thing off at once," blazed Beryl, her
tone thinning into virulence as the muscles of her mouth, tongue
and throat contracted to the touch of acid secretions, "I'll go
downstairs this minute, and I'll tell my mother——"

"Aw, put a sock in it!" her brother advised her.

These exchanges, uttered in the flat-vowelled and even
truculent intonations of West Scotland, suggested a certain
gracelessness in Lily Rolland's children, and there was decidedly
about the youth called Cha, short for Charles Stuart Macaulay
Rolland after Lily's father, a head sorter in the Post Office, the
look which would have suggested to a sergeant of the Guards
the need for a brisk, bracing course of drill.

The boy was sufficiently personable as to facial appearance,
if with a faint suggestion of weakness about the mouth that was
hardly corrected by a smear of dark hair above his lips. The
shoulders of his double-breasted jacket in light grey were

enormously padded to suggest breadth, but the physical reality beneath them distinctly drooped, and the deep thrust of his hands into their pockets had the quite eccentrically wide legs of his trousers sagging over shoes of brown suede. Even while he exchanged insults with his sister, these feet executed a dexterous little dance to the tune of *Begin the Beguine*. Mr. Jack Buchanan was one of this young man's idols.

Lily Rolland's appearance on the scene of strife was brisk, decisive and conciliatory all at once. She was a woman who had been forced to lead, as it were, a double life. For one part of her spiritual existence she was in the continuous state of sombre hostility towards her husband, while the remainder was passed in the sunshine of her children's company. (" Me and my three chicks are good pals," was one of her gambits in congenial company.) Her ambition for them, whatever the level of taste it occupied, was the only projection of her personality now permitted to her by circumstance ; and this vigorous, cheerful Mama of theirs did in fact command the affection and respect of Cha and the Twins.

" Now, now, you three ! " she cried, bustling in upon the acrimonious situation. " That'll do the lot of you. You learn to keep your temper, Miss Beryl, or you'll be in for a lot of trouble one of these days. Cha, switch that thing off at once. You're a bad boy to stop the Twins practising. You'd better stop altogether, the lot of you, or you'll have your father up."

Having thus swiftly disposed of the quarrel, and ignoring the pout of Beryl's underlip and the faint groan that was wrung from Cha by the mention of his father, she presented her children with a bright proposition.

" What about us having a wee supper to ourselves up here ? I baked a bit of gingerbread this afternoon—lovely, with lots of raisins. Cocoa for you two girls. I suppose it's Camp Coffee for you, Cha, though how you can sleep on that stuff——? Now, keep quiet and I won't be a jiffy."

She left them with a smile, having succeeded as many a time before in subduing the hostilities that so frequently broke out among her far from reticent offspring.

" Good old Ma ! " said Cha, and then facetiously addressed his sisters. " Never mind, chicks. When good old Uncle John rolls up from China with the doings you'll be off to London and rattling the ivories till you're blue in the face. Thank God I won't have to listen any more ! "

" It would be a good thing if Uncle John would get you a decent job," retorted Sybil, whose temper was rather more sullen than that of her sister.

Cha executed one of his lissome, silent *pas seuls*.

"Don't worry about the job, Faceache," he counselled the older Twin. " I know what I want out of old man Cram. Know that wee car of Jerry Martin's ? M.G. Nine : a beauty. Sixty an hour as easy as kiss-me-hand. That's my little game, and next year's model, too. You watch me."

" You've a right neck on you," said Beryl, but not without admiration of her brother.

Waiting downstairs for the kettle to boil, Lily Rolland was thinking of her firstborn. Now and again the problem of his future would occur to disturb her, a small cloud over her sanguine spirit. It was a crying shame that in Cha's last year at school the Leaving Certificate papers had been so difficult and unfair, that he never got started as a real apprentice with that old snob Aitken, the C.A.—keeping a clever boy on as a junior clerk, and him nearly twenty-one ! It was no use expecting a miserable old skinflint like his father to do anything, but we'd see when Uncle John came home from China. Lily could hardly conceive that any right man could fail to be taken with a nice, bright boy like Cha. Full of ideas, if he had only a wee bit capital behind him.

5

The *Matamoka Maru* steamed on through the night, pitching more and more wildly into the increasingly steep seas. Even a traveller so experienced as Mr. John Rolland Cram was wakened, from midnight onwards, by an occasional movement or noise of unusual violence—the vertiginous thud of the whole mass of the ship as she came down from the peak of one wave on top of its follower ; the slither of one of his heavy boxes across a foot or more of his stateroom floor. This equable and happy man, however, was never thoroughly roused by the commotion that so greatly alarmed most of his fellow-travellers and invariably dozed over again, modestly unaware of the thoughts, indeed the passions, that so many of his own folk at home were in that moment projecting towards him.

If he could, fully awake, have easily appreciated the interest of his closer relations in his return, as his own return to their firesides was of passionate interest to himself, he could never have guessed that one ageing person on an exalted level of society sat long after midnight in a deep armchair in the library of a country house and considered, with some dry amusement but not a little alarm, the approach of something like a family ghost.

Mr. Tertius Troquair Bannerman was a party of distinguished appearance, even if a close analyst of his features would have discerned a streak of inner remorselessness, if not cruelty, in the long, convex curve of his upper lip from the root of the bold nose to the thin upper lip, an untidy auburn-grey moustache intervening. He was a gentleman of sixty-odd years, tall and loosely built, and he wore his dinner jacket and the tie over his soft shirt-front with just that picturesque and elegant looseness which is, in the English tradition, one hall-mark of the cultured well-to-do. One might well imagine this figure adorning (as indeed it had often enough done at decent intervals) the Senior Common Room of a smallish but distinguished Cambridge college.

Mr. Bannerman was really a not uncommon product of the Industrial Revolution, one of those intellectual and æsthetic sports, in the genetic sense, thrown up by a family of engineers in the fourth generation and cushioned by quantities of inherited and acquired wealth so considerable that high taxation could only corrode the shell of it.

His paternal great-grandfather had been the village blacksmith of Killogie Old Cross, the farming parish of which Tertius Troquair Bannerman, sitting in the library of Killogie Old House, was now the laird. The blacksmith's second son, his grandfather, had gone down from the backblocks of the country into Garvel to follow fortune in the new engineering, and in the roaring 40's had formed with his workmate, Finlay Tod (third son of the skipper of a coal gabbart) the engineering and shipbuilding firm of Tod & Bannerman, which, greatly prospering by the excellence of its products and the native caution of its founders in the surging days of Victoria the Good, became in the Jubilee Year a limited liability company with capital to the tune of £225,000. His father, christened plain John Bannerman but all too familiarly known as Jumping Jack, succeeded to the nominal control of the business in the year of Victoria's death ; and then, as Tertius saw the historical process with a dryly amused detachment, the vital spark of creativeness in the Bannerman line of engineers started to flicker.

Something reckless and coarse, his son decided—something out of the rude peasant ancestry—had informed Jumping Jack's progress through life. Unlike his forebears, he had not been called upon to serve any sort of apprenticeship in the shops, nor had he been directed, on the other hand, towards the higher learning. There was some record of a Militia commission, briefly held, but the third of the Bannermans, so far as his son could remember and ascertain by research, had been a rough, hearty foxhunter and chucker of barmaids' chins, living high and coarse. It was he who, the last of the diligent Tod line dying out in 1910, had sold out to the Liverpool combine, accepted a knighthood in part-payment for a not ignoble inheritance, and retired to become a country gentleman of the beefier order on the estate of Killogie Old Cross, acquired by the second Bannerman in the 80's from the trustees of the 7th and last Baron Kilcart of Cart, Killogie and Troquair.

Tertius poured himself a last half-glass of the Cockburn '08 and smiled wryly into the depths of the wine that so deliciously caught and enriched the glow from the log fire. It was all delightfully odd. History, as his studies had taught him, had this queer way of working in circles. It was an exquisite adornment of the situation that he himself was not Jumping Jack's born heir.

The first-born, Bob, had gone down under a hail of Mauser bullets at Elandslaagte long ago, a girl-faced subaltern of the Gordons not long out of school dying for the sake of what was called the Empire. The second-born, Sandy, had indeed succeeded, when Jumping Jack died of a stroke in the year of the General Strike, and perhaps as an emotional consequence of that damned insolent upheaval ; but Sandy, a man after his father's heart and habit, had in 1929 driven a car of enormous power at excessive speed towards a road-bend in the Belgium Ardennes, failed to negotiate it, torn away some fifteen yards of wooden fencing, and ended up in the bed of a stream with a broken neck but

without issue. The cynical Fates were surely laughing when they
inducted to the superiority of Killogie Old Cross a younger son
with the spirit of an antiquarian and the training of a historian.

He had not coveted the position, but it gave him comfort and
security and a rich field for specialized research under his hand.
Long ago he had made testamentary provision of £5,000 for the
posthumous publication of " Killogie Old Cross : A History and
Survey of a Scottish Parish." It was nearly finished, the long task
of working through archives, parish records and the musty files
of the Register House and the National Library ; of collating the
six-inch Ordnance Survey with all the maps back to the Harding
Chronicle ; of repeating in the Twentieth Century the work
initiated by Sir John Sinclair in the Eighteenth. And now an
eminently respectful letter on thin foreign notepaper came at the
last moment to complicate the theorem.

Mr. Bannerman's left hand, somewhat unsightly with its
knuckles red and swollen with rheumatism, picked it up again
from the table by his chair. He smiled once more over the stiff,
businesslike phrases and especially over the formal subscription :
" Yours respectfully, Sir, Jno. Rolland Cram." The spirit of the
letter, on the other hand, greatly pleased his sense of history. It
was written by one who shared his feeling for form and continuity.

This was one of Tod & Bannerman's men, one of thousands
of such men, formally making his signal to the hereditary head
of the old firm ; one who, knowing well that the old associations
were invaded and broken, still cherished such loyalty to the
traditional order of things that he asked leave to be allowed, " at
such time as may suit your convenience," to present himself at
Killogie Old House and " pay my respects to the grandson of my
old master, one of the finest gentlemen, not to mention a very
able engineer, that ever stepped." Charming ! And this decent
man almost certainly did not know that he proposed to come,
respectful hat in hand, to meet his own half-brother, or whatever
the phrase was !

If he had not been trained in historical method, Tertius
reflected, he might not himself have lighted on this interesting
fact. To the considerable concern of the family solicitors, however,
he had insisted on having for the purposes of his study the estate
accounts for all the years the Bannermans had held Killogie.
The recurrent entry had caught his eye and sharpened his

curiosity : £100 per annum for " Sundries " to a Mrs. Elizabeth
Rolland in Baker's Loan, Garvel. It was not difficult to trace the
explanation of the entry, even if those grey-faced lawyers sank
deeper into evasive profundity at every one of his eager questions.
There were still old folk about the estate who would talk, either
out of senility or when suitably flattered by the laird's off-hand
condescensions.

She had been a pretty dairymaid about the Home Farm, and
Jumping Jack still an urgent man after the birth of his third—
and last-born—Tertius Troquair Bannerman, had sent his long-
suffering wife into a decline. There had been two bastards, a boy
and then a girl, off this stock ; and they had duly passed, by a
process Tertius had not troubled to investigate, into the custody
of this Mrs. Elizabeth Rolland, of Baker's Lane, Garvel. It was
only right, as in a Victorian novel, that the boy should be found
an obscure place in the family works.

The last twist of the joke was that the bastard boy had
prospered. The family talent for engineering had been in him,
also the devotion to hard duty that had dwindled (Tertius
admitted to himself with his wintry smile) in the fourth generation of the Bannerman line direct. It would be diverting in the
extreme to have a visit from this old figure in the saga of Killogie,
and the encounter would have the special flavour of risk. The
paternity of this Jno. Rolland Cram apart, one never quite knew
where one was with Florence in the matter of people returning
from the East.

Florence, his wife, was a Birch-Pitkeathly ; that is to say,
of the Scottish family of merchant princes that dominated the
commerce of a sub-continent of rich, wet country from Assam
south to Rangoon and even Singapore. More than that, her
mother had been of the purple, daughter of a titled A.D.C. to
the Viceroy. Her attitude to all things Eastern was thus apt to be
authoritative ; the centre of her world, the repository and fount
of all the standards she lived by, was India or, as she chose to
pronounce it with a curious snap of the tongue on the last
syllable, In-jah.

Tertius had proffered her the respectful letter from Mr. Cram
over the tea table, and she had read it carefully, her fine, bold
nose twitching a little over and above the sheets of rather inferior
paper.

"Who is this person?" she had asked at length and in her viceregal manner; for she had some others.

"Rather an interesting case," Tertius had explained. "His mother was a woman about the Home Farm. He served his apprenticeship with our people in Garvel. The perfect specimen of the successful Scots engineer. You observe, my dear, the feeling for tradition?"

"Quite," Florence had agreed and then seemed to sniff inaudibly. "Dockyard Superintendent on the China Coast? Not quite *pukka*, I shouldn't think."

"Certainly, certainly!" Tertius had hastened to agree. "Probably not quite *pukka*. Interesting, nevertheless."

Florence had then helped herself to a chocolate biscuit and, as it were closing the Cram affair, remarked on the shortcomings of the new kennelmaid, an experiment. She made it clear that she preferred her dogs to be handled by a man. And there it was. The most detached student of history could never know when it might not come at himself round a corner.

CHAPTER TWO

FAMILY GATHERING

I

THE TRAIN burst out of the tunnel at Bishopbank, and even before the swirling smoke had cleared from about the swaying coaches John Rolland Cram had the window down and, the rush of air ruffling his white hair, was doting on the reality of the scene that had been for so many years his sustaining dream.

There it was exactly as it had been imprinted on the tablets of his memory, as deeply and accurately and lovingly as the old engraver's tool had pictured the Customhouse Quay and the Five Arches on his precious bank note ; and now the richness of gold in the light of a September morning brought the cherished picture to such a fullness of reality that the late Superintendent Engineer of the Kwanghai & Shangchuan Dockyard was simultaneously afflicted by a constriction in the throat, as painful and embarrassing as tonsilitis, and by an even more embarrassing filling of his lower eyelids with the tepid wash of tears. In the midst of his emotion he was aware of gratitude to the Inscrutable for alloting him a compartment to himself on this early forenoon train.

There was the rock across the River, the cluster of military buildings at its base taking the morning light on their unequivocably Scottish frontage. Beyond the Rock were the gantries of the shipyards, and beyond these again, in a cleft formed by the Vale's green hillsides and to be glimpsed for only a few seconds by alert train-travellers—and he had rehearsed the moment for half a lifetime—was the conical peak of the Ben, aspiring thousands of feet into the powder blue of the northern sky, waiting for the snows to give it its winter covering, as a woman might dream deliciously of the first cold spell and of her ermines.

The ship channel was as it had been since he could remember, that curving double line of buoys and miniature lighthouses perilously founded on artificial islands, which weaved a pattern of curves among the sandbanks. Yes—there were three lighters high and dry on the yellow dunes of the Great Bank, steam jetting from their sides as the donkey-engines raised the hoppers of sand to be emptied into their holds ; and there was the inevitable hopper barge, the gleaming black funnel set far aft on the eccentric red hull, away down on the tide to dump the overnight dredgings in deep water between the islands. He could not yet see the anchorage where the ship-channel ran into the open Firth, but he saw the Highland hills that guarded it on the North, and his being was filled with happiness.

The impact of these familiar sights on an ageing party was so powerful that John Rolland Cram was fain to turn from the window, sit down on a middle seat with his back to the engine, and wipe his eyes. He was crying as, nearly forty years before he had secretly cried to be leaving it all and off to join his first ship at Liverpool. This was it : this was the decisive, incredible moment of coming Home for good ; and it was dreadful to be unmanned at the very moment of achievement. Old fool—after having knocked about the world and fought for his place in it all these years ! Better collect his things and get ready to get out at the Main, looking like a sensible chap in command of himself and less like an auld wifie at a christening.

This task, for his packages were numerous, he made so absorbing to himself that he hardly glanced at the shipyards as the train passed through the Port and completely forgot that, as it slowed down for the Main, a hollow thundering below announced the crossing of the viaduct above the Five Arches.

There were not many people on the down platform to meet the 10.47, and John, the seasoned traveller, was first concerned to hail a porter and give him a series of crisp orders. Then, suddenly feeling a little frustrated, as if the rhythm of a well-rehearsed plan was somehow faltering, he stood at the open door of his compartment and looked about him.

It was the same old Main he had always known, the same damp and sooty sandstone walls, the same sulphurous reek from the tunnel at the western end, the same old automatic machines and advertisements in enamel, all sadly in need of a wash or a lick of paint. But where . . . ? Ah, there ! His sister Beth was hurrying down the platform to greet him.

" John ! Home at last ! O dear, am I going to start crying ? "
" Beth ! Man, it's grand to see you again, lass ! "

His impulse was to kiss her, but he was quick to perceive her involuntary faint reaction to the velleity, and he appreciated that she still held by the undemonstrative code of the Scots working folk from whom they had both sprung. They shook hands ceremoniously.

"Well, well!" cried John with a heartiness he realized to be really rather empty.

Beth sniffed and wiped away a tear with the back of a black cotton glove. The moment was awkward. Fortunately, the porter came up from the luggage van with a laden truck, and there was a welcome distraction as the hand-luggage was piled on the trunks and packing cases and the disposal of this mass of belongings was discussed.

"That's the lot, then," said John at length. "Come on, Beth. I ordered a car, and I'll give you a run up the hill. You'll want to be back to get Davie's dinner ready. It was real nice of you to spare the time to meet me. Tell me now, how are Davie and the bairns?"

But as they walked the length of the long and now empty platform together he was still groping in his mind for the significance, the explanation, of something—well, what would you call it?—something missing in the quality of his return home.

Beth was always a queer stick, of course; as straight as a die but of the worrying kind, too modest for her own fine qualities of industry and simplicity. She was talking freely now, giving him all the news, but as he smiled and nodded his interest John was subtly unhappy within himself to see his sister so plainly, nay dowdily, dressed in the worn blue costume, the lisle thread stockings and the cotton gloves of the working chap's wife, while he, the well-to-do man from the East, sported a heavy frieze coat over a new suit in light grey Cheviot, carried a new raincoat from Haymarket over his left arm, and could look down on the gleaming toes of shoes that had cost him four guineas in Piccadilly. He suspected, accurately, that Beth skimped herself for others, probably to save against the old age of which the menace haunted her kind, and it was a pleasure to think that he could perhaps do something about that.

There was, however, the factor of Beth's pride that could take the aggressive form he had so often seen displayed in the old days by his Grannie. Beth had often enough written to protest against the unseemly lavishness of some of his gifts sent home, as if a moral issue had been involved. A queer stick ! Now, seeing the splendour of the Daimler that awaited her brother at the station entrance, she had to exclaim :

" I'm not used to riding in a swell big car like this."

" Get in," he retorted half-angrily, half-affectionately : " I'm paying for it, amn't I ? "

Beth sat upright beside him on the back seat, her feet amid the clutter of luggage on the floor but her bearing uneasy. It was deliciously plain to John that she did not like being driven up to the mouth of a tenement close in an equipage so haughty, and he could easily imagine her fear of the comments of a host of neighbours with sharp eyes. Showing off—he knew exactly the deadly phrase she feared. Poor Beth !

He got down on the pavement of the steep street to hand her out, saying :

" Well, I'll see you all in the evening, Beth. I thought that was the best way to arrange things. Tell Addie to put on her best bib-and-tucker."

" We'll wear our best, John," said his sister with great gravity, " and I don't think we'll disgrace you. But Davie and I are working folk, not like some of these——"

John's hand took her shoulder and gave her a little shake. He peered into her grey eyes, so wide and steady, and he saw that her face was still fresh and comely.

"You're an awful fool sometimes, Beth," he said kindly and fell back into the speech of their childhood. " I'm your big brother, am I no' ? "

" Yes, John," she said, having suddenly become, as it seemed, a good little girl surprisingly scolded.

Poor Beth ! She did not seem to realize that that touchiness of hers must make him feel unhappy in the very hour of his return. It was heartbreaking if money and position were to count for so much among his own people, even if he could appreciate how hard work and good fortune had allowed him to grow out of these anxieties of the near-poor.

Through the windows of the Daimler he stared a thought morosely at the drab, upper streets of his native town and saw that the clotted tenements and little shops lacked order of arrangement and grace in themselves, that dilapidation had grievously

overwhelmed them, and that the hasty, thoughtless building of
the age of industrial expansion had left the place with a monstrous
burden of inglorious decay. There even passed through his mind
the treacherous thought that what he had so long believed to
be a fine town as seen through the haze of nostalgia was in
bitter truth a mean town on a fine site, criminally meaner than
the splendour of its position on the hillside above the Firth
demanded.

The little wave of depression passed as the car slipped under
MacCallum's Clock on its high kirk steeple and round the corner
of Regent Square, passing in a flash from East End into West
End, from the grubbiness of narrow, cobbled streets and tall
tenement buildings into a region where you could see the sunlight
on the greenery of old trees and on the mellow sandstone frontages
of churches and solid villas. When it drew up at the door of
Blackwood's Hotel he was pleased to see that its grave Italianate
façade, with the two wings that curved so sweetly to meet the
broad pavement, had lately been cleaned with steam and wire
brushes. It was fresh, calm, dignified ; and while his driver and
the hotel porter grappled with his luggage, he lingered on the
kerb to take pleasure in the assurance that the bowling greens
and the tennis courts still formed a secure patch of greenery in
the middle of the quiet square.

And yet again he did not seem able to escape entirely from
the feeling of anti-climax, at least, that had come on him when
he parted from Beth. There was a day, he could not help remembering, while old Tom Blackwood was still alive, when he had
been, " my friend, Mr. Cram, home from China. See that he
gets the very best of attention ; " when there would have been
the immediate opening of a bottle and much honour done to
him in Tom's private room ; when he would have had a little
table to himself in the bow of the dining-room window and
Charlie, the head waiter, always at his elbow with a special bit
of cheese or a slice off the breast, and always bedroom Number 8,
with a view across the chimneypots to the Firth and the hills on
the other side of the water. The new company had made a rare,
bright job of the old hotel, but it was a wee thing daunting to be
received in what had been a home from home by a polite but
impersonal girl who made him fill up a form and sign a book
and coldly intimated to the porter " Number 32," which turned

out to be a small room on the second floor, overlooking a garage and the sidings behind the Marine Station.

John Rolland Cram smiled wryly to his own image in the mirror. This was a rare way to come home, wasn't it? This vague frustration was what happened to a silly old fool who, with the orderly mind of the engineer, must make an elaborate plan for his first day at home, writing letters to all and sundry concerned.

Rabbie was about right; the best-laid plans gang aft agley. Now he had only gone and left himself with an empty day before him. All very fine to be met by Beth at the train in the privacy of their special relationship; but then to be left after twenty minutes in her company without a crowding of congratulatory friends, a shouting of welcome about his ears! It was somehow not what you had dreamed of for years on end.

All his own fault. It was John's experience that it did no man any great harm to realize his own relative unimportance. There would be the Party in the evening. Then the friends and relations would come gathering round him as he had so carefully planned, then he would have the time and the opportunity to get the hang of his relationships, and have a good look at the young folk, and size up the community of blood to which he had chosen to return. They would make an evening of it with a right good feed, a distribution of gifts from China, a drink for the older folk, a song or two for auld lang syne, and mebbe a bit of a dance for the youngsters for an hour before midnight.

He had formally bidden those he knew to attend this family reunion at 6 p.m. on the evening of September 6, 1937, and left it to Beth to pass on the good word to those of their small family circle of whom he could not remember the addresses, even the names. It would be a rare good night, if care and affection and money—in reason, of course—could make it so.

This hope and preoccupation did indeed help to fill the long day he had left himself. The hour or so before lunch was pleasantly taken up with a partial unpacking and an arrangement of the gifts he had chosen for his people. The meal was good and served by a sensible lass, able to take and give back a bit of harmless chaff with an old lad who could have been her grandfather. After that the hotel manager, in striped trousers and black jacket, couldn't do enough to please Mr. Cram about the lay-out of the big private room for the Party and getting a piano carried in from his own sitting-room and seeing it placed by the porter, boots and a couple of dim men from below stairs precisely where Mr. Cram thought it would be most advantageously placed, across the corner between the fireplace and the window. Anything that Mr. Cram wanted done . . .

It was to be a slap-up high tea with fried fish and chips or bacon and egg, or both for those who could get outside them. The manager ever so delicately intimated, as if he insisted on making a contribution to the feast at his own expense, that he had arranged for silver dishes of sweets and crystallized fruits to be on the table. " The ladies appreciate a little touch like that."

This was all very satisfactory, but when John left the hotel in mid-afternoon for a turn along the sea front it was with a certain apprehension. His mood was much that of one who has been ill for a long spell and, venturing out of doors for the first time, wonders what he will make of the once-familiar world and it of him. Moving down the steep street towards the Queen's Pier he saw that his appearance did indeed attract some attention, especially from errand boys with large wicker message-baskets over their arms, who almost stopped to stare at his approach ; and he did not realize that the broad-brimmed Stetson in light fawn he had bought in Singapore was the true object of their interest. On his own part he observed with a pleased particularity the changes amid so much that was familiar.

There were no electric trams along the main road now, only motor-buses that seemed in an almighty hurry to get to their destinations. Ah ! So somebody had made a garage and service station out of the old low building in which Joe Morton had striven so long to perfect, manufacture and sell his fancy stone-cutting machine : a hopeless job from the beginning, as John could have told another old Tod & Bannerman lad. And they had put up a big milk-handling depot in staring concrete on the old Fair Ground ! He wondered vaguely if the Town Council had the right to hand out the common land in this fashion ; but then he found himself round the wide corner of the Esplanade, and these small concerns passed from his mind, for there before him was the sea, the unchanging.

It changed only with the weather and the tides and the ebb

and flow of shipping along the trade routes of the world. This September afternoon, as it chanced, the anchorage was nearly empty, with only a couple of old Levantine tramps snubbing on their chains against the last of the ebb and a new two-funnelled ship of size—she looked like a City liner—apparently swinging compasses far away on the other side, in the mouth of the loch. It was too hazy now for a man to be sure about such things. The anchorage might be a vast and tideless inland lake in an alpine region, so calm did it lie under the dreaming mountains on the other shore.

As he stepped along the sandy walk on top of the sea-wall, and saw how the action of salt was always eternally corroding the iron railings, and smelt the stink of weed from the foreshore (for all the world like cabbage being boiled, he reflected) John thought with pride and pleasure how this upper anchorage was only, as it were, a quiet, upper pool of the ocean waterway that turned into another, wider, rougher leg beyond the point at Kempock, and was then tempestuous, broad and deep beyond the islands, until at length the estuary spread its gaunt arms wide open to the swell of the Western Approaches and the shipping of all the nations.

He walked westwards smartly, a man proud of an inheritance regained, but soon it came upon him that the broad promenade was nearly deserted. On every second bench or so, each at a hundred-yard interval, there seemed to be a young woman reading a book, while her child or her charge slept in a perambulator at her elbow. John smiled to these young women and only once, from a plump little nursemaid with a close grin about her snub nose, got more than a lifting of carefully doctored eyebrows.

The forenoon feeling of frustration gathered over his spirit again. His impulse was to go up to one of those young, disdainful mothers of the new generation and say : " Excuse me, madam, but I am an oldish man who has just come home after the best part of a lifetime in the East. I have few friends, but I belong to this place, as it belongs to me in a way, and I think that you might, out of the kindness of a woman's heart to the ageing and lonely, give me back at least a smile for the smile I offer you and your baby."

Thus in his simple heart he did want to appeal to the young

women he passed. But of all the daft notions ! He must really try to get it into his old nut that the wonder of returning home was his own wonder exclusively, and that these young women who read books so patiently beside their sleeping infants could not, in the most extreme extension of reason, be expected either to recognize the return home of John Rolland Cram or, even if they perchance had heard of it, to regard it as being of the slightest importance. In his decency Mr. Cram concluded that his own emotions on revisiting the familiar scenes were just a bit too much for the common sense he had so long prided himself on possessing.

He reached the half-way mark of the Red Lamp. As he had done as a child more than fifty years before he bent his head to listen to the ticking of the clockwork mechanism that turned the lamp on the tall pillar and warned the mariner of a reef and shallows running out from a blunt point of land. That pleased him with its old assurance of continuity, but as he walked on beyond the Red Lamp he had the feeling of walking into a vacuum.

So far as his eye could see along the half-mile curve of the embankment to the Boat Club not a living soul was in sight ; not a vehicle, not an errand boy on a bicycle moved along the carriage way. Smoke curled in the windless air from the chimneys of the villas set back from the other side of the roadway, but their windows were as sightless eyes staring across the water. It was as if this part of his native town were atrophied, dying for sheer lack of vitality and interest in the world that was to him so exciting, and John's spirits sank again under the senses of age and loneliness and disappointment.

At length, however, he did discern a figure coming towards him down the slight slope from the Boat Club corner. It was clearly the figure of an old man taking his daily exercise, and as they approached each other John thought to see something familiar in it despite the passage of years and the havoc they had wrought in the person of his fellow-traveller. They were within twenty yards of each other when John decided that this was indeed Rab Ballingall, who had been foreman patternmaker with T. & B.'s outbye when he was an apprentice fitter ; and a right smart tradesman he had been.

A hearty hail was on the tip of John's tongue when he saw

it was only the shell or ghost of Rab Ballingall that passed : an exhausted, indifferent thing with a sagging mouth, dull eyes that looked straight forward with no hope of recognizing or of being recognized, and knees that jerked stiffly upwards in the mere effort to progress. Some sort of stroke had turned the brisk, pawky journeyman of forty years before into a pantaloon, no doubt dismissed the house by a sharp-tongued daughter-in-law, an old dog sent out to exercise in the sun and, if it must be, die among the bushes.

They passed on the empty stretch of sandy footpath, and not a word, not even a small hesitation of footsteps. What had been the glowing coals of life in 1895 were ashes now in 1937 ; and John Rolland Cram was suddenly afraid, seeing in the passer-by the eternal but eternally agonizing tragedy of old age. A man was of use to his kin so long as he had productive power, of interest to his friends so long as he had strength of mind, but after that was nothing but pity or, at the best, the faithful care of women in whom the Lord had implanted the gift of (what they themselves so much required) kindness.

Was this the shadow in the fourth of the Five Arches ? John Rolland Cram stopped short of the Boat Club and, from the outermost bend of the Esplanade curve, a foot up on the sandstone plinth that supported the decaying iron railings, looked across the water. Even through the autumnal haze that was gathering over the Firth, it might be towards fog and even an early frost, he could discern the white gleam of cottage walls five miles away along the coastwise road that runs round the Strone. There he was going, with a plan for living in his mind. A trig cottage, a nice bit of garden, a motor-boat for the fishing in the long summer evenings of the North. Peace. Yes. But was it not perhaps escape, the lazy and self-indulgent rearguard action before such an attack of physical and social facts as had overwhelmed Rab Ballingall ?

A wooden gate on the other side of the carriage way clicked twice as it was opened and shut. John turned from his brooding and saw a young woman in tweeds, a bundle of letters in her gloved hand, come out of a villa front-garden. A mongrel dog, of which the mother had probably been a collie and the father an industrious fox-terrier, bounded through the gate with the girl and then across the roadway to make friends and play with the stranger from China. Leaping and licking and fawning, his paws on John's thighs, he would not obey the whistle and then the sharp voice of his mistress.

John sent the mongrel off with a gruff but friendly command. The young lady proceeded up the road to post her letters, her tweed skirt swinging gracefully. The dog, having investigated with his nose the base of each tree on the landward side of the Esplanade, duly signified his satisfaction with the *status quo* by a grave and philosophical raising of one or other of his hind legs.

This small encounter greatly raised the spirits of John Rolland Cram, and helped him to forget almost completely the imponderables of life. Where the Esplanade resigns its unique command of the Firth and merges with the main coastal road, he turned eastwards and hurried towards Blackwood's Hotel, thinking at once anxiously and eagerly about the Party.

2

He was downstairs and ready for his guests half-an-hour before the first were due to arrive. In a pleasing ferment of pride and anxiety mingled he surveyed the private room, the table with its twenty covers, the flowers and the lighting. He struck a tentative note on the piano, and the fact that it yielded an agreeable noise satisfied him. Twice he had the manager in : the first time to order a box of cigars and a supply of cigarettes, the second to request an interview with the waitress who would be in charge of the feast. After this the woman concerned—a veteran campaigner called Mrs. McIlmoil in private life but professionally Kate—remarked to the two girls who were to assist her : " He's a right nice old gentleman, but he's an awful footer." She reckoned privately, however, that the old chap would be good for a solid tip if he got the friendly sort of service she knew so well how to provide when in the mood.

The excitement worked so strongly in John Rolland Cram, the time seemed to pass so slowly, he found his way into the bar and ordered himself a glass of whisky with a drop of water. Young and middle-aged men from Garvel's West End glanced curiously at this ageing party who wore a black velvet jacket with

trousers so light in hue that it might be lavender, patent leather
pumps, and a polka-dotted bow tie in blue and white over the
collar of a white silk shirt ; but when they heard Sophy the
barmaid's whispered explanation that this was " a Mr. Cram,
just home from China," their curiosity was completely satisfied.
Old jossers retired from the East were a common species in Garvel
and apt to get themselves up like that.

John, on the other hand, had upon him a higher emotion
than the loungers could understand : the deep satisfaction of
enjoying his first dram of the native beverage on Scottish soil and
among his own people. Good stuff it was, too ; mellow ; none
of that fiery, if not fabricated, muck they handed out at ransom
prices in Japanese ships and London hotels. The real Mackay.

The drink restored his surety of grasp over his own position.
With a lively sense of well-being, of the personal power that is a
necessity of living in the male order of things, John returned to
the private room, exchanged some homely remarks with Kate
and the girls, and, his hands locked behind his back, presented
his posterior to the fire in the right attitude of a host benevolently
awaiting the coming of his guests.

The first intimation, however, took him somewhat by surprise,
for he had been watching with an engineer's delight in such
things with what dexterous delicacy Kate and the two young
girls were turning folded napkins into decorative fans of starched
linen. The door swung back with a violence that sent the hinges
biting into the soft wood of the jamb and a small boy in a much
be-buttoned but ill-fitting tunic of cavalry pattern stepped in and
bawled at the pitch of his voice, and in the thickest accent of
industrial West Scotland :

" Muster and Mustress Bryden. Muss Bryden. Muster Curly
Bryden."

It was Beth and Davie and their bairns who were thus
vociferously announced, and John was happy that they had come
first among the guests. He advanced with the glow of happiness
in his face, his two arms outstretched.

" Beth ! And it's you, Davie ! How are ye, man ? It's grand
to see you again, the same old sixpence ! "

" John ! Welcome hame, man ! "

The two artificers wrung each other's hands. It was good for
John to feel the honest grip of a strong and steady kinsman.

"And these are the bairns?" he asked eagerly, turning to the young people. "This'll be Addie. She was no' much more than a baby when I saw her last." The vernacular idiom came easily to his tongue in this moment of reunion. "And how are ye, lass? You're your mother all over again!"

"I'm very well, Uncle John, thank you," said the girl, demurely reciting her piece; and she bobbed a funny little curtsey before him. "I can just remember you, and not much more."

"Ye'll get to know me better now, Addie," said John happily. "And this is Curly? That's a queer name for a lad that was christened plain John after his old uncle! How are ye, son?"

"Fine!" said Curly with a grin.

"That's no way to talk!" protested his mother from the background.

"I mean I'm fine," the boy persisted, "and I'm hoping Uncle John's fine. It's nice to see you, Uncle."

John laughed and patted the youth's shoulder.

"That's champion, Curly!" he approved. "You were kicking a dirty paper ball along Palmerston Place when I saw ye last. We'll have a talk about things, you and me . . . Now, John—Beth—tell me all your news."

Davie Bryden had much to report. He was a cheerful and equable man of great vitality, gifted with the natural actor's trick of miming unconsciously, so that as he talked away of this and that he unconsciously delighted John with living pictures of relatives and their little oddities of behaviour, of old workmates in T. & B.'s, of the town's surviving characters. (It would no doubt have interested Mr. Tertius Troquair Bannerman to see one of the firm's foreman blacksmiths give an admirable lightning sketch of one of his very occasional, baffled peregrinations through the family shipyard.) Davie became quite extravagant in some of his reminiscences, and Beth tut-tutted and cried "Wheesht, man!" and John laughed all the more to encourage his good-brother's exuberances. At the same time, the inner, considering part of his mind—that part which must now make an adjustment to a new sort of life at a late stage of any man's calculable stay in the world—was diving, as it were, beneath the flood of Davie's happy reminiscences in the effort to understand how it was with his sister Beth and her children.

She and he were kith and kin in a unique, lonely relationship. Those other nominal cousins who were still to arrive were wholly outside this special intimacy. He wondered if she knew, if she had ever troubled to wonder, of what line they had both come. She was meanwhile the perfect, canny wife of a decent, well-doing Scots working man. The dress she wore was black and plain, of a material he could not put a name to. Her unbarbered hair was combed down tightly about her head. The only decorative thing she wore was the golden wedding ring on the third finger of her left hand. These hands of hers were rough and red with much work in water and soap and soda. But Beth was still a woman out of the ordinary—and what a pity in some ways that she did not know it !—with her pale but clear complexion, regular features and those wide and ever-steady grey eyes.

John considered the person of young Curly, christened John Cram Bryden. He brooded on the closeness of a relationship unsuspected by the boy, who was nevertheless the nearest to a son Mr. Cram, late Superintendent Engineer of the K. & S. Dockyards, would ever have.

In his neat blue serge suit the youth seemed remarkably short in stature, but there was clearly unusual strength in the broad shoulders and the long arms that hung down below the hips, clenched fists facing inwards and elbows slightly crooked outwards. The small face was smooth as to the texture of the skin and bright in its expression, with a bird's alertness in the brown eyes below the black hair plastered down flat with an unguent and parted in the middle as became an apprentice plater in his fourth year. A good boy, this ; John liked the look of him.

He was still more profoundly interested in the quiet girl they called Addie—Adelaide, after Davie's mother. John found indeed that his encounter with the maiden he was really seeing for the first time was in some mystical way disturbing.

On the surface of things he was delighted to see her, as he thought, very prettily and suitably turned out for the Party in a plain dress of Quaker grey with a little frill of lace about the neck and no fal-lals save a cameo brooch pinned between her young breasts. It somehow delighted him to see that the lass, taller and straighter than her older brother, was neatly stockinged and well shod ; and it was a special pleasure to see how, while her elders talked and laughed and talked, she could stand still and silent without awkwardness, as if fortified by the strength of an inner quiet.   Like her mother : her mother refined, her mother more securely poised.   Watching her sideways and furtively, continually turning to glance at the pretty, quiet girl and win one of her rare but shining smiles, John was visited by the queer feeling that, in his new life, he would dearly wish to have Addie near him, always.   But perhaps he was just only a selfish old man.

The buttoned boy threw open the door, tilted back his bullet head, and gave tongue in such a loud and glottal announcement that John could not comprehend it.   He turned to Beth and whispered rapidly :   " Stay here with me and tell me who the folk are ; I won't know the half of them."   The plea was uttered too late.   John found himself stormed by four aged females all in black, down to black button-boots, black coats, black boas and a proliferation of black plumes on their antique hats.

These ladies were all yellow and lined with age, all bent and twisted in one degree or another, and the stink of napthalene and fustiness mingled which they brought into the room with them was a threat to any sensitive person's enjoyment of the feast in prospect.   Apparently they were sisters.

Of this quartette of females two seemed utterly mindless and silent, lost in a world for which their physique and talents were inadequate.   It was immediately clear to John that these—the odd, unwanted women of an industrial society, lacking the brains, the education and the spirit to fight for a positive place in it—had surrendered to their more vital sisters the whole responsibility for communicating on their behalf with the other inhabitants of a complex and daunting universe.   The other two—the oldest and the youngest of the sisters, as John guessed rightly—closed on him, exuding waves of the moth-ball odour.

" John Cram ! " the eldest croaked at him.   " And to think that I used to change yer nappies ! "

John found himself recoiling a little from the attack of this aggressive old party with a nose that hooked over an almost toothless mouth, lips that twisted with the soulless motions of rubber and one apparently sightless, bleared eye.   He contrived to laugh, only to be assaulted even more stridently by the youngest of the sisters, who wore silver-rimmed spectacles, one of the broken arms mended with insulating tape, awry across a nose bolder and ruddier than her sister's.

"He doesny ken us! He canny tell who we are!" she exulted, emitting a laugh that sounded like the screech of a macaw in some impenetrable jungle.

"Wait a minute, now," John temporized jocularly.

"Who made yer first wee suit for ye?" the youngest sister persisted. "Who used to carry ye down to the Betty Burn to paddle, and a right wee rascal ye were?"

The laugh ripped the air again, and the intermission allowed John time to make a swift recognition.

"I've got you now!" he cried. "Grannie's cousins in the cottage on the Peat Road! Man, it's a pleasure to see you again. You don't tell me? Still in the same old house? Well, if that's not a record. . . . You'll excuse me a minute."

The door had opened again, and John passed the virginal quartette into the care of Davie, always willing and able to act cheerfully as assistant master of ceremonies. Beth was at his ear with a quick, explanatory whisper:

"Those were the Grosarts. I had to ask them. This is a great night for them, and it's not many they get, poor souls."

"Quite right, quite right, Beth! Who's this?"

"Peg Rolland and her husband," his sister muttered hastily. "Dan Rolland's half-sister."

The boy in buttons proclaimed the news to the assembly in much more telling tones.

"Muster and Mustress Alexander Lightbody," he yelled. "Mr. Sam Lightbody."

The chatter in the room was suddenly hushed by the mention of this last name. A detached observer of the scene would have concluded that while Mr. and Mrs. Alexander Lightbody might have been expected at the feast, Mr. Sam Lightbody was a stranger, unknown, and something of an interloper.

He was a fat, hearty-looking man in his sixties, a grey moustache of extreme luxuriance falling to the level of the first of several folds beneath his chin, a gold watch-chain, hung with a constellation of badges and medallions, stretching far and wide across the expanse of white waistcoat over his paunch.

"I knew you wouldn't mind, John," Peg explained in her

prim way when she and her husband had been duly greeted,
" but Alec's father is staying with us for a while and we knew
you'd like to meet him. He was a long time out East himself."

" Is that so ? " cried John hospitably. " Glad to see you,
Mr. Lightbody, glad to have you join the family party. So you're
like me, another old-timer ? "

" Aye, man ! " bellowed Sam Lightbody, pumping at his
host's hand. His voice was at once loud, wheezy, harsh and
genial. " Thirty-seven year foreman sugar-boiler wi' the Taikoo
in Hongkong. Retired these five years, and enjoyin' every
minute of it."

" We must have a yarn sometime. I used to work a lot with
the B. & S. boys. Yon was a regular Garvel colony you had at
Taikoo Bay. . . . Now, Peg and Alec tell me all your news."

Peg had been an elementary school teacher and, a late
marriage having failed to set the blood coursing through her
veins with any degree of joyfulness, still looked it at the age of 44.
John always thought of her as the woman—neat, prim and a
thought self-satisfied—who continued to wear rimless pince-nez
fifteen years after they were out of fashion, down to the thin
chain and the gilt button-spring on the shoulder that hitched
them safely in when, as frequently happened, they were shaken
off her short nose by the corkscrew action of sniffing, a habit to
which poor Peg was much addicted. Her husband was the obvious
mate for such a woman—quite unlike his full-bodied begetter,
tall and a thought bleak, but quiet and serious-minded withal.
He was manager of the Co-op. furniture shop in the High Street ;
and both spouses were regarded regretfully by their relatives as
being suspect of Socialist leanings.

John and Beth were in conversation with these newcomers
when the door was flung open and the boy in buttons threw back
his head to make the final, loud announcement of the evening.

" Muster and Mustress Daniel Rolland. The Musses Rolland.
Muster Charles Rolland."

This entry had a wholly theatrical effect, for as Peg later
confided to Beth with one of her sniffs, the other women of the
clan felt strongly that the Dan Rollands had come to the feast
" a good sight too dressy for my taste." Even John in the full
flush of his happiness as host was alarmed to hear how a silence,
complete and abrupt, fell upon the rest of the company at their

entrance, and was a little embarrassed by the physical ebullience of Lily as she bore in upon him at the head of her brood, making excited noises of welcome and surprise.

Her form was tightly sheathed in apple-green velvet, and she supported in front a snowy plateau of bosom, its essential curves and shadows not wholly concealed within the upper line of the corsage. The thin gold strap of a wrist watch and a variety of rings were embedded in the flesh of her plump upper limbs.

"Well, John! Back again! And not a bit changed!"

"Lily! It's nice to see you. And here's old Dan!"

The epithet might have been chosen ironically. If Dismal Dan Rolland had deliberately made himself up as the mourner at the feast he could not have looked the part to greater perfection. He was in black morning coat with striped trousers, a dark tie caught within a broad golden ring under the wings of his collar. The dull face, with the narrow fringes of hair running from ears to nose, suggested the presence of one who would have been equally happy at a funeral, and probably more so.

"But here's the Twins, John!" Lily interrupted brightly.

Twins they unmistakably were as John saw them for the first time as ripe young women. Their mere appearance had a positive, dynamic impact, as of an individual with double the normal power of personality. It was not merely that they were dressed exactly alike in full frocks of blue taffetas with roll collars in orange velvet and silver shoes; it was not that they almost invariably spoke in unison, as if their bright replies had been exactly rehearsed. John was really a little stunned and confused by the impression of sheer, bold, feminine nakedness conveyed by the lengths of bare arm and bare shoulder these two sizeable and nubile wenches displayed.

"Beryl! Sibyl!" he repeated the introductions overcoming his surprise. "I hope I'll come to know which is which, my dears."

"Thank you, Uncle John," the Twins replied in perfect unison.

John was turning to see if the party was now complete when Lily caught him by the elbow in a grasp as of old familiarity.

"But you haven't met our Cha, John."

"So this is Cha, is it? How do you do, son?"

He thought the boy's hand was flabby and unresponsive in

his. His survey of the person of Cha, though swift, was penetrating, cataloguing the smear of callow moustache, the drooping shoulders, and the soft silk shirt he wore with a dinner jacket, the flabby black tie over a down-turned collar, all as popularized among many young males of the period by the princely example of him who was now Duke of Windsor. Just a halflin boy in the silly stage, thought John charitably, but he was visited by an uncomfortable memory of the type of dancing boy familiar in every public ballroom from London to Tientsin.

But now it was surely time to be sitting down to table, and Beth's tap on his arm drew his attention to the reproachful face of the manager in the doorway, worried like all hotel managers over the passage of time, temperamental cooks, dishes to be washed and the take-it-or-leave attitude of part-time labour.

" Right you are, boss ! " he assured the management. " Fire ahead."

He clapped his hands and, that failing to subdue the rising clamour in the room, beat on his plate with the bone handle of a knife.

" Ladies and gentlemen ! Good friends all, will you please take your places ! Just sit as you like. There's no standing on ceremony in my house."

He stood at the head of the table and, with pleasure, watched his guests settle themselves down to eat. Beth alone took her pre-arranged place as his hostess at the other end, but the absence of a table plan quickly produced alignments of a surprising kind.

Thus Davie Bryden had placed himself between the oldest and the youngest of the Grosart sisters, and, being a man wholly without inhibitions and superiorities, was already plying them with so much banter that the parrot-cries of the youngest were heard again. On the other side of the table Dan Rolland between the two middle sisters formed, as it were, an enclave of gloom unrelieved. John chuckled inwardly to see the bright-eyed, bullet head of Curly between the effulgent shoulders of the Twins, and he was amused to wonder how our Cha would enjoy conversation with Mr. Alexander Lightbody of the Co-op. up at the far end near Beth. On the other hand, he frowned to see that Addie, the quiet one, had patiently suffered herself to be pinned between the bulk of Sam Lightbody and the dumb nonentity of one of the middle Grosart sisters. That was all wrong; the young folk should have been put together, Addie with Cha, though he could have wished for her something with a bit more guts to it. Too late; and he was a man who hated fuss.

That was why he had decided that there would be no saying of grace, though that would have been fully in keeping with his own profoundly humble sense of gratitude for this privilege of cordiality. He had thought of giving them, half-facetiously, the old Covenanting toast, *Some hae meat that canna eat*, but some instinct had moved him to drop this item from his otherwise careful plans for a gathering of people he scarcely knew as individuals. So, while Kate and her helpers surged in with the food, each performing a small feat of prestidigitation with a cluster of plates held like a hand of cards between strong fingers, he sat down at length to discover that his table companions were, on his left, Peg Lightbody and, on his right, Lily and her considerable bosom.

"That's fine, then," he said. "Everybody settled down nicely."

"It's been wonderful, John, perfectly wonderful!" cried Lily. "I don't know how you managed to think everything out so nicely. Do you, Peg?"

"It's very nice," said Peg judicially.

John got the feeling that perhaps Lily, as he might have phrased it to himself, was laying it on a bit thick, but he charitably put it down to excitement. He had not observed (as Peg, and Beth, grimly had) how Lily had adroitly manœuvred for that place beside him and pounced relentlessly when the signal was given, and he listened tolerantly to the flow of her talk. But was it not just a wee bit too much about her unique children, the difficulties of financing their higher careers, Dan's business troubles and, always, how wonderful it was that he was home again and what a wonderful party he was giving his poor relations!

"Of course, you'll have to do your round of visits, John," she chattered on. "You can't stay in a hotel for ever. It's a nice hotel, but you'll want something homelier like. I tell you, Dan and me will be mortally affronted if you don't come to 'The Neuk' for a while—until you find a place of your own, of course."

" That's very kind of you, Lily, indeed," he spoke sincerely. " We'll think about that later on. But, Peg, tell me . . ."

He turned to his neighbour on the left with a spontaneous question and only then realized that he might seem to be snubbing poor Lily. Fortunately, in precisely the same moment, Mr. Sam Lightbody turned from Addie to Mrs. Dan and, with a vulgar jerk of his fork up the table towards the Twins, demanded to know in his wheezing growl :

" Those your two lassies ? Are they workin' yet ? "

" Certainly not ! "

Lily was offended, but Mr. Lightbody had raised an issue very near to her, and since the late sugar-boiler was an argumentative party, John was free for a space, while carrying on a desultory conversation with Peg, to look down the table again and consider the nature of the party he had convened.

He was well content, even if he was also entertained in his detachment. Out of his knowledge of the world, and of the larger social experience his relative success had brought him, he could mark and compare with tender amusement the little pretensions that had developed in some of his people and the absence of these that marked the naturals among them. It was a bit of a joke really, to turn from the Twins, who ate genteelly with little fingers decoratively outspread, to Davie Bryden, honest man, who pointed with his fork, brandished his knife and, through a clot of food in his mouth, laid down the law across the table, presumably to Alec Lightbody, about the merits as a pugilist of Joe Beckett. It was a more bitter joke to move the eyes from the Grosart sisters, who bent low over their plates and wolfed the victuals in a frenzy of release from the hunger of poverty, to the slack figure of our Cha who, the knife propped against his plate in the American fashion, rested both elbows on the table and with a slack wrist and an indolent fork raised an occasional gobbet of food to his mouth. That lad wanted a bit of discipline : a conviction which grew importantly in John's mind when Cha lit a cigarette and, before anybody else was finished, blew a plume of smoke across Beth's face.

Even so, John's view of the gathering remained benevolent, though the benevolence was tinged a little with sympathetic pity. He saw that, for all the silly little pretensions to manners and competitions in female dress, his own people had moved little, either upwards or downwards, in the economic scale in thirty years. They were inveterately of the working folk, even if the Twins would have been horrified to be told so, and none the worse of that. They belonged to him ; they were absolutely all he had now. It pleased him to be the patriarch among them, the man who had been lucky enough to do well, and to know that, without undue sacrifice, he could help so many of them.

Would a pound a week to the Grosart sisters, just to buy a drop more food or a warm garment now and again—would that hurt him ? Not a bit of it. To help Beth and Davie out of a small tenement flat into a decent bit bungalow with a garden— would that not be a happiness ? But his most thoughtful looks fell on the young people, the only hostages to fortune he would ever have now, and he was profoundly moved to think that he might be the means of helping them on to do credit to the family, to be of use in the world, at the least to escape the dreadful negation that had overtaken such as the Grosart sisters. Education . . .

Suddenly something that had been haunting the back of his mind came into his consciousness, and he turned eagerly to Lily, still vivaciously engaged with old Sam Lightbody.

" Excuse me, Lily, but where's Effie Templeton to-night ? I wrote her specially."

" Och, you'd never get her to a party like this." Lily dismissed a triviality. " I'd go mad if I had to live up yonder."

" I don't think Effie has her troubles to seek, poor soul ! " observed the more temperate voice of Peg on his other side.

" Oh ! I'll have to look her up."

And why was it, John often wondered afterwards, that in that precise moment he decided not to make the distribution of gifts as he had so fondly planned : firmly, stubbornly decided to leave them where they lay spread out in his room upstairs until such time as he might see fit to give them over privately on his visits ? He supposed that he must have subconsciously perceived then the elements of competition, even antagonism, especially among the womenfolk of the clan, and the sheer danger of appearing to make such preferences as their sharp eyes would think to observe and their various prides would almost certainly magnify. What really surprised him afterwards was the firmness with which he had come to the decision.

By now, however, most of the clan had had their fill. A look from Beth had even arrested in mid-air the hand young Curly had put forward to seize his seventh chocolate biscuit. Davie Bryden, his firm chin indrawn as if to imprison a belch, smiled down the table to his host and handsomely declared :

" Man, John ! That was a rare tightener, I will say."

Beth rose abruptly—" black affronted," as she told Davie much later in the evening—and there was a rustling and a whispering and a nodding as the women gathered and in a body trooped out of the room, more or less successfully looking as if they were really off to see an exhibition of fine needlework in a neighbouring place. The enemy thus out of the way, Davie Bryden laid a hand on the door-knob and, with a violent jerk of his head, silently indicated to his brothers that he had, by the earlier exercise of prudence and enterprise, discovered a place to which the males might with equal propriety resort.

When the party reassembled it was to find the room completely transformed. A feminine fugue of " O my's ! " and " Isn't that nice's ! " and " Fancy that's ! " hailed a miracle whereby the long tea-table had vanished and, apart from a crescent of open space before the hearth, the room was now filled with card-tables and a variety of chairs, including some of the easy order for the older folk. Little squeals of pleasure from Lily in particular saluted the excellence of the management that had set out on the tables a proliferation of crystallized fruit and such in bon-bon dishes, with here and there a split-new pack of cards. Such as old Sam Lightbody observed with approval that a table in the corner by the fireplace carried a promising collection of bottles and glasses.

Happily, a box of fine cigars in his hand, John moved among his guests and urged them to be at ease.

" Make yourselves at home, make yourselves at home ! No standing on ceremony here . . . A cigar, Davie ? All right, you stick to your pipe . . . Those that would like a hand at whist or that, just carry on. The rest of us will not bother about you . . . O, you're going to have a cigar, Cha, are you ? Well, it's no worse than those coffin-nails you usually smoke . . . You don't smoke at all, Curly ? That's the boy ! The only sensible man in the room . . . A cigar, Auntie ? "

He facetiously offered the box to the Grosart sisters and

evoked from the youngest one of her more piercing skirls of laughter. It was all great fun. Sam Lightbody selected a weed with care and rolled it between his fingers before a hairy ear.

" That's a good article," he pronounced loudly ; then his voice dropped to a confidential wheeze. " Ye're doin' yer folk well, John Cram, but be careful, man, be careful."

Mr. Lightbody winked, but the graveness of his unexpected warning completely escaped his host at the moment. He was in among the ladies again, urging them to enjoy themselves. He noticed with a dry amusement that of all his womenfolk only Lily and the Twins smoked cigarettes, observing also that Lily's performance at least was a somewhat awkward business of holding the weed between two stiff fingers, sucking it violently and spasmodically, and then holding it away from her face. He saw a four for whist settling down at a table in the corner by the window—Mr. and Mrs. Alec Lightbody, Dan Rolland and Charlie Rolland. But our Cha should have been among the other young folk, making a night of it.

John was momentarily exasperated. Did this young whipper-snapper think he could detach his elegant self from the ruck of poor relations ? One hour of the night watch in the engine-room of a tramp walloping in the grey seas off Cape Agulhas . . . O, well ! It took all sorts to make a world.

" What about a bit of music now ? " he addressed the company.

" The very ticket ! " Davie Bryden backed him up, himself breaking jocularly into song with a snatch of *I'll sing thee songs of Araby.*

" Davie ! " Beth, scandalized, cautioned her spouse.

" Davie's fine," laughed John. " Come on, now ! Who's going to break the ice ? "

" I think the Twins might do something," Lily suggested modestly.

It appeared that Beryl and Sibyl were not lacking in alacrity to oblige. With that air of having successfully rehearsed a drill movement their joint actions were always apt to suggest, the Twins rose simultaneously and, their taffetas rustling, advanced upon the piano. While Davie Bryden hurried forward with an extra chair they stood awhile, tall and cool and purposeful, and stripped their wrists of watches and bangles. The adjustment of their persons to the chairs seemed to increase suspense by a nicely calculated deliberation. Four hands, sixteen fingers and four thumbs were to be seen poised above the keyboard. They fell together in a precise and crashing chord.

It was playing such as few there had ever heard before. A master might have smiled over the flashy technique of the Rolland Twins, a dilettante sniffed at their choice of pieces, but it was in its sort playing of a brilliant order. To the poor and lonely and untravelled among those who listened it had a quality of the miraculous in its precision and dexterity ; and the selection of tunes they played had been so arranged, accidentally or cunningly, that they ravished the emotions of those in whom the restatement of an old air created an inner warmth of romance secretly cherished : old days, old friends, lost loves, fleeting but lovely triumphs.

When the players modulated into *Just a Song at Twilight*, Sybil softly enunciating the melody on the rich baritone notes below middle C and Beryl decorating it with all manner of gentle runs and cascades in the treble, the receptive hush was no less rapt, or less sincere, than that which falls in a metropolitan concert hall when the great voice of a Beethoven or a Sibelius speaks through a hundred instruments. Tears coursed down the ludicrous cheeks of Sam Lightbody and dropped on his great moustaches.

This was the music of the lonely, the uncultured, the penurious. If the Twins passed all too oleaginously from *Just a Song at Twilight* to *O Sole Mio* ! with a most abominable dragging-out of the emotional entrails of that Mediterranean confection, they were still soothing the souls of the wounded and the feckless ; and when they wound up their recital with a dazzling version of *El Relicario*, their fingers nimble, strong and accurate, they were in fact restoring to a few weary spirits the senses of gaiety and confidence.

One last smashing chord and the Rolland Twins stood up together, bowed in unison, and proceeded to adorn themselves again with their bangles ; and they heard about their ears a clamour of applause. Old Sam Lightbody was up on his feet, waving the stump of his cigar and shouting "Bravo ! Bravo ! " Beth and Curly and Addie were clapping in unison with Mr. and Mrs. Alexander Lightbody at the card-table. From the same corner our Cha shouted " Attaboy ! " and Dismal Dan actually appeared to be pleased. The youngest Grosart sister said something and laughed at it, harshly. Davie Bryden, the natural man, advanced on the Twins with his arms open, drew them into his embrace, and hugged them back to their seats.

"Upon my living Sam ! " he cried. " Youse two can fair tickle the ivories, and that's the God's truth ! "

John found that Lily was beside him, and he turned to her generously, his heart and eyes full.

"Lily ! I never realised. These girls of yours, they're . . . they're as good as you'd hear on the concert platform. Upon my soul . . ."

"What they really need," said Lily carefully, " is some proper professional training."

"Well, we'll have to see about that," declared John with some vehemence.

He turned to the door as a white-jacketed young waiter entered the room, and John answered the question in the youth's eyes with a curt nod.

The hour of refreshment had arrived ; and never before, it may be recorded, had the women of the Rolland-Cram clan known such a bold refinement of hospitality. To have a foreign young man in a white jacket bowing before you and, in a soft voice, asking : " What will you have to drink, madam ? Whisky, port, sherry, or a liqueur ? " !

The delightful, expensive peril of it ! The allure of the sin into which they were being so smoothly tempted !

On his own part John watched these proceedings with the tolerantly amused eyes of experience. He had known that the women would squeal and make excessive protests and giggle and then fall. A macaw-cry of particular loudness from the youngest Grosart sister neither surprised nor annoyed him. In fact, he chuckled to see how these simple people for the most part chose to drink port, in the curious common belief that this insidious beverage is really a harmless drink of quite considerable respectability. A glass of port each for the ladies, and three whiskies for old Sam Lightbody, Davie Bryden and himself. John was pleased to see that Curly and Addie and the Twins were delighted with long glasses of orange squash. He was equally annoyed to hear our Cha order what he called " a wee Benny " and see the waiter make a special journey to fill and serve to the gallant a glass of the delirious syrup from Fécamp. Pup !

But it was nice to see everybody relaxing and having a good time, and soon the alcohol was working merrily on many an unseasoned metabolism. The jungle-yells of the youngest Grosart sister increased in frequency and force. Now Lily, flushed, linked arms with Sam Lightbody and, dancing skittishly from table to table, toasted this person and that sentiment with a glad freedom from inhibition. The most surprising moment arrived when Alec Lightbody arose from behind the card-table in the corner and, clearing his throat, with the sure air of one who has studied the rules of procedure and put them into practice on many a political and fraternal occasion, begged leave to suggest to the company that this seemed the right, he might even say the appropriate, moment in which his good friends present there that night might see fit to join with him in honouring a sentiment that, Alec dared to think, was very near the hearts of all present ; and, if they would see to it that their glasses were charged, it gave him the greatest personal pleasure to ask them to be upstanding and to drink—a warm welcome to Uncle John and a happy and contented retirement !

The passion with which this sentiment was received and honoured had on John Rolland Cram the effect of a shock. In a trice the party had ceased to be a merely amusing and sentimental occasion. It suddenly seemed a profoundly moving fact that these dear folks of his bore him true love and respect, and that he had indeed come home to a security of affection. He was hard put to it not to cry openly, and he took refuge from his emotion in a raising of his own glass and a bow all round.

" Thanks, friends ! Thank you one and all ! And you, Alec, for a nice speech. But what about a bit more music now ? A song ? I'll be singing myself if you're not careful."

His eyes ranged over the company and rested ultimately on the small, eager face of Beth's boy.

" You, Curly ? Or are you too shy ?"

With remarkable promptitude the boy stood up and grinned.

" I'll give ye *Thora* if ye like," he announced.

Curly felt in a jacket pocket for a much-folded sheet of music and looked about him hopefully.

"Beryl—or Sybil," commanded Lily with decision. "One of you play the accompaniment for your cousin."

Curly's performance was as remarkable in its own order, and as successful with the given audience, as that of the Twins had been, for he sang according to a code sincerely regarded by the meek and simple as effective in the extreme. Its chief quality was extreme loudness. When Curly sang there could be no doubt at all as to what he was about. He forced what might have been quite a good tenor voice at high pressure through his nose, so that the quality of penetration was added to that of loudness. More blatantly (and more innocently) than any Italian he used the trick of slurring, so that his work in the more emotional passages bore a whining menace his listeners found extremely effective and moving, just as they thought the words and general sentiment of the ballad impressive beyond the ordinary. When it came to the climax,

Child of my dreams ! Light of my life !
Angel of love to me-e-e-e,

with Curly threatening to yell his head off and Beryl, on behalf of the Rollands, punishing the pianoforte with pitiless fingers and wrists, it seemed to some among his listeners that music had no more to offer.

Beryl's last chord was followed by a hush. This in turn was followed by an outcry of applause led by old Sam Lightbody who, adroitly and simultaneously, moved towards the table that carried the bottles, as if to suggest that his exhaustion through refined emotion could only, at his great age, be relieved by another whisky. As it chanced, the clumsiness of the move was lost in the concern created by one of the middle Grosart sisters, who, emerging for [once in a lifetime from nonentity, started to howl and sob. The demonstration was so loud, so awkward, that a paralysis overtook the company for many seconds on end.

As John saw it, Beth and Peg handled the crisis with admirable calm. He even saw Peg smack the unhappy woman's wrists, as you might smack the hands of a naughty child. It was all very awkward and alarming. The Grosart sisters had to be shepherded from the room in what John felt to be a rather shabby sort of way. It was as if they were being ejected, and John had to endure the feeling that his party had collapsed in sordid fatuity.

Davie Bryden, making for the door, muttered confidentially :
" I'd best walk up the road with these old bodies. They'll lose themselves."

" No, no ! " said John impatiently. " Ring for a taxi and get them sent home properly."

He realized afterwards that he could not bear to lose Davie's support. With Davie and Beth gone to the succour of the Grosart sisters, the whole delicate edifice of his homecoming arrangements must come crashing down.

Everybody was very nice about it, of course. Lily dismissed it as a case of excitement and spoke tolerantly of those whose social opportunities were limited. Alec Lightbody recalled strange cases of collapse and hysteria among the female customers of the Co-op. The most useful, and quite umpremeditated, distraction was provided by Curly, who, while his elders were thus pre-occupied, stole to the piano and picked out on one finger the air of *I hear you calling me*, a ballad he was then earnestly rehearsing in private.

John excused himself. He slipped out to the vestibule to find the Grosart sisters being packed into a Daimler of monster proportions, Davie Bryden's friendly jests evoking from the youngest those eldritch peals of laughter. The roof-light within the cab seemed to reveal the sisters as four black animals in transit, as it were, from zoo to zoo. When the car rolled away even Beth laughed at the concern on John's face.

" Don't worry about them," she said. " It's been the greatest night of their lives, and just a wee bit too much for them."

" And more food in a day than they're used to getting in a month," added Peg shrewdly.

" And a wee port ! What with that and goin' home in a Daimler," cried Davie with glee, " they'll talk of nothing else from here till Doomsday ! Man, John, ye'll never know what ye've done for these poor old geezers this night."

" But I think we all ought to be getting home now," suggested Beth in her prim way.

" Nonsense ! " John protested.

" Havers, woman ! " Davie added. " The fun's just startin'. And I tell ye what—" he winked maliciously at John—" I'm

going to have another of John's good drams, even if you and
Curly have to carry me home."

" Ye're just a big fool ! " said Beth, but tolerantly. .

The second dram worked so agreeably in Davie Bryden, a
temperate man, that, after wickedly inviting Dismal Dan Rolland
to join him in *Larboard Watch* or any other duet of the latter's
choosing, he announced that he would give the company *Roamin'*
in the Gloamin' as sung by Sir Harry Lauder.

Perhaps only John and old Sam Lightbody fully appreciated
this performance. For them, exiles over many years, the readiest
possible victims of sentimental nostalgia, the ditties of the great
comedian ranked in loveliness and authority next to the works of
Robert Burns and Holy Writ, in that order. Sincerely they sang
the essential poetry of the working Scot, the superb artisan so
strangely fated to the rough service of Empire and, by an
exquisite irony, therefore blunted in his tastes. They sang the
chorus with Davie so selflessly, they never knew that of all the
party only young Curly sang with them, and that such as Lily
smirked her tolerance of their folly, seeking all the time to catch
an equally superior eye, while our Cha winked at the Twins
and Mr. Alexander Lightbody appeared by his bleak look to
regret, faintly, this lapse from the standards of an organized and
forward-looking democracy.

But even Alec Lightbody was of a people that put solidarity
and the social obligation in the forefront of their code of
behaviour ; and when John, having heartily served Davie to a
third and old Sam to a fifth dram, called on him for a contribution to the evening's fun, Alec strode purposefully into the
open space by the fireplace, cleared his nostrils with a gustier
sniff than even Peg could compass, grasped the lapels of his
jacket with both hands, and announced :

" *Invictus*. By W. E. Henley."

Alec had taken classes in public speaking and elocution, and
this was the fairest fruit of his studies. He gave forth the
impeccable sentiments of the poem with vigour, conviction
and some few but energetic gestures, notably the pointing of a
long and vibrant forefinger. This digit quivered to the ceiling
of Blackwood's Hotel as he thundered in conclusion a more
individualistic *credo* than the Co-operative Society might have
approved :

> *I am the master of my fate :*
> *I am the captain of my soul.*

Everybody, save the elocutionist's father, thought the performance first-class. They clapped. Lily was heard to congratulate Peg and say : " I like a bit of good poetry, don't you ? " Davie Bryden shook his head in the manner of one who has just received a communication, dazzling but beyond the power of a simple chap fully to understand. " Who d'ye say was the chap that wrote it ? " he earnestly asked of Alec. On the contrary, old Sam Lightbody, shaping up to the table for his sixth dram, confided in John's ear, sourly :

" Ye'd think the silly —— was a minister at a burial."

John did feel indeed that Alec's grave performance had been in the nature of a benediction ; but as he cast about, fumbling for the next move, his eyes fell with pleasure on Addie Bryden and he called out to her without thinking :

" What about something from you, Addie ? "

The girl rose promptly. She blushed, but she was of a people who believed profoundly in the importance of sociability.

" I could sing *The Lea Rig*," she said.

" That's the lass ! " roared old Sam Lightbody appreciatively.

" Sibyl . . . Beryl . . ." Lily commanded her daughters to oblige at the piano.

" We don't know any of that old-fashioned stuff," said Beryl petulantly on behalf of the Rolland Rhythmic Twins.

" I don't need the piano," said Addie serenely.

So, her hands folded demurely, she sang as probably Robert Burns would have wished his simple little lovesong to be sung, modestly, in a small, clear, true soprano. As compared with her brother's all-in wrestle with *Thora*, it was a miracle of unsophisticated sweetness. It was of this sort of girl, one might have guessed, that the poet was thinking as he fashioned to the old, true air his wistful lyric of rural courtship :

> *When owre the hill the eastern star*
> *Tells bughtin' time is near, my Jo,*
> *And owsen frae the furrowed field*
> *Return sae dowf and weary O !*

The homely, familiar words, the air that he must have heard sung over his cradle, brought the tears back to the sentimental eyes of John Rolland Cram, but again he was most deeply moved by the warmth of his own feeling for this child among all his relatives. She was Beth's child, but so was Curly ; and he knew only that something in and about her, as it were an aura, rendered her a person apart. He was conscious of a positive, outflowing love for this girl in the dress of Quaker grey, with her shapely face and steady grey eyes.

The three short verses of her song duly sung, Addie bobbed a little curtsey to the company and, blushing again, sought an obscure seat beside her mother. Old Sam Lightbody's voice prevailed above the polite clapping that saluted her performance. He raised a brimming glass towards her, his great face flushed.

" Well done, lassie ! Well done ! And the best turn of the evening, never mind what they say ! "

" Well done, Addie ! " John interposed more mildly. " And a great treat for old chaps like Mr. Lightbody and me. Now——"

He looked about him rather helplessly. Lily's voice sounded over his shoulder.

" The Twins could play again," she suggested.

" That would be nice, Lily," he demurred, " but I think the hotel people will be worried about their guests upstairs. It's been a wonderful night for me, but I think we might——"

He looked towards Beth who, ever watchful, rose and said in her firm voice :

" I think it's time we were all going now."

" What's your hurry, woman ? " cried Davie, who had been deep in an entrancing debate on football with Alec Lightbody.

" Have you looked at the time, Davie Bryden ? "

" Time ! " Davie dismissed that element with a wave and one of his enchanting grins. " Nobody'll stir a foot out this room till I've made a speech."

" O dear ! " wailed Beth, but with resignation.

So Davie made his speech, which was almost word for word, the oration delivered earlier in the evening by Mr. Lightbody of the Co-op. but now the speaker was such an honest chap, his grand phrases so unexpected, his mortification over his own confusion so comic, nearly everybody was reduced to laughter, and tears were rolling down even Beth's cheeks. Finally, he had them all singing *Auld Lang Syne* and was only by Beth's firm-ness restrained from leading a chorus in *For He's a Jolly Good Fellow*.

When the womenfolk were gone at length to prepare them-selves for the road, John found himself near the bottles, towards which Mr. Sam Lightbody had also converged while opportunity prevailed. John beckoned to Davie to join them, saying :

" Come on, lad ! One for the road."

" Great idea, John ! That sister o' yours'll skin me, just the same."

" Aye, man ! " Mr. Lightbody repeated himself. " You've given your own folks and me a rare treat this night. But mind what I told ye. You and me should be havin' a bit yarn."

" We should that," John agreed in the vernacular. " Where can I find you, Mr. Lightbody ? "

" I'm with Peg and Alec till Tuesday, but after that," announced the obese veteran almost majestically, " you'll find me at Sunnyside Cottage, Killadam. If you're ever takin' a bit sail . . . Sunnyside Cottage, Killadam."

" I will ! " cried John. " I'm thinking of buying a wee place that way myself."

" I'm your man," said Sam Lightbody, raising his glass. " Your verra good health, sir."

" And, John——" Davie Bryden cut in eagerly, " if you're doing nothing else on Saturday there's a rare fitba' match at the Potteries. Me and Curly——"

Beth's head appeared round the edge of the door.

" At it again, ye old fool ? " she addressed her husband tolerantly. " You'll be in a rare state to walk home, won't you ? Away and get your coat and hat, man."

" No need to walk, Beth," John intervened hurriedly. " There's a taxi for everybody."

He found himself alone with his sister.

" Was it all right, Beth ? " he asked anxiously. " The party ? "

" It was a fine party, John," she replied honestly. " You've given a lot of pleasure to a lot of plain folk."

" It was a pleasure to me," he said. " And I wanted to tell you, Beth, I think that's a fine girl of yours, Addie."

" Addie's a good girl," her mother stated. Suddenly she clutched at his arm and whispered vehemently, " But I want to talk to you, John. Not about Addie. About yourself, and all these folk——"

Lily burst in upon their momentary privacy, luscious in an evening cloak of black velvet with a pink satin lining.

"There you are, John ! Now you won't forget what I told you. There's open house at 'The Neuk' any time you want. Plenty of room and a warm welcome. Any time."

Then he was out on the doorstep, shaking hands and receiving thanks and joining forces with Beth in suppressing Davie's last hearty bid to raise the chorus of *Will ye no' come back again* ? Then he was alone, the last red tail-light sailing sidereally round a corner of the square.

When he returned to the room in which the feast had been held the young waiter in the white jacket, collarless now, was clearing up.

"Anything you want, sir, before I put these away ? " he asked, indicating the bottles.

"I don't think so. Yes—just a nip of whisky and a drop of water. We weren't too much trouble, were we ? "

"Not at all, sir," the youth politely replied, handing the glass. "That's what we call a nice, quiet family party. A sing-song and a drink or two. Nothing like some of the do's we have here when they start smashing the place up. Makes you a bit sick sometimes, sir."

"I'm sure it does."

John felt in his hip-pocket and brought out two notes between his fingers. He knew that he was grossly over-tipping the youth, but he must thus express his own satisfaction.

"Thank you, sir. Thank you very much indeed, sir ! "

"I'll get to bed, then," said John, draining his glass.

"I'll take you up in the lift, sir," the waiter insisted.

It was long before sleep overtook John Rolland Cram. He was much aware of the janglings and bumpings in the marshalling yards by the Marine Station. He heard the early morning milk train pull out for the city. He also heard, and with pleasure, the deep boom of a great ship's siren bellowing for a pilot to come out and take it up-river on the flood.

It was the cinefilm of the party, however, that kept turning over and over in his mind, with all its bright and comic and pathetic pictures, with all the puzzles and problems it presented to himself, from the near-tragic penury of the Grosart sisters to the ambitious ebullience of the Rolland Twins, from the uncomplicated heartiness of Davie Bryden to the miasmic, autogenerated misery of Dismal Dan, from the quiet anxieties of Beth to (as he shrewdly guessed) the equal but more flashily-suggested anxieties of Lily, from our Cha's limp handshake and his final, casual " Thanks a lot, Uncle," to the brave and honest simplicity of Beth's girl, Addie.

It would take an old chap just home from the East quite a time to get the hang of things. But that Addie girl was something special and, the picture of her virginal figure in his mind, John ultimately fell asleep ; but not before his professional ear caught the rattle of the riveting machines borne on the easterly wind from Tod & Bannerman's yard. Even through the night the shipbuilders were working against this war that some chaps insisted was coming. This Hitler chap ; and those damned little yellow beggars he knew so well. The Japs in China. My God, if people only knew !

He made a mental note to ascertain to-morrow, on the strictly professional basis, what Admiralty jobs T. & B. had on hand. Davie Bryden would know, Addie's father.

3

A first-class compartment of the 11.55 out of the Marine had as its sole occupant Mr. John Rolland Cram. The guard, an observer of considerable experience and with an expert eye for the main chance, had himself opened the door, indicated the unique comfort the compartment offered, and assured the company's patron that he could count on being undisturbed. For this act of perspicacity and consideration he felt himself well, but only properly, rewarded with a half-crown piece.

The guard had seen in Mr. Cram a gentleman of some consequence proceeding to a social occasion of moment. His shrewd and parasitical eye had acutely discerned, and in a flash, the significance of the heavy overcoat in fine frieze, the ample lines of the Stetson hat, the sharp crease on the trousers of a light suit in expensive cloth, and the beautifully polished black shoes beneath them, with purple-shot silk socks intervening. The guard knew a well-to-do gentleman just home from the East when he saw one ; and he assured his patron that the moment the train stopped at Killogie halt he, the guard, would appear to see that the process of alighting might be carried through with the least possible inconvenience.

The railway line out of the Marine to the city pursues a fantastic course. For nearly two miles on end it is carried quite steeply uphill and along deep tunnels, of which the driving through deep igneous rock could have been possible only in an age of optimistic expansion and cheap labour. Out of the tunnels the engine has still a climb of several hundred feet up a track cut into the steep hillside before it achieves the plateau ; so that while the down-trains have the speed and fire of rockets as they plunge towards the riparian terminus from the heights, the up-trains puff mightily in labour to conquer the formidable gradient.

This circumstance was rather more pleasing to Mr. Cram than otherwise, if only because he was still savouring the exquisite sensation of one lately returned from a long sojourn abroad. Even the bite of the sulphurous fumes that seeped through the frames of the shaking windows was an old and familiar experience gratefully renewed.

In the blindness of the tunnels he reflected pleasantly on what, in three days, he had been able to contrive towards his resettlement in his native town—notably, an interview with what seemed to be a very decent and reliable sort of solicitor chap and a flattering talk with the youngish man who had just taken over the agency of the Linen Bank at Petrie's corner, vastly delighted to acquire a new customer with a fat pension and a tidy bundle of Policies of Assurance and gilt-edged script. He had ordered a daily delivery of the *Glasgow Herald*, in the columns of which, under the headings of PROPERTIES FOR SALE, he fully expected, and with good reason, to discover ultimately the advertisement of the right wee cottage at the Coast ; and he had also satisfied himself that the *Herald* was sound on Japanese aggression and the Imperial problem in general.

When the 11.55 ultimately burst out of the tunnels and painfully breasted the slope in the pale sunlight of a showery autumn day, John became more than ever enchanted with his situation. From this point onwards the line, sliced out of the foothills, commanded what for many years he had reckoned to be the finest view of the anchorage and the mountains on the other side. He had even maintained against rabid and touchy Australians that his own bit of northern firth was, in the considered view of any reasonable party, finer than Sydney Harbour. Just look at it now—some six miles by three of fine, deep tidal water shelving swiftly from under the roots of the hills ; a jagged and romantic pattern of wooded peninsulas and sinuous lochs ; a real picture laid out on the flat, with a new cruiser on trials, a twin-and-yellow-funnelled C.P.R. ship, a red-and-black-funnelled Cunarder, and a black-funnelled Anchor liner out in the fairway four hundred feet below : for this was Saturday forenoon, the big day of the North American sailings, as it always had been.

John's affectionate eyes then came ashore, so to speak, looking down on the small forests of cranes and gantries that marked the shipyards stretching along some three miles of beach, the red-leaded hulls looking like models, or even toys, from the heights. It gave him a deep, warm satisfaction to boast to himself that he knew every shipyard of a baker's dozen, its history, capacity, average output, management and relative efficiency—aye, even how the common five-eights of a shipyard worker rated it as a place of employment : whether it was " Klondyke," where wages ran high in the old days of free enterprise, or " Siberia," cocked out on the spine of the Neb and eternally castigated by whistling winds.

They all built ships, good ships : the best ; and it was grand to see, and hear, them working at full pressure, even if most of the construction was naval—cruisers, destroyers, minesweepers and what not—and the rest tankers. During the three days since his return John had made it his delightful business to visit most of them, the card of the late Superintendent Engineer of the K. & S. readily admitting him to managerial and drawing offices presided over by chaps who had served their time with him in T. & B.'s or came of the families that had led the industry ever since John Wood built Henry Bell's *Comet* at the very spot on to which, looking from the carriage window, he felt that he could toss a stone.

The most confidential blueprints of the Admiralty had been passed to him for his experienced consideration. Harassed yard managers had found time to conduct him over vessels which, fitting out, were on the Secret List. In one of these a young technician, regular R.N. at that, had made no bones about explaining and demonstrating the Asdic device. Wonderful things the young scientific chaps were up to nowadays ! Even in the plain business of shipbuilding, all the new applications of power from relatively small units to the paramount problem of answering the call for speed and economical running seemed very wonderful to an ageing man brought up in the heyday of triple expansion. Clever lads ! But behind them always was the fundamental power of superb craftsmanship in the Black Squad, the inherited knowledge of how a ship should be built to fulfil her prime function of seaworthiness.

As the train scaled the heights Mr. John Rolland Cram was, in short, a man in a high state of satisfaction with himself and the world about him. He had been received back into his own professional fold with the consideration due to a successful veteran and trusted ex-official of a great British corporation operating overseas ; and now he was on his way to answer a bidding he regarded as other men might regard a command to present themselves at His Majesty's Court of St. James. He was going to have luncheon with Mr. Tertius Troquair Bannerman, hereditary head of T. & B.'s, and his lady at their great house at Killogie Old Cross. Mr. Bannerman's invitation to this feast, written in an eccentric but neat script that suggested the ancient Greek calligraphy, had been couched in the friendliest terms of equality.

If John had been a more egotistical, more astute and less honest person his pleasure in this outing might have been qualified to some extent. It was rather beyond the range of his apprehension that, having given his relatives a glimpse of glory through the Party and conferred on at least a few of them a sense of valuable possession, he had promptly returned them to a state of frustration by attending to his own affairs for three days on end. He had not perceived in his simplicity and modesty that he and his reputed wealth were factors in a whole complex of private, and pathetic, schemes of development long cherished and hopefully elaborated.

It would have touched him to have seen, for instance, the look of boyish disappointment on the face of Davie Bryden when, on

his return from work that Saturday forenoon, Beth handed him
the postcard on which John, remembering a half-promise, had
explained why he could not attend the football match.

"That's a pity," Davie mourned sincerely. "He's missing
a great game. He's got some swell friends, eh, Beth?"

"Is the man not to have a life of his own?" asked Beth with,
in her tone, that unfortunate tendency towards the belligerent.
"It's a great honour for John. And he has earned it."

"That's right, lass! He's a fine man is your brother John!"
said Davie handsomely. "I was just thinkin' . . ."

Prudently, Davie did not go on to particularize about what
he had been just thinking and, stripped to the waist, bent over
the kitchen sink, to rid his person of the grim and grease of the
blacksmith's shop in a prolonged, noisy and energetic series of
ablutionary processes. It might have comforted him, and it would
certainly have amused him sardonically, to know what pangs of
frustration were simultaneously troubling Lily Rolland in "The
Neuk" at the other end of the town.

Lily had been assiduous in her attentions to Cousin John.
With the unswerving concentration of a mother of talented
children, her own life of passion foundered on the mudflats of
Dismal Dan's preoccupations, her personal ambitions transferred
to the Twins, she had cherished one of John's enthusiastic phrases
and, essentially a simple and single-minded woman of tough
fibre, was bent on having its general intention realized. She had
made and, as it were, caressed a plan. John should come to
Saturday night supper. The Twins would play for him again at
their most brilliant. The discussion of their development, properly
financed, could then proceed.

On the morning after the party Lily was down at Blackwood's
Hotel in her best tweed costume, the green one with the leather
buttons, only to learn from the distant girl in the office that Mr.
Cram was out and, so far as she, the receptionist, could know,
would not be back until evening. At about five o'clock that
afternoon Lily deluded herself into believing that she had some
shopping to attend to and, just while she was passing, looked in
again to ask for Mr. Cram; again to be told by another but
equally cool miss in the office that he had not returned and, so
far as the staff could know, might come in any time between
now and midnight. No, said the chit in a final salvo, Mr. Cram

had not said anything about being in for dinner. He would know perfectly well that Blackwood's, under a new management, had dinner always ready for residents from six until as late as nine. Perhaps Madam could ring Mr. Cram—and poor Lily cursed the lack of a telephone in " The Neuk."

She tried once again on the second day, quite early in the forenoon, and Mr. Cram was out, and after a torment of hesitations and anxieties she decided to write John a nice note, inviting him to supper on Saturday, and posted it herself after midnight in the pillar-box at the corner of Pitt Street. She had thus failed, however, to allow for the vagaries of the local postal system, so that John's reply on a postcard did not reach " The Neuk " until the second delivery on the Saturday morning.

Lily had already ordered a boiling fowl from Fletcher's, and she had hopefully but unwisely encouraged her confidants, the Twins, to believe that their higher tuition in the art of rhythmic pianism was as good as guaranteed ; and when the girls saw Lily hurry to answer the second postman's ring they naturally followed her and scanned her face as she read the few lines on the G.P.O.'s somewhat shabby oblong of yellow board.

" What does he say ? " asked Beryl.

" He can't come," replied Lily, tightly, between her teeth.

" Why not ? " asked Sybil in her blunt way.

" Because he can't," her mother snapped back, adding bitterly, " It might have been on something a bit more private than a postcard. I suppose the postman has it by heart now."

She remembered then her ideal position in the eyes of the Twins, the clever, cheerful Mummie who was also a good sport and a good friend, and she added, bitterly blithe, mocking the cultured accent :

" Seems we've got to go visiting our grand friends in the County, Mr. and Mrs. T. T. Bannerman, all very posh."

" But you said he would be coming to talk about us ! " bleated Sybil, an unsubtle child.

" A little less impertinence out of you, Sybil Rolland—— " blazed Lily, her temper rising again.

All innocent of any sense of responsibility for these disappointments and asperities, John contemplated with pleasure the upland scenes that unfolded themselves when the train, having won its daily battle with the foothills, scudded across the plateau through the dormitory towns that city-made wealth had created on the very edge of the moorlands. Plenty of retired chaps like himself had settled down in these agreeable communities of red-roofed bungalows with harled walls, and good luck to them! His own fancy was for a seaside place, but he enjoyed this journey as revealing to his eyes, so long homesick, another well-remembered aspect of his native land. An agreeably proprietary sort of feeling was upon him as the train, having dashed through a stretch of woodland, slowed down for Killogie Halt.

The guard was at the carriage door, touching his cap with the rolled green flag, before John had got a hand properly to the strap. Then a hugely tall young man, in black leggings and a tidy grey uniform with a tight jacket of hussar pattern, blocked the platform to salute and ask if he was Mr. Cram, sir. Admitting the identity, John was led through the tiny booking-hall of a wayside station and herded into the interior of a limousine infinitely more luxurious in its dove-grey upholstery and actually more comfortable than the first-class accommodation provided by the railway company.

The Rolls-Royce moved off with hardly a murmur, and John felt mightily pleased with his situation. He recognised in the exquisite vehicle a glory of British achievement, matching in his engineer's mind the efficiency of the London Underground system and the powerful splendour of the great ships built by his own people. Forty-five horse-power in eight cylinders under that long bonnet, but so sweet and flexible that the driving of the limousine was in fact infinitely easier and safer than the management of a small family car. With a boy's delight in such things he watched to see how the tall chauffeur could slow down to the pace of a pony and yet, without changing gear, get the bulk of the car smoothly round one of the abrupt bends of the tortuous route from the station to Killogie Old House. He thought happily of such considerations as carburettion, injection, pressure, timing and torque.

The drive of some two miles was thus a technical treat, but if John Rolland Cram could have been interviewed at almost any moment while it lasted he might have admitted that a certain feeling of social consequence was at the back of his happiness. He could not help feeling that his bidding to lunch at a County seat was a reward of modest distinction honourably earned, and still less could he help thinking, though with the kindliest tolerance, how strangely the gathering in prospect would compare with the Party he had arranged for his own people only three nights before. He actually chuckled to think what Mr. Tertius Troquair Bannerman would make of the four Grosart sisters, and he smiled to envisage Davie Bryden, at that precise moment probably bent over the kitchen sink in his semmit, vehemently and noisily cleansing from his person the oils and grimes of his forenoon labours as a foreman blacksmith.

The car had no sooner turned in through the gates of the Killogie Old House policies and passed the lodge than it slowed down and stopped. John was puzzled to know why this should be, for he was rehearsing the manner of his entry to the mansion-house proper, when a high clamour of barking and bowfing and yapping of terriers outside drew his attention to the fact that his host, the unmistakable Mr. Tertius Troquair Bannerman, had walked down to the gates to meet him and was now, a churn of small dogs about his ankles, signalling him to dismount.

" My wife's dogs," explained Mr. Bannerman with a wan smile as John put a tentative foot to the ground, fearful lest, on the one hand, he might injure a pedigree Cairn of priceless rarity or, on the other, have his ankles and the ends of his trousers chewed to bits by these spirited and belligerent animals. " This is my daily duty. And how are you, Mr. Cram ? It is extremely kind of you . . ."

" Very well indeed, sir. And it is very kind of you."

Mr. Bannerman then surprised his guest by clutching his stick about the ferrule, swinging it back to the full extent of his arm and sending it whirling through the air ; whereupon the terriers streaked off in pursuit of it, fought for its possession, and fought again for the honour of returning it to their master.

" A cowardly device," Mr. Bannerman admitted wistfully, " but my only *modus vivendi* with these ferocious creatures. At least," he added optimistically, " it always takes us towards the house."

Their progress up the long drive was thus contrived in due course. A singularly good throw of his stick by Mr. Bannerman might gain as much as twenty yards, while host and guest might make another ten by overtaking and outdistancing the Cairns as they wrangled and snarled and snapped for possession of the

ashplant. Conversation was difficult, however, in this world
where dogs were kings, and John was greatly relieved as they
approached the terrace before the big house to see a kennelmaid
in khaki breeches appear round a gable and, with one clear
call, attract the terriers towards her in one urgent, yelping
stream.

"That's better," said Mr. Bannerman with relief. "The girl,
of course, feeds them ; hence their attachment to her. But let
us go in, Mr. Cram, and refresh ourselves."

In the library an agreeable array of glasses, decanters and
syphons on a low table took the lights from a fire of logs. John
lowered himself with conscious pleasure into a deep chair
upholstered in leather.

"Sherry, spirits, one of these gin affairs ? " Mr. Bannerman
suggested. "A cigarette ? "

"A drop of whisky and water, if you please," John agreed.
"And I'll stick to my pipe, sir, if you don't mind."

Thus the two ageing gentlemen settled down to mature and
agreeable conversation, starting with a few polite inquiries and
replies as to John's recent experiences and concentrating on the
theme of Japanese expansion : a topic that was apt to recur in
the ex-Superintendent Engineer's reminiscences of the East. Mr.
Bannerman had an historian's interest in the subject and questioned his guest with some thoroughness.

"Yes," he summed it up at length, passing the glass of sherry
from side to side under his hairy nostrils. "The typical bid of
the half-baked for domination by force. A recurrent theme in
human history, Mr. Cram—the dirty boy at the bottom of the
class determined to get his own back. As with this ranting
pantaloon in Germany."

"That's just about the size of it, sir ! " cried John, greatly
struck with the figure of speech. "Since the Manchurian
affair——"

He was about to elaborate the theme when the door opened
to admit a tall female in a tweed costume, goffred tongues hanging
over the fronts of her brogue shoes. A long face with a curious
hint of masculine modelling about the jaw matched her general
appearance of open-air austerity, but this impression was offset
in a rather puzzling fashion by the fluffed curls of a great head
of greying reddish hair and by the copious frivolity of a triple

string of pearls about her neck and a longer superimposed necklace
of fine filagree work in silver that extended downwards almost to
the lower extremities of her fluffy jumper in angora wool, dyed
a somewhat girlish carmine-pink.

"Ah, my dear!" cried Tertius as the men rose. "Allow
me to present an old friend, Mr. Cram. Mr. Cram, my
wife."

The lady's handshake was indifferent, as it were a brief loan
of three lax and uninterested fingers.

"Ah, yes. Mr. Cram! Heard of you. How do you do? See
anything of In-jah on your way home?"

As he fulfilled his part of the polite conversational bargain, John
classified Mr. Bannerman's lady to his own satisfaction. She was
memsahib to perfection in her clipped, automatic mode of speech,
inveterately of the Ruling Class in her probably quite unconscious
tone of ever-so-subtle condescension. While the party settled
again round the fire he felt himself, his clothes, his manners, his
speech, to be the objects of a superior but careful scrutiny. He
hated to suspect it, but Mrs. Bannerman made him aware of a
distinct hostility, perhaps not so much towards himself as towards
the sort of person she took him to be, and he was aware at
the same time of a lack of interest on his own part to break it
down, except in so far as it complicated his relationship with his
highly respected friend, Mr. Tertius Troquair Bannerman, titular
head of the clan to which he owed a willing, even a wilful,
obedience.

They were almost like two rival claimants for the sovereignty
of the East; and then the lady quite suddenly surprised John by
addressing her husband in a voice and manner startlingly different
from those of the aloof and soldierly *memsahib*.

"Terty, darling!" she wooed her husband in a caressing
mezzo-soprano. "What has Lionel brought for a poor woman?"

"My dear!" cried Tertius, jumping to his feet. "How very
foolish of me! Unforgivable . . ."

John could not help looking round the room for this person
called Lionel, but he quickly perceived from Tertius's movements
that Lionel was the code name for the heavy decanter that contained the sherry. Anything but an anthropomorphist, he
perceived that his hostess, in the girlish phase that was also
represented by her redundant necklaces and bright jumper, had

this, to him, baffling trick of giving pet-names to the familiar objects of the household. He was thus to learn before the day was done that a poker might be Toddles in the domestic vocabulary of Killogie Old House, or Snooks the local byword for a silver cigarette box.

It was clearly observed by John, however, that this diction was exclusive to Mrs. Bannerman in direct communication with her husband ; that the historian was hardly enthusiastic in his responses ; and that this variant of Ogham or Choctaw, while intended to enchant the guest, rather deliberately excluded him from the confidence of the household. This feeling was strengthened in John when his hostess, fortified by a sip of the liquid from the belly of Lionel, turned on him strongly and demanded :

" Now, tell me how are things in the East, Mr. Cram ? "

While John hesitated, Mr. Bannerman demurred :

" Surely rather a tall order, my dear."

" Why ? " cried his wife with the bold diphthong of the Ruling Class. " I thought Mr. . . . er . . . Cram has just come home from China. It *was* China, wasn't it, Mr. Cram ? "

" Well, madam, it's all very difficult . . ." John began.

Fortunately for him, the deep voice of a gong boomed in the hall and, dropping the subject with that lightness of mind John had always noted in the females of the Ruling Class (to whom conversation seems to be a sort of drill exercise carried out at high speed and in loud tones) his hostess led the way to the morning-room.

This was a delightfully bright chamber with quite a small round table of gleaming mahogany, nicknamed Honeybun, drawn up near the high French windows. The grave and anonymous presence of a manservant was noted by John with some appreciation, but he was much less favourably impressed to see that, on a large cushion before the fire, lay an aged and nearly hairless terrier with bleary eyes and the elongated teats of accouchements innumerable sagging from a revoltingly bald belly in black, blue and buff.

" Darling Miffy ! " said Mrs. Bannerman, tickling the historic bitch in the midriff with the toe of a stout brogue, over which the unhappy brute slavered lavishly. " Too many babies, sweetheart ! Getting old and mumpy ? "

As he took his seat in these elegant circumstances John was

aware that confused feelings, some amusement, and sharpened powers of perception were at work within him all at once. He thought again of the simplicities of the family party in Blackwood's and wondered how the Grosart sisters would approach this table with its complex array of instruments and its strict code of service. He was most acutely and even deliciously aware of the contest of personalities between his hostess and himself, of the scrutiny to which he was being subjected, and of his own reserves of experience in the social conflict.

Wet wedges of honeydew melon were already in position before them, and when the manservant indicated a helpful presence at his elbow John remembered previous experiences at the seats of the mighty and was careful to help himself well to castor sugar, sparingly to ground ginger. When it came to the soup he felt he scored substantially off Mrs. Bannerman by choosing the consommé, but found himself mysteriously losing ground again as, with the arrival of the cutlets, he was careful with the carving of these awkward articles, whereas his hostess sawed great gobbets off them and, with her mouth full of the exquisite home-fed mutton, maintained a flow of abrupt questions and dismissive comments. The ways of the Ruling Class seemed to him all the more mysterious when, having picked up a bone in her fingers and wrenched at it fiercely with her teeth, she tossed the rest to the decrepit dog on the cushion and there-after appeared indifferent to the creature's slaverings over the morsel.

John's last stroke in the battle was to resist all the butler's blandishments and accept only a glass of water, but when they returned to the library and a fat bottle in a wicker jacket was produced under the name of Tubby, he accepted a thimbleful of a very fine old brandy with his coffee. Sunk in a deep club armchair, soothed by good food, the suave spirit of Cognac, and an excellent cigar, amused by his hostess's kittenish play with the nicknames of cream jug, sugar bowl and percolator—Bubbly, of course—he realized too late that the lady, upright in a stiff-backed chair above him, had him at her mercy. Quite suddenly she emerged from her girlish phase and challenged him in the relentless tones of the Birch-Pitkeathlys in the female line.

" You were talking about the situation in the East, Mr. Cram. Why difficult ? "

John hitched his person forward to the edge of the armchair. He had found that with his girth tending to increase, the upright position was essential to clarity of brain and voice.

" Because, ma'am," he answered gravely, " the Japanese are making it so."

" R'ally ! Why ? "

" My dear ! " Tertius protested wearily. " Their obvious policy of imperialistic aggression. It is all on the record. Clearly."

" Clearly ! " repeated John, gratified for this meed of support. He appealed to his adversary : " You must remember, ma'am, that they walked into Manchuria in '31, and nobody stopped them : not ourselves, not the States, not the League of Nations —nobody ! "

" Beastly sort of place, Manchuria, I should think ! "

" That may be, ma'am," observed John warmly, " but you know the East as well as I do, or better, and I think you must see that every time we fail to face up to the Nips, bang goes so much of our Face ! They're all over China now. They own Shanghai—*Shanghai* ! They're picking up islands all over the Western Pacific, and hardly anybody here or in the States seems to know or care a docken about it ! "

He was aware of his own increasing excitement, and it was helped to hear Tertius declare with a vague, oracular detachment:

" The footsteps of Clio are apt to be muffled. Most interesting what you say, Mr. Cram. Yes ! The processes are almost invariably imperceptible except to an enlightened few, and these are usually powerless. How very odd ! "

" Don't know much about China myself," his wife bellowed defiantly. " Don't quite see what it's got to do with In-jah."

" Small matter of geography, my dear," muttered Tertius.

" Ah ! " cried John simultaneously.

Seizing in all innocence his small bit of advantage, he leaned forward in his chair and pointed his cigar at the long, unfriendly face of his hostess.

" That's just the Japanese plan, ma'am ! India's their prize silver teapot, surely. Hold off the Yanks in the Pacific. Occupy China. Jump on Australia. Mop up Indo-China and Siam as easy as winking. Cut off Malaya. Then India . . . That's the scheme the little beggars are hatching. It will be a nice day when we have the Nips sitting on the banks of the Canal, won't it ? "

A painful hush followed this outburst. Mrs. Bannerman sucked loudly at her coffee-cup.

" A bold scheme," observed Tertius at length, easing the tension of silence in the room. " Fantasy, if you like. But feasible. That is, in the face of universal inertia. There's one prime factor, I think. The inertia of the theoretically responsible. Thus we have Clio in snowboots ; if the phrase is not too flashy. I think, my dear "—he turned happily to his spouse—" Mr. Cram has made some very interesting points. I hadn't myself apprehended the significance of the Pacific islands."

This woman of the Birch-Pitkeathly's, however, was not so easily to be put down.

" Mr. Cram seems to have forgotten Singapore," she said.

John sipped at his brandy and considered the length of ash on his cigar.

" No, ma'am, I have not," he demurred gravely, " for the very reason that I happen to think, and so far do cleverer men than I, that Singapore is the blindest of our blind spots, the very place where we'll get the biggest shock because we least expect it."

" Ah ! " exclaimed Tertius.

" R'ally ! " observed his wife.

" Yes," John resumed eagerly. " Singapore's a wonderful job as a naval base, beautiful ! But it's only a naval base, planned by chaps who think every war is decided by a fleet action. The next one isn't going to be. I'm a sailor of sorts myself, but I'll maintain that the aeroplane will make places like Singapore look silly in a week, once the fun begins. And all that opens up the spine of the Malay peninsula behind it ! "

John Rolland Cram finished his last small drop of brandy.

" And it's a mighty flabby spine," he added, sadly bitter.

His hostess, now far removed from the kittenish mood, screwed a cigarette into the long holder she affected, but she contrived to be reasonably urbane in her counter-attack on John's position.

" So you think we're going to lose In-jah ? " she laughed conventionally and with complete disbelief.

" Mr. Cram hardly went so far, my dear," muttered Tertius.

" No, ma'am ! " John insisted warmly. " I'm simply trying to point out what seem to me serious dangers. The Japanese are on the war-path ; there can be no arguing about that. I think very seriously that Singapore is—what would you call it ? "

" A legend. Or myth," suggested Tertius.

" The very word, sir—a legend. That's the point I was getting at ! There's far too much taking things for granted, out there as well as here at home. I'd go so far as to say that it's even worse out there than here. The British people in Malaya are just fair rotten with complacency and too much comfort and too much cheap native labour. It's bad enough in China, goodness knows, but when I saw those people in the Straits Settlements nowadays ! "

" What did you see, Mr. Cram ? " asked his hostess icily.

" Ma'am, I saw a great many spoiled people, a lot of people rotting away in a bad climate with too much easy money to their hands. No, no ! I don't mean responsible folk with a big stake in the country, like your own relatives or case-hardened old-timers like myself. I mean the younger folk who came out during the past twenty years or so to jobs in rubber or tin. And I particularly mean, ma'am, if you'll forgive me, the women."

" R'ally, Mr. Cram."

" I mean that, Mrs. Bannerman, with all my heart. Poor lassies ! I'm sorry for them. The monsoon in Malaya would take the heart out of a professional boxer in a fortnight. But it's the easy-come, the easy-go in a way they never knew at home. It's their plain confounded ignorance of history and geography. It's the mere clapping of hands that brings a dozen servants running to them."

" Power always corrupts," observed Tertius helpfully.

" Aye, and drink," said John harshly.

Both his hostess and host raised curious eyebrows.

" I'm no teetotaller myself," John went on gravely, " but I'm as certain as I'm sitting here in this fine old house that too much cheap drink is the undoing of far too many of these young people. The swank of it, the forgetting it brings ! Och, we needn't blame the poor souls ! But I tell you, Mrs. Bannerman " —and he turned earnestly to his hostess—" it takes a hard head and a stout heart to keep the old flag flying in the East ; and I sometimes wonder, much against the grain, if just a good deal too much gin and whisky isn't going to be the death of us out there."

If he expected an answer to his rhetorical question he did not receive one. Mrs. Bannerman had exhausted her interest in the more remote aspects of imperial integrity. She rose and addressed her husband exclusively.

" Got to dash off to a W.R.I. meeting in the village. I'll send the car back in time to get Mr. Cram to the 4.8. You can expect me for tea."

She turned on John, extending a quite hearty hand.

" So nice to have seen you, Mr. Cram ! Most interesting to meet somebody home from the East. Good-bye ! "

John was not a whit downcast by the abruptness of this parting. His dealings with the womenfolk of the Ruling Class had been quite extensive, and he had a shrewd feeling for the instincts of possessiveness and continuity that haunted all females. What he could never understand was why these upper-class women never hinted, even as a matter of form, at the possibility of a future meeting. John generously supposed that this came of meeting a lot of people.

" And now," said Mr. Tertius Troquair Bannerman, " I think we might have another glass of brandy."

" Well——" John hesitated.

" It is a very good brandy, I think."

" It is."

" *Ergo*——"

Mr. Bannerman returned to his chair, allowed his face to sink into his bosom, and finally grunted " Yes "—as if an unbroken argument was still proceeding.

John did not pester his host to amplify this enigmatic statement. He extinguished the butt-end of his cigar, took a sip at the second glass of Cognac, and then started patiently to fill his pipe. It was a queer thing, but he felt completely at ease with Tertius Troquair Bannerman in his most elusive moods.

" Yes, indeed ! " remarked Mr. Bannerman again.

He picked up his glass and drained it clean in one swallow.

" History repeats itself, you see," he confided to John. " The *motif*, as the musician would say, is recurrent. I am merely an historian. You understand that ? "

" Certainly, sir," John hastened to agree.

" But we have to take the economists into our confidence. I think we have to see that any fine romantic battle with flashing spears and noisy trumpets happened simply because a lot of people lacked the wherewithal to fill their bellies. Fame out of Famine —or is that too flashy, do you think ? Clearly, I suggest, your Japanese are seeking to expand in search of food essentially, like this mountebank Hitler in Germany. Mackinder said some very useful things on this point. Where is it now ? "

While Tertius short-sightedly perused the shelves of his untidy library, John took the opportunity of saying :

" I hope I didn't put it too strongly or upset Mrs. Bannerman in any way."

" The imperatives of history can never be put too strongly. My wife naturally takes a somewhat—shall one say ?—traditional view of these matters. Nor has she had your advantage of having lived in the East lately . . . But no, my Mackinder seems to have disappeared, like every other one of my books I happen to want immediately. Shall we have a walk in the park before the car comes back ? "

The two elderly gentlemen, so strangely related, so differently constituted as adult citizens, walked in the parklands about Killogie Old House in their heavy overcoats and found each other's company highly agreeable as they chatted of this and that out of their parallel series of memories and experiences.

It was for John a particularly pleasant circumstance that they were not now obliged to be accompanied by the raging tornado of terriers that had greeted his arrival. He was more impressed, more deeply moved and even troubled to think that he, John Rolland Cram, son of the People, who had deliberately returned to the People by the mere act of giving the Party to his nearest relations, had been by his own experience of living rendered more fit for, and even more sympathetic to, the urbane, remote and smoothly conventionalized life of the well-to-do. It gave him positive pleasure to walk by the side of an educated gentleman ; the spacious peace of the parklands, the mere extent of the natural grass under his feet, the age and loveliness of the trees, ministered pleasantly to his spirit.

At the same time, he was taking a considerable amount of amused delight in the unpredictable actions and statements of his host. Mr. Tertius Troquair Bannerman was one of those who wonderfully diversify the common life by departing naturally but spasmodically from the normal. He would break off a nice bit of talk about famous ships built by T. & B. to fumble for a penknife, slice a chip of bark off a tree, hold it close to his eyes for a full minute and then throw it away, as if he had satisfactorily checked the conclusions of the botanists. He would suddenly point his stick to the skies and shout : " One crow, sorrow ! Ha—two crows ; that means joy. Where are we ? " At one point of their journey John was greatly alarmed to see the historian run forward towards a molehill, scatter it in one devastating kick, then fall flat on his face as the result of this violent action.

" Parasites ! " he declared angrily as John helped to pick him up. " I hate the little brutes. They throw up their beastly mounds on my lawn. My lawn, I ask you ! Ah, well ! I suppose they are just like those Japanese chaps of yours and rather more innocent of malice aforethought."

It had already become alarmingly clear to John that his own views on Japanese Imperialism had quite profoundly disturbed his host. When they heard the car returning up the drive and started to move slowly towards the house, the afternoon sunlight had caught and isolated a clump of sycamores in the yellow loveliness of their early decay. The trees seemed to be on fire among their darker, hardier neighbours.

" See ! " cried Tertius, pointing his stick. " The ancients would have taken that for a sign."

" They are beautiful trees," agreed John. " There's nothing to beat the trees we have at home."

" Change and decay," his host pursued his own line of thought, wistfully. " Though so beautiful, autumn is always so damnably portentous to men of our age, my friend. And when I think of your Japanese acquaintances and what I know to be happening in Germany now—and the Good God alone knows what may be happening within the Russian concentration camp !—my heart, I must confess it, sinks. Decay and darkness ! Why, it is perhaps the twilight of civilization you and I see falling across these parklands in front of the old house ! The lights go out one by one, and I am afraid."

When he was at length in the train, throwing itself down the slopes into the pit from which the town of Garvel faces the Firth, John had no eyes for those scenes that had enchanted him on the outward journey. He found himself in a low state of mind that utterly baffled him to understand. It was not that he was aware of a positive unhappiness. It was least of all any considerable sharing of those historical preoccupations that so greatly concerned Mr. Tertius Troquair Bannerman. It was more like a feeling, as he might have phrased it to himself in his plain engineer's way, that the wonderful, long-planned homecoming was not working out very well. In his honest mind he searched for one simple explanation of his unease and could not find it.

He could hardly know that he was only that sad, recurrent figure in human history : the one who had thought too long and fondly and generously of a return to a self-created heaven on earth. His was the commonplace fate of those who, throwing off their own burdens, are foolishly if innocently blind to the human weaknesses behind the smiling faces in the imaginary scene of welcome ; forgetful in their own hopefulness of the preoccupying struggles, pains, ambitions, passions, desires and hostilities within all but the odd saint among suffering and sinful humanity. Being a plain man, marvellously uncomplicated, John could not see that the indifferent hostility of a Birch-Pitkeathly had only completed a process of disillusion through which he had been passing for just about four days.

He therefore did not apprehend that a struggle to make a choice or reach a compromise still lay before him. As he walked uphill from the Marine, a drizzle of rain hazing the nap of his fine frieze overcoat, he was conscious only of a premature deepening of the shadows within the fourth of his Five Arches. Back in Blackwood's Hotel he could hardly bear the notion of spending a long, empty evening within its walls, and he found equally intolerable the idea of going out in the rain to visit any of his relatives unannounced. It was a pity he could not get Beth and Davie on the telephone and have them along for a bit talk. The best thing, the right thing, would be to go over those advertisements of Properties for Sale at the Coast he had methodically cut from the *Herald* and get some inquiries going. It was time to get something started.

Thus quite a number of people in that northern seaport wondered what had happened to John and even vaguely feared that they might lose him to his fine friends. Up in " The Neuk " her children had a difficult evening with Lily in one of her snappy moods and could not fully appreciate that she was a worried woman who, fighting a battle, greatly feared an early reverse after a promising attack. Even his sister Beth, a woman wholly innocent of greed, having bought in food on the chance of John looking in for a bite, was patiently disappointed when nine o'clock struck and not a sign of him. After all, she and John hadn't had a right talk since he came home.

CHAPTER THREE

DECLARATION OF DIVIDEND

I

IT was Sunday morning in Blackwood's Hotel. Even at ten
o'clock the place had that air, common to most catering
establishments on the Sabbath, as of an organism which,
exhausted after the profitable excitement of the working week,
unwillingly faces the boredom of an off-day.

As Mr. John Rolland Cram made his way down the side-stairs
to the dining-room, ten minutes before the hour, he observed
that the chambermaids were not yet astir, and that bedroom doors
hung open, revealing hillocks of tumbled, untended bedclothes,
clothes in disarray on chairs and floors and even an occasional
stranded and abandoned utensil in earthenware, a bleak island on
an ocean of worn carpet and mutely eloquent of the simplicities
normally obscured by smart hotel routine.

Reaching the ground floor, he saw an ancient troglodyte
sweeping out the bar and seeming to sweep into the main building, with the sawdust and the cigarette ends, the sour stenches,
imprisoned overnight, of stale tobacco and the heeltaps of beer.
The young waiter, who had so smartly served the drinks at the
Party, was to be seen polishing glasses in a service pantry, the
splendid shirt-front of his public appearance revealed to be but
a paper dickey worn over a thin striped shirt and deplorable
braces mended with bootlace. Only one unsmiling girl served the
breakfast tables, and she, when John boggled over her curt offer
of porridge and kedgeree, snapped " The gong went at nine,
didn't it ? " and John had to check his rising temper and remember
that he dealt no longer with Chinese menials but with dour
individualists of his own race.

Even the lounge, an agreeable chamber in its chintzy way, with
plenty of light from high windows and a great coal fire blazing,
had in its atmosphere the nip of Calvinism. The regulars had
been reduced by the week-end exodus to seven or eight aged

female parties and their middle-aged spinster daughters, all disposed towards the cosier sort of conversation, and one sour-looking person with a goatee beard and the air of a professor of one of the bleaker sciences (he belonged in fact to the esoteric, highly-skilled, respectable and profitable profession of average adjuster) who held that day's *Observer* at arm's length before him, stared at it angrily, and ceaselessly gnashed and clicked with his dentures as if the editorial opinions were intolerable to a man of his scientific training. The only casual was a commercial traveller, stranded in Garvel for the week-end by a highly complicated set of circumstances he was all too willing to explain to his fellow-guests.

It was perhaps the commercial traveller who, by one of fate's eccentric and unreasonable caprices, forced John Rolland Cram into a line of action that was to prove portentous. If the choice John had seemed to see before him on the previous evening, returning in a mist of disappointment from Killogie Old House— if this vaguely-understood choice really had to be made, then it was almost certainly the commercial traveller, a Mr. Tweedie, who intervened and, by dint of being a decent bore, sent his fellow-guest along one given track through the unchartable jungle men call life.

He was a well-furnished person in a black morning-coat and a wide-winged collar which, in a thoroughly statesmanlike manner, framed a heavy, pink, friendly face in the Roman mould. When John entered the lounge and bowed to the company, Mr. Tweedie's bob of acknowledgment was far and away the most unrestrained. When John walked to one of the high windows before deciding on a seat (for all those by the fire were securely occupied as according to proprietary right by females) it was not long before Mr. Tweedie was up behind his shoulder, making friends.

" Damp, this morning," he observed in a rich voice. " Of course, as they say, it's always raining in Garvel."

" That's the story," John agreed with a civil little laugh, though he had been a little damped himself by the wet greyness of the sky and the shallow puddles on the pavements.

" Where I come from," suggested Mr. Tweedie, " it's likely to be a fine day. Sunshine and a rare breeze off the North Sea."

"Where's that?" asked John, almost willingly falling into the trap.

"Haddington."

"Oh?"

"Yes. I should have been home last night. My little lady will be wondering what's come over me. Of course, I gave her a tinkle last night, but I don't think she believed me; thought I was on the skite or something. A 'smatter of fact, it was the funniest thing you ever heard, the way it turned out. Garvel's the end of my round, of course. Always, invariably. Start from Edinburgh and work West. Three weeks, I always reckon. Got it taped. Kitchen soaps, washing powders, bleaching agents— that's the line. Anyhow, yesterday afternoon——"

The tale of delays, important discussions and missed trains was long and detailed. In patience and silence John listened to the recital, and only when Mr. Tweedie started to repeat himself and looked like going over the adventure once more, with details omitted from the first version, did he turn away from the window and say politely:

"It must be very awkward for you, sir. But now, if you don't mind, I must have a look at the papers."

The sheet he picked up and took to a remote chair lacked the power to interest him. It is the paradox of news, which can seem so entrancing when fresh and intimate, that it loses all savour over quite short distances of time and space, and actually acquires the faintly repulsive quality of the leftovers from yesterday's supper that have passed the night uncovered on a table nobody has troubled to clear.

Not yet accustomed to the rhythms of life at Home, John merely glanced at headlines in which the words "Germany," "Hitler," "Society," "Crisis" and "Sensation" were the most frequently recurrent, considered with a faintly ironic curiosity a photograph of Royalty in one of its interminable exposures to the Press camera, skimmed an article of an extremely alarming but equally speculative nature on the strength of the Luftwaffe, and finally threw to the floor that finished work of hundreds of men and women which had failed to hold his individual attention for five minutes.

Warily watching the attitudes of Mr. Tweedie, now telling the story of his strange misadventure to one of the unmarried daughters, the one with the moustache, John slipped out into the entrance hall. Even as he did so all the kirk bells of the numerous tabernacles of several denominations in the Presbyterian way of worshipping the one Christ started to clang and compete almost simultaneously; and John's heart swelled to hear that confusion of noises, for it was as it had been in his childhood.

He could still identify them—the deep, funereal thump from the Mid and the lighter tongues from the Free West confusing the issue, even as their sectarian refinements did; the pleasant if monotonous minor third from the two tenor bells in Beaconsfield United persisting through the appropriately frivolous drip of chimes from St. Michael's, the English Church. So it went on from nearly two-score spires and steeples perched along several square miles of precipitous hillside until the mariners in the ships at anchor in the Deeps, waiting for the tide, must have stirred in their Sunday morning sleep to such a clamour.

For the late Superintendent Engineer of the K. & S., by no means a churchgoer, it was a joyful noise, and he stood behind the swing doors of the hotel to watch Garvel going to Kirk as by custom severely ordained. There they were—the elderly couples tottering along together, the aged spinsters clutching their Bibles and hymn-books, the youngish families of father and mother with their infants. He observed that there were fewer frock-coats and silk hats on parade than he would have expected twenty years before. There was now no boy encased in the Eton suit that had been strict West End fashion for the adolescent male in 1910 or thereabouts; the nice little boys of 1937 wore kilts and Harris tweed jackets with Balmoral bonnets that had the strange effect of seeming to flatten out their faces in the semblance of frogs.

Only the women and their daughters were consistent, with due regard to current fashion dressed in their very best: the faithful conservatives, by their fidelity sustaining the old order, even if it was only to make, in effect, a competitive fashion parade of the approach to the House of God.

John then thought, however, of the long services of worship to which these good people were submitting themselves: of the succession of metrical psalms, prayers, readings from Scripture and hymns that, devised in defiance of ritual, had itself become a ritual, and of thirty minute Presbyterian sermons, thoughtful, learned and sterile. He remembered the long, quiet Sabbath afternoons and evenings that had made the inhibited day the slowest of the flying weeks of childhood ; and he thought suddenly and with wry amusement of what he would have been doing on such a day in the sunlit and pagan East—cruising down to the Club about noon for a drink or two, watching tennis or cricket after lunch or perhaps out in the native sampans for a spot of duck-shooting, then dinner and two or three frames of snooker.

At this point in his reflections John became aware of Mr. Tweedie's emergence from the lounge and his genial approach from behind, and he turned to the desk with a swift affectation of intense thoughtfulness, asking the girl in the office if Blackwood's Hotel was in touch with a good motor hire service. On being assured that it was he said :

" Would you tell them to send a car here at two o'clock sharp ? A big one—Rolls-Royce if they've got one. I'll want it until the late evening."

" That will be quite all right, sir," replied the girl to John's faint surprise and the awed interest of Mr. Tweedie in the background.

It was then easy to pass that hapless traveller with a nod, spend a pleasant hour in his bedroom among the gift-parcels he had brought home, and subsequently enjoy the excellent lunch with which Blackwood's Hotel, emerging from its Sunday morning sourness of temper, offset for its resident guests the drabness of the day. It was a singularly pleasing circumstance that the head waiter, urbane but firm, headed off an attempt by poor Mr. Tweedie to take the other place at his own table in the bow of the window.

The sweep of the Rolls-Royce through the shabby, cobbled streets of the upper town made quite a stir in those regions of narrowly financed respectability. John noted with sympathy how the decent couples, setting out for a walk in the Cemetery with their carefully-dressed children, involuntarily halted to watch the passage of such a resplendent vehicle as his, the very symbol of plutocracy in the English mode. (John never came to realize the exotic prominence of his large Stetson from Singapore.) When it drew up at a close or entry to one block of tenement houses in a rank of tenements, a horde of small boys and girls swiftly gathered about it to speculate shrilly on its provenance and its mission.

"It's a hearse!" cried one.

"No it's no'!" countered another. "It's a doactor!"

"Mebbe it's a merriage," piped a small girl hopefully.

"Ye canny get merrit on a Sunday, silly!"

"Will ye get to hell oot o' here, the lot of ye!" pleaded the driver, not unkindly, as he jumped out to open the door for John. "Ye've saw a motor before, haven't ye?"

Descending with such dignity as he could muster amid the clamour of the children, John said:

"Bring these parcels up to the second flat, right. Bryden's the name."

"No' me, sir," the driver demurred respectfully. "Leave this motor a minute, and these wee devils wid have it oot o' gear and runnin' backwards doon to the Square. They'd have the straps cut off the windeys before you could say knife . . . Tak' yer fingers aff that door, ye wee besom! . . . A Rolls," the driver added apologetically, "is no' safe up here, sir, without there's somebody bye to keep these wee beggars aff it."

So John had to convey his own considerable burden of parcels up the worn and odorous stairs. Beth seemed to see a ghost when she answered his ring.

"John! What on earth . . ."

"Lay hold of some of these parcels," he begged her, "or I'll drop the lot."

They got them safely to the kitchen table, on which they made a noble pile indeed. Davie Bryden swung himself from the great bed in which, apparently, he had been awaiting the oncoming of his afternoon nap.

"John!" he cried jocosely. "Or is it Father Christmas?"

"Never mind the parcels just now," said John. "We're all going for a run first. I've got a car waiting outside. Hurry up now, everybody! Where's Curly? Where's Addie?"

"Curly!" said Beth. "You'd never see him at home on a Sunday these days. He's away at this hiking all the young folk have gone daft on. Addie's in, but," she hesitated anxiously, "she's got her Bible Class at four."

"If Curly can go hiking, Addie can miss her Bible Class once in a blue moon."

"Go and get her, woman, and don't waste time," Davie urged his spouse. He winked at John. "That woman'll stand arguing with Peter at the Golden Gates. But this is a great treat, John! And where's that dashed collar and tie of mine?"

The Brydens did not take long to prepare themselves for the outing, Addie already attired for Bible Class in a modest costume of grey Cheviot, to which she now added a ginger tammy that, in John's admiring eyes, admirably contrasted with her auburn hair and brought up the light in her grey eyes. The street children were still milling about the car, and the appearance of the party was greeted with a babble of comment.

"Help the blind!" screamed one female child sardonically, "it's only the Bryden's! And see the size o' the old man's hat!"

"I'll Bryden ye, ye rascal!" retorted Davie genially. "And a Rolls, by God! I'll get in in front wi' the driver chap."

John watched with amusement the embarrassment these too public proceedings caused Beth in her humility, but he was pleased to be paying his sister and her people a proper compliment, and he waved the big hat when, as the car started off, the urchins raised an ironic cheer.

Their passage out of the town along its southern edge was swift, and as the car started to pick up speed along the valley road to the sea, John began to appreciate the change that had come over the customs of his own people since he had last watched them at close quarters. Their own majestic vehicle was continually cutting out of and back into a nearly unbroken procession of lesser fry, almost every one containing a suburban family of the sort that, twenty years before, would have held this Sabbath holidaymaking to be mortal sin. The black tops of the small saloons made something like a procession of beetles that could find the satisfaction of their mysterious needs only on the beaches. Among the beetles was an occasional caterpillar— the long cavalcade of a cycling club, perhaps forty young men and women in double file, all in the skimpiest of khaki shorts and open-necked shirts, heads down almost on their handlebars and their legs—skinny, hairy, red, fat, long, short—whirling furiously as if the urge to flee the crowded places was nearly a dementia.

On the footpaths, sitting on gates or clambering up the slopes, were the hikers, most of them in shorts but many in the kilts of a dim, renascent nationalism.

By these belated by-products of the industrial civilization John was almost horribly fascinated. He noted the obvious passion in them for near-nakedness and, at the same time, the willingness with which they transported their heavy packs. He wondered why they should apparently rejoice in and plan for eccentricity of appearance, so that the prettiest girl among them must look a hoyden at the best. With elderly concern, and not very hopefully, he speculated on the state of sexual morality among these children so ebulliently returning to nature.

" My Goodness ! " he turned to Beth. " Sunday seems to be a public holiday in Scotland nowadays."

" There's been a big change these last ten years," his sister agreed. " Whether it's for the better is another question."

" No hiking for you, Addie ? " John turned to his niece, demure by his side.

" I'm not allowed," she said in her steady way.

" Well, perhaps there's some sense in that. I'm not sure . . . But tell me, lass—I've been waiting for a chat with you—what are you doing with yourself these days ? Still at school ? "

" I haven't been back this term," she replied.

John might have guessed from the hint of bleakness in the girl's tone, still more easily from the awkward silence that followed her brief speech, that he had blundered on an issue of difficulty among the Brydens. Perhaps it was his affection for these two women and his simple delight in their company that blinded him to the subtleties.

" Are you doing something else, then ? " he asked bluntly.

" No, Uncle John."

This was puzzling indeed, and John turned to his sister.

" It's that man through there," she said, but not at all harshly, pointing to the figure of her husband who, on the other side of the safety glass screen, was greatly enjoying a conversation with the driver about football, boxing, the wild chances of the Pools and cognate subjects.

" But why ? "

" You know what it is," Beth explained patiently. " Davie's a plain working chap—and one of the very best—but he's got the old working man's notion that a girl has to go out to a job and earn a wage as soon as she's able, and nothing will budge him. So Addie's got to go into the Mill, he says, and that's that."

" Into the Mill ! " cried John. " Minding a loom ! A girl like Addie ! Nonsense ! "

" Just you tell that to Davie," suggested Beth grimly.

" I will, and this very night, too ! Just nonsense ! " He turned to his niece. " Have you any notion what you'd really like to do, lass ? "

" I'd like to be a nurse."

" That's better," said John happily. " That's a fine profession for a girl. I've known many a grand woman in it out East, holding down responsible jobs at that. The very best ! You'll need your education for that, Addie."

" The headmaster says I should take my Leaving Certificate."

" Quite right, and so you will." He dropped happily into the vernacular. " Wait you till I get my hands on that father of yours. I'll sort him . . . But now we'll enjoy the scenery. Isn't that grand ! "

They had come down from the hills to the road which runs so close to the sea that in brisk weather the spray breaks on red rocks and soars above them and the interstitial seapinks in such iridescent clouds that, however bright the day, the pedestrian may be soaked as by a fine rain and the driver at pains to clear his windscreen.

This day was grey and still, but you could feel the creep of the unresting tides, and the westering sun was suffered to pour through barred clouds a lurid if occasional gleam along the spines of the islands, on the yellow-and-black funnel and varnished bridge of a pleasure steamer, on the white pillar of a lighthouse six miles away, and on an odd planting of yellowing trees on the near hillside. If the mountains to the North had their boldness momentarily subdued by the prevailing conditions of light, they gained all the more in remote mystery.

John was seeing the open Firth for the first time in many years, and Addie beside him knew that emotion was filling his lungs and gripping him by the throat, and she could hear him softly ejaculate : " Wonderful ! Wonderful ! Nothing else like it ! "

Soon, however, they had slipped with the stream of traffic

going in, and against another coming out, along an esplanade to the heart of the seaside town where, over the length of a wide front before a low range of rather old-fashioned buildings in red sandstone, the driver had to search for a niche for his car amid score upon score parked to face the sea.

Again John was astonished, though by no means scandalized, by the Sabbath stir in a place which, at a corresponding hour in his childhood, would have appeared deserted and asleep behind blinds drawn in a sourness of the spirit. He saw that the boat-hirers were doing a brisk trade with the handless lubbers from the inland towns. He noted that others than mere Italian Papists had opened their shops. He observed that, thanks to the operation of the *bona fide* clause in Scotland's licensing system, the convivial were able, and willing, to sit openly at the windows of hotel lounges with whisky glasses and tankards before them.

The party from Garvel walked the length of the front, noting this and that and dutifully enjoying the sea air. They sat on a bench and watched the antics of children, happy even on the nobbly beaches of the upper Firth. They walked anon to the pier and, after a brief struggle with Beth's scruples, enjoyed a trip in a motor launch at sixpence a head across the sound to the inner island and back. Returning to dry land, the men actually per-suaded Beth that a foursome on a municipal putting green was neither a shameful act of exhibitionism nor a mortal sin, though she was mightily disturbed when Davie, a high-spirited man, shouted encouragement, waved his putter or danced a jig on the green as one of his more adventurous shots dropped into the cup.

They had high tea with cold salmon and potato salad in a sound hotel—" a rare good feed," Davie pronounced it to be. While the ladies retired, he and John enjoyed a glass of good whisky, Davie insisting now on paying his small share of the treat ; and as they all walked along the front in the pearly evening light to find the car, John was touched to see with what solid kindness Davie took Beth's arm and to hear his earnest question :

" Have you enjoyed yourself, lass ? "

" Every minute of it, Davie ! " was Beth's rapt reply.

They found the car, now a monstrosity stranded on an empty and oily beach of concrete. John made his dispositions with firmness.

"Into the front seat with you this time, Addie. You'll see better from there. In the back with Beth and me, Davie."

The Rolls swung massively into the straight and headed for home.

"A great day!" sighed Davie, feeling for his pipe and pouch. "I haven't enjoyed myself so much for a long time."

"Aye, man!" agreed John with a chuckle, "and now you're going to pay for it. I'm going to talk to you like a Dutch uncle."

"What's all this?" Davie's innocent face took on a boyish look of puzzlement.

"It's about Addie. What's all this nonsense about her going into the Mill and not going back to school?"

"Have these two been getting at you?" asked Davie, rueful.

"They have not. I had to get it out of them. Addie's my only niece, and I can ask questions about her future, can't I? You'd make a fine job of it, wouldn't you, you and your Mill!"

Davie puffed at his pipe, his fine face suddenly wistful.

"I'm a plain working chap," he finally stated with dignity, "and I know my place. I was brought up to believe that a girl should go out to work as soon as she's able and bring her own share into her mother's house. My grannie worked in the Mill. My mother worked in the Mill, and——"

John interrupted him with a laugh.

"Man! Isn't that the best argument for keeping Addie out of the Mill?" he cried. "Your grandfather was a labourer. Your father was a craneman with the Harbour Trust. But you're a foreman blacksmith with T. & B. Dammit, Davie! Are you going to tell me that you need the wee bit wages Addie would be able to bring in? Does he, Beth?"

"He does not. And we can save, too."

"Two against one!" protested Davie, his sporting instincts stirred. "It's all very fine, but——"

"No 'but' about it! I'll tell you this, Davie Bryden," said John vehemently. "It's been the curse of the working classes for generations—and I'm one of them—that the bairns have had to be sent out to work far too young. Take myself. Up at five every morning, and me just a child of fourteen! It was criminal, not that my poor Grannie could help it. It's fourteen by law now, and it's still far too young. If I had my way . . ."

"Aye, but Addie's sixteen," Davie argued, "and a strong girl."

"And therefore she's got to go and work in a hosiery factory ! " snapped John, getting heated now. "Preposterous ! Is her education costing you anything ? Have you got to go to the pawn for her keep ? No, you haven't. Here's a girl that wants to improve herself and go into a fine profession, a clever girl, and her silly old fool of a father tells me she ought to go into the Mill. Davie, you're daft ! "

John laughed again and, leaning forward to where his brother-in-law sat on a folding seat, tapped him on the knee.

"Let me tell you this, Davie," he said earnestly. "You'd call me a pretty successful man. I've done well, occupied a good position, saved a bit. But believe me, man, if there's one thing I've missed all my life, cursed and kicked myself for wanting, been ashamed of not having . . . Education, Davie. Learning. Not for the money it can make, but for—well, just having it."

This confession was followed by a slightly embarrassed silence, broken at length by an enigmatic " Ah, well ! " from Davie. It was not an open acknowledgment of defeat, but John, a man of some experience in negotiation, knew to drop the argument there. Quite dexterously he changed the subject to sport, and the honest blacksmith's lean face lighted up, and before they were home John had solemnly engaged himself to witness—but from a covered stand, he insisted—next Saturday's match between Palmerston and the fabled Rangers.

Two hours later—the car having been dismissed, a light supper eaten at Beth's table, the presents distributed to a highly satisfactory accompaniment of gasps and " My's ! " and thanks—John said that he would walk to the hotel, the night being fine, and Davie said that he would walk a bit of the way with him.

The latter's silence during the first minutes of the journey was mildly surprising. The blacksmith was first and foremost a cheery, chatty sort of man, and John wondered if his own intrusion in a family matter had hurt that simple spirit. You had to laugh at Davie ; he was honest and open as the day. John waited patiently for the revelation.

"About Addie, John," it came at length. "I've been thinking you're mebbe right."

"Good, Davie!" John quietly encouraged his friend.

"Then there's Curly . . . Not, mind ye, John, that I'm wanting to worry you, or needing money or anything like that."

John chuckled into himself. He had long ago perceived that this man of sanguine temperament was always reaching out like a boy for moral support against the rigours of Beth's code. But he replied gravely.

"Yes, we'll have to have a talk about that. I'd like to have a yarn with the boy. But he's doing well at his trade?"

"It's not just that, John," Davie temporized awkwardly. "I don't know if you follow the game, but the fact of the matter is that Curly's a rare wee boxer."

John had to laugh then, stopping in the middle of the pavement, his shoulders shaking.

"O Davie, Davie!" he gasped. "You're a real comic sometimes."

"But it's the God's truth, John!" Davie insisted, absolutely refusing to see anything funny in a matter so fundamental. "Curly's no' juist an ordinary wee puncher. He's champion at his weight in the Y.M. and the Rovers and the Welfare. He might be a real champion if I could only get him started. You can ask Slugs Macluskie himself."

John could only guess at the identity of this legendary person, but he did suddenly apprehend the passion in Davie for the advancement and triumph of his dear son according to his own ingenuous lights.

"I didn't know that, Davie," he observed gravely. "We'll have to look into this. Mind you, I'm dead against taking any boy from his trade . . . But here we are at the hotel already! It was nice to have your company, Davie. See you next Saturday. Goodnight, lad, goodnight!"

A quiet glass of whisky-and-water in the lounge, Mr. Tweedie being now the life-and-soul and the only male of a four of whist by the fire, and John went to his room, humming happily, his mind full of agreeable notions and his body pleasantly tired after exposure to the sea airs. If he had been a more introspective sort of man than he was, he might have known that since the irritable and empty morning he had experienced a change of life; he might have realized that his afternoon with the Brydens had surprisingly given purpose, shape and interest to his new existence.

(Fine, modest girl, Addie. It would be a pleasure to see her get on.) If he had been a person of sour spirit he might have realized that he had exercised and was now enjoying the power conferred by his position and his means.

Being not unduly introspective and certainly not sour, however, he declaimed his evening prayer (to the vast interest of the assistant housekeeper, who happened to be passing at the moment) tumbled into bed, enjoyed the feel of a good old-fashioned pig at his feet, and shortly fell sound asleep.

2

Mrs. Daniel Rolland, the mother of the Twins, was having a busy Monday morning in the back premises of the villa called "The Neuk." Over and above the chores of every normal household day she had on hand the dishes rather foolishly left over from Sunday's supper and a washing, which included the long and heavy winter woollens adopted by Dismal Dan in early September as protection against the chills he saw bearing down upon him with unique ferocity. She was alone in the house, the Twins being away down to the Lyle Hall to rehearse for a production of *Love in Old Japan* in aid of the League of Pity, in which their four competent hands and twenty nimble fingers and thumbs were to deputize (and very adequately, as the event proved) for a full theatre orchestra.

For more than an hour that Monday morning Lily was continually on the go, as she would have phrased it, between the sink in the scullery and the tub in the wash-house, with an occasional dash into the living-rooms to scoop crumbs off a cloth, to shake and pummel cushions, to tug at curtains, and to slash at mantelpieces and occasional tables with a feather duster.

As she bent to the washing, over a tub set quite absurdly low by a Victorian builder with no feeling for economy of effort on the part of the slave race of females, her pleasure was to think of the distinguished prominence the Twins were about to earn ; that they were not at hand to help her about the house would have been the last of her grievances.

It was a pity that Cha did not more frequently take a bath

and change his underclothes ; getting the dirt out of them was an awful job and sore on the material ; but Cha was the artistic sort and, her only son, to be forgiven almost everything. The bitterness was to have to pound away at Dan's long and heavy drawers ; the mean old devil who wouldn't let her have a proper maid to live in, as was due to their position, even if it was no fault of his that the daily woman, Mrs. Balharrie by name, had failed to turn up. All the same, these chars ; you couldn't trust them an inch, even if you gave them the very best of the cast-off clothes and a bowlful of good stock now and again.

Lily's back was sore. She was concerned that her hands were red and soft and swollen, her arms wet to the elbows. She was conscious of untidy hair under a mob cap, of a hole in the right heel of her cashmere stockings above slippers burst and sprouting their stuffing at several points. The day's duties before her were still a confusion in her mind—all the beds to make, the potatoes to peel, apples to core and bake to go with a milk pudding. (It would just have to be rice, whether Dan liked it or not.) Then there was that length of elastic for Beryl's brassiere : an awful girl to burst things ; if it wasn't her brassiere it was her breeks or her suspenders. All that hard work at the piano ; it was a strain on a young and still-developing girl.

The front-door bell rang, urgently intruding the claims of the larger world upon Lily's preoccupations. That would be the squinty-eyed boy from the greengrocer's ; and she had told Miss Dobbie in the shop not to send on Monday. She hurried through to the front door to give him a piece of her mind.

On her doorstep stood Mr. John Rolland Cram, solid in his frieze overcoat on this pleasantly frosty morning of September. He raised his great, wide-brimmed hat with a deference of courtesy that had her completely melted.

"John ! What a surprise ! Come in a minute and have a cup of tea."

"No, no, Lily. You're busy," and his eyes, taking in her person from the burst slippers to the mob cap, made her feel, as she phrased it later to the Twins, black affronted. "I just looked up to make sure you'd all be at home to-night. I've got some wee things——"

"Now, isn't that a crying shame !" mourned Lily. "I wonder—No. I couldn't, John ! The Twins have a rehearsal for that show in the Lyle Hall, and I solemnly promised Lizzie Macpherson I'd sit with her mother while she went to the Pictures. It's not often the poor soul gets an outing. And Dan said he might be going to Glasgow . . ." she almost sobbed : " Ugh, isn't it too bad, John ! "

" Nonsense, Lily ! " he laughed. " I've got plenty to do. Any night suits me."

" Could you make it Thursday, then ? " she asked eagerly. " Supper here at six. We'll have a sing-song."

" Grand, Lily ! And many thanks. I'll look forward to that. Yes," he added sentimentally, " I'm just making my rounds and enjoying every minute of it. We had a grand day at the Coast yesterday—Beth and Davie and Addie and I. Drove down and back again in style. I think it did Beth a lot of good. She doesn't get out much, poor lass. But you're busy, Lily. I think I'll just go down this afternoon and see my old friend Effie Templeton at Corsewellhill. Then I'll see you all on Thursday. Cheerio, then, Lily ! "

" Thursday at six. Cheerybye, John ! "

Lily returned to her surging preoccupations. He was coming on Thursday, definitely ; and would she make it the usual high tea, with a nice bit of fish or something, or go for a real evening dinner ? She would wear her nigger brown frock with her best Aristocs at fifteen-and-eleven the pair and the suede shoes. The Twins always looked nice in those girly checked gingham dresses in grey, Auntie Pearl sent from America ; you didn't want to make a show at a family party. But he had already taken Beth and Davie Bryden and that stiff Addie of theirs to the Coast, had he ? And now, if you please : just because the hellish luck of things went that way, he was off to visit that Effie Templeton at that dirty farm ! Lily supposed bitterly that these other women would make choices and prefer claims before she had a chance to speak for herself and her own.

Thinking thus, she fought angrily against the deadweight of Dan's drawers, little knowing that the sense of urgent competition which troubled her was matched in John Rolland Cram, as he walked back to Blackwood's Hotel, by a return of the elusive sense of frustration that had dogged him since his return. An engineer, he liked things to go by plan, and he was quite absurdly put out by the failure to fix up with Lily for the evening, especially after starting off so well with Beth and Davie and getting Addie fixed. It was going to be a fine thing if he was to have to spend the half of every day in mooning about and looking for something to do : not to mention asking people to give him an evening's entertainment. The sooner he found a place of his own and made a life of his own, the better.

The girl at the desk in Blackwood's was quite taken aback by the abruptness of Mr. Cram when, on his return, he instructed her to ring the hire service people and tell them to have a car at the door at three sharp, and, if possible, the same driver as he had had yesterday.

"Just like that," the girl complained to her afternoon relief. "A right shirty old devil, if you ask me."

"Rolling in it, I suppose," the relief rationalized the case. "Think they can buy everything."

It was thus in fact that John unconsciously enriched the legend that was already building up about his innocent self. His supper party had been little enough to the hotel servants, who had their own views as to the standing of his guests, but the weight of his tips was bruited about below stairs. Then the office girls, however defensive of their own dignity, could not think lightly of a gentle-man who hired a Rolls-Royce two days running and insisted on having the same driver. This got to the barmaid, who retailed the facts to her intimates among the customers. In his turn the driver boasted among his mates and fellow-workers for other companies.

It soon got about in several wide and overlapping circles that this old chap Cram just home from the East was, as the relief girl in the office had put it, simply rolling in it. Even when Lily reached Lizzie Macpherson's that evening it was to hear from the latter, in a curiously Scottish mixture of congratulation and sneer, how, looking from her mother's bedroom window that afternoon, not thinking of anything in particular, lo and behold ! she had seen that swell relation of yours, Lily, rolling along towards the Glen Road in a great big motor with a chauffeur all to himself : all very rich and grand, Lizzie was sure.

For John the drive was another simple joy of rediscovery. It followed for some three miles the road they had traversed the day before, but a swing to the left before the highway started to dip down to the sea transformed the Rolls-Royce and its occupants into a monstrous caravel and an innocent crew exploring narrow and uncharted seas. The size of the vehicle, and its metropolitan elegance, were too great and too splendid for the narrow, rough roads that twisted here and there among the whitewashed farm steadings. Farm workers backed their carts at its approach, pulling harshly at the mouths of their startled Clydesdales. Servant lassies forgot the hens they were supposed to be feeding to watch it pass ; so that a thick cloud of curiosity as to the identity and destination of the visitant covered many square miles of countryside before evening fell. Even the dumb, castrated bestial, fattening for the winter market, looked up and blearily pondered the nature of this incursion.

From within the great car John enjoyed the spectacle in reverse. He recognized the lower farms one by one and spoke their fine names into himself—Thornalees, Pomillan, High Holm, Bargane, Finnockend and The Crooks—good solid two- or three-pair horse Lowland mixed farms, living largely by the trade in milk to Garvel. That was always a right bonnie turn of the Kett Water through the gorge under the Bluebell Hill ; and John noted with approval that Sir Peter had been planting since the glen was shaved blue in the last war. It made you think of Switzerland or Norway, not that John had visited either of these fabled countries. And down there to the right, suddenly, was the frail arch of the old Cadger's Bridge with the ruins of the old meal-mill beside it, all as they had been fifty years before.

The car continued to climb out of the valley. The countryside began to look barer, the fields browner. The old thorn hedges of the richer lands gave place to fences of stark wire. There were no natural trees up here, only the dull, regimented green of conifer plantations, strategically arranged up and down the hill-shoulders, like so many infantry battalions arrayed for battle, to provide shelter for bestial.

The car slowed and stopped on a stretch of narrow roadway between open fields, grass between the worn tracks taking the occasional drip of its elegant oil. The driver pushed back the sliding screen that separated him from his patron.

" I'm sunk, boss," he confessed, but in a very friendly manner. " If ye told me we was in Palestine I'd believe you."

" I'll come in and guide you," said John, not a little proud of superior knowledge. He hopped out of his privileged chamber and took the place beside the driver, whose Christian name, he shortly ascertained, was Ernie.

" Straight ahead and up the second road on the left," John advised. " It's a sharp turn and a pretty rough track."

" Never had a job like this in ma life," said Ernie with the defensive sourness of his kind.

They had two miles and more to go, through gates that had to be laboriously opened and carefully shut, over small and narrow bridges and by the edges of rough fields on which the moorland heather, defying the cropping of blackface sheep, had established itself in dark, parasitic tufts. It was such a bleak passage that Ernie expressed his surprise when, over a rise, they saw the whitewashed steading of Corsewellhill in its oasis of arable land, a little fortress in the shadow of the Scourie.

Conned by John, the great car heaved along a length of rutted road and turned into the close within the low ranges of farm outbuildings. A tall and burly young man, busy unloading turnips from a cart, turned to stare with hostility at the vehicle which so arrogantly dwarfed this unexpected setting. He advanced as John got down.

" Ye'll be ma mither's kizzen John," he suggested in uncompromising dialect, " the man frae Chiny ? "

" That's me ! " John admitted cheerfully. " You'll be Tam ? "

They shook hands warily.

" Ye'll find ma mither in-bye," the young giant explained. " She's at the bakin'. Juist gang ben through the boilerhouse and gi'e her a yell. Ye'll be staying for yer tea, man ? I'll see ye then."

Obedient to the terms of this rough welcome, John passed into the concreted gloom of the boilerhouse and was shaping for what he knew to be the living quarters of the farmhouse when a large, full-blown girl with a scarf wrapped turbanwise round her head came charging out of the shadowy dairy, stopped to stare, and blushed.

" Hullo ! " she said guardedly.

" Hullo, Mary ! " responded John. " You're Mary, aren't you ? I knew you from your brother. I'm your Uncle John Cram, just back from China."

The girl quite abruptly turned her back on him and hurried indoors, shouting in her singularly shrill, rough voice :

" Mither ! Mither ! Here's thon kizzen o' ma feyther's, the man frae Chiny."

While he stood awkwardly, pondering his new status as the legendary man from China, the remote and unreal abstraction of the primitive folk of a hill farm, John became aware of the figure of Effie Templeton filling the narrow doorway leading into the kitchen.

" Effie ! "

" John ! "

Once upon a time they had been sweethearts, and the consciousness of the fact lay between them still. He saw her physically as any overworked woman beyond middle-age, her figure squat, her face roughened and coloured by hill weather, but he also thought to see with the fading eyes of his youth the ghost of an old prettiness, and he did see a sweet and intimate beauty in the dusting of flour that whitened her plump hands and arms up to the elbows. Her eyes were still grey and clear, like Addie's, but wistful, telling of an inner loneliness.

" Come in, man, and sit ye down till I finish this batch of scones," she bade him.

" Ah ! That's lovely," he said, sniffing the exquisite odours of a country baking. " This is the nearest home I've been since I got back last week, Effie."

" You're always welcome here, John," she said, firmly rolling a slab of dough on the virgin wood of her baking board.

The big farm kitchen, warm and scented from the baking, did give him the feeling of having come home, even if that feeling was no more than a wishful return to the simplicities of childhood. He confessed to himself that this setting was in fact nearer his private ideal of home than even the bright, spotless kitchen of his sister Beth, filled with kindliness and affection as he had felt it to be. It might be just the old-fashioned range and the big, wasteful fire of glowing coals ; it might be only the simplicity of the great Culross girdle hanging from the swee— how proud he was to remember the old word !—and the good scones baking in the right heat upon it. It might be (though he did not allow himself to frame the thought exactly) the kindly comradeship of an old sweetheart, unashamedly floured to the elbow, getting on with her work while he sat by the fireside, just as if they had been there together in solid loyalty for all the long years of their separation.

"You'll be staying for your tea with us, John," Effie repeated her son's invitation.

"I hope so, if you can have me," he responded. "But I wonder about that driver of mine."

"If there's a man in it," said Effie with a flash of the rustic coarseness, "you can trust oor Mary. She'd smell yin across a hundred-acre field."

So it turned out. John quickly satisfied himself that Ernie was delighted to spend the afternoon gathering eggs, seeing to the lamp in the incubator, and assisting at the evening milking, all in the company of a buxom girl, who did not in the least object to having her plump upper arm pinched at intervals or even, in the flickering radiance of the incubator chamber, having her waist encircled by a cunning arm and her mouth well kissed with an exciting brush of Ernie's small and carefully trimmed moustache. When John asked Ernie if he was in any hurry to get home, the latter said that it was okay by him ; that he had never before seen a farming joint ; that the car was his, John's ; and that in short he, Ernie, was delighted to make a day of it.

So John sat comfortably and happily by the fire while Effie baked, both of them with plenty to talk about and all manner of old friends and shared episodes to recall ; and John thought again what a fine, comforting thing it was to have a woman about the house, never mind the passionate side of it. It was pleasant at the fall of evening to hear Tam's great boots clumping across the boilerhouse floor and the noises of splashing, gurgling and sucking produced by his ablutions at the sink in the scullery. A coarse devil ; he took the head of the tea table, and roared at his mother and Mary for their domestic shortcomings, and laid down the law in a series of bellows that were not any easier to understand or endure for being delivered through the enormous mouthfuls of food he simultaneously masticated. In answer to his mother's question he intimated with an almost splendid crudity that he was going wenching over to Tullybog that evening, and that the movements of the man from China held little or no further interest for him.

John enjoyed it all ; at least you knew where you were with a peasant like Tam. It also pleased and amused him that the custom of Corsewellhill assured Ernie's presence with the family at table ; and Ernie gave quite a wonderful display of table manners, holding his knife and fork ever so politely between thumb and forefinger as if they were writing implements, always ready with what he knew as a wisecrack for Mary and, the earnest child of the machine age, took up with vigour one of Tam's wilder pronouncements on the superiority of draught horses over tractors. When the meal was over he insisted on helping Mary and her mother to wash up and then, with a roguish wink of masculine confidence to John, accepted Mary's suggestion that they might go for a turn round before darkness fell—along the edge of the moor to the Daft Doctor's Well, she suggested.

The fire had been lit in the front room, and there Effie Templeton and John Rolland Cram sat down together, facing each other in worn armchairs under a steel engraving of a Covenanters' meeting that hung above the mantelpiece.

The evening gathered outside and little enough of the failing light came through the narrow, eastward-facing window. It was the hour and setting for confidence, for remembrance, but John was more eager than his companion to canvass the news of the day, and it was with some alarm he came to realize that in this worn woman, who had once been bright Effie Templeton, he was dealing with one sentimental, dispirited and perhaps even a thought self-pitiful. It vaguely alarmed him that her memory of their old boy-and-girl affair had apparently increased in warmth while he himself had long ago shaken off the very last vestiges of disappointment and wounded vanity.

He was sorry for Effie ; her lot was thankless now. Even if she had not told him, he had seen for himself and could have guessed that life in the upland farm with Sandy Rolland's coarse son and rough daughter was hard in terms of labour and harder for its utter lack of grace and love and respect. He understood perfectly the harsh logic of the peasant law whereby, when Tam chose to give his doxy his name and a fireside of her own, Effie must be a slave on sufferance and utterly without economic rights.

" Well, we'll have to think about all that, Effie," he said to cheer her up—and a little to rid himself of embarrassment. " There'll be ways and means, you needn't doubt."

It occurred to him to think how often lately he had had to assure members of his renewed circle of friends that they would have to think about all that, as they came to him one by one with their problems. He was, however, simple and vain enough to enjoy the patriarchal emotions these approaches conferred on him. He was now more immediately concerned to hear Effie's voice break on a sob and see her eyes shining wet in the fire-light.

" The whole trouble is I married the wrong man ! " she mourned with alarming candour.

" Now, now, Effie ! That's an old story," said John, annoyed and peremptory. " It's the future we've got to think of, not the past."

He was more astonished than ever to see Effie jump up from her chair and stand rigid, a hand at her throat. He thought that he must, by his brusqueness, have wholly maddened her.

" What is it, Effie ? "

" Wheesht ! Listen."

She slipped behind his chair and swiftly but silently lowered the blue linen blind on the window, and with unsteady fingers she lit the lamp that stood ready on the table. John stared at her, but then he heard what sounded like a large sliding door being shaken somewhere towards the back of the steading.

" That'll be Mary and my driver coming back," he said.

" It isn't. Listen," she hissed at him.

Down the side of the house and round the gable end came the thudding crunch of heavy footsteps in the gravel. John rose and made towards the door.

" What the devil's all this ? "

Effie's strong hand gripped his arm and held him back.

" He's mad," she whispered, and her almost rapt expression held him.

She leaned forward and turned down the wick in the lamp. The footsteps stopped outside the window with a coarse scattering of the gravel. The stranger's knuckles rapped peremptorily on the pane.

" In Heaven's name——" cried John.

He was out of the room before Effie could intercept him and into the little, rarely-used porch, struggling to turn the stiff mortice lock. When he had the door wrenched open and the night air on his face it was to hear only the end of the stranger's run along the gravelled terrace, the thud of heavy feet landing on the turf of the Laigh Park, and then nothing but the crepitant silence of the upland fields in the thickening dusk.

"Get to hell out of this, you dirty blackguard," he shouted in foolish anger into the mocking darkness, "or I'll have all the police in the county after you ! "

Effie was waiting for him in the porch, the pedestal lamp in her trembling hand.

"It's a madman that lives up the Quarry Glen. It goes on like that night after night, whenever he thinks I'm alone. Do you wonder I'm nearly driven mad in this house ? "

"And can your son do nothing about it ? " John asked harshly.

"He just laughs."

"I'll talk to that young man. You can't go on like this, Effie, that's plain. We'll have to get you out of here somehow, or get that rascal locked up, at least."

The sheer, cold terror of her situation was now clear to him. He was an honest man who could not bear the thought of woman or child being lonely and afraid. He followed Effie slowly back to the room, pondering the problem he had set himself on her behalf, and then normality quite suddenly returned with the laughter and banging of Mary and Ernie coming in through the boilerhouse.

"Well, that's Mary home," said John, "and it's time for me to be getting back. And I won't forget my promise, Effie. You can depend on that."

"Thank you, John," she answered quietly.

Homeward bound, Ernie was grieved that his boss did not come and share the front seat, for his day in the country had been for him a novel and amusing experience about which he was very willing to talk. A sociable man, he was conscious of his fare's remoteness in the depths of the cab and, when they came to the door of Blackwood's Hotel, of his preoccupation.

3

Lily and the Twins had cleared away after supper in " The Neuk," and now John sat on with his host in the dining-room, the only other place of reception in the villa, the drawing-room upstairs being now occupied by Cha, who could be heard picking out by ear the air of *Smoke Gets in Your Eyes* on the piano.

It had been a good supper, the table so rich and varied that even such a candid man as John Rolland Cram had wondered a little if the scale of the feast had not been just a thought on the ambitious side for folk like Dan and Lily. Salted almonds all over the place, if you please ; finger bowls beside the covers and crystallized fruits in bon-bon dishes. What had most interested John, however, and faintly embarrassed him in fact, was the band or sash of yellow satin with which Lily had decorated her table, laying it diagonally from one corner to another over the white tablecloth. A bit roary, he might have described it to himself, but he supposed in his uncritical way that this was the fashion.

Still, the small awareness of a certain ebullience lingered in his mind now that he was obliged to sit and listen to Dismal Dan. For John his cousin had never possessed the true essence of humanity. Since he could remember, Dan had been a phenomenon, an accepted figure of fun, with his mournings about his health and his fortunes. To sit and listen to the lugubrious voice of the poor chap, sunk in a spiritual abyss of his own creation, was just like listening to the telling of an anecdote that had been amusing enough but had gone stale with repetition. Only the almost theatrical funniness of Dan's figure—the long grey cheeks with the fringe of hair from ear to nose, the lack-lustre eyes fixed on the fire, the ragged moustache—kept it tolerably comic.

Thus, by virtue of life's haunting irony, John attached no importance at all to what Dan was saying between awkward puffs at one of his guest's best Manila cigars. It was just the sort of stuff Dan had been girning about all his life—lack of capital, the sharpness of his wholesalers, the dishonesty of assistants and the unhappy inability of his own sorely-tried physique to master these handicaps. The tale was so familiar that the man who had just come Home from China did not even perceive that it was directed towards himself. He found himself at length becoming impatient, and he burst out with :

"Capital can't save a business, man, if your own heart's not in it ! You've got a rare old-fashioned shop down there, Dan, and what it needs, if you ask me, is new ideas—launching out—not just sitting on your backside and waiting for something to happen."

He threw the butt of his cigar into the fireplace.

"I'm telling you bluntly, Dan," he half-apologised, "and I'll tell you what I'd do. I'd take that boy of yours, Charles, out of a dead-end job, and I'd send him to one of the big stores in Glasgow or London to learn the trade thoroughly and get all the new notions, and then I'd take him in and turn him loose on the business."

Dan shook his head, a second each way from side to side.

"Our Cha hasn't the taste for it," he grieved. "The iron-mongery's not his line. If I could only lay my hands on a bit of capital——"

John speculated rather vaguely on this topic, realizing that no exhortations of his could change Dismal Dan from what he always had been. The way some of these chaps talked about capital, as if it was something you could claw out of the air without working to create it ! Nobody, friend or stranger, would get a penny of capital out of John Rolland Cram for fancy new companies or for the succour of old ones. The late Superintendent Engineer of the K. & S. had worked damned hard for his savings, which, solidly invested in gilt-edged or nearly so, would remain there for the support of his old age and the benefit, ultimately, of such young folk and poor old people as he might deem deserving. The very idea of old Dan thinking that people were going to break up their estates to relieve him of his confounded worries !

Lily came in then and indicated that the low concerns of the kitchen had all been disposed of, and wouldn't John like to come upstairs to the drawing-room where it was all nice and cosy ?

"Fine, Lily !" John approved this agreeable suggestion, rising to his feet. "And I wonder if these two clever girls of yours would play for me again ?"

"Surely !" Lily guaranteed brightly.

Dismal Dan did not follow the party upstairs, but they were all content to leave him among the bleached bones of his pre-occupations and assemble in a happier fireside clime in the drawing-room, the light from a single standard lamp with an orange shade so falling on the dresses and complexions of the women and on Lily's somewhat exuberant choice of cushion-covers and such as to give John, at least, the impression of being once more in a close-knit family circle, intimate and secure and reasonably decorative round the sort of blazing coal-fire that had been for so long one of his most precious symbols of Home. He noted with approval that Cha was quiet and hospitable, very courteously arranging the guest's armchair at the right angle to the fire, while the Twins were solicitous to a degree over the arrangement of cushions behind his head. Lily had to secure the comfort of his legs with a footstool affair that had a suspiciously frivolous look in John's eyes.

" That's our Bobby ! " she cried happily, wedging it under John's heels ; and he suddenly remembered Mrs. Tertius Bannerman's trick of nomenclature. "And only our favourite guests ever get it. Isn't that right, kids ? "

This proposition having been heartily supported by Cha and the Twins—by the former with a crisp " I'll say ! "—the party settled down nicely to a chat. Anon they listened to a vaudeville programme on the wireless, and at length the Twins, stripping themselves of their bangles and other impedimenta, sat down at the piano. His pipe going nicely, John leaned back in his chair, his eyes upturned to the ceiling, to enjoy the treat of the evening.

His enjoyment was in fact complete, his pride in it abundant. The Twins' act—for so they called it with near-professional cant and as such it was deliberately rehearsed—seemed to him quite wonderful : beautiful music beautifully played. He was apt to describe himself as a plain man who knew nothing about all this highbrow stuff but, on the other hand, knew very well what he liked, and the playing of these two girls was thus for him within the order of genius. It gave him what he liked with a hard brilliance of polish he took to be unique. It was wonderful to him that such talent should have manifested itself in the family to which he had returned from exile.

When the Twins, having battered their way through the

waltz called *Missouri* to a triumph of chords in F major, John rose in his emotional enthusiasm and led them by the hand back to their seats, saying :

" Splendid, girls ! A treat ! Thank you, Beryl ! Thank you, Sybil ! "

With an avuncular tenderness that filled Lily's heart he kissed the blushing cheeks of the Rhythmic Twins.

" And now, for that, I'm going to give you a present."

" I'm sure you've given them lovely presents already, John ! " Lily protested virtuously.

" Ah, but this is really a present for myself. I want to have some nice music in my old age," cried John, enjoying his own generosity. " We want to find a teacher for these girls, just to give them the last wee bit of polish."

" O, Uncle John ! That would be *won*-derful ! The Twins achieved in speech a unison as remarkable as their precision on the keyboard.

" John ! That's far too much." Lily was insistent.

" Attaboy ! " said Cha loyally.

" The question is," John developed his theme magisterially, " who's the right man ? "

" Billy Mayerl," said Cha promptly and with the gravity of a deep student. " It's their syncopation and cadenzas that want jazzing up a bit."

" They speak very well of Willy Klein," Lily hazarded with modesty.

" A Yid ? And are these chaps both in London ? " The questions were sharp.

" Yes, but of course——"

" No, no ! " said John decisively, shaking his whitening head. " I wouldn't have a couple of young girls going up there on their own, not into that line of life. It's a bad place London for those that haven't knocked about a bit first of all. Especially girls."

The firmness of this demurrer was taken by the Rollands as quite a distinct set-back, but his next question slightly relieved the strain.

" Surely there's somebody nearer at home ? There must be a good man in Glasgow."

" Bud Bell's the chap," said Cha. " Conducts the Bellringers

in the Studio. And can he tickle the ivories ? I'll tell the world !
He's a wizard."

"That sounds more likely," John allowed, turning to his
hostess. "There it is, Lily. If you can see this Bell chap and
get the Twins fixed up for a real set of high-class lessons, it's my
party. I've half a mind to go with you . . . Anyhow, I'd like the
girls to stay at home for a bit yet and travel every day—we'll
see about seasons—and anyhow, you go ahead."

The enthusiasms and thanks of the Rollands surged in gratifying waves about his ears ; and John said it was nothing, a pleasure
and—what was more to the point—only right. And then Lily
rose crisply from her chair, and gathered her Twins with her
unresting eyes, crying :

"Come on, girls, and help me to make a cup of tea. And
you, Cha," she turned on her son, "you should have a talk with
Uncle John."

Mr. Cram perceived that, by the force of this device, he had
subtly become involved in Cha's future as in that of the
Twins. Left alone with the youth, he felt distinctly ill-at-ease ;
the more so since our Cha, deprived of his familiar background
of pliable females, had clearly lost in assurance. Another of
John's difficulties was that he had little recent experience
of dealing with halflin boys, especially of this new sort that
seemed to be more taken up with jazz and picture houses than
with learning an honest trade. Breaking the ice with Cha,
therefore, he sounded much more formidable than he would
have wished.

"And what are *you* going to do with yourself, young man ? "
he began.

"I'm not right sure," faltered Cha, taken aback.

"Not doing yourself much good in that accountant's office,
are you ? "

"O, I don't know, uncle ! " the youth rallied. "There's
accounts and audits and that. You see, the boss isn't Chartered ;
he's just Incorporated. It's not exactly the same."

"You've got to study and pass exams nevertheless, haven't
you ? I hope you're doing something about that."

"Well. It's kinda difficult . . ."

"I never found anything worth doing that wasn't," snapped
John. "To tell you the truth, Charles, I wonder you don't go

into the shop with your father and learn the trade thoroughly. You could make it a rare business again."

" Gees ! I'd sooner be seen dead than go sweat my guts out in that joint."

" Many a better man than you has made a decent living and done a good job in an ironmonger's shop."

John was immediately sorry that he had spoken so harshly. It must be that silly wee moustache, or the boy's trick of slumping in his chair as if a code of manners were beneath the contempt of his small egotism. Or was it this trick of vulgar, near-American speech borrowed from the films ? John contemplated with alarm the fantastic possibility that this provincial youth saw himself as a star frustrated ; and the longer he considered it, the more credible did the theory appear. When he studied the boy's huffed, averted face he was sorry, and he thought to see the inevitably unhappy child of Dan and Lily, of a defeated father and a mother not always wise in her ambitions. He also thought honestly that the ordinary parental duties had in a way fallen upon himself.

" Look here, Cha," he began again kindly, leaning forward to tap the boy's knee with the stem of his pipe. " Do you know what I'd do if I were you."

" No. What ? "

" I'd go abroad and start again. All on my own."

" Abroad ! " cried Cha, his languor falling from him. " You mean China or one of these places ? "

" No . . ." John demurred. " I wouldn't suggest China or anywhere in the Far East, for that matter. I was thinking more of India or Ceylon. Tea-planting ; that sort of thing. It's a good life for a young man, Cha. Learning how to manage labour —learning how to manage yourself, for that matter. Nice social life. Horses. A pony of your own to ride round the gardens. Maybe a bit of polo . . . There's a lot in it for the right sort of chap. That's where this accounting business might help you a lot."

" O boy ! " cried Cha. " That's an idea, Uncle."

Poor Cha had suddenly seen a vision of himself on horseback against a frieze of distant mountains in translucent blue. In his little dream, innocent if pitiful, he had seen himself like Bing Crosby in the saddle, fluting his love-song to the hills : the handsome and lonely Man contributing his quota of energy and beauty to the stream of life.

" I'm pretty sure I could arrange it, Cha," said John, catching his own infection. " I've a lot of friends who would help to place you. It would mean going to London for an interview likely, but that can wait. Just you think it over for a bit, Cha : have a talk with your father and mother. It's worth considering."

Just then Lily providentially reappeared, bearing a laden tray and followed by her daughters with plates of eatables in their hands. Her eyes were bright with curiosity as to the atmosphere prevailing between her first-born and his potential benefactor, and she perceived that it was at least hopeful. She made a merry song of having the occasional tables laid out to her liking, of borrowing Bobby to take a cakestand, and of having the teapot set close to the fire on the hearth—" nice and cosy."

" There we are now ! " she cried happily. " We always have our wee picnic about this time, John. Sugar and cream for you ? I couldn't do without my cup of tea, could you ? "

" That's right, Lily," John agreed, though he would much rather have been facing a good tot of grog.

" O, and Cha ! " Lily added. " Give your father a cry and tell him the tea's ready."

Dan joined the company, moving slowly and warily into this bright world in which people were reasonably happy. He remained himself, however, his long person folded up on a low chair drawn back from the circle about the fire, and with long sucking noises at his cup occasionally he continued there to commune with himself. It occurred to nobody to toss the ball of conversation towards that preoccupied intruder ; Lily's inveterate brightness led the field ; and when Cha switched on the wireless to let the party hear a programme of Hawaian melodies given forth by a plangent assembly of steel guitars, Dan rose and excused himself.

" I'll have to go now, John, I'm afraid," he explained himself to his guest. His right hand was brought across to rest over the region of his heart. " I doubt I may be in for a bad night with the palpitations. It's my heart, you understand ; the doctors tell me I've got to go very carefully. Very carefully. And I've noticed," he added for good measure, " a late cup of tea is terrible apt to repeat."

When Dan was gone Lily recaptured the attention of the circle with a smile and a wink.

"There he goes !" she trilled. "He'll be an hour in that bathroom if he's a minute."

Her tone indicated a willingness to resume the chatter and the music, but John rose massively, ignoring protests and blandishments alike.

"No, Lily ! Thank you very much, and I've had a grand evening, but I never like being late, and I ordered the car for eleven. Is it there yet, Cha ? "

Cha opened the curtains and peered into a thin fog that moved lazily in the pallid beams of the incandescent street lamps.

"Car's there," he announced, "and a Rolls ! O boy ! O Boy ! "

As John and Lily stood on her doorstep in the last formal scene of the evening Dismal Dan's wife was still capable of a hopeful advance.

"I wonder, John, that you don't think of getting a wee car for yourself. These hires are awful expensive, and you're never just your own master, are you ? I'm sure Cha would love to drive you about whenever you wanted. He's an awful clever driver, our Cha."

"I don't see Cha getting off the office to drive me for the afternoon," John laughed easily, "or waiting for me outside offices. No, no, Lily ! I've no ambitions that way. These hiring people here are a pretty smart lot, and they'll do my turn till I get a wee place of my own. And good-night again, Lily, and thanks for a grand evening."

While the man of the house still laboured in the bathroom amid the confusion of syringes, measures, bottles, suppositories, unguents and tonics he deemed necessary to the continuity of personal existence, Lily and her children sat around the sagging fire in the drawing-room and, as any adult group will after a common endeavour of unusual scope, sought to sum up, with due modesty, the relative success of the entertainment. A satirical ear behind the curtains might have caught a few of the more significant phrases, thus :

"Anyhow, we're going to get our lessons." That was Beryl.

"I wish it had been London, just the same." That was Sibyl.

"I wish your Father wouldn't keep nagging about the business."

"Did you see the old man trying to smoke a cigar?" asked Cha blithely. "Uncle John didn't offer me one."

"The fish was nice, though, I thought."

"We'll have to get season tickets."

"And he's not buying a car, isn't he? Too bad. Never mind, Piefaces," Cha addressed his sisters. "What about me on a pony in India or wherever it is? Ride 'em, cowboy, ride 'em!"

"Well, I must say, Cha, that was very kind of Uncle John," Lily protested, "and I won't have you making fun. There's any amount of money out there, I've been told. And now, girls, there's the plug. Help me to get this stuff down to the kitchen."

On the whole, striking the cash balance that is always ciphered in letters of dully glowing fire on the dark and confused background of the lower middle-class life, the Daniel Rollands' reckoned a distinct credit balance on the night's proceedings. Romance was at hand to make them happy with the vision of the Twins as platform artists, and that of Cha as a crisp and sunburnt servant of Empire.

4

The snowy cone of Fujiyama, albeit in a cheap print rather unimaginatively framed, suggested a rare Buddhist serenity from above the mantelpiece in Beth's kitchen. At the level of the table, from which the dishes of the Saturday evening meal were now being lifted by the mistress of the house and her daughter, Addie, however, the latent thunder of unphilosophical and wholly personal rancours shook the atmosphere of what should have been an hour of well-fed, domestic contentment. Seeking an object for the gaze that would rather not betray neutrality by looking at either Beth or Davie as they bickered; anxious most of all not to appeal to Addie in her tortured quietude; John considered the peak as limned in the print and reflected sadly that it and the philosophy it symbolized were very far away from this tenement kitchen in industrial Scotland and the attitudes to life that, contending sharply, made enemies for the time being of one good man and one good woman (who loved each other dearly, as the gods would have it), an unhappy and helpless child of their daughter and an uneasy clown of their relative and guest.

As John saw it, they were both at fault : Davie fair daft on his bit of sport and insistent on his consequential rights as a male ; Beth in her Puritan reaction to all free, wild undertakings and nippy about the rights of a housekeeping woman to see her menfolk once in a blue moon and be reasonably entertained by them, especially on a Saturday night. If he had only had the wit, John reflected, he could have stopped all this nonsense with a laugh and an exercise of his own authority as guest and rich uncle from the East. He must have been talking to Addie. Anyhow, he had missed the moment ; and there they were at it, hopelessly involved in the ancient and intractable rivalry of the sexes.

" I would have thought," Beth was saying firmly, " an after-noon at the football was enough for ye, Davie Bryden. Now ye've got to go dragging John to this boxing nonsense, and Addie and me will have to sit here and twiddle our thumbs, I suppose ? "

" But John wants to go," Davie protested. " He's never seen Curly in a fight. You and Addie can go to the Pictures. Dash it, Beth ! It's juist once in a while, and we'll no' be late."

" Wastin' your time on that dirty, brutal business," Beth persisted blackly, sweeping away all the knives and forks along one side of the table in an angry, comprehensive gesture. " And gettin' poor wee Curly mixed up in it, to get bashed about and tied up with a lot of blackguards."

" In the Welfare ! Ach, for Heaven's sake, woman, chuck it!"

It was this undue bitterness that disturbed John. The pretence of hostility was an old convention between these spouses, but here was the confession of an open and profound difference. Its elements were obvious. Davie's passion for what he called a bit of sport had carried him too far, even to the point of deceit. It was one thing, as Beth had maintained, to arrange an afternoon at the football match, another to book ringside seats for the boxing tournament in the evening and announce the fact to the women-folk only at the supper-table. Even John himself had understood the expansiveness of poor, innocent Davie's programme only as they were coming away through the puddles outside the football

ground on a dark autumn afternoon with a drizzling rain from
the East.

Big babies, both of them ! If he had not been overtaken by
the little crisis unprepared, John could have laughed to realise
that Davie's small deception had been conceived entirely in his
fear and respect for Beth's authority. He was the eternal boy,
plotting clumsily in the matriarchal shadow. Then Beth in her
turn was the housekeeping woman who must hold the reins tight.
John remembered his Grannie like that, seeming to frown
automatically on simple pleasures, seeing evil in all departures
from the normal. If he could not have related the tendency to
the religious experience of the Scottish people, he did perceive
it to have some of its roots in an economic concern that must
at all costs preserve the sanctity of the hearth and had had, in
fact, the sorry effect of turning generation after generation of
working-class women into shrews, too soon.

John was himself a male and therefore on Davie's side, but
as he cast about in his mind for the easy, avuncular phrase that
would ease the strain, and as his eyes lingered on the remoteness
of Fujiyama's peak, he had to confess to himself that he would
very willingly abide by Beth's ideal programme and stay at home
before the fire that blazed so happily in the range with its
burnished fittings.

The football match had been very well in its way as a
spectacle, but John had found it a little difficult towards the end
to maintain his first eagerness. His powers of partisanship or
local patriotism, he discovered, had dwindled, and there were
latterly moments when he was almost nauseated by the unreasoning partisanship of the angry, roaring industrial mob in
their dripping tweed caps on the terraces, even by the comic
agonies, groans, gasps and shudderings of Davie as the crises of
the game tortured his innocent mind and racked his powerful
frame. It was as if the foreman blacksmith, somehow denied
active and competitive exercise on his own account, had transferred all his love, passion and loyalty to the eleven young men
in maroon jerseys and white pants who, facing another eleven
in black jerseys and blue pants, were the ingenuous and admittedly
skilful hirelings of a limited liability company with a board of
directors recruited largely from the licensed trade.

The East Wind, however, was the real trouble, the East Wind

in its bearing on John's habitual, old-timer's concern for the state of his liver.

He had insisted on Davie booking seats under cover, and he had swathed his middle in a flannel body-belt, but the seats had turned out to be high up at the top end of the stand, and the wet wind which swept across the ground from the North-East so swirled and gathered force and chilling power within the gaunt angularities of the edifice that John sat throughout the last half-hour in an agony of apprehension, feeling the cold get at his vitals through the last defence of the belt, accepting miserably the certainty of such " a go of liver " as his eastern experience had taught him to be one of the most miserable states of physical man. Now to go out in the rain again, probably to sit in another draughty hall, when he might be enjoying a cosy hour before the fire and have Ernie to take him home in the Rolls in time for early bed and a hot-water bottle !

He was all the more annoyed by the preposterous smallness of his dilemma, but therefore all the more eager to have it resolved and be at peace among his friends.

" You see, Beth," he turned from Fujiyama to mollify his sister, now savagely engaged with the dishes in the sink, " I promised Curly I'd come and see him box. He'd be disappointed if I didn't. Not that I want to be late."

" But you won't, man ! " Davie protested. " This is just a wee amachoor show in the Welfare. It'll be finished long before ten."

" Well, that suits me," said John, gently sweeping aside the possibility of further trouble. He turned with a smile of relief to Addie, calmly drying the dishes as her mother thumped them on to the drying-board. " And what picture do you want to see to-night, lass ? "

" I don't know, Uncle John," the girl returned his smile. " I'd just as soon stay at home and read."

The exchange of smiles greatly comforted John. It restored proportion to a situation into which, as the unwilling witness, he had perhaps read too much gravity. That girl had her head screwed on the right way, he reflected. Indeed, he would have been surprised, if he could have read into it, by the tolerance and justice of Addie's mind. He would have found that, as a woman, she was on her mother's side, but also that she loved her

father's enthusiasms and gawky subterfuges, and that she did not
make anything, save the small social awkwardness, of a tiff so
characteristic of the contrasting virtues of the parents who had
given her her comely body and her good sense. If John could
have gained the girl's confidence he would have learned much in
explanation of Beth's unwonted petulance.

He might have seen for himself the drift and clash of the
little human emotions between the spouses as the time drew near
for him to go out into the rain again. These were to be seen
in Davie's fidgetings, in his glances at his watch ; in Beth's
brooding look, distributed equally between her husband and her
brother. He might have seen, what Addie saw with the un-
sentimentality of the young, Beth's dark eagerness to get John by
himself for a minute or two and Davie's determination to prevent
such a dreadful thing happening to spoil the evening. But John
was a simple man, pleased to be over an awkward moment,
and he was talkative and reminiscent about sporting events
he had witnessed in the East until Davie rose and said, clumsily
enough :

"Well, it's about time we were getting down the road,
John."

The Welfare Hall that Messrs. Tod & Bannerman (Garvel)
Ltd. had fashioned for the benefit of the more sociable among
their thousands of employees, out of a building once dedicated
to the worship of God in the United Presbyterian convention,
turned out to be a much brighter and more agreeable place than
John had envisaged and, to his supreme reassurance, had been
equipped with central heating. Trust T. & B. to have everything
shipshape in proper engineering style ! More than that, much
more—Davie must have been talking—the reception offered to
himself was of the most gratifying kind. The officials of the
Welfare were at the door to receive him—Mr. Balhardie, Chairman of the Club and Chief Draughtsman, no less, of the Firm ;
the Hon. Secretary, Mr. Gavin Downie, a thin-faced and
sardonically smiling statistician from the Estimates Department ;
a burly foreman plater on the Committee—a word he accented
on the last syllable—called by everybody Big Joe, and two or
three other less prominent parties but all decent shipbuilding men
by the cut of their jibs.

It was pleasant to be led ceremoniously to the Staff Room,

once the ministerial vestry, to be helped off with his overcoat and given a seat of honour before an electric radiator that rather unnecessarily supplemented the excellent central heating.

"You'll feel it cold here after so long in the East, Mr. Cram. It's really the damp rather than the temperature," said Mr. Balhardie.

Yes, these chaps knew how to pay decent respect to one of T. & B.'s men who had done fairly well for himself. John's heart warmed to them for being still the plain, common, realistic five-eights the heavy industries of Britain keep throwing up : the solid non-commissioned officers, as it were, the backbone and salt of a mighty army. It impressed him deeply that such well-paid chaps as Mr. Balhardie and Mr. Downie should desert the comforts of suburban villas to supervise the recreation of the workers.

He said so to the statistician and Hon. Secretary, Mr. Gavin Downie, adding : " There was nothing like this in my time," and watched a grave smile ripple down the muscles of that long, tolerantly sceptical face. John liked this chap, Downie.

" Yes," agreed the latter in a plain, clear Scots voice after due consideration of the thesis. " Welfare's a new idea, and some of us think it's not a bad one. It's obviously worth the firm's while to pay for it, but some of us—like Balhardie and Big Joe—think it's a good thing on its own. It's not just that it helps to keep the youngsters off the streets, mucking about in pubs and ice-cream shops ; it gives them a sort of idea of order. At least, we hope so. Don't look for a hundred per cent result, Mr. Cram. But if you get twenty, that's really not bad going, considering," Mr. Downie added with a bitter twist of his muscular face, " the filthy mess our forefathers made of this town. Ever looked at the slums about the Five Arches ? "

John would have gladly taken up this point, but he was attempting simultaneously to take in the advices of Mr. Balhardie on his other hand, a graver and more portentous man by far than Mr. Downie.

" We'll show you round the place later on, Mr. Cram," he was saying, " but we'll have to be getting to our seats soon. You understand the system, of course ? "

Mr. Balhardie knew very well that Mr. Cram did not under-stand the system and greatly enjoyed explaining to the guest how the fights that night would be for the championships at various weights of the T. & B. Welfare Club, whereupon the winners would proceed to fight the chosen warriors of other Clubs and so, by a complex process of elimination John found it difficult to follow clearly, might crown the work of a winter in the ring by appearing in what Mr. Balhardie called the Nationals.

"Strictly amateur status, of course," the latter explained primly, "but you will see some rare good boxing."

"And ye'll see, Mr. Cram," roared the foreman plater they all called Big Joe, "some rare good slugging and a lot o' ruddy wallops ! These wee beggars would tear the tripes out of each other if we didny get them into the ring and make them fight proper. That's the idea of the Welfare, isn't it, Mr. Downie ? "

"Quite right, Joe."

"I wish we had had it in my time," John repeated sincerely.

"It might have made a difference," Gavin Downie agreed, flashing him a smile. "Here we're really working overtime on a repair job . . . But it's about time we were getting in, Mr. Balhardie."

"Aye, Mr. Cram," added Big Joe through a wheeze, "and now ye're going to see that wee nephew of yours knock bluidy hell oot the whole jing-bang o' them. Thon's a Holy Terror. Talk aboot Benny Lynch ! "

"That'll do, Joe," said Mr. Balhardie tolerantly. "This is not the plating shed."

"I only said a bad word oncet ! " Joe pleaded.

"Once too much in the Welfare ; and it won't be the last to-night, if I know you. If you're ready now, Mr. Cram ? I don't think you'll need your coat."

"I'll carry the man's coat," puffed Big Joe, at once recovering his position on the Committee and expressing his independence of these chaps with the white chokers in the drawing-office.

It was then an extremely pleasant experience for John to march down the main aisle of the area behind Mr. Balhardie, and see the white faces of the shipyard workers and their apprentices stare at him in the shadow of the bright lights over the ring, and even hear the preliminary lowings of such a cheer with which the Scots, a people with few loyalties left to them, may occasionally greet a stranger they believe to be worthy of respect. He was happy to be ushered into the obvious seat of honour at the ringside between Mr. Balhardie and Mr. Downie. An eager whisper in his ear assured him that Davie, whom he had been inclined to forget, was accommodated in a seat immediately behind him and was clearly impressed by the success of his own negotiations.

"How's this for a show, John ? " Davie asked with an anxious, hushed hopefulness of whisper.

"It's wonderful, Davie ! Wonderful ! I wish we had had it in my time."

The reiteration of the phrase confessed a really profound emotion. He was proud that T. & B. had made a bright place of this old kirk, with the billiard and ping-pong tables shoved back into the shadows and the white lines of badminton courts and what-not under his feet : decent chairs and forms arranged to frame the lighted platform of the evening's sport. With a pang of envy he thought of what this sort of communal centre might have meant to him in his overworked, all-too-anxious boyhood. There were almost tears in his eyes to think that all the men and boys about him, rough lads of the Riverside, were all T. & B.'s men and boys : the best builders of the finest ships in the world, or so John Rolland Cram believed, as more refined men might believe in the uniqueness of Shakespeare's genius. This Welfare business was new-fangled and all that, but it expressed to an ageing man a lovely and perdurable idea. This was one of the real acts of Coming Home : this consequential reception into a society of engineers.

John saw Big Joe climb into the Ring, greeted with hoots and low remarks from the body of the hall, and in the midst of his amused delight in the spectacle of the big, puffy plater turned public announcer he suddenly, irrelevantly but vehemently, thought what a damned fool was his sister Beth to make a domestic drama out of her husband's wish to attend at a gathering so respectable, not to say distinguished.

Big Joe's roar from the upraised platform fortunately distracted him from the bite of inner thought.

"Gentlemen all ! " he began like the Bull of Bashan.

"Speak up, Joe," piped a wit at the back of the hall. "We canny hear ye."

"Awa' and see a doctor, then," retorted Joe, bellowing

louder than ever, his face purpling with indignation. " Or mebbe a plumber would suit the likes of you better."

The crowd roared its delight in these familiar sallies, and John rocked with mirth, enchanted to hear again the rough, familiar idioms of Riverside humour. Shortly, however, Big Joe was allowed to proceed with his announcement, his foreman's voice slapping against the vaulted roof of the converted kirk and sweeping all interruption aside.

It was to the effect that the evening's programme would be short, consisting of two postponed ties over four rounds each, two semi-finals over six rounds each for the Featherweights, and then —" and this'll be a fair smasher," promised Big Joe—the final over eight rounds for the Bantamweight Championship of the T. & B. Welfare Club. As usual, Joe added for the benefit of a distinguished visitor among us this night, and to whom they would all offer the right hand of friendship ; and he, Big Joe, could tell a lot of the young chaps present that a lad who served his time with T. & B. could look the whole world in the face as an honest craftsman, never mind politics or, as Rabbie had put it in one of his pomes . . . This exordium being drowned in ecstatic cheers, Joe concluded cheerfully :

" Anyhow, if youse mugs would stop yer roarin' and nonsense, I'd explain to our guest to-night that the boxing here is conducted according to Amachoor rules ; that is, no referee in the ring. As usual, gentlemen all, our good friend Staff-Sergeant Popplewell from the Drill Hall is with us at the referee's table, and what he says goes ; and any snash from youse guys at the back and ye'll be oot on yer ears and nae bother."

John saw a uniformed Warrant Officer in the portly and moustachioed tradition of the English county regiments rise and bow to right and left, acknowledging cheers that bespoke his popularity.

" And now, gentlemen all—and youse holeborers at the back "—Joe concluded amid laughter, " we'll get crackin'. The first bout is between wee Jimmy Macandrew of the Pattern Shop and red-heidit Tam Heenan oot o' the Paint Store."

Through the thunder of partisan cheers Joe worked to his artistic climax.

" Come on, chaps ! Get tore into it. Hit hard but hit clean, or I'll belt the backsides aff ye. And may the best man win !"

Through the clamour aroused in the audience by these remarks Gavin Downie explained quietly :

" That was Big Joe's stock turn, and the boys wouldn't miss it for anything. He's a wonderful asset. Your nephew, by the way, won't come on till the last bout, the final."

Meanwhile, two small boys in shorts, singlets, socks and sand-shoes had clambered into the ring and, at the stroke of the bell, set about each other with a will. However they may have shaped as scientific boxers, John had no means of knowing ; he merely reflected that he had many a time paid guineas to watch renowned professionals give infinitely more tedious displays.

Here was neither caution nor fear ; these working boys were as terriers, chasing each other round the ring, thumping each other's persons with their huge gloves, letting not a second pass for even the deliberation of sparring if the narrowest opening for an urgent fist presented itself. The louder the crowd roared and laughed, the wilder did the battle become. The urchins lost their tempers frequently and then, always at a sharp bellow from our old friend Staff-Sergeant Popplewell, shook hands with a grin and resumed the scrap. When it was all over, Tam Heenan from the Paint Store adjudged the winner, the infants quitted the ring in a fond embrace, bare arms about each other's shoulders.

" Gracious me ! " gasped John, wiping his eyes. " I've never seen a better scrap in all my days."

" Good, isn't it ? " approved Gavin Downie. " And it lets out the black blood."

When at length it came to the announcement of Curly's bout, however, an almost palpable atmosphere of tension developed in the hall. John could hear that the cries of partisans carried a faintly alarming note of savagery, while the polite committee-men at the ringside seemed to hive away from the clamour into discreet silence. Big Joe's announcement included a rather less than usually facetious warning to the boxers to hit cleanly, to the spectators to be moderate in their comments ; and no laughter acknowledged it. John was aware of Davie's lips at his ear, whispering :

" There's a wee bit of a grudge in this."

When the fighters clambered into the ring it was to be seen that Curly's opponent was the taller, longer in the reach and looser of limb. His body was dark and hairy, and a slack underlip gave him an unfortunate look of truculence.

"That's a tough customer," John could not help remarking.

"And that's about all," commented Mr. Downie drily. "Curly's the boxer. Just watch his feet when he gets to work."

The bell sounded, and John's heart was in his mouth. He was at once proud and fearful to see Beth's boy up there in battle. Just a small young chap, but taut of muscle and sweetly built. The good-tempered grin was always on his little round face ; the plastered hair remained unruffled as he danced about his more cumbrous opponent. Go on, Curly lad ! he wanted to shout, but restrained himself for the sake of the family's dignity. He found himself full of concern for Davie behind him, normally the highly vocal partisan but now silent in a private agony of concern. There were plenty to shout for Curly, plenty in that crowded hall to roar when, tripping lightly aside, he would flick his slower opponent on the jaw with a flashing left and jump round again to ride the heavy counter-attack.

The justice of Gavin Downie's observation grew on John as he watched his nephew's feet. They were as those of a dancer, deftly and swiftly serving the balance of the body they carried. John perceived that Curly's essential strength lay in this nimbleness ; he perceived for the first time the rightness of the old phrase about making rings round the enemy. That was precisely the boy's natural, inborn technique ; and his anxious uncle came to see that the issue between the dark lad and the fair was the latter's ability to score point after point as against the former's chance of landing just one decisive blow.

In one sudden, horrible moment he thought to have seen it reach the mark. The crowd roared in sharp unison. Curly was bending low, his gloves folded to protect his stomach. The dark boy stood menacing above him, steadying himself to launch the fatal punch.

Miraculously, blissfully, the bell tinkled sharply from the referee's table. The hoarse voice of the Regular Army rebuked the dark lad for hitting low.

"Another like that, my son, and you're disqualified, see ? " said Staff-Sergeant Popplewell severely. "Box on."

"And now," announced a still more wheezy voice from somewhere over John's left shoulder, " now ye'll see some ruddy fightin' that'll make that hairy-chested mug look like yesterday's dog's breakfast."

The speaker, John discovered later, was a large person of middle age with a deformed ear that confessed much practical experience in the Ring and small eyes so reduced to slits amid hillocks of pasty fat that he might indeed have just emerged from a gruelling bout.

For the time being, however, John was completely lost in the spectacle of his nephew, John Cram Bryden, turn himself into a fighter bent on the punishment of evil. He had noticed that the boy, recovering from the near-foul, had not thrown his customary grin at either the spectators or his rival. Instead, the small round face set with purpose, while the lips twisted in the ghost of a faint smile ; and then Curly was in at his man, his arms working with redoubled speed, his dancing feet all the nimbler for being touched by passion.

In that moment the pleasant boy, Curly, shed something of his natural self to let some hard, relentless quality within him emerge. The fighter became embodied through the boxer's shadow, and now he was fighting to hurt, to win, to be done with the enemy.

" Boys, O boys ! " the wheezy voice behind John rejoiced in the display. " Look at it ! Gees, chaps, just look at it ! One-two, one-two, and every point a winner—and there, for Gees' sake, a clip under the heart for luck as he comes out ! Fight ! That hairy-chested guy doesn't know if he's in hell or Halifax, and he's goin' to take the rap one minute from now. Watch it ! One-two, one-two . . . There's a fighter for ye ! Gees, if I had the training of that boy Curly for a year, then ye'd see a world-beater ! "

Mr. Balhardie turned to reprove the commentator primly, and Gavin Downie winked to John, whispering :

" That's the renowned Slugs Macluskie. And he really does know what he's talking about. But look . . ."

The dark lad was now but a sluggish target for the dancing Curly ; it was all he could do to revolve slowly on his own axis, as it were, and somehow face the flailing fists of the smaller, fairer boy. His face seemed to have turned foolish and damp ; now and again he shook his head like a sick bullock ; and at length he sank on his left knee, his swollen lower lip hanging.

Curly stood back, his arms by his sides, the smile on his face once more.

"Bide where ye are, ye big mug," Slugs Macluskie hoarsely advised the dark boy, "or ye'll be fair murdered."

A towel fluttering through the air and Staff-Sergeant Popplewell's bell brought the affair to an end. Big Joe climbed into the ring with a great puffing and blowing, but few listened to his closing formalities, and few indeed could catch even the drift of his loud announcements. Those of the crowd who were not making for the exits were blocking the alleyway up which Curly, his jacket round his shoulders, made his grinning way back to the dressing-rooms. John rose and turned to Davie, and the good-brothers shook hands with a profound and joyous solemnity.

"You must be a proud man, Davie," said John gravely. "So am I."

"And now I expect you'll want to get home, Mr. Cram," Mr. Balhardie intervened. "We always try to close early. After all, we've got to start building ships again at eight on Monday."

"Quite right, Mr. Balhardie," John approved. "It's wonderful of you chaps to spare the time for this sort of thing. There was nothing like it in my day."

He did admire men like Balhardie and Downie, now putting on their raincoats and bowler hats and heading belatedly for the suburban homes they had deserted for the sake of an idea and an ideal, however vaguely envisaged. While they all hesitated in the entrance, waiting for a shower to lessen, John found himself edged apart from the rest by Gavin Downie.

"I'm glad you saw that, Mr. Cram," said the statistician with his awkward smile. "Curly's such a wonderful wee fighter, heads above the average amateur, that there's likely to be a bit of a fuss about him. It's no business of mine, of course, but . . ."

"Here's the car, Mr. Downie," the authoritative voice of Mr. Balhardie interrupted the talk. "Can we give you a lift, Mr. Cram?"

"No thank you. I'll be walking up the road with Davie . . . If we could have a word some time, Mr. Downie."

"Surely."

But Mr. Downie was in duty bound to follow his superior to the handsome car supplied by T. & B. for the convenience of their servants, and John was left to look round for his brother-in-law ; and there was Davie at his shoulder, saying with modest pride :

" I'd like you to meet Slugs Macluskie. Slugs, this is my good-brother, Mr. Cram, John Cram."

" Shake ! " said Slugs Macluskie heartily. " Proud to meet Curly Bryden's uncle. Is yon no' a fighter, eh ? Boys, O boys ! I'll tell the world . . . Could ye be doing with a bucket, Mr. Cram ? "

So many things were passing over John's head at once, so deeply was he committed to the rushing stream of life, he found himself walking with Mr. Macluskie and Davie across the dark square and up an alleyway in the shadow of T. & B.'s erecting shop to where an incandescent lamp on a bracket wanly lighted a board which, above a low door, indicated that here were the premises and registered office of the Deerpark Gymnasium and Recreation Club, Ltd. The cautious, prudent part of John knew that he ought to be at home in Blackwood's and shaping for bed, but the excitements of the night had put him in a reckless mood, and he enjoyed the feeling of being a character in one of those stories of the Chinese underworld written by chaps who wouldn't know the difference between a godown and a junk.

Slugs Macluskie's private office, into which they were ushered, seemed a deliberate parody of an executive's sanctum : the consequence of an untidy roll-top desk offset by a pair of men's underpants hanging over one end of it, the massive security of the safe by brown paper over a broken section of the skylight window. While Slugs fumbled with keys to get at a bottle in the safe, John floundered almost ankle-deep through sporting periodicals that littered the floor between the door and a basket chair of advanced decrepitude. Davie had to perch on the edge of a cluttered table and there sat obviously awed, gazing with the rapture of a devotee at the framed photographs of pugilists that covered the walls.

" The glassware's no' very bonny," their host wheezed amiably, " but the stuff in the bottle's the Real Mackay."

John was given the only tumbler and saw it filled four-fingers deep with neat whisky before Slugs would desist. He and Davie drank out of cracked cups.

" Salue ! Hair on yer chest ! " cried Mr. Macluskie heartily. Then, when he had sunk his drink in a gulp, his narrow eyes on

John's face, he gasped immediately : " And what are we going to do about this young chap, Curly ? "

" That's hardly my business," John hesitated.

" But ye seen him for yourself ! " the host protested. " Ye seen a champ in action, or did ye not ? Surely to Goad we're no going to leave it there ! "

John felt a little bit nettled at having this responsibility apparently thrust upon him.

" I know nothing about that, Mr. Macluskie," he said. " That's Davie's business, not mine. I'll tell you frankly, I don't like the idea of taking any young chap away from his trade. And if I don't know much about this boxing business, I know it's a short life for the professional. What's the future in it ? "

Slugs Macluskie looked through his puffy eyeslits with the innocent wonder of one who encounters a freak of nature.

" Help the blind ! " he prayed in a wheeze.

He reached for the bottle on the top of the desk, grasped it by the neck and half-filled his cup again.

" See here, Mr. Cram," he said gravely. " You haven't got this right. What's it got to do with Curly's trade ? His training'll no' interfere with that. And if he gets into the big money—and I'll bate ye a hundred quid he will—he'll no' need to worry about a trade for the rest of his natural. See here, Mr. Cram "— and he leaned forward to tap John's knee—" we're not talking about the future of a clever wee amachoor. Ye can pick that kind up by the dizzen anywheres. We're talking about a boxer, a fighter. We're talking about a lad in the class of Benny Lynch, Elky Clark—anybody ye like. *We're talkin', son, about a boy in the class of Jimmy Wilde.*"

Slugs uttered that last sentence in the consciously prayerful tones of one who knows that, in a sacred cause, he comes near to apparent blasphemy. John was impressed. He respected the fact that a professional of experience and even international repute should go so far as to claim so much for Curly, Beth's boy, his own nephew. It was hard to think of a high talent in the family thrown away for too much prudence. After all, Lily's Twins were to have their chance.

" I don't understand, of course," John said, " how these things work. What would you do, for instance, if you had the training of Curly ? "

" What would I do if I had the training of Curly ? " repeated Slugs as if it were a lovely line of poetry. " I'll tell you what I'd do . . . Pass me yer glass."

John having declined the invitation, Slugs refilled his own cup and Davie's, leaned back in his swivel chair, closed his eyes and started to intone something like a piece rehearsed.

" If I had the training of Curly Bryden, he would have a year of it before he saw his first big fight ; and he wouldn't turn pro till we had it fixed for a cert. Three nights a week in the gym here. Two nights of the usual stuff—skipping, the bag, shadow boxing an' that—and one night in and out the ring with a bunch of old pros. Not in his class, mind ye, but as fly as foxes and up to all the tricks."

" Then," said Slugs with a degree of self-congratulation, " while we was workin' him up, I'd be watchin' form—seein' who was the likeliest of the young pros ; seein' who was shapin' to have a crack at Benny Lynch ; and *then*, when they wereny lookin', I'd announce Curly as a pro and a challenger. They wouldny know, see ? We've been keepin' Curly quiet as an amachoor down here, see ? Then . . . one-two, one-two . . . and the block's out for keeps."

Mr. Macluskie's pantomine of these processes was alarmingly realistic.

" And then," he resumed, winking one of his puffy eyelids at John, " then we have the Press boys down to ask who's this Curly Bryden, and I sell them the dope, and there's a build-up, and then there's a real match, and then we're into the big purses— five hundred a twist, it might be—and Bob's your uncle. Gees, it's a dawdle ! With a born fighter like that . . ."

Sincerity rang in Slugs Macluskie's enunciation of that last phrase. Such as John had to eye this rough customer with many reserves, but he caught then the authentic accent of the expert who recognises genius in his own line. He rose to his feet.

" It sounds fair enough," he announced cautiously, " but it's Davie's business, as I said, not mine. Now we'll have to be getting along the road ; and thanks for your hospitality, Mr. Macluskie."

" Call me Slugs and be done wi't. Will ye no' have another bucket afore ye go ? "

The night had faired, and John and Davie walked westwards

under stars in a new-washed sky. The former felt tired, pummelled
by the events of a day unusual in his experience, but oddly
uplifted in his mind by its strangeness and by Curly's brilliant
part in its most brilliant moments. The brothers-in-law walked
for a time in silence, the awkwardness of a family issue between
them ; and John thought ruefully how blandly he had lied to
Slugs in saying that it was Davie's business, not his. He broke
the silence tentatively at length.

"Our friend didn't say anything about the costs of a boxer's
training—gym fees, prize money and all that. Does he just
expect to get it all back out of the purses later on ? "

"That's the usual way of it," Davie agreed eagerly, adding
defensively : "But that's not just Slugs' idea for Curly. He's put
it up to me many a time, but to tell you the truth, John, he'll not
take the boy on without a bit of a guarantee. He wants a lump
of cash down—but a proper contract, of course."

"How much ? "

"He said a hundred pounds," faltered Davie.

The nature of poor Davie's dilemma was thus made clear to
John, and he wanted to laugh with affectionate pity for this
simple man who went in fear of an upright wife with an imperfect
sympathy for his dearest aspirations. The old problem of poverty ;
the old story of the wage-earning artisan and the decent woman
eternally burdened by her anxiety to get him out to his work
each day in time and keep up simple appearances ! And wasn't
it just fair damnable to think that their precious hundred pounds
did not matter much to him who would, for all his disclaimers,
have the deciding of the domestic issue ?

"The way I see it is this, Davie," he resumed at length. "If
you're dead keen, and if Curly really wants to go on with the
boxing, we can easily find the hundred pounds. That's a present
from me to you and Curly, and with pleasure. We can't keep the
boy back if that's his line."

"O, John——"

"Just this first, Davie," John fenced anxiously. "I won't
have the boy taken from his trade, and that's flat ; and I won't
have him boxing as a professional for at least a year. More than
that, Macluskie will have to sign a proper legal contract before
he gets a penny. That'll keep us all right for a year . . . and then,"
he added rather weakly, "we'll see where we are."

They had reached the windy corner by the West Station, the expanses of the road junction deserted at this lateish hour of night and ghostly under the furtive gleams from incandescent mantles that swung in a rising wind. It was one of those empty moments of the long northern day when the inexorable timelessness of things urges itself against the human illusions. The high tenements above the odorous tunnels of the railway under the hillside might have been convict prisons in Siberia or the abandoned fortresses of a dead civilisation. Still it was here, at a corner, that Davie Bryden stopped to shake his good-brother by the hand, the pressure of his blacksmith's fingers vibrant with such an emotion other men might express in a symphony or a sonnet.

"Thank you, John!" faltered Davie huskily. "You're the best friend Curly and me ever had. Curly'll not let you down."

"No, no!" John reacted a thought testily to this tribute. He took refuge in the easy vernacular. "You'd best turn back here, Davie. It's only a step now to the hotel. Good night, lad! Not another word."

He hastened through the quiet streets alone, his mind busy. It was grand to give pleasure to a decent chap like Davie; grand to be able to help a fine, clean, manly boy like Curly. It would be fine some day to sit at a ringside in, say, the Albert Hall and hear the cheering and know that a wee bit of a loan made long ago had made him the honoured uncle of a champion. More to the point: he had tied the thing up shipshape and Bristol fashion; the conditions would be firm, and there was a year to play with. If it came to the bit, what about the Rolland Twins and giving Cha a recommendation on his own word for a job at the tea-planting? It was just the same sort of thing; a chap had to distribute his gifts as they were needed.

It was pleasant to be received into the security and warmth of Blackwood's Hotel, especially since he had now persuaded the manager into allotting him a big room to the front. He found, however, that he could not get to sleep; and he also found in the early hours of the Sunday morning that there was no honesty in attributing the fact to the unwonted excitements of the day. The funny thing was that all his thinking seemed to be watched and judged by the steady grey eyes of Addie, Curly's sister. That was queer.

5

The little steamer paddled daintily across the Firth, heading from Kempock towards the riparian settlements which look so oddly like suburbs that have strayed from their proper places on the outskirts of cities and surprisingly come to rest under the Highland hills ; their great sandstone villas in the Victorian tradition suggesting an orgy of inept and expensive building by the industrialists in an age when money was flowing and skilled labour cheap.

The steamer was small, a pier-to-pier ferry and not one of the great, rushing turbine vessels that carried the summer holiday traffic on quite extensive and voluptuous trips into the nearly open seas of the outer Firth. The railway combines set little store by the winter trade, being held to maintain it, and a thought unwillingly, only under the obligations of the Mail Contract.

On board the *Duchess of Buccleuch* that dull October forenoon, so far as John Rolland Cram could make out, were only himself and Addie, Beth's girl ; a commercial traveller in an obscure brand of confectionery ; two dim, blackly-dressed women, probably returning from the beds of relatives in city hospitals ; a Scots Guardsman, the peak of his cap obscuring his nose, no doubt hastening on leave to some shepherd's cottage in the glens, and an Ayrshire calf, sewn up to the neck in a bag, its large, frightened eyes inviting the kindness it would certainly not receive from the realistic deckhands of the railway steamer. The more important elements of the ship's burden, casually but conveniently arranged behind the ship's funnel in tactical proximity to the forward sponsons, consisted of the Mails, bread in boxes, sausages in cartons, and half-a-dozen odd parcels of fresh fish dispatched, by a freak of modern economics, from city shops to well-to-do dwellers by the seaside.

Mr. Cram, a portly figure in his frieze coat and stylish withal by virtue of a white silk scarf about his neck and the splendour of his Stetson, stood in the lee of the funnel and enjoyed the scene and the experience. If the Firth was shrouded in the early winter haze, the hills no more than gigantic ghosts to the northwards, he rejoiced in the space and freedom of the waterway. The little paddle-steamer, as modern in design as they made them, was but a perky young granddaughter of the boats of yesterday that had carried him on many a fondly-remembered sail through the enchanted summer days of childhood ; the paddles still churned sea water into ginger beer. The officers and deck-hands were as of yore heavy men from Lochfyneside, given to comic turns of Highland-English phrase. Even the commercial traveller, the sombre women and the calf were permanent figures of the immemorial scene. The round of calls was as he had recited them in his boyhood—Ardhallow, the Bay, Killadam, the Strone, Kilbride, Sandpoint and Hamilton's Quay. It was all as he had dreamed over so many years in exile ; this was one of the bits of Home.

He smiled to see Addie almost on her knees by the calf, stroking its long brown ears and speaking to it in those foolish terms women reserve for the lonely, the young and the unhappy. A nice girl that, and a picture in her tweed costume with a nice fur-collared tweed coat over it and a brown tammy on her bright head. John thought particularly well of her legs in nice fawn stockings and sensible tan brogues. Trust Beth to get her girl out in good trim ; he was a proud man to have such a lass for company—my niece, Miss Bryden. He had wanted Beth to take the day off and come with them, and Beth had indignantly asked how he thought Davie and Curly would ever get their dinners if she were to go gallivanting here, there and everywhere. Beth's sense of duty was a bit overwhelming sometimes, but Addie could cross the Firth with him on the Saturday morning, and John was content.

They were going to see the cottage. It had turned up out of the blue, as it were, in a telephone message from his lawyers in Garvel. The death of an elderly spinster and the provisions of a Trust Deed and Settlement had suddenly put on the market the desirable property known as Penang Lodge at the Strone ; and the senior partner thought it would be the very thing for Mr. Cram. It was an old cottage, enlarged and brought up-to-date some thirty years before by the late Mr. Mungo Peddie, who had made his little pile in the East. The senior partner felt sure he could persuade the Trustees to accept a firm offer of six hundred ; and he added his honest view that, if Mr. Cram could spare a couple of hundred extra to modernize the place, he would acquire a very tidy property indeed.

John could have bought the house offhand for the sake of the name alone. He liked the notion of the late Mungo Peddie—he had once met a nephew of the old chap's in Lappa—coming home to rest and giving his seaside cottage the name of the strange, distant place in which he had spent the best years of his life. Penang Lodge—that was good ! It was almost as good as the fancy of old Pete Skinner who, retiring from the important position of foreman plater with T. & B. years ago and buying a cottage on the shore near Hamilton's Quay, proudly renamed it " Bulkhead Bank." John chuckled to think of the sentiments that, in simpler days, had inspired such eccentricities.

He and Addie were the only animate items of the *Duchess of Buccleuch's* complement to go down the gangway at the Strone, though they were followed by a bag of Mails, the inevitable carton of sausages, a crown wheel for the repair of the doctor's car, a box of kippers and a cardboard box which, though mysteriously marked " Knickers, Beige, O.S.," appeared to contain two pairs of pigeons, permitted to breathe through a series of casual punctures in the lid.

" And where," said John, addressing Addie when they had set foot on the rutted baulks of the pier, " where do you think this Penang Lodge may be ? "

The piermaster in a tweed cap paused in the task of releasing the steamer's stern-rope from a bollard.

" Is it Penang Lodge—old Mr. Peddie's place ? " he asked sympathetically. " You'll be the gentleman inquiring from Garvel ? Go you up to the Post Office at the head of the pier, and my wife will gif you the keys. And that will be tippence each for the pier dues."

They discovered that Penang Lodge was fully a ten-minute walk from the pier and round the spine of the Strone, so that it faced a trifle East of South rather than slightly westwards as John had hoped, but he was utterly conquered by acquisitiveness at his first sight of the whitewashed front behind a formidable monkey puzzle.

It was not the cottage of his dreams. It was not on the seaward side of the shore road, which hereabouts ran on an embankment built out of and above the boulders of a stony, tide-fretted beach. There was no level lawn before it, for the original cottage had been built on a steepish slope, its back walls apparently hard against the precipitous eastern face of the Strone Hill. It was larger than the cottage of his dreams in that a second or, at least, attic floor had been added by the throwing out of dormers from the 45-degree angle of the slate roof.

John's mind had to make only a small adjustment to see in Penang Lodge a covetable improvement on his dream-dwelling. Against the rocky hillside, with a nice scattering of young larches behind it, the house had a pleasing flavour of the romantic in the Alpine or Norwegian convention. If the lawn in front of it— heart-shaped between twin, curving paths, the majestic araucaria in the middle of it—if this plot was steeply graded, it had been carefully tended ; and it was wonderful what you could do with one of these new motor-mowers. Joy of joys ! A little burn ran down the side of the garden from the hill.

John's craftsman's eyes saw that the paintwork on the doors and sashes of the house was fresh, a bright lime green contrasting piquantly with the white walls. A glance assured him that a flight of concrete steps, if a thought battered by the sea, ran down from the embankment to a stretch of foreshore that had been cleared of boulders to allow for the beaching and mooring of a boat.

" This looks the very ticket, Addie," he said, surveying Penang Lodge from the gate in a wall topped by a hedge of escallonia.

" It's nice," the girl agreed ; adding, in her capacity of Beth's daughter : " But wait till we see what it's like inside."

There was both a Yale and a good mortice lock on the front door. (Old Peddie hadn't kept house in the East for nothing !) The visitors were met in the lobby by a sullen front of that lifeless air which gathers in any house untenanted. Addie sniffed.

" I don't think it's damp, just the same," she announced, as if she had fully expected to encounter that prime objection. " We'll throw up a window or two."

Both were faintly depressed to find that the sitting-room, first on the left, was crowded with furniture of the Victorian age in its most fussy, ornate and depressing mood. A soot-powdered spray of crinkly red paper filled a fireplace framed in pictorial tiles. The yellow satin drapery over an upright piano—described in Gothic lettering as an Iron Grand—was held in position by the weight of studio portraits in fancy frames, all the simpers and attitudes of forgotten and unimportant uncles, aunts, nephews and

nieces witnessing pathetically to the frailty of human aspirations.
These yellowing photographs spoke more direly of mortality than
the exhuasted atmosphere in which, with intolerable cynicism,
they displayed personal and never very striking charms long
written off in the massive accounts of life. There was even a
horsehair sofa against the inner wall, a florid Burmese scarf
draped across its back.

"I'm not buying any of this junk," said John defiantly.

"No, but it could be made a nice room," said Addie less
emotionally. "See, it runs the whole length of the gable, and
you've those two side-windows looking out to the sea. If you
could build one of these new fireplaces in brick . . ."

John cocked an amused but respectful eye at his niece. It
was a fine business, indeed, when he had to have a schoolgirl to
point out what he had missed for himself. It must be this domestic
science stuff all the girls got nowadays. A cool customer, Addie.

They looked into the small dining-room on the other side of
the lobby and saw it to be adequate. Beth's daughter was more
firmly bent on inspecting the kitchen and scullery behind. She
paused by the kitchen table and looked round.

"It's a bit dark," she pronounced, "and just look at that
awful old-fashioned range !"

John was again enchanted to witness the emergence of Addie
as a decisive domestic character. He chuckled.

"Just imagine, Addie, that you had a hundred pounds to
spend in here, and no questions asked. Tell me what you'd
do."

"I'd gut that old thing out first of all," said the girl, pulling
off her gloves and smacking them on the table. "A terrible waste
of coal and a perfect heartbreak to any woman cooking, never
mind a supply of hot water. There's no gas, I suppose, and you
don't want one of those stinking paraffin contraptions. What we'd
want is one of the new slow-combustion stoves with a cooker
attached. Hot water *all* the time and a nice oven and hot-plate,
and they'll run on a shovelful of anthracite a day. And I'd want
white paintwork and a primrose distemper on the walls."

"Would you, now !" cried John, delighted. "What about
the scullery ?"

Addie followed him into this somewhat dank chamber and
looked about her with displeasure.

" The places they expect women to work in ! " she exclaimed.

" Just what's wrong then, lass ? "

" Nearly everything. Look at the level of that sink ; a woman would break her back washing up. And just the one cold tap. Do the fools never see that you can't run a house without hot water everywhere, all the time ? There's no rack for the plates ; just a greasy old draining board, far too narrow. That's how crockery gets broken. Look at the pots and pans on one shelf, and then their lids hanging from pegs a mile away on the other side. The light's behind anybody working at the sink ; it should be right above it . . . My, if I had only a week in here ! My mother would have the place about her ears in five minutes."

" You can have a week in here any time you like, my dear," said John with a depth of emotion that surprised himself. " I promise you, Addie, I won't do a thing that you and your mother haven't passed first of all. But come and we'll have a peep upstairs."

The three bedrooms on the upper floor were as might have been expected—pleasant little chambers with the peculiar charm of camceiling—and the visitors had fun deciding which was to be John's and which Addie's by prescriptive right whenever she should come to stay at Penang Lodge. They allotted the smallest room at the back to the housekeeper and agreed that the bath-room across the landing was the most pleasant and up-to-date of all the offices in the house. The inspection was completed when John, opening his pocket-knife, jabbed a blade into sundry lengths of woodwork and pronounced them sound, good stuff, free from dry rot.

They stood in the roadway and looked back and up at the white face of the house.

" I think the place would do me fine, Addie," he said, but tentatively.

" Yes," the girl agreed slowly. " It's a nice house, and it could be improved quite easily. There's just one thing, Uncle John . . ."

" Eh ? " he asked anxiously.

" I was wondering about the light," the girl suggested quietly. " These back rooms are a bit dark, and if you look now—and it's not one o'clock yet—you see that you're going to lose the sun behind the hill quite early, even on a summer's day. It's not much perhaps, but . . ."

" Och, we're not going to worry about wee things like that ! " John interrupted impatiently. " Come on, Addie, and we'll walk up the road to Killadam. We should get a bite to eat in the hotel there. Then I thought I'd look up old Sam Lightbody before the afternoon boat."

They marched along in silence. The girl who had been so communicative when challenged by a domestic arrangement seemed to have turned shy and remote again, and John felt uneasy, wondering if she had conceived mental reserves as to the suitability of Penang Lodge she was unwilling to mention. For his own part, if he could have been wholly honest with himself, he was utterly consumed by covetousness and could not brook the notion of being put off his bargain. Penang Lodge was going to be his house, his own. Much could be made of it ; Addie had admitted it. He toyed happily with the idea that the little hill-stream which tumbled and tinkled through the garden on its way to the sea might be somehow harnessed to supply Power . . . A wee arrangement of pelton wheels, or a turbine below a small dam at the top of the garden . . . He saw a whole decade of happy work before him.

The hotelkeeper at Killadam had neither food nor the will to prepare any, and John had to remember that he was no longer the man of position in the obliging East but a stranger in Scotland in the off-season. A decent woman in a tidy tearoom at the pierhead, however, agreed to run them up a plate of canned soup and a dish of beans on toast, and while this was being prepared John fumed and grunted on the topics of hospitality, starvation and enterprise.

" Everything out of cans ! Do they never cook a plate of broth ? "

" I don't suppose they see a stranger once a week now the holidays are over," said Addie calmly, " but a hotelkeeper should be ashamed of himself. Do you know, Uncle John," she added rather wistfully, " I'd like to run a restaurant ? "

" And I'll bet you'd make a rare job of it, Addie ! " cried John loyally. " And why not ? A bit of training at one of these domestic colleges, and then, if you were looking for a drop of capital to get you started——"

" Not me ! I'm going to be a nurse."

The firmness of his niece pleased him, even if he saw in it something of her mother's inveterate dourness, and the canned soup turned out to be smooth and palatable after all. He watched the girl's face as he asked carefully :

" What do you think of Curly as a professional boxer ? "

" O, that ! " Addie appeared indifferent. " We'll see."

" How did your mother take it ? "

The girl surprisingly grinned, her face lighting up in wrinkles of amusement.

" There was a rare row, I can tell you ! " she chuckled. " You'll get what-for when my mother gets you alone."

" I suppose I will. She's a warrior, your mother."

" Of course," explained Addie calmly, " you've got to make allowances just now. My mother's going through a very difficult time in a woman's life."

John was enchanted and scandalised at once. This was your modern girl for you ! A lass of seventeen to up and explain to her uncle the physiological background of her mother's moods. His own Grannie would have beaten the life out of Beth had she been heard whispering a hint of the mere knowledge of such dreadful intimacies. Still, the lass was straightforward and sensible about it ; no silly giggling or blushing ; and her statement did abate in John a trifling irritation he was unhappy to entertain at all.

Meanwhile, the woman of the tearoom had obligingly sent one of her children to advise Mr. Sam Lightbody that Mr. Cram was in the neighbourhood and eager to see him ; and shortly that massive man arrived to suggest that, if they were finished, they might repair back to the hotel where, if not food, a good dram was always to be had. There, in a fusty sitting-room, the elderly gentlemen from the East settled down while Addie excused herself.

" A nice girl that," allowed Mr. Lightbody hoarsely, filling a monstrous calabash.

" One of the very best ! " declared John proudly.

" Not like some of them, as I expect ye've found by this time."

" How do you mean, Mr. Lightbody ? "

" What I discovered when I first came home. That most of

yer dear relatives is just a lot of spongers—juist a lot of bluidy spongers."

"I haven't quite found that . . ."

"You will, then."

Mr. Lightbody set fire to the vegetation in his pipe with mighty, wet puffs and went on to develop what was clearly one of his favourite themes.

"It's not the folk like my boy Alec and his wife, Peg. It's the far-out ones that hasn't a real claim on ye worth a damn. Hintin' at this for the girl, that for the boy—a bit loan for Uncle Peter— and there's aye somebody wantin' to start a chicken-farm or some damned nonsense and looks to you to put up the cash for it. If you haveny found it yet, ye will find that they think ye're made of money. No, no ! Dear Uncle Sam, juist back from Hongkong. . . . But it's no' you they care a damn about. It's yer siller they're after. You mark my words Mr. Cram. Would they look at you twice if you came home a pauper ? Nut on yer life ! "

Fortunately for John's peace of mind, Addie reappeared then to say that she would like to have a walk, and that she would warn them when she saw the steamer coming across from the Bay ; and with Mr. Lightbody thus distracted from his obsession, he and John had an agreeable conversation about Penang Lodge and its possibilities, old Sam agreeing in his capacity of native by residential qualification that it was a tidy bit house of which much could be made. They had an eager discussion of the technical sort as to the possibility of harnessing the burn, and Mr. Lightbody promised that this problem would be the matter of a survey by himself on the spot and of close thought, to the end of producing for his friend what he called " a bit plan."

As the steamer made homewards across the greying Firth John looked back over the taffrail to pick up the white front of Penang Lodge in its sub-alpine setting. That was the house for him ; he firmly intended to clinch the matter by letter that evening. Then his eyes wandered to see Addie's trim figure, virginally alone in the bay behind the starboard paddlebox, the wind from the ship's passage making play with the natural curls of her bright hair. The emotion of protective love stirred in him, and he mildly wondered why this child, alone within the family group, should so engage his interest.

The train of vagrant thought brought him back to Sam

Lightbody's sour generalization on the values of blood relationship, and he could not wholly drive it out of his mind. It remained a furtive ache, like Beth's refusal to be free and happy. The inexhaustible human power of self-deception came slowly to his aid, however, and before the little ship had started to swing in towards the terminal pier, John Rolland Cram had it fairly firm in his mind, that by his acquisition of Penang Lodge he had somehow cut himself free of the first, faintly shabby entanglements. He had now made all his grateful dispositions. Now, in Penang Lodge, he was to be the man who had come Home for good.

CHAPTER FOUR

A HOUSE AT THE COAST

I

ON A FORENOON of January, 1938, one of those winter days
that carry in fitful sunlight and an unexpected gentleness
in the air the assurance of spring's eventual return, three
elderly male persons stood in obviously serious and occasionally
heated conference on the gravelled terrace before the house or
cottage known as Penang Lodge in the sub-Highland parish of
Finlas.

One of them was the new owner of the property, Mr. John
Rolland Cram, distinguished in that small company by the size,
scope and colour of his American hat, bought in Singapore. The
largest and by far the noisiest of the trio was Mr. Sam Lightbody,
attending in his self-appointed capacity of Clerk of Works, as it
were, to his new friend and prospective neighbour. With them
was Mr. Macfarlane—strangely named in full Giuseppe Garibaldi
Macfarlane—of the building and contracting firm of Macfarlane
& Son of Hamilton's Quay.

An interloper on the scene about nine minutes past noon that
day might have heard Mr. Lightbody holding forth on the right
way to line a kitchen recess in which an old-fashioned range had
recently been replaced by an up-to-date slow-combustion stove
of half its size and some ten times its efficiency.

" I'm telling ye, man," Mr. Lightbody addressed the builder
in a wheezy roar that horribly suggested a flood of rheum over
small boulders in his bronchial tract, " there's a rare new material
on the market. It's an asbestos board, mebbe three-eight-parts
thick, with the one side high-polished to look like tiles or a mirly
kind o' wallpaper. Can be fitted as neat's Katie's leg, and a
woman can clean it in one wipe wi' a damp cloth. What do you
say, Mr. Cram ? "

" I haven't seen the stuff," said John, temporizing. " If my
niece were here, Addie Bryden . . ."

"And mebbe," said Mr. Macfarlane, polite but dry, "you could be telling me where to get this wonderful stuff?"

This speaker in the accent of the Highlands was a tall and loosely-articulated man, obviously aged but somehow jaunty in appearance, perhaps because of the Donegal hat in light tweed he wore. He had the brooding manner of one who, beyond optimism either in faith or business, still takes a sardonic interest in the distant and faintly absurd struggles of his contemporaries. A Highlander born, perhaps he had fallen between spiritual stools in setting up in competitive business within the Lowland sphere of interest. Perhaps his spiritual integrity had been obscurely affected by his Christian names, given him by a father who, deserting a shepherd's cot for the railway service in the abundant '50's, had become the most intractable of Radicals in a non-industrial county and a somewhat tedious worshipper, in the recurrent British way, of him who wore a Red Shirt against tyranny abroad.

John got a lot of quiet fun out of the conflict between old Sam and Giuseppe G. Macfarlane. Sam was always so full of bustling, urgent notions; the builder so sceptical and slow, filled with the Highland mistrust of the time-element in human affairs. The one roared and wheezed and spluttered; the other hummed and demurred and ironically questioned, as in the matter of the asbestos boarding. The result of this battle over two months of time, however, was that a new fireplace in brick had been built in the sitting-room according to Addie's ideas, a new stove and boiler established in the kitchen, and a new sink, with hot water laid on, put into the scullery.

Skirting a sort of volcano of cement within a low crater of sand, created by Mr. Macfarlane's men outside the back door of Penang Lodge, the three elderly persons peered into the scullery and saw that a plasterer and his apprentice boy were smoothing off a new floor.

"Well, that's that about finished," Mr. Lightbody allowed grudgingly. "That's the plumbers a' done and the plasterers near done. What about yer painters now, Mr. Macfarlane?"

"Don't ask me," replied the builder, shaking his head over the folly of looking to sub-contractors for any satisfaction. "That man Gourlay and thon kizzen of his from Aberdeen-way is a law aal to themselves."

" I'll sort Gourlay and his cousin, Aberdeen or no'," promised Sam grimly. " But come and we'll see about the dam."

The three gentlemen, who were all enjoying themselves thoroughly in these unhurried considerations of what Sam called " the job at the Lodge, Mr. Cram's new place," now proceeded round the back of the house and saw again how what had been but a precipitous patch of drying-green had been dug away, and the young trees above it cut down, to allow more light into the back windows of the house.

" Now, that's what I call a big improvement," said Mr. Lightbody with pride. " That muck we dug out is a bit of an eyesore, I'll allow ye, but ye see, Mr. Cram, I was keepin' it back for the dam. It would be rare stuff for filling a retaining wall."

Mr. Macfarlane coughed politely in John's direction, asking :

" And would you be serious about a dam, sir ? "

" Serious isn't just the word, Mr. Macfarlane," John demurred. " The fact is, I haven't gone into the technical side of it. But if we could get a drop of cheap power through a pipe into a wee bit turbine, charging a range of good batteries . . ."

" And a right bonnie bit o' the garden ! " Sam added enthusiastically. " You could have lilies and deucks and goldfish and . . ."

His invention exhausted itself at that point, and a silence, strangely imposed by the aloofness of Mr. Macfarlane, held the little gathering in a momentary trance.

" I would have nothing to do with a dam," declared Mr. Macfarlane at length, morosely.

" Nonsense ! " cried Sam, and " Why not ? " asked John, simultaneously.

Mr. Macfarlane raised his eyes to the hills and spoke, in fact, with a kind of prophetic vehemence.

" There's no trusting these mountain burns," he said, pointing a forefinger up the line of the stream that normally ran like a toy thing through the grounds of Penang Lodge. " They are pretty and pleasant in quiet weather like this. But come you to the spring and the late summer, and I myself have seen this same burn come down like a waterfall, washing half the hillside on to the shore road so that a horse and cart could not get past. You make a dam at the top of your garden, Mr. Cram, and get one of these storms on you, and you'll be up in the attics there, shouting for the Riccar lifeboat."

John laughed at this fantastic forecast.

" Well, we won't worry about that just now," he said. " The thing is to get the house finished first."

" And I don't agree with a word you say, Mr. Macfarlane," Sam protested. " Do you mean to tell me that you and me and Mr. Cram couldny build a dam, with sluices and overfalls and a' that, that couldny take a bit flood from the hill ? Away with you ! "

" We haven't time to argue that now, Mr. Lightbody," said John equably, pulling out his watch. " It's time we were going up to the hotel for a dram and a bite of food."

Having thus dealt with the problem of the dam, and not for the first time, the associates wandered amiably round to the front of the house and were scanning the façade as if in search of fresh themes for technical discussion, when the click of the latch on the gate brought them round simultaneously to see what stranger came among them.

" My Goad ! " breathed Sam Lightbody heavily. " If it isn't that Spring-heeled Jeck o' a sky-pilot. Watch yerself wi' this one, Mr. Cram."

A clergyman with an extremely jaunty step was approaching them up one of the pathways, his rolled umbrella digging into the gravel and then pointing sharply forward with the rhythmic precision of a rifleman's weapon at the trail. When he saw that his approach had attracted attention, indeed, he waved this object in the air with the boyish gladness of one who is confident of his own fitness as a bearer of glad tidings, a happy man among men. As he approached closely John observed that this ordained servant of God, a person of less than middle height, had a thatch of russet hair which looked uncommonly like a wig, upon which was comically perched a small hat in light grey felt. He wore brown spats over black shoes.

" Well, well, well ! " cried the newcomer, as if he were really making an entry into the Sunday School Heaven of harps and angels. " Caught you out, pretending to be busy ! Mr. Macfarlane. Mr. Lightbody. How nice ! And this must be Mr. Cram, of whom we hear so much ? "

T.F.A.   L

"Mr. Kiddie, the parish minister," the builder explained in an embarrassed mutter.

"How do you do, sir?" said John heartily.

"Now, this is nice," Mr. Kiddie rattled on, pointing his umbrella at the dumb fabric of Penang Lodge. "Nice to see the old house open again. Yes, yes, yes. Mr. Peddie was one of my pillars, Mr. Cram : a great influence for good. Is that not so, Mr. Macfarlane? We look to you, sir. Your experience and influence . . . And we have to find a County Councillor for the next election. The very man, I think, yes. Don't you agree, Mr. Macfarlane?"

"You might do worse," the builder admitted with embarrassment.

John laughed outright then. He laughed at the notion of himself as a County Councillor-elect before he had so much as half-a-foot in the province ; and he laughed at this arch homuncule who, self-removed from the apprehension of realities, arranged a parochial world of his own in quick, cackling phrases.

"I think I'd better get to know something about the County before you think of putting me on the Council," he said. "Is it a fill you're looking for, Mr. Kiddie? Try this of mine."

The minister had produced a briar pipe from the pocket of his shabby grey raincoat and had tapped his person, cocking his head comically as if he might hear the rustle of a missing tobacco pouch, then frowning petulantly in self-criticism.

"It will be my head next," he cackled. "Left it on my study desk as usual, I suppose. Dear me, dear me! Sermons, Mr. Cram; the poor parish minister's mind is apt to be confused by so many things to think of. So many things. Now," he added practically, poking his sharp nose into John's pigskin pouch, "this smells good. This smells *very* good indeed."

Having filled his pipe and returned the pouch, Mr. Kiddie appeared to be overcome by a fit of abstraction. John, who had a box of matches ready, watched the filled pipe being returned to its pocket in the rusting raincoat. The minister turned, apparently to consider the mystery of the sea.

"Yes, many changes," he remarked portentously. "Great changes. But here you are among us, Mr. Cram," he added briskly, his pastoral gaiety returning, "and our quiet country life will be enriched, I am sure. Don't forget the County Council," he raised an arch, quivering forefinger. "Most important. We need our best minds. But there we go—a quarter-past twelve, and I promised a visit to Mrs. Rigby of Whindene before lunch. Off I go—always on the trot, Mr. Cram. Good-bye ! Good-bye, gentlemen ! "

And with a florid wave of his rolled umbrella the little minister shot off down the northern path, his progress so rapid and precise, so unnecessarily violent in the given setting, that the three older men were held in a trance of wondering silence until the gate clicked behind the Rev. D. MacGilchrist Kiddie and the urgent footsteps of that divine faded out of hearing along the shore road.

"My Goad ! " cried Sam Lightbody again, breaking the silence. " If that isn't the damndest wee sponger in Christendom ! Did ye see him workin' his old pipe trick on Mr. Cram, Mr. Macfarlane ? "

" I did," said the builder with a slow grin.

" I'll bet ye he gets the best part of an ounce of tobacco a day that way, the same wee twister. See here, Mr. Cram," Sam turned kindly to his friend, " you've got to be fly for that chap. If he comes to see ye—and he will, b' Goad !—never offer him a cup of tea. Never offer him a fill. Never offer him a cigar or a cigarette. For if ye do, I'm tellin' ye straight, he'll never be out yer house. The poor wee rat's juist built that way. Am I right or am I wrong, Mr. Macfarlane ? "

" He's a queer wee man, indeed," the builder allowed cautiously, much disliking the challenge to his native respect for the collective ministry. " But I must be getting back along the road."

John and Sam saw Mr. Macfarlane off in a T-model Ford of great antiquity and turned together towards Killadam and its hotel, gravely following in the hot footsteps of the Rev. D. MacGilchrist Kiddie.

They marched in silence for a while, enjoying the mildness of the day and a vision of Highland peaks revealed to the northward by a sudden splitting of the clouds that mysteriously lumbered and blundered among them. John was quite startled by a sudden and carefully-pondered pronouncement by his friend.

"The fact of the matter is," puffed Sam, "ye've got to get used to a place like this."

"I've seen that," returned John dryly.

"Take that wee runt, Kiddie," Sam pursued his argument. "He's what ye seen for yerself—juist a miserable, spongin' humbug with the gift of the gab. The poor devil's got about three hundred a year and a manse too big for him, so what could ye expect? The real point is, Mr. Cram," and here Mr. Lightbody waved his calabash towards the glorious hills, the gold of the sun upon them, "Kiddie's here because he isny fit for a better job; and he's here because the folk *don't want a better man*. Wouldny have him, wouldny pay for him; suits them best to have a bletherin' mug who kids himself on he's a kind o' bishop and would run for his bluidy life if a drunk navvy put up his dukes to him."

"I don't think I'm going to lose sleep over Mr. Kiddie," laughed John.

"No," Sam agreed gravely. "What I was kind of getting at was the queerness of a wee place like this. It takes a mighty lot of gettin' used to after the life men like you and me had in the East. Man, ye've got to understand from the word 'Go' that Kiddie's nearly normal compared wi' some of them. Did ye ever see a bairn about the place, except among the locals? No, ye did not! We're juist a collection of old, retired, eccentric nobodies—everybody sticking to his own bit house and garden, his own bit rights, his own bit weys o' doin'. Freaks and frumps, the whole bluidy lot of us. Wait till ye see some of them; Madame Tussaud's isny in it. They're fair daft, most of them. They should build a wall round the place and pit up a sign 'Loonies—keep out.'"

John found his friend's vehemence amusing, but he could have acknowledged to himself that this fantastic picture of a seaside community had the bite of basic truth which undermines optimism. He had already felt in himself sometimes a queer, uncomfortable sense of—what was the word?—desolation when, walking along the shore road, he had seen each cottage or villa or mansion to be an isolated community, mute and enigmatic and silent. He had got the feeling of stringency and small snobbery and pride that informed the life of the settlement, which failed to be a community precisely because, built round a subservient nucleus of native tradesmen and shopkeepers and jobbing gardeners, it consisted of the retired and displaced and dis- oriented, along with a number of genteel spinsters who looked to their summer lets to keep them from starvation during the long Scottish winter. He had even been troubled by the servile assiduity with which the grocers along eight miles of coast, the smart and helpful vanmen of distant butchers and bakers, had stopped outside Penang Lodge to solicit his custom and give large assurances of flawless service.

"I see what you mean, Mr. Lightbody," he said, "but isn't it what you would expect? We're retired folk, and that's that, and we needn't look to have something like the Canton Club in a Highland village. No: I'm ready to be as eccentric as the rest, keeping myself to myself. If one or two old chaps like you and me can meet now and again for a dram and a yarn; if I can have my folk from Garvel across for the day off and on; if I'm left in peace to work in the garden and potter about—well, that's my choice. It's peace I want."

"If they let you have it," interjected his friend enigmatically. "But as long as you know . . ."

Thereupon they turned into the hotel, of which the proprietor, now fully informed as to John's status and means, was delighted to put on an adequate meal whenever he cared to leave word on coming off the morning boat.

2

On a day of February, cold and lowering with the wind from the East, Mr. Giuseppe G. Macfarlane lingered in the small entrance hall of Penang Lodge and, twisting his long neck, looked round its walls and cornices as if in search of flaws hitherto unobserved.

"Well, there it is, Mr. Cram," he said at length and almost regretfully. "The job's done to the best of my ability, and that's your house ready for you."

"Yes, Mr. Macfarlane," John agreed, but with the faint impatience of one who would have the interview at an end. "You've made a tidy job, and I know good workmanship when I see it. Now——"

"And I'm obliged for the cheque," the builder insisted on adding. "The like of that hasn't happened to me since—no, not since I was in business."

"Well, I can't bear having accounts hanging over my head. Now——"

The insistence of the lean and honest man on this single point had John fairly bewildered. This was the appointed day for a final inspection of the works on the new house and the handing back of the keys, and he had written the contractor to come to the meeting with his bill made out in full. Having asked for it and scanned it cursorily, John had brought out cheque book and fountain pen and paid it there and then. This was as he liked business done; and it was as if he had administered a real physical shock to Mr. Macfarlane. He was embarrassed. The slip of pink paper trembled in his great hand; he was excessive in his apology for not having on his person a stamp for the receipt.

"Well, you can post it to me, can't you?" John had observed calmly, adding jocularly: "Do you never get your bills paid round about here?"

"That's just it!" Mr. Macfarlane had cried with sudden candour. "It's all credit, credit, up to a year, mebbe two years. There's not a tradesman on this side of the water could live if it wasn't for the Bank. You see, sir," he explained anxiously, "it's the dividends."

"The dividends?"

"Yes, they're pensioners, the most of them here, or the spinster women of folk that once had money. They get the dividends in June and December or their wee bit allowances at Whitsunday and Martinmas. Mebbe they'll pay you a bit then, but you can whistle for your money in between times. Not in all my time have I had anybody but yourself pay on the nail, and that's the God's truth."

This peep behind the façade of the sort of life he had chosen to share seemed to John at the moment not much more than amusing. If he was touched, it was only by the faintly comic pathos of the shifts and pretensions of gentility seeking to maintain position without economic substance and at the expense of the small tradesman. In another mood he might have reflected on the decline of the Victorian standards of security that had left this tidemark of pretension within poverty on the outer fringes of every industrial area.

At the moment, however, he was more concerned to get Giuseppe Garibaldi Macfarlane off the premises and, by a private act of symbolism, take conclusive personal possession of his own bit of landed property : this precious realisation to his hand of so many years of saving, planning and dreaming.

He had urged the builder out of doors on to the gravelled terrace and was itching to shake hands in farewell when their parting was ludicrously interrupted by a swishing noise through the air and the fall at their feet of a metal object.

John looked down to see that an empty sardine tin had been thrown with fair accuracy in his direction. Glancing to determine whence it had apparently come, he saw soaring towards him, with the erratic but impressive purpose of a glider or kite, one of those heavy paper bags fashioned to contain cement. This missile fell short, but the period of its flight allowed him to perceive that these strange objects were being thrown into his property over the boundary hedge of privet by a woman from the house next door to the North. He had always been vaguely aware of the existence of a neighbour ; and now, over the hedge and at the extreme end of the kitchen garden between it and the gable of her dwelling, there stood an angry woman, now heaving crusts and cigarette cartons and empty match-boxes across the frontier of her threatened property.

John saw a woman of nearly sixty, perhaps : a short woman with a fresh face under a wild thatch of nearly white cropped hair, parted in the middle. The freshness of her face was as that of a robust schoolgirl who has been sledging throughout a winter afternoon in the rapture of her first affair with a personable boy. Through this abnormal mask there goggled a pair of wet, pale blue, exopthalmic eyes. She threw the stalk of one of her own savoys at her enemies, shouting all the while :

" That's enough from you ! Take your dirt back where it came from ! Don't you imagine you can make a midden out of my garden. It's you, Macfarlane, you and those dirty men of yours. I'll have the law on the lot of you, messing and dirtying. You and your fine new house," she appeared to address John directly, " take that ! "

Now a pebble of size, quite accurately aimed, whizzed over

the heads of Mr. Cram and his contractor, causing them to duck sharply, and chipped the rough harling on the northern gable of Penang Lodge. The wild lady then turned away and marched back to her house, talking loudly as she went, in her desperate loneliness telling the sea and the hills and the birds what a terrible life was hers among so many enemies, each bent on her destruction.

"And what on earth's all this?" asked John at length.

"It's that poor creature, Kate Clapperton," Mr. Macfarlane explained tolerantly. "She's fair demented, living there alone since her sister drowned herself. Plenty of money, too; their father was head of thon big firm of City Mercers in Glasgow, you may remember; shops all over the place. But there it is; shuts herself up and won't have a soul near the place. These men of mine," the builder allowed mildly, "are untidy beggars just the same."

"They're all that," John agreed. "I'd be confoundedly annoyed if they chucked that stuff into my place from the other side of the fence."

"Ah, well," said Mr. Macfarlane, "it's not easy these days, whichever way you look at it! And now I'd best be stepping along the road."

They shook hands, and John watched the builder swing down the path and climb into his antique car.

This was positively the last act of the small drama of possession. He, John Rolland Cram, was now the man in full ownership of Penang Lodge; and he felt in that moment a man utterly alone. He turned and thoughtfully picked up the bits and pieces of rubbish thrown back across the hedge by Kate Clapperton. (It was a pity this had happened.) He then carried the shards round the back of the house and dumped them on a pile of rubbish that had been assembled there, to be carted away in due course. Mr. Macfarlane's lorry was coming for it on Monday—if you could trust those Hielan' tradesmen to remember.

It was all very well to be concerned with little details; all very well to be a retired gentleman who, having paid the contractor's bill, now entered into possession of his property; but John's heart was sinking as he passed through the back door into the renovated scullery. The house now seemed so big and empty, so cold with the East wind blowing under the doors and no woman

about to light a fire and create the circle round a hearth. The
very newness of scullery and kitchen was surprisingly bleak ; the
smell of fresh paint and plaster was repulsive. He should have
brought Addie with him. But Addie was at school, working with
that queer intensity of hers for her Highers. Beth and Davie
and Addie were far away, busy with their own affairs, not
knowing at all how lonely Uncle John was feeling in this moment
of time ; and, if they thought of him at all, no doubt envying
his means and his happiness in taking possession of the new
house.

John passed through the kitchen and lobby to what he now
called the lounge, the long sitting-room on the South side, away
from the searching East wind. He carried with him a small parcel
of sandwiches, his lunch made up by the nice girl in the stillroom
at Blackwood's. He looked about him and realised that there was
no place to sit, save a narrow window-ledge : no chair, no table :
nothing but the vacuous aridity of an unfurnished room. The
importance of furniture in the scheme of things dawned upon him.
He was like a hawker at a sale, eating a tu'penny pie on a bare
window-ledge.

As he chewed the sandwiches without appetite, his dentures
making heavy weather of so much glutinous bread, John thought
of furniture, of the bits and pieces of fashioned wood and carpet
and rug and ornament that make a room. He thought of the
great packing-cases of his own stuff from China due by N.Y.K.
almost any time ; probably kicking about the London Docks
at the moment, if he knew these little yellow beggars and their
worship of a system which never functioned properly. And that
led him to think of Sam Lightbody.

This was a bad business. Sam should have been with him to
take over the house and see Macfarlane's bill paid. Sam had been
a pillar of strength while Penang Lodge was being done up :
always on the spot to keep an eye on Giuseppe Garibaldi Macfarlane and his men. He had shrewdly foreseen the nature of all
John's furnishing problems ; he had envisaged great shopping
expeditions in search of bargains, indicating in detail what he
would look for and where, how he would deal with backchat from
smart shop assistants. Sam's attitude towards retailers was
invariably bellicose, wary.

" And we should be lookin' out for ads of sales and roups in the papers," he would say hopefully. " Many's a good bargain ye can pick up at a private sale, and it's always a bit of sport."

Then they had quarrelled, two foolish old men falling into a tiff over nothing. In his zeal for his friend's interests Sam had marked down in a second-hand shop in Doon a display cabinet that seemed to him of singular beauty and a thief's bargain. They took a morning off to go in by bus to see it, and when the object was pointed out by Sam with quiet pride John had been unable to find words to express tactfully his revulsion against its heavy Victorian elaboration.

" Do you no' like it ? " Sam had asked suspiciously.

" Good Heavens, man ! " John had laughed too carelessly. " I wouldn't be seen dead beside that bit of coffin-work."

" O, if you're going to take it that way . . ."

They had returned in silence, John dropping off the bus at the gates of Penang Lodge, while Sam continued the journey in a private vacuum of offended dignity. Two foolish old men, pathetic pantaloons in the twilight of life ; and the very triviality of the episode had now the power to heighten John's feeling of loneliness as he stood uncomfortably eating without appetite in the house of his long, fond, sentimental dreaming.

He saw, belatedly and with alarming clarity, that he had made a decision without knowing it. He was leaving Garvel now, cutting himself off from his small, precious circle of friends and relations. Often enough he had told them impatiently that he was only moving five miles across the Firth ; that there were plenty of steamers and a hearty welcome for anybody who took the notion of a sail and a visit to Uncle John ; but now he knew that the kindest people do not readily stir out of routine, that they are held back by a complex of hesitations and prides and pruderies, and that he would more likely have to tempt his visitors than to repel surprise invasions . . . unless, his secret mind cruelly suggested, Lily was out for something. The mere certainty of having to leave Blackwood's Hotel was discon- certing, now that it occurred to him. An oldish sort of chap liked, needed, the assurance of warmth, good service, things done for him without fuss and paid for at a proper rate. He had got to know and like the servants about the place. He had his chair of honour in the manager's sitting-room in off-hours ; his little table by the dining-room window was defended as a fortalice . . . "Mr. Cram—one of our regulars—a real nice old gentleman."

But this would never do; and a sudden blatter of easterly rain on the window restored his awareness of time. Twenty minutes before the afternoon bus would pass the gate to take him to the afternoon boat for Garvel. He looked quickly round the house, locked up thoughtfully, and marched away down the path. From the shore road he turned in through the bedraggled iron gates, their stone pillars bearing the chiselled legend AVOCA, of the house next door.

The instinct came out of his honest courtesy and of his will to be a good neighbour; it was also partly born of pity and sympathy for the lonely. But there was no answer on that level to the bell that jangled in the back premises of " Avoca " to his pull at a handle in tarnished brass. It seemed to be a dead house, and his engineer's eye saw the stigmata of decay in the parched wood of window-sashes that had not known the lick of paint for years; he had time to look round and see that the front garden was a jungle. He rang again, and a window opened above his head. He looked up to see the lurid face of his neighbour in its setting of wild white hair glaring down upon him.

"What do you want? What are you doing here?" she challenged him shrilly.

"O, Miss Clapperton," said John, raising his great hat, " I just wanted to apologise for the trouble those builder's men gave you. It was wrong of them to throw that rubbish over your fence, and I wanted to tell you it won't happen again, or anything like it."

"It better not! It better not!" cried Kate Clapperton in a high state of indignation. She gabbled ferociously: "You'll get a lawyer's letter, that's what you'll get. I'll get damages. I'll take you to the Court of Session, so I will. Get out of here! I don't want you. Leave me alone."

"Very well, madam," said John, raising the Stetson again. "I just wanted to apologise. There's no bad feeling on my side of the fence."

"Go away, go away!"

John did so, confused and unhappy in his mind, the daft voice following him down the path; and when he was just ten yards from the gate the afternoon bus, with a fine Highland disregard for exact timing, went hurtling past, its wheels throwing out cascades of water from the puddles on the ill-surfaced road.

It seemed a very long walk to the pier in the rain and the darkness which comes with wind from the East. John's mind was filled in the front part of it by exasperation with the burden of his frieze overcoat, which was but a trap for the relentless driving rain. In the back of his mind, however, there worked unhappily his new awareness of loneliness and abnormality about him : of crazy lives and haunted souls, offcast from society. Once again he considered the cottages and villas along the line of the shore road, each in its considerable plot of ground, each a private fortalice, each probably a species of madhouse. He had the feeling of one who has unintentionally blundered into a mental colony.

He felt the wet getting down his neck and into his underwear, the puddles splashing over the tops of his otherwise strong shoes ; and he was worried about his health. He made a note to acquire a stout raincoat. Or would an oilskin and gum-boots be the thing ? He must ask Sam Lightbody. But old Sam was no friend of his, for the time being. It seemed to be a proper mess all round, whichever way you looked at it.

He was relieved to get on to the boat at length ; and it was a queer thing that he was in fact delighted to get away from the place where he proposed to make his new home and to be making again for Garvel and the comforts of Blackwood's Hotel. The rain had a lot to do with it, of course. Anyhow, he went below to see the chief engineer, an old T. & B. lad, and got his sodden overcoat hung in the stokehold, drying quickly enough while he and the chief shared the wooden bench under the cabin companionway and, with the gleaming crankshafts tumbling over before them and the array of gauges flickering to the pulse of the machinery's complex life, chatted agreeably of this and that.

A taxicab was on the pier, dropping a passenger for the steamer's evening run, and John claimed it with loud cries and large wavings of his hat. A glass of spirits in the manager's room at Blackwood's, a hot bath, and a complete change of clothing all helped to lap him once again in the insulation of security. He saw from the menu posted outside the office that the evening meal was to be a good one ; roast duck was a real treat ; the rich smell was already in the alluring act of escape from the kitchen.

When at length he tried to settle down in the lounge with the evening paper, however, he knew that there was upon him a restlessness he could not endure alone until it was time for bed. Something from the day's experiences over at the Strone must irk him. He thought of the Pictures and considered the advertisements in the *Courier*. He wondered if he could try to get in touch with that clever young chap he had met at the Welfare on the night of Curly's fight ; he could not remember the name. At length, after giving her quite a bad time with his fidgets and queries, he got the girl in the office to ring the garage for Ernie and a car to be waiting for him at half-past seven.

It was always easy with Beth and her man : no nonsense, no ceremony.

" Come in, John. It's a pleasure to see you, though it's a wild night."

" Thanks, Davie, I thought I'd look you up and give you the news. I took over Penang Lodge to-day."

" Did ye now, man ? Beth'll want to hear all about that. Give me that coat of yours till I find a peg."

Ah, the comfort of the small, uncritical exchanges ! It was a joy they would never understand just to see Beth at her darning in a chair before the kitchen fire, Addie's bright head bent over her books at the bare table, Addie's slow, pure smile. There were Rabbie's words for it—" a happy fireside clime for weans and wife." They would never know how vulnerable was a wifeless man growing old, for all his means and a cottage by the sea !

The talk round Beth's kitchen fire was all of the new house. Davie Bryden had been across the water on two separate Saturday afternoons (his team playing away from home on these days) and had developed something of Sam Lightbody's proprietorial interest in the place. As with Sam, Penang Lodge was for Davie " a job," something new and interesting to be put into order by the application of hard-headed foresight and mechanical skill. Strange, thought John, chuckling into himself, how the acquisition of a house, the creation of a home, stirred in the honest members of the clan something fundamentally helpful and constructive !

" It'll be a job movin' in," opined Davie, puffing thoughtfully at his pipe. " All these carpets to be laid, the stair runner and that."

" You don't worry about that sort of thing nowadays, Davie," John dismissed the difficulties. " These removal chaps'll leave the place so tidy you could walk in ¡and put the kettle on for tea."

" I wouldn't trust any removal men," Addie put in vehemently, " to arrange my furniture and my kitchen for me."

" O, I'll be on the spot, of course," John fenced.

" And your removal men," added Beth in her tart way, " won't hang your curtains or make up your beds for you."

" That's true, but——"

" I tell ye what, John," Davie put in eagerly, " I think I'll come over and give ye a hand myself. I'm due two or three days from last year. It would be a rare holiday for me, I'm telling ye."

John glowed with pleasure and gratitude at the thought. He and old Sam were splendid gaffers, but when it came to a bit of real hard work the help of a lean and knacky man like Davie would be invaluable.

" That's a grand idea, Davie, if you could spare the time," he exclaimed. " What do you think of that, Beth ? Here—could we not all take a bit of a holiday at Easter ? I could book nice rooms in the hotel at Killadam, and if we could all spare an hour or two a day at the house we'd have it shipshape in a jiffy."

" That cistern under the roof above the bathroom," observed Davie, " is juist not right somehow. I'll have a good go at that one of these days."

" You and your cisterns ! " Beth scolded him with that unfortunate snap returning to her voice. " It's a woman you need. And do you think I can leave this house ? Who's going to look after Curly ? "

" Well . . ." John, abashed, allowed the point.

" But Addie could go," Beth relented, " if it's in the holiday time and she wants to."

" Yes, I'd like to," the girl admitted. " I want to see that new stove working properly."

" The very ticket," Davie exulted. " This'll be a right bit of sport, John, eh ? "

" Sport ! "

Beth rose and seized the kettle from the hob and made for the sink to fill it for the ritual cup of tea. The copious water from the hills bubbled noisily within it.

" The fact of the matter is, John," she said, returning to put the kettle on the fire under the sleeping crater of Fujiyama, " your next real job is to find yourself a good housekeeper."

" O, we'll manage that ! " her brother declared, waving a casual male hand. " In fact, the hotelkeeper down-by is looking about for me already. I'll bet you an advertisement in the *Herald* will bring in dozens of applications."

" Aye, no doubt it will," his sister agreed, " and a bonny lot of dirty, untidy old trash they'll be, likely. I'd like a good long look at the woman who's going to keep house for my brother."

" Well, you will, Beth, you will ! " John laughed the demurrer aside. " You and Addie can form a committee if you like. I'll take what you send me."

He watched her closely and saw, however, that this was for Beth no laughing matter. She frowned as she went to get the cups and saucers from the cupboard and laid the table with the look of one unhappily obsessed. Davie winked to John. He and his brother-in-law, being males with a liking for a bit of sport, could not possibly entertain the foolish feminine notion that the opening-up of a house—" a flitting," Davie called it—and the engagement of a housekeeper constituted a problem or was indeed anything but a diversion of the most agreeable nature.

" O, by the way, John ! " Beth suddenly changed the subject. " Do you remember the Grosarts—those old bodies that were at the Party ? They were taken away to Hagshaw yesterday."

" Hagshaw ! You don't mean to tell me. Could we not have done something, Beth ? Why didn't anybody tell me ? "

John spoke out of an alarmed concern. Hagshaw had been a name of dark omen even in his childhood, much used by his Grannie in both her scolding and self-pitiful moods. For all who lived within the parish of Garvel it meant the poorhouse and asylum combined. You did not go to Hagshaw except in the direst distress, and then with the mantle of shame over your bowed shoulders.

"No, no, John!" said Davie gravely, his fine face thoughtful in the firelight. "There's nothing you could have done, short of a fortune. That oldest one was just daft, plain gyte, and certified. Yon other one, with the laugh like a hyena, kept them goin' somehow with her knitting for the Gryffe. They'll be better where they are. They'll be looked after; they'll get their meat regular. The poor craturs couldn't look after themselves."

"Davie's right," said Beth with quiet decision, laying out on a metal stand the knitted cosy in green wool with a cock's head in red and yellow for decoration. She added viciously: "Knitting for that Gryffe lot is fair murder."

"If you make a single mistake, maybe just a dropped stitch, the inspectors pull the whole thing out from the beginning, even if it's at the end of a jumper."

This statement, clear and hard, came from Addie at the table, her head now raised from her books, her eyes bright with indignation.

"Did you ever read a book called *The Odd Women*?" this strange girl challenged her elders, whose apologetic looks confessed that they had not. "That shows you what can happen to women who are only fit to sew and skivvy for other people. Not me! I'm going to learn a job that'll keep me."

"Good old Mrs. Pankhurst!" cried Davie, fondly satirical. "D'ye remember the Suffragettes, John?"

"No, no! Addie's right," said John impatiently, thinking of Kate Clapperton. "Every girl should be able to stand on her own feet, marriage or no marriage."

A scud of rain, hurled on the wings of the gusting wind, threshed on the window-panes and howled in the chimney, sending a back-blast of smoke to irritate Beth as she was in the act of warming the brown earthenware teapot from the kettle now near the boil.

"That's a right dirty night," Beth exclaimed impatiently. "I never hear these noises but I think of the poor lads out in the ships at sea."

"Aye, it's sore on the boys on a night like this," Davie agreed sanctimoniously.

John was thinking rather uneasily of what it would be like to be alone in Penang Lodge on such a night with a strange woman as housekeeper, the wind howling round the spine of the Strone, rushing among the small firs behind, and the rain sweeping the coast road as if through a hose, the great gobbets rebounding to gleam in the lights of a solitary, late bus that seemed itself as lost as a truck on a Burmese jungle track in the monsoon.

And that reminded him : he must look out for a first-class wireless. Voicing this intention, he started Davie off again on a bright, congenial line of technical talk ; and John was enfolded once more in the warm security of his own family circle, well content about the bright fire of the kitchen, itself surrounded closely by hundreds of kitchen fires in the small homes of decent, patient people.

3

Lily Rolland was ready for her visitor. The tea things were nicely laid out on a small table in the drawing-room, and though the afternoon of early April was mild, the coals blazed in the fireplace and she had an electric kettle on the hearth so that she might brew the tea all nice and cosy and not have to be running up and down to the kitchen like a skivvy.

Lily's eagerness was such that she spent much of the time while she waited taking cover, like a soldier, behind the edge of one of the draw-curtains, in a rather fanciful cretonne, that flanked the bow window. Her gaze along the surburban street, however, was not so much bent on the approach of John Rolland Cram as upon the possible advance of some curious neighbour. John's note had been brought up by a page from Blackwood's Hotel, as smart as you please in his buttons, white gloves and pillbox hat. At the time, about eleven o' clock that forenoon, she had thought that that would be a rare smack in the eye for some of the folk who would be watching from behind other but more sinful blinds along the street, and she had been moved to present the page boy with a banana and a sixpence all to himself ; but she had reflected since then that they would all be dying to know what was in the wind. She wouldn't put it past that nebby old wretch, Susie Pratt in " Mossgiel," to make it the occasion of an apparently casual, friendly call. Well, she would just not answer the door until she was sure it was John himself.

T.F.A.

M

His note had been of an exciting character. In his bold script John, first pleading that he had an evening engagement, had asked if Lily could receive him over a dish of tea about four o'clock, he having just received word from London, at last, about a possible opening for Cha on a tea estate in Assam. That matter would have to be discussed and arranged quickly. He would also like to take the opportunity of seeing all his friends before settling into the new house at the Strone, not that he did not look forward to having them all across the water whenever they cared to look in. He added his regret that the business of getting the house done up had perhaps made him something of a stranger these last few weeks, but he nevertheless begged to remain, with regards to all, " Yours affectionately, Jno. Rolland Cram."

He was hers affectionately ; she was going to receive him alone—even if it was a pity in some ways that the Twins were away at their lessons in Glasgow. These circumstances were of some moment to a woman of Lily's adventurous vitality.

From behind the curtain she saw the first wave of red-capped schoolchildren from the Grammar School playing their way homewards along the street, and Lily remembered with a little pang of tenderness how often as a fond young mother, if a trifle more candidly, she had from the same window watched for the return of Cha and the Twins. At length the dome of the noble Stetson could be seen cruising above the line of the privet hedge at the corner outside Miss Younie the music teacher's, and anon John swung into sight. She noticed that a knot of schoolboys on the opposite corner paused in their horseplay to stare at the passage of this distinguished stranger, a striking and faintly exotic figure indeed in a double-breasted suit of fine cloth in a bright pearl-grey such as befitted a gentleman from abroad on encounter-ing his first spell of really mild weather at home. Lily hoped, and was tolerably certain, that that Miss Pratt in " Mossgiel " would be looking.

She behaved like a girl, for in fact she felt like one, as she settled her valuable and celibate guest among the cushions on the chesterfield, and when she sat down in the chair by the fire while the electric kettle hummed hospitably she did not grudge him a view of a length of her not unshapely legs in her second-best pair at eight-and-eleven in J. & M.'s.

"And now, you naughty man," she chattered, " where on

earth have you been ? We haven't seen you for ages. The Twins were saying only the other night . . ."

" O, it's that house over there ! You've no idea, Lily. If it's not the painters, it's the plumbers, and if it's not the plumbers, somebody wanting a subscription for the Cottage Hospital."

" I know, I know."

The small change of conversation on a topic as arid and familiar as the peeling paint on the sashes of " The Neuk's " windows passed easily backwards and forwards between them until the kettle boiled and Lily became the careful hostess again.

" But you haven't asked any of us to help you," she hazarded as she spooned the tea into the pot of Chinese silver that had been one of John's presents to the household ten years before. " I'm sure I would have been delighted . . ."

" Well, it's wonderful, Lily," John explained innocently. " Old Sam Lightbody—you'll remember him at the party—he and I work away together. Of course, I had my niece down to see the place ; give it a bit look-over from the woman's point of view . . . You'll remember Addie at the party . . . That's a very fine girl : got her head screwed on the right way."

" Yes, quite a nice girl Addie. It's a pity they never sent her to the Grammar School . . . Cream and no sugar, John ? That's right, isn't it ? . . . But if I can do anything when you're moving in. You want a woman about the place. I'm sure the Twins and I would be delighted. Not that Sibyl's really good about a house," Lily giggled happily. " If there's a bit of china to be broken, that girl'll break it. But I'd be delighted, John."

" Nonsense, nonsense, Lily ! "

John's innocence was as a rock. Lily was spinning her heavy web before one in whose elderly world webs were no longer valid.

" I wouldn't dream of it ! You've got a house here and Dan and Cha to look after. As a matter of fact," John added generously, " Davie Bryden and Addie are coming down for a day or two at Easter—a nice wee break for both of them—and that'll be me moved in. Then we'll have to have a housewarming some time."

" O ! Yes."

" But about Cha. I've got a bit of news at last."

Lily was elevated in a trice from the depths of envious disappointment to those heights of romantic optimism that were all easily within the scope of her sanguine temperament.

" Aw, it's far too good of you, John ! " she protested.

" Nonsense," her guest returned a thought snappily. " This is business, and we've got to get it straightened out at once. In fact, I want you to send Charles down to see me at the hotel about half-past six to-night, if he can manage it."

" O, isn't that wonderful ! "

John meant what he said. This was business in his most serious view. A young man was not casually given an introduction to a high-class firm in London ; the late Superintendent Engineer of the K. & S. did not lightly recommend a young man to his more important business associates ; sending a young man abroad, perhaps for life, was not just a story in the *Strand Magazine*. This woman was a nice enough creature, but she ought to know when to lay off the girlish line.

" Here's the letter," said John severely. " It's from my old friend Tommy Bell, the London manager of my Bank—the Amoy and Singapore. Now, Tommy has arranged for Charles to see a Mr. Ferguson in the London office of Ballingall's ; and I can tell you that Ballingall's are big people, very big people. But the point is, Lily, we've got to arrange for Cha to be in London on Wednesday next week without fail."

" O, dear ! O, dear ! Isn't that just wonderful ! How on earth I'm going to manage——"

" We'll manage all right," John waved an impatient hand. " That's why I want you to send the boy down to see me this evening. What I wanted to impress on you was this, Lily," he added more tolerantly. " This is a big chance for the lad, and I'd like to see him shaping up to it. Don't think I'm being personal at all, Lily, but these big firms will look for a young chap decently dressed, quiet, manly, nicely spoken, modest, but able to keep his end up. It would be a good thing," he appealed to her, " if you would have a quiet word with him, use your influence, and get him in the mood to put his best foot forward. It's always the mother's influence that matters in these things."

" O, I wouldn't worry ! " cried Lily, happy and blithe again. " If ever there was a good mixer it's our Cha."

John frowned, and he spoke a thought stiffly again.

" I don't think this Mr. Ferguson will want any mixing. He'll be looking for a young man who can keep his place, whether it's with his own seniors or with native labour. However "—John rose to his feet—" there it is, Lily, and though I say it myself, Charles is having a fine opportunity. But you'll send him down this evening ? I must be getting along."

She saw him away from " The Neuk " in a clatter of her grateful and fundamentally innocent fuss ; declaring again and again what a wonderful uncle he was, and how pleased Dan would be, and what a pity it was that the Twins were not present to play for him. As they stood on the topmost of the short flight of sandstone steps before the villa, John was overtaken by a waft of pity for Lily, seeing momentarily that she was excessively arch and talkative only because she was vulnerable.

" That's all right, Lily," he assured her kindly. " That's all right. We'll get this thing fixed, and don't you worry . . . And look at those daffodils ! It's a long time since I've seen the spring flowers at home."

" Yes, I love the daffies," said Lily wistfully, and she seemed for one fleeting moment to be talking from the heart, her posture of bright matron lost in the sad, recurrent mystery of the seasonal rhythm.

Her only son presented himself at Blackwood's Hotel that evening at precisely the right moment. The head waiter announced his waiting presence in the lounge as John was polishing off the Angels on Horseback that applied a sharp full stop to a meal of Scotch broth, whiting with its tail through its eyes, leg of Canterbury lamb and a fruit salad piled high with cream.

" Ask him to wait in the lounge for a minute. Then coffee for two."

The head waiter bowed from the waist to the bidding of the rich man from the East, and John enjoyed the feeling of power. It was quite seriously in his mind that Lily's boy was being granted a high privilege, and he intended to make the youth understand that an introduction to Ballingall's was no trifling novelty. To keep him waiting on his elders and betters was just the medicine for brash young men like our Cha.

When at length he sailed portentously out of the dining-room

through the swing doors held open by the head waiter and an
acolyte, as he proceeded gravely among the tables and plants and
standard ashtrays of the lounge, his evening paper under his arm,
John atracted indeed much attention from his fellow-guests,
and greying female heads bent close together to speculate on the
nature of the encounter between this important-looking gentleman
and the boy who had been waiting, fidgeting with a cigarette
case, at the table in the corner. The situation was capable of the
most romantic interpretations.

John's technique of patronage had in fact already succeeded
in reducing Charles Rolland from his familiar stratosphere of
smart fantasy to his natural level of sanguine, puzzled, ill-educated
youth. He rose courteously as John approached his table, and it
seemed to the latter that his handshake had acquired the beginnings of a certain nervous strength. John also noted with approval
that his words to Lily had not gone amiss. Charles was dressed
now in a discreet blue suit with a white linen collar and a dark tie.
His patron could criticise only those unfortunate suede shoes and
the hint of whisker under the ears the deluded stripling persisted
in wearing.

"Well, Charles, here we are!" John began briskly. "Your
mother will have told you what's in the wind."

"I should think she has! And it's grand of you to get me
the chance, Uncle John."

"That's all right, my boy," said John, not without a little
complacency. "And now, Charles, there are one or two
things——"

He felt compelled to say a great many things to this youth.
John delivered there and then what was in truth an admirably
cogent lecture on the science, the rewards and the responsibilities
of Empire-building. It was for him, untouched by either the fever
of jingoism or the bile of the newer cynicism, a serious subject.
Before Charles now was a job, an opportunity, that might lead
to responsibility. The late Superintendent Engineer of the K. & S.
could not but expand in the warmth of success remembered ; no
more could he fail to be touched by the callowness of the boy he
was now urging along the road that must lead far from home and
the amenities of "The Neuk." Even if it reflected not un-
pleasantly on his own influence, he was at pains to impress on
Charles (a youth whose sense of values he did not wholly trust)

that Ballingall's was a firm in the very first flight of East India merchants, and that an interview with them was in the character of a bidding to Court.

Charles having indicated again and again that the importance of the business had sunk into his mind, John said :

"Good ! As long as you understand. Now we'll have a small drink."

"O, I'm quite happy with the coffee," Charles hastened to say.

"Nonsense ! This is a celebration. Waiter ! A Benedictine for my guest here, and a large liqueur brandy for me—the old Otard and none of your grocer's stuff, now."

In the intimacy so curiously established by the mere act of drinking together John continued to press his authority on Lily's boy.

"Now, Charles," he began, raising an avuncular forefinger, " there are two wee things I'm going to tell you plump and plain, and I know you're a good enough man to take them in the right spirit. First of all—those hairy shoes of yours. That's just the sort of thing Ballingall's wouldn't like. Get your mother to look you out a nice quiet pair of black shoes ; Good ! I'm glad you see the point, son."

"The next thing, lad," and the forefinger was emphatic again. "Those side-levers of yours. It may be a bit of a fashion among you young chaps nowadays, but I'd—well, I'd shave them off and be done with it."

"I was going to do that, Uncle John," pleaded Charles, now almost a dutiful schoolboy again.

"That's the boy, that's the boy ! " John approved. "Now, your expenses in London. Let me see . . ."

"My mother said I wasn't to take anything from you."

"Nonsense ! This is my do, Cha—a wee bit of a present. Let's see now. Your fare ; two or three hotel nights in London ; you'll want to see a show . . . I think fifteen'll do the trick."

He clawed in his hip pocket and, a thought breathless from the effort, produced such a wad of notes as had Cha's eyes goggling. John counted discreetly by touch under the edge of the table.

"Fifteen, son. There you are, and don't starve yourself, and don't be foolish either. Wait a minute ; better safe than sorry.

We'll make it twenty. You can square up with me when you come back."

It was easy and pleasant to be able to wave aside the lad's not notably fluent expressions of gratitude : easy to protest that a car was just coming to take him out for the evening, and to imply that he had merely transacted a normal bit of business between friends.

When, however, he reclined in the back seat of the Rolls with Ernie at the wheel, driving him to a long-postponed party in the West End villa of Mr. Balhardie, T. & B.'s chief draughtsman and chairman of the Welfare, his inner mind was haunted by the slender figure of our Cha as he had watched it pass through the entrance hall of Blackwood's towards the door with twenty unwonted pounds in its pocket—the boy who was lonely and weak for all his flashiness, the provincial lad whose vulgarity must be harshly tested by the trials that Empire and its ruling caste imposed on their recruits : Lily's boy, indifferently equipped for the battle ahead.

It was only when he had got back to Blackwood's after midnight that John was able to abate the significance of that figure in his mind : saying to himself, perhaps a trifle defiantly, that, well—he had now done the best he could according to his lights and means for all his relations who needed the aid he was able to give them. As he slipped the upper denture into the brass bowl and stood by the bedside table to repeat the prayer of childhood, it was in the back of his mind that he could now very decently retire to Penang Lodge and have a bit of time to himself.

4

The mists of the late April morning dissolved from the face of the waters at the touch of a sun that was warm within an hour of its rising. Their disappearance left the Firth a glassy pond which reflected the eggshell blue of an utterly cloudless sky and, along its edges, mirrored the shapes of the coloured hills. It was so still and sweet that you could imagine this inner reach of an arm of the turbulent Atlantic to be a mountain lake uplifted into the windless realm of a poet's fancy. The cry of a bird across six miles of water carried with the force of a rifle-shot. Each splash of the tide on the beach of shingle below the hotel at Killadam was portentous in the larger silence.

Turning in his bed within that establishment Davie Bryden put out a hand to touch the shoulder of his wife, reached only an emptiness, realized that he slept alone in a narrow bed, and remembered that he was a man on holiday, giving his good-brother John a hand with the flitting into his new house at the Coast.

He sat up promptly, the early-rising habit of years allowing him no peace, and saw from the watch he had hung by its chain from the bedpost that it lacked ten minutes of seven. He then jumped from the bed to the window and, drawing a curtain aside, perceived that the morning was fair. Next, he washed and shaved with speed and skill, using the old-fashioned basin and ewer of cold water on a washstand, and as he worked with his cut-throat razor he heard the beat of a steamboat's paddles carried from far across the water. That would be the morning steamer with the Mails and the newspapers crossing from Kempock to Ardhallow ; he must hurry.

A quick and sinewy man, Davie was soon completely attired in flannel trousers, tweed jacket, open-necked shirt and brown sand-shoes. The first person up in all the hotel, he moved silently downstairs, unlocked the front door and let himself out into the mild brightness of the morning. Only a few chimneys in the cottages at the pierhead were smoking ; on the pier itself were Johnny McGill the piermaster and Neil Mackinven the post, both at their ease on the latter's red truck. Davie joined them and passed round a packet of cigarettes, and when the steamer came about in a sweet curve to take the pier, neatly checked at precisely the right moment by a touch of the paddle-wheels in reverse, he caught a rope thrown from her bows, hauled in the dripping hawser of thick Manilla hemp, and heaved the bight of it round an iron bollard.

Davie Bryden was one in whom the instinct to assist in physical enterprise was automatic. He was the man who helped to push broken-down motor-cars and sat on the heads of fallen horses. This was not out of any feeling for display ; it was, on the contrary, the natural expression of his simple, kind and tidy nature. Now he helped the longshoremen to unload the bags and parcels, slipped the hawser from its bollard at a nod from the skipper on the little ship's bridge, then hurried to help the Post with his heavy barrow along the spine of the pier and up the brae to the low, white cottage that served as Post Office and General Stores in one.

Here he waited until the newspaper parcels had been cut open and, having collected those ordered for the hotel, he sauntered thither, merely glancing at the headlines in one of the penny sheets, which told of the bellowings of this daft German chap Hitler, and turning quickly to the back pages and the grave prognostications of the experts in racing and football.

A smoking chimney in the hotel building told him that the establishment was slowly coming to life. That would be Mrs. Rose, the cook. He strolled round the back of the building, past an untidy drying-green, a kitchen garden littered with the runts of cabbage and brussels sprouts and barren of any sign of spring cultivation, and an old iron bath that had been thrown out to rust by the back door. Within her kitchen Mrs. Rose, a dark and angry sort of woman, fumed amid the smoke from an old-fashioned range with a stubborn temperament.

" If you get your breakfast before ten this morning," she flamed at Davie, " you'll be lucky. This dashed thing'll break my heart. But His Lordship upstairs and that fat baggage of his will do nothing."

" Here, let me have a go at it."

Since his arrival in the hotel three days before, Davie, having struck up an early-morning acquaintance with Mrs. Rose, had studied the vagaries of the range in several conditions of wind and stoking and had, he fondly believed, got what he called the hang of it. On his knees before the fire now, poking at the cinders, opening vents, rattling away at shutters, he expounded his theory of range-management to the cook, dropping naturally into the tradesman's vernacular.

" The bother wi' an auld-farrant range like this is that it needs to be hotted up right afore it'll draw. It gets choked through the night, see, and it's near cold by this time o' day, and if there isny a right draw of heat up the vent ye might as well spit. See—she's beginning to draw now. That's wi' me clearing the clinkers from the bottom o' the basket and giving her the gun through this shutter here."

He stood upright and considered the range with a sort of tender pride.

" That's her away now," he pronounced benevolently. " But she's a right cranky piece o' machinery just the same."

" You'll not see me breaking my heart over it much longer," Mrs. Rose protested. " But thank God for one man with some sense in this house ! "

" And now I'll get ye some nice kindling, mistress," said Davie.

He filled two large buckets of coal from the dump behind the house, a dump that added its own quota of untidiness to the squalor prevailing in the territory outside the back door, and carried them into the kitchen. That done, he returned to the more agreeable public side of the house, now warmed by the morning sun, crossed the reasonably trim lawn and took a hard seat on the supporting wall, his feet swinging over the footpath.

Davie Bryden was in that moment the perfectly happy man. Out of his bed an hour now, he had assisted at several interesting operations essential to the conduct of the orderly life. The mild April sun and the promise of a long, full day ahead put an edge on his always eager appetite for living and doing ; and he had sworn to himself that the cistern at Penang Lodge would that day be reduced to submission. The sea and the hills—man, but they were bonny ! Soon his dear daughter Addie would be down, and then John ; and then they would have a right good tightener of ham and eggs, rolls and strong tea, and then along the road for a morning of work in Penang Lodge. This was a rare holiday he was having, thought Davie to himself ; never had a better.

Addie came down and out to sit beside him at the back of eight o'clock : Addie cool and remote and bonny in a little summer frock of cretonne. They sat silent and content on the wall together, the girl giving the morning papers a more earnest scrutiny than her equable father could ever give to anything save the late Saturday sports editions ; and then, at half-past, John came hailing them across the lawn : asking them why they were not long ago at table, as if he, Mr. Cram, were the pattern of orderliness and punctuality.

Mrs. Rose served the breakfast to this contented trio, the hotel's only guests, muttering angry comments on kitchen fires, the young girls of the day and her own intolerable conditions of employment. If John and his friends had lacked the distractions of fine weather and an absorbing task they might have taken a morbid satisfaction in cataloguing within that dining-room alone the stigmata of a basic disease within the management of the house, visible in the broken slats of Venetian blinds hanging awry, in the streaky yellow of plated ware on the heavy Victorian side-board, in the fustiness of atmosphere that pervaded the chamber. They were birds of passage, however ; the hotel provided but a roof for the nights of enchanted days ; their life was a mile along the road in the rooms of Penang Lodge, now taking on the shape of a fixed order and the glow of a life of its own.

There was no moving thither until John had taken the con-siderable measure of his *Glasgow Herald*, with particular attention to Births, Marriages and Deaths, the Shipping Movements, the Wills and Estates, and the Prices of Dominion and Colonial Stocks. Then they must pay the ritual holiday visit to the pier to watch the first of the forenoon steamers come in, John curbing Davie's impatience with : " There's no hurry, man. You're on holiday. Enjoy yourself."

Davie really enjoyed himself best when at length they reached the new house and he had invested himself in a boiler-suit and gone with his bag of tools into battle against a variety of fittings that appeared to him to be lamentably below T. & B. standards of efficiency. Then Addie donned an overall, wrapped her bright head in a coloured handkerchief, and with much of her father's intensity struggled with the new stove in the kitchen and, between its tantrums, put away crockery and glass in cupboards or cased the slender rods through the new curtains of muslin. Invariably, the morning's work ended with a conference between John and Davie as to the project for a dam, regarding which the latter was as enthusiastic as old Sam Lightbody.

" It would be a rare classy thing up at the back there," he would declare again and again, " let alone a bit power through a turbine or that. It would be real nice with ferns and things. Man, if I could have a week in the summer, with mebbe a labour-ing chap to give me a hand, I'd run ye up a dam ye'd be proud to launch a cruiser into ! "

They were back at the hotel before one for the midday meal, and that was late as usual. At twenty-past the hour a girl, on whose face a scaly layer of powder and rouge stopped abruptly above an unwashed neck, banged a gong at the door and brought them in from where they sat on a garden-seat with a defective leg. Two letters lay on the soiled tablecloth at John's place.

"Bit late in the day for the Mail, surely," said John. "Excuse me."

Addie watched him as he read. Over one long letter on thin paper and in a scrawling hand of write she saw him frown. He folded it quickly and thrust it into a pocket. When the waitress came with the soup, he asked quite sharply :

"When do the letters usually arrive in the morning ? "

"That lot came in with the morning boat about seven," Davie explained. "I gave Postie a hand with the bags myself."

"Yes, but at the hotel here ? "

"About half-past nine," the girl admitted.

"Then why don't I get them till after one o' clock ? We were about the place till after ten."

"You can ask the boss yourself," the girl suggested pertly "All the letters go up to his room first of all."

"O, they do, do they ? "

Addie became aware of tension in the air. She saw her uncle turn grave and preoccupied, perhaps angry, and she felt unhappy and uncomfortable. It was easy to guess at his regard for the importance of His Majesty's Mails and for the sanctity of his own correspondence in particular. Intuitively she guessed more miserably at bad news in the long letter on cheap paper. She hated this silence of suspended tension that held even her father in its grip. They were at the second course before her uncle emerged from his remoteness.

"Well, it looks as if I'll have to go across to Garvel this afternoon and leave you."

"O, dear ! " cried Davie with concern.

"Yes, it's an old friend in trouble, and I'll have to run across and try to sort it out."

"Man, I'm sorry to hear that ! "

"I could hardly manage back to-night, but I shouldn't be late to-morrow. You'll excuse me, Addie and Davie ? Why not take a sail down the water this afternoon and enjoy yourselves ? "

"No, no ! " Davie protested with a serious shake of his shapely head. "Addie and me'll put in an hour or two at the new house, and mebbe we'll run round to the Pictures in Doon after our tea. We're fine, and don't you worry, John. Never had a holiday like it in my life."

When the meal was over, having ended a thought ingloriously in tinned apricots with a smear of commercial custard over them and hunks of sapless, greasy cheese with biscuits that smelt and tasted of damp, John rose with the majesty of the Eastern official from the table.

" And now," he announced, " that so-called hotelkeeper is going to get a piece of my mind."

At that Addie fled out of doors with her book, apprehensive of such a row as might be created by her important Uncle John in a temper.

She need not have been afraid. Having made his way through the empty cubbyhole of an office to a dark sitting-room in which the landlord and his wife, a large and ornate blonde, were sipping glasses of port amid the shards of their meal, John stated that he had a complaint to make regarding the handling of letters. Reasonably but firmly he declared his view that the prompt distribution of the Mail was a first charge on the management of any proper hotel, and that any unreasonable delay to do so might complicate an urgent issue, as had indeed been the case with one of his own letters that day. He put forward the suggestion that the incoming letters should, immediately after arrival, be laid out in a conspicuous place where guests might pick them up promptly.

" They were on your table by eleven," said the hotelkeeper sullenly, stung on one of the spots most rawly exposed by his infrequent self-examinations.

" And they arrived in the house at half-past nine. And I was still about the place after ten."

" O, if you're not pleased you can find somewhere else, I suppose."

" I'll go on Friday as arranged in our letters," said John calmly. " I am drawing your attention to something that shouldn't happen in a properly-managed hotel."

At that he marched away, and the landlord turned with an uneasy grin to his lady.

" And what do you think of that ? "

" Snooty old bastard," said the lady indifferently, popping

a crumb of the hard cheese between the incarnadined portals of her mouth. " And that's a proper couple of kikes he has with him."

" Properly-managed hotel ! " repeated her husband. " I'll give the old b. a real telling-off before he goes."

He rose from the table with a lurch and passing through a swing door into the public bar, there filled himself another glass of Real Old Tawny.

5

When the little steamer stood out to round the Strone, and he saw the figures of Davie and Addie marching along the road to their tasks in Penang Lodge, a handkerchief waving from the girl's hand, John felt as wistful as a schoolboy going home after a happy holiday. These last few days, he reflected deeply, had been the happiest he had known since his return Home ; they had been the coming-true of the ancient dream. It was heart-breaking that the trance of sunlit happiness should be shattered by the burden of a letter from a distant harsh world.

There lingered with him his irritation over the matter of the morning post. He was more exasperated now, as one who must have order in everything, that he should have been obliged to leave his guests behind, even if they were his closest relations. All the illuminated splendour of the Firth on this April afternoon could not distract him from the unhappy, though suppressed, feeling that perhaps just a little too much was being asked of him. It was a queer thing that a chap, not getting any younger and looking for a bit of peace after a lifetime in the East, should be dragged into every bit of trouble that cropped up. It was not as if Effie Templeton were a blood relation or that her husband had been anything but a remote connection, rather a minor entry in the family ledger than a person with a known and identifiable personality.

He went below into the cabin, stuffy and musty in the warmth of the day, and in one of its alcoves in crimson and tasselled plush sat down to read her letter again.

It was a right mess when you looked at it coldly ; Effie had fairly laid it on, the wild phrases and desperate appeals repeated again and again. It was hard to see that the situation she described could have the calamitous implications she feared or could wholly justify the high pitch of the cry for aid she uttered. It was that quality in the epistle, rather than the marks of tears on the thin paper, which sustained John in his enterprise. Being a simple man, he concluded that there must be more to Effie's plight than she could explain ; having a tidy mind, he agreed with himself that it was best to tackle this problem at once and get it settled before he came to a quiet settlement on his own account in Penang Lodge.

He went on deck again and saw that the steamer was making eastwards once more towards the point where, in a notch under the Lowland foothills, the industrial smoke of his native town drifted above the piled tenements on the slopes. There was little traffic on the Firth, only a few nondescript tramps at anchor in the Deeps, their snub noses towards the tawny deserts of the Great Bank, now exposed by the ebb. He studied with professional care a stocky ship with a strangely-marked funnel going out, her scuttles boarded up against the heavy seas of great oceans, and learned with mild interest from the mate that she was a new coasting vessel for a Tasmanian company out of Leitch's yard in the Port. His real mind, however, was busy with schemes for the removal to security of an ageing and penniless acquaintance. His heart was troubled too, for he could never bear to think of woman or child lonely and unhappy.

Ernie was on the pier to meet him with the Rolls. He had told Addie to telephone for this service, and Ernie explained that he had been kept off for a funeral to oblige the firm's valuable customer.

" They're feart to let you loose without me to look after you," added Ernie with the blithe, familiar and indestructible jocosity of the Scots working man.

The Lowland countryside was fair as the great car skimmed along the upland roads. Passing through the valley of dairy farms, John reflected that a herd of brown-and-white Ayrshires in a field bright green with spring grass made as pretty a picture as you could see anywhere. Even as they struck in towards the hills the tracks of the small glens through the pastures were dazzling in lime green against emerald, with the young foliage of hazel and saughs and hornbeam along the banks of the upland streams. Roadside dells and ditches were blessedly lighted by the sheen of primroses in their multitude, and every cottage garden flaunted the trumpets of daffodils or the golden eye of the narcissus amid petals intolerably white.

On the moorland level of Corsewellhill, however, the April sun had made little impression so far. For a mile or more before the steading there still stretched the hopeless, spasmodically-drained expanse of coarse and tussocky grass, like straw in its saplessness. In the heart of it the cluster of farm buildings was as remote and pathetic as a frontier outpost ; the hillside of the Scourie behind was as a glorified slagheap, meanly turfed with rushes and heather and criss-crossed by the immemorial tracks of the blackface sheep. The brighter patches of arable fields about the steading emphasised the farming folks' insecurity of tenure in this upland holding. On the tall ash trees that in a loose row protected the buildings against the sou'-westerly gales the black buds were still dormant, the sap only starting to rise.

As he got out of the car in the close John was immediately aware of the difference of atmosphere about this remote steading and that of the region from which he had come by sea. Barely eight miles separated the points as the crow flies, but over there by the sea's edge was the pervasive softness of the Highland scene, the Highland air, the Highland speech and the Highland attitude ; while here there was a harshness about : a harshness of line, of life, of accent and of circumstance ; almost a stridency that proclaimed itself in the very stink of decaying organic matter in the close itself and in the noises of shouting and of trundling iron wheels on concrete that proceeded from the byre within. He had the feeling of having passed in the course of a short afternoon from one country to another, and the experience moved him to forget his personal irritations and, suddenly, to range himself on Effie Templeton's side in the mountain warfare she had waged so long at Corsewellhill.

He let himself into the steading through the boilerhouse door and saw in a glance to the left that most of the shouting and clangour in the byre was being produced by Tam Rolland, Effie's son, now busy, with a ragged boy to push the galvanized hopper, feeding sliced swedes and oilcake to young bestial. The smell from the byre was sweet and warm, but John noted with what roughness, as of a jealous hostility, the farmer shoved the

T.F.A.   N innocent, appealing brutes aside to get at their troughs. The smacks of his great hands on their trembling flanks seemed to be paying off old scores against the hardness of life on a small hill farm.

As he passed from one stall to its neighbour Tam followed the stare of the ragged boy and, instead of cursing the half-witted loon, wiped his hands on the seat of his trousers and advanced to deal with the uninvited visitor in his fine city clothes ; and in that setting, indeed, John Rolland Cram cut an inappropriate figure with the light fawn raincoat he had lately acquired and the lofty Stetson upon his head. Tam did not offer a hand, and it was not for any fine feeling about its condition.

"Aye, and here ye are, man ? " was his greeting.

"Your mother got my wire ? "

"She did that, about an hour past. And has she gone girnin' to you, noo ? "

"Your mother and I are very old friends, Tam," said John with all the calm and dignity he could muster. He added rather aggressively. "Have you time to come outside for a word ? We can't talk business with that boy listening."

Tam's stare indicated that he thought himself to be dealing with eccentricity. The excessive loudness of his own voice and the delicacy of the situation as John saw it were not within his peasant understanding. However, he followed the visitor out through the close to a corner of the stackyard where the moorland airs would carry their voices away across the tussocky spaces of the laigh pasture.

"I'm not here to interfere," said John, reasonably but stoutly. "It's just to see what I can do for your mother. You're getting married ? "

"That's the wey o't," Tam agreed. "At the Whitsun term."

"And does that mean your mother's got to leave the place ? "

"Dammit, man ! There'll be nae room for her when I bring the wife hame. There'll be me and the wife, and then there's Mary, and when the bairn comes alang, and it's on the way noo," Tam chuckled and winked at John with a roguish eye, "there'll be nae place to pit her."

The man spoke honestly. This was crudity but not cruelty in any wilful degree.

"T'hell, man ! " Tam added earnestly. "I offered her the

cothoose up the loan there, but no—she couldna bear to live alane. Weel, if she canna bear to live alane, and there's nae room for her in Corsewellhill, she'll just hae to find a place o' her ain."

" But how's she to keep herself, man ! " asked John, dropping vigorously into the vernacular. " If she's got to go out, is there not a bit allowance you can make her, even if it's only a pound a week ? "

" Damn the hait ! This," said Tam, waving his arm to indicate the wide boundaries of his impoverished holding, " is nocht but a poorshouse. The wey it is wi' the hill-sheep nooadays, it's like to be sheer bluidy bankruptcy."

" I see," said John at length, turning back towards the steading.

He saw with a dismal clarity the hopelessness of Effie's position and of his own as one dragged in to share it. They were both in the clutch of the cold logic of the peasantry, to whom tenderness was an irrelevance when the issues of property were concerned. He saw how simply and remorselessly Tam's mind worked on the economy of Corsewellhill, so that the able-bodied Mary was still an asset and worthy of house-room as compared with an ageing and enfeebled mother. The law was precisely that of the byre— care and good feeding of the bestial in immaturity, the brief summer of productivity, and then the slaughterhouse.

As they came back through the close Mary, her face flushed with excitement at the appearance of Ernie, that subtle gallant from the town, was out to call them in for tea. Thus John met Effie decorously with a handshake in the shadow by the kitchen fireplace. The tea-table was loud with Ernie's quips, Mary's rewarding giggles and Tam's earthy embroideries on the prevalent theme of courtship and mating. It struck John with sadness that he and Effie were futile mummers at this feast of youth, both preoccupied with their elderly worries and incapable of communication through this babble of those who had not yet felt the chill of life's complexity.

Ernie, a shrewd cockney among the bumpkins, observed that the Boss was preoccupied, but he could not know to what extent John Rolland Cram, normally a person well in command of himself and his own affairs, was floundering in his mind for a good way out of the tangle in which he had been involved : this

sordid tangle with the stink of dung upon it that so strangely
threatened the perfection of the dream of peace in decent retirement he had built up about Penang Lodge.

Through the cracklings of Ernie's sparrow wit, behind his
dumb observance of the primitive table manners, he was wildly
estimating the financing of Effie's future, at so many shillings per
week and so many pounds per annum ; calculating them in
relation to his own pension from the K. & S. and his own savings ;
and wondering all the time, bleakly, why he should be dragged
into the business at all ; desperately planning, indeed, a decent
way of escape from something like a trap. He saw frequently
through his thinking—and this seemed to him odd—the figure
of Addie in her cretonne frock, moving like a taught featherweight
along the shore road to her tasks in the new house only eight
miles, and yet a lifetime, away from where he was imprisoned in
the kitchen of the farm on the moorland's edge.

When the meal was over at length he observed with some
elaboration of a casual manner that he would enjoy a turn out
of doors before going home, and perhaps Effie would care to
walk with him on such a fine evening. She said she would also
like a bit walk ; and soon, she with a grey shawl about her
shoulders and he with the high American hat completing a comic
contrast, were moving at a mature pace between the thorn hedges
of the loan that ran uphill towards the high pastures.

" It was good of you to come, John," she whispered intensely,
as if their communications could still be heard from the steading.

" That's nothing. It's a real hard problem you've got, Effie,
and," he added with deliberate candour, " it beats me to think
what I can do about it."

A sniffing at his shoulder informed him that Effie had taken
to tears, but he kept his eyes averted from her face as stoutly as
he sought to keep his mind and hers on the practical issues.

" Have you no savings of your own at all ? " he asked.

" A pound or two ; it might be ten. And where would that
take a woman of near sixty ? "

" But Tam offered you the cothouse. That would be a roof
for you and your keep, surely, and when Tam's bairns come along
they'd need you about the place . . . Something to interest you."

" John ! John ! " she pleaded with him in a wail. " That
madman from the quarry would have me out of my mind."

"Is he still about? Very well," said John angrily, "if Tam will do nothing, I will, and just as soon as I get back to Garvel. We can't have that sort of trash frightening you out of your life. We'll soon fix him."

The sniffing at his side had not ceased, and now it hardened to a sob.

"You don't understand, John. Whatever happens, I couldn't stay on here. They don't want me now, and they'd never stop letting me know it. O, it's a terrible thing when your own bairns turn on you! Terrible, terrible!"

He perceived clearly the cold truth of her assertion, and he was profoundly touched by pity, but still he deemed it necessary to hold to the facts. Indeed, he was too innocent to discern the motive, powerful if subconscious, that inspired it, but he was irritated by her stubborn defeatism.

They had come through a small spinney of birches and by a sheep-track to the top of a knoll, from which the prospect was suddenly splendid. For from this height, beyond the rusty pastures about the steading of Corsewellhill, the pure green of the foothills and fields on the slope of the escarpment came into view, vivid in the evening light, with the peaks on the other side of the unseen Firth between taking the afterglow of the sunset in fabulous yellows and pinks. The long northern evening was mellowing towards gloaming, and the light, though still full of its daytime quality, was gradually being tinctured with that golden glow which has in it the evocative suggestion of sweet sadness.

"No," said John quietly, after they had stood up there for a time, "I can't quite see it yet, Effie. It's not as if a wee bit present would tide you over, or a small loan set you up in a place of your own. And you're not due for the Pension yet."

His companion wept again, and still he remained aloof.

"We'll have to think again," he said. "Give me a day or two."

"Ye'll not get me into the poorshouse!" Effie cried bitterly. "I'd sooner put myself over the quarry."

"No, no, no! There's no question of that. Pull yourself together, Effie. Do you think I'm such a poor friend as all that? Come, we'll have to be getting back. I was thinking more of a place where you could give some help for your keep and a wage.

. . . In an Orphan Home or something, where there would be bairns to keep you interested. I'll make inquiries."

They made their way downhill, Effie still tearful behind him as they threaded the sheep-track in single file, and they were passing out of the small birch wood on to the hedged loan when a shot was fired from near at hand, blasting open the secret world they shared.

John saw the flash of the gun, aimed from the root of the thorn hedge where it grew out of a retaining wall above the level of the field, and felt the blast of the discharge. There was something like the lightning sting of a wasp at the back of his neck ; he swung round and then steadied himself to see that his great hat had been blown off his head. His eye caught a figure running like a hare across the Laigh Park, a gun in its hands.

Effie was on the ground, kicking and screaming. Her screams were so loud and unrestrained that his instinct was to smack her face, but the real John dropped on one knee beside her and raised her head, looking for the wound. There was no sign he could see that she had been touched.

" Effie, Effie ! " he begged her to be quiet. " It's all right. He's gone now."

Running footsteps came up the loan. Ernie and Mary had been interrupted in dalliance in the barn by the shot and the screaming.

" Is she hurt ? " panted Ernie, arriving first.

" I don't think so. Just fright," said John, much aware of the trembling of his own person.

Mary came panting and bawling : " It's that mad devil from the quarry. I seen him running into the Cadger's Strip. O, mither, mither ! Has he shot you ? "

" No sign of it," said Ernie competently. He touched John's shoulder. " He's got you in the back of the neck, Boss."

As he bent over Effie a trickle of blood had meandered down John's neck and along the line of his jaw to gather on the point of his chin. He brushed it impatiently away and was then disgusted to see the red smear across his fingers. He wiped the trickle with his handkerchief and dabbed tenderly at the nape of his neck.

" I don't think it's much," he said. " And now, Mary, give me a hand to get your mother into the house. You, Ernie—away down to the village in the car as quick as you can and get a doctor and the policeman."

Effie's distress had moderated to a low moaning as they shouldered her back to the farm, and when Mary had taken her upstairs to put her to bed there was silence in the kitchen where John sat alone, patting ruefully at his wound while his mind turned over and over in its effort to comprehend the enormity of his experience. He felt sick in body and at heart. A good glass of whisky might have put the former to rights out of hand, but he was miserable under the sense of dirt in the world about him and a dim, intuitive knowledge that the half-wit's shot had somehow complicated the pattern of his life, he could not guess how.

Mary came rattling down the bare wooden stairs from the upper rooms.

"There's not a scratch on her," she declared, rather indignantly. "It must be the scare she got. I think I'll juist make ye both a cup of tea."

"Not a bad idea," John agreed.

Ernie came back, followed by the policeman and the doctor in the latter's car. While he was upstairs with Effie, John had to endure the making of what the village constable called a formal statement, a tedious process involving the writing of John's answers to ritual questions in a slow, large hand in a ridiculously small notebook ; and he did not in the least hasten it by insisting irritably that the policeman would be better employed in rounding up the culprit.

"We'll come to that," said the officer equably. "I know where to lay my hands on that same gentleman when I want him. Now, you were saying that you and Mustress Rolland had come through the birches and was turning into the loan . . . You wouldn't be arm-in-arm or the like of that ? "

The doctor, returning, heard this and laughed.

"But go on, Peter," he encouraged the policeman, and turned to John. "Not much wrong upstairs. A sharp shock, naturally, but I've given her a sedative, and she'll rest now. Let's have a look at this neck of yours. Turn the lamp this way, Mary, and give me a bowl of boiling water. H'm . . . just one wee pellet in the muscle, I think."

"Did you see the mess he made of my hat ? " asked John indignantly.

" I dare say," said the doctor absently. " I think we'd better pick this out now. It'll sting a bit . . . There !"

He dropped the pellet on the deal table for John to see, then dabbed the tiny wound with iodine, cut a square of plaster and pressed it with comforting results against John's neck.

" That should do you just now," he said. " Better get your own doctor to look at it to-morrow. And I don't mind saying, Mr. Cram, you had a slice of luck this evening. One inch to the right . . ."

" The funny thing," said John, soothed by the dressing, " is, I don't think he was shooting to kill. More the idea of scaring me off. He couldn't have missed if he had been trying."

" High time he was certified and locked up just the same. If you're nearly finished, Peter, I'll run you down the hill. I suppose you'll want to get the Flying Squad cars out."

The house seemed very quiet after they were gone. Darkness filled the kitchen window beyond the range of the lamp's soft glow. John addressed Mary anxiously.

" I ought to be getting home myself. It wearies you, a shock like that. Will you be all right, Mary ? "

" Me ! Anybody that comes near the place this nicht afore Tam wins hame will get a dose from that," and she nodded her round head towards the 12-bore gun that rested against the wall above the mantelpiece on a series of nails.

" That's the girl ! " John approved. " Now, just a word with your mother before I go."

Effie lay under a patchwork quilt on one side of the double-bed in the poor little attic room she shared with her daughter. Candle-light on the angularities of the ceiling conveyed to John a sad sense of claustration ; the stuffiness of the chamber, as of a female den, spoke to him of peasant ignorance. He saw poverty in the bareness of a small dressing table with a man's old circular shaving mirror on its top, in the absence of any fabric covering on it, in a couple of chipped saucers cluttered with pins, hairpins and wisps of hair, in the lid of a cigarette tin holding the candle.

" Well, Effie," he began awkwardly. " Feeling a bit easier now ? "

The head shook slowly from side to side within its framework of grey hair on the coarse pillowcase.

"That was terrible, terrible, John!" she quavered.

"Yes, but it's all over now," he assured her gently. "That's the end of your troubles with that fellow; he'll be locked up before the morning. And now I'll have to be getting up the road. Just one thing before I go, Effie. I've been thinking . . ."

His fingers played restlessly with one of the untidy saucers on the dressing table.

"I've been thinking that I'll need a housekeeper for the new place across the water, so I thought, Effie, if that would suit you for a while until perhaps something else turns up . . . I thought you might like to come over and give me a hand and have a bit rest and peace until . . ."

"O, John, John!" Effie sighed.

"Well, think it over," he quite abruptly rid himself of strain. "Don't worry now, I'll say good-night."

He held out his hand, and she pulled an arm from under the bed-clothes and seized it in nervously strong fingers. He felt it pressed close against her hot cheek.

"You're a good, good friend to me, John, better than I deserve," she protested, weeping again.

Sitting alone in the back of the Rolls as it sped towards the town, feeling intolerably weary, John struggled in his mind to place in order and understand all that had happened to him in the course of a day that seemed now as long as a lifetime. It was in another existence, surely, that he had been so well content in the company of Addie and Davie over at the Strone. It was fantastic enough to have moved from that mild shore to the harsh uplands within an hour or so. But still that was not at the root of his bewilderment.

It was that lunacy had intervened : sheer, dark, incalculable lunacy, tainting those it touched, involving them inextricably, it appeared, in its own sinister chaos. Now its victims were the sharers perforce of a dark secret, fantastically wedded in a communion of horror. There was no simplicity in life, no prospect of peace even in age. It was as if the mad fellow's gun had been loaded with an explosive latent in an affair that had ended forty years before and had been nearly forgotten.

As the car entered the town and turned eastwards along back streets John reflected how curious it was that he had told Ernie to drive him to Beth's place. There would certainly have been a room for him at Blackwood's, but no ; something had prompted him to go to his only sister, to Beth.

She opened the door to him and stared, but recovered herself sharply.

" John ! What on earth ! But come in at once."

With a woman's instinct she had perceived that something was amiss, but when she saw him in the light of the kitchen, an ageing man with a grey, shocked face and a smear of dried blood about his neck, she sprang into alarmed but tidy action.

" Sit down in the big chair at once and get your shoes off. Undo that collar. I've got a drop of brandy in the cupboard here. Here, John, drink that. Let me look at your neck. In God's name, Johnnie——"

It was long enough since she had called him that, his Grannie's pet name for him. The cordial refreshed him swiftly.

" There's nothing in that, Beth," he assured her, " though there might have been, but I've had a very ugly experience this day. I feel I've been in the mud, Beth, all the life trampled out of me. It's a queer story . . ."

She listened in silence as he told it, her dark gaze on the fire. An exclamation now and again alone told of her concern. When he had done she spoke gravely.

" What a business ! What a thing to happen to you, John, when you were looking forward to a bit of peace ! But why you should get mixed up in Effie Templeton's affairs . . ."

" You're forgetting the mind of a madman, Beth, if you can call it that. And Effie Templeton hasn't her sorrows to seek."

" No, no ! I'm heart-sorry for her, poor soul."

" And I may as well tell you, Beth," John broke out in sudden candour. " Perhaps it wasn't wise, all things considered, but she was in distress, and I was upset myself, and I wanted to help her a bit . . . Anyhow, I told her she could come as my housekeeper across the water for a bit, until we get all this straightened out. I just had to find my own way out of the rotten, dirty mess, if it comes to that."

" Oh ! "

Beth rose quickly to fill the kettle at the sink and to place it with some vigour on the fire. She spoke over her shoulder at length.

" That's your business entirely, John," she said. " It might turn out quite well, and we'll see. Now you're going straight to your bed, in Addie's room, and I'm going to bring you the rest of this brandy in a good hot toddy with three aspirins. Curly will be in soon, but he's always quiet. Off you go, now. We'll see what's what in the morning."

"Yes, I'll be glad to lie down," he wearily agreed, adding with a wan and rueful smile : "Dear knows I'll be happy to see Addie and Davie to-morrow and get a bit of peace for a change."

CHAPTER FIVE

THE SUMMER PASSES

I

ON A PATCH of shingle hard by the pier at Killadam, just below the ragged line of wrack that marked the limit of the tide's last advance, two elderly gentlemen in brown boiler suits laboured in and about a boat that had there been beached for repairs.

This was a shapely craft of some 18-feet overall, clinker-built, and its smooth sides gleamed with a recent coat of white paint of the finest quality, contrasting nicely with the red of a duller bituminous preparation on the under-water parts. Now the boat's pleasing appearance was being heightened, as to the point of coquetry, by the application of a ribbon of gold to the grooves in the gunwale strokes. This was being laid on with exquisite care by the older and more corpulent of the two workers, who had been obliged, indeed, to go on his knees to his delicate task.

The other intent labourer sat on a ground-sheet near at hand and, a neat kit of tools by his side, dismantled a carburettor with a nice regard for the placing to his hand of all its tiny parts. He had the absorbed air of one who patiently seeks an elusive but definitely ascertainable truth. Like his companion, he worked with the careful confidence of the trained craftsman. The two ageing gentlemen were in fact easily recognisable as parties who, retired from the hurly-burly of the economic struggle, vastly enjoyed the exercise of skill and the illusion of being busy, even on a holiday task.

They worked away in silence under the forenoon sun of a fine June day. The little waves of the loch, fretted only by a mild wind from the South, plashed daintily on the shingle a few yards away, still withdrawing in ebb until, after a strange moment of hesitation, the flood would mysteriously start at noon. Raucous and greedy gulls, an occasional pert sandpiper and fluttering flocks of dunlin would frequently move and call near them.

Steamers put in at the pier and put out again, and knots of children on holiday occasionally gathered to stare. The elderly workers, however, were secure from these distractions in their serene absorption ; these utterly happy men formed a group as immemorial in quality as the soaring, steep hillside of the Strone behind them.

This prolonged trance was broken at length by a little cry of pleasure from the engineer on the ground-sheet.

" Here's the whole trouble ! " he announced. " Look at this, Sam."

" What's that, John ? " asked the other, turning unwillingly from his decorative subtleties.

His companion advanced the blade of a knife with a tiny pile of sand on the point of it.

" This old packet must have been under water some time," the engineer explained, " or the last owner was mighty careless how or where he filled his tank. The filter's choked with sand."

" No wonder she wouldny start," observed the painter mildly.

" No wonder," the other agreed. " But I'll have to get that tank out this afternoon and see that it's clean. I'll bet you we'll get her going this evening."

" I'd like to see my paint dried proper before then. O, my Goad ! " groaned his friend, rising heavily from his kneeling position, " I'm stiff in every bone, and that gravel's fair bored holes in my knees. What about knockin' off, John ? I could be doin' with a pint of beer."

" Not a bad idea."

Mr. Cram and Mr. Lightbody had been reconciled more than two months now, after an estrangement that had lasted little more than a fortnight all told. It had been sensibly brought to an end by John, who had one day penned a note to say that he intended the next morning to sail down the Firth to Port Gordon to inspect in Maclachlan's Yard there a motor-boat he had seen advertised for sale, and that he would value Sam's company and advice. Before they returned from the expedition they had come to a warmer understanding than ever and a natural use of Christian names.

They had not bought the boat as advertised from Maclachlan's Yard, and it would have been nearly impossible for

them to bring an agreeable quest to such a quick conclusion.
They were elderly parties with time on their hands ; they needed
the illusion of purpose in what remained to them of life. A score
of yards up and down the Firth came to know them, those two
funny old boys who came clambering over logs and slipways and
under the hulls of yachts drawn up for the spring overhaul, to
inquire after the bit boat they had seen advertised or had heard
through obscure longshore channels was for sale. Usually it was
too big, or too expensive : not the sort of thing at all, Sam would
say, his powers of sales resistance being much more formidable
than those of his friend.

This pleasant game they played for weeks on end, until the
promise of May could be resisted no longer and the manager of
Samson Bell's round the corner of the Norloch, a quizzical
humorist, and more for his own amusement than with any hope
of a deal, took them into an outside shed and showed them the old
open boat known somewhat grandiosely as the *Golden Girl*.

John and Sam had then eyed the boat and peered inside her
with a blend of gravity and covetousness that vastly amused the
boatbuilder. While John tested the propeller shaft for suspicions
of play, Sam jabbed the point of his knife into the planking. They
stood back and regarded the vessel with heads cocked to the side.
Then they walked round her again. At length their eyes met in a
mildly emotional haze of agreement. Shortly in the manager's
office, lapped by the lovely aromas of wood shavings and archangel
tar in redolent blend, John had written his cheque. Sam failed
to gain the last satisfaction of getting a pound or two knocked
off the price, but the manager agreed instead that he would
throw in an anchor for the fishing and arrange to have the
Golden Girl towed down to Killadam next afternoon by a lighter
which was coming in with a deck cargo of oil drums and going on
to Hamilton's Quay with coal for the shooting lodge up the
glen.

They had a boat of their own. Before noon next day they had
supervised the laying by the piermaster of moorings for her,
complete with a bright green buoy and a running-line of fresh
hemp. They waited on the sea-wall until the lighter *Sweet Afton*
of Garvel came panting down the Firth with the motor-boat in
tow and her own dinghy stringing out behind. It touched John
that the skipper of the *Sweet Afton,* with the always surprising

Highland delicacy, refused a tip but would be very glad, along with the three members of his crew, to have a dram with the gentlemen at what he called the Inns. This was a prolonged ceremony, much decorated with Gaelic toasts and Highland ceremonies ; and the gloaming was down before the lighter panted away and John and Sam could look again at the *Golden Girl*, snubbing to her moorings against the first of the ebb out of the loch.

" She'll be taking in the water," said Sam thoughtfully, " but that'll tighten up her seams. If it's fair to-morrow I'll get the floorboards and that out of her. We'll mebbe have to borrow a bit pump."

" And we'll need to hire one of Neilie's boats until we get a dinghy," John added. " I'm going to lift that engine right out of its bed and take it down in the smiddy."

Three weeks they had laboured on the *Golden Girl*. Often John paused at his work to look round the waters and up at the hills and think how happy he was without knowing it, as it were. He often pondered the nature of happiness and vaguely perceived that the elements of it, for an old chap at least, were in the feeling of timelessness in which he was lapped throughout those long days of an early summer fine beyond the average. An absorbing task, but without urgency beyond what his expectation of mild pleasures urged him to put into it ; the quiet, occasionally explosive, always industrious companionship of old Sam, usually lost in the rapture of a job ; the mild sun, the mild rains, the mild winds of West Scotland ; the healthy weariness of the body when the evening came ; the freedom to forget the boat when the fancy took him— all these things were elements of his palpable happiness.

He gravely concluded, however, that the essence of happiness lay in the suspension of the sense of time. He was curiously pleased one evening, getting the last ounce of interest out of his *Glasgow Herald* and turning a thought unhopefully to the Book Reviews, to come on lines quoted from one of those Irish poet chaps about a place where " peace comes dropping slow." That was the very idea ; and anyhow, he was at length living the dream he had cherished among the vilest stinks of Chinese cities.

Meanwhile, the afternoon tide crept up and over the patch of shingle hard by the pier at Killadam. The *Golden Girl's* petrol tank and its connections had been unshipped and cleaned. Sam

Lightbody had completed his nice work with the gold paint and thanked his Maker for sparing him such a shower of rain as might have ruined the living handiwork. With the natural helpfulness of all country folk and longshoremen the Piermaster and the Postie had come down to lend a hand, to advise, applaud and bless the undertaking : the former bringing with him a new pair of oars John had prudently ordered from Samson Bell's. Now the wavelets came plashing up to the line of the little boat's sternpost, sending out flat streamers to lick her flanks. A knot of children gathered to take part in the ceremony of shoving-off. The tide increased. Soon the shell of the *Golden Girl* was quivering and starting in the pregnant beginnings of buoyancy. The infants then wanted to push her off with a shout, but Postie told them not to be daft ; this wasn't a rowing-boat. John and Sam climbed in over the bows, round which the water was now gathering.

The *Golden Girl* was eventually launched by the Piermaster, who put the sole of a gum boot against her stem and, with a negligent heave of his leg, sent her shooting out with pretty curtseys into deep water. John stood by the engine. Sam, in the stern sheets with the tiller to his hand, poled the boat out with the butt of one of the new oars. She swung broadside on to the shore and seemed to sulk in the mild chop. This was a great moment in the lives of both members of her crew.

" We'll try her out now," said John tautly.

" I'm ready at this end," said Sam.

John had seen to it that the carburettor was primed. Puffing a little, he bent low and swung the starting-handle. The engine fired at once, making a rare racket until he threw in the clutch and the sinking stern brought the exhaust under water. The *Golden Girl* dashed off with a verve that considerably startled the ageing gentlemen in charge of her, but Sam at the tiller contrived a surging turn that swung the little boat's nose out to the safe expanses of the Firth.

" How's that ? " shouted John to his friend, his face glowing.

" She's a fair topper ! " cried Sam in return.

John clambered over a thwart to be near his companion amid the noises of many waters and the rush of air.

" I'll give her a good ten minutes on the petrol to warm up," he remarked, "and then we'll see how she does on the paraffin."

" She's going a fair dinger now," said Sam.

The *Golden Girl* was in fact capable of only a very moderate speed, but Sam would have it that she was doing a good nine knots. To this John demurred, pointing out that one was apt to get a false impression of speed in a small craft and doubting if they were doing more than six. It was agreed that they would one fine day carry out a trial run between points carefully measured on the shore ; and so they settled down to enjoy their hour on the water.

The boat was a frail and tiny thing on the expanses of the Firth, a dwarfed fragment of civilization under the high, steep hills. As boys, however, the ageing men were without any sense of their world's littleness and vulnerability. This was a rare bit of sport, in Sam's phrase ; this was an amazing escape into a free element. They lit their pipes in an almost ostentatious profession of contentment. John hovered over the engine, quite unnecessarily lavish with a long-spouted oil-can and many anxious pressures of his palm on the water-jacker, and Sam conned the boat as he pleased ; up the loch and down again, round the Strone point and across among the moored yachts to Hamilton's Quay, even out from the northern shore and a couple of miles across the main estuary towards the Riccar Light.

" I'd watch where I was going, Sam," John suggested. " You're into the big-ship lane. I don't want to end my days with a clout on the head from one of Paddy Henderson's propellers."

" There's nothing near us, and we'll easy jink if there is," said Sam, confident in his command. " But it's mebbe gettin' late. There's the *Duchess* comin' out of Kempock on the five-forty run."

So they turned in a fine circle for home and the moorings by the pier, and as they came in towards the green buoy the *Duchess of Buccleuch* overtook them, and Captain Macglashan on the bridge, who had been a helpful critic of the venture from first to last, gave them a series of hearty blasts on his vessel's whistle and raised his braided cap in salute to the *Golden Girl* returning from her trial trip.

John and Sam had a pleasantly fussy time putting the boat to rights for the night and running her out on the endless line to ride the tides alone. They stood on the beach regarding her with affection before they could bring themselves to turn and walk up to the store on the pier with the new oars.

" Well, will we have a dram in the hotel now ? " asked Sam ceremonially. He had in him the longing to describe the afternoon's triumph to the longshoremen in the bar.

" No," said John, " we'll get a better dram at the Lodge, and the more I see of him, the less I like that manager chap."

" Thon's a twister," Sam agreed.

" You'll stay for your supper, Sam ? "

" If it's your pleasure, and thank ye."

Question and answer had the ring of mere formality. Sam was only a lodger at Sunnyside Cottage, and old Mrs. Gunn was getting frail and tetchy. On most evenings of the week now Sam came to Penang Lodge for supper. It was the comfortable understanding that, as the evenings lengthened, he was John's adviser and helper in the garden now taking shape again. There was also the Dam. So they marched together down the shore road, talking contentedly of the *Golden Girl* and what might yet be done to bring her to a condition of invulnerable perfection.

" What ye'll need now is a bass," Sam was saying, " a nice bit of coconut matting to put down if you was havin' ladies on board and them steppin' on the thwarts. These fancy heels weemen wear nowadays is fair ruination to varnish, and I was thinkin' it wouldny be a bad idea to lay on another coat this week-end."

" Quite right, Sam," John agreed, losing himself willingly in the fond dreams of age. " We might run round to Doon to-morrow and see what we can pick up."

Effie Templeton was out at the door of Penang Lodge to greet them.

" Well, there ye are at last ! And how are you to-day, Mr. Lightbody ? "

" Fine, Mrs. Rolland, fine ! We got the wee boat goin' at last."

" Isn't that nice ! Now, what do you want for your supper ? You can have ham and eggs, or I've got some nice kippers off the van."

John and Sam agreed that kippers would be the very thing, and Effie disappeared into the kitchen, assuring them she wouldn't be twenty minutes. The friends passed into the long sitting-room, now always referred to as the Big Room, and settled happily to noggins of whisky and water poured by John from a bottle with an almost ostentatiously austere label.

"Aye," observed Sam, recovering with a sigh of contentment from his first swallow, "that's a better dram than ye'll get at the hotel."

"I wouldn't have that man's firewater in the house if I was paid for it."

"Just so," agreed Sam with a sly closing of the small eyes in his wide face, "but he'll no' like ye any the better for givin' him the go-by. But as I was sayin', John, if we're goin' in to Doon the morn for those odds-and-ends for the boat, we'd best lay in some fishing tackle when we're there—penny flies for the mackerel and that."

This led to another agreeable debate as to the best lures for the local waters : whether the white fly was better than the yellow, the yellow better than the red, the red than the white, or whether the spinning sand-eel was not better than the lot put together, with some reference to the virtues of the silver minnow. Effie appeared at length round the edge of the door.

"Your supper's on the table."

"Thank you, Effie. Come, Sam."

When they were settled in the little dining-room and Sam had his napkin securely tucked under his ample chin, he remarked sententiously :

"Aye, Mrs. Rolland lays a nice table." Then he glanced sideways at his friend and took a liberty of confidence. "She's suitin' ye all right, John, is she ? "

"Very well indeed," said John hastily. "Help yourself to toast, Sam."

"I will say," Sam blundered on, "she's twice the woman she was when she came here first."

The metaphor was just in its intention. Effie Templeton, another trope would have more accurately summed it up, was a new woman after these weeks in Penang Lodge. Her face was fresh again, her eyes bright ; she seemed to have thrown off completely the self-pitiful fear that had almost irritated John whenever he had seen her at Corsewellhill. In person she was a woman renewed, a woman with a new individuality in the black dress and neat ruffed neckband of the professional housekeeper.

Throughout that single meal, however, eaten in celebration of a triumph as it were, even old Sam Lightbody, who was far from being a sensitive recorder of the velleities of human conduct, wondered why his friend should go quiet all of a sudden after the mention of the woman's name. Was she just the usual sort of middle-aged besom after all, and up to all the old tricks with a decent, innocent, loyal chap like his friend, John Cram?

In due course Effie came in to ask if they were finished, and could she clear away and wash up? She had a notion she would take a walk along the road and call on Mrs. Mactaggart at the Pierhead; and John said that was a good idea; it was a fine evening, he and Mr. Lightbody had some jobs to do about the garden, and there was nothing more they would need. And old Sam, with the grim intensity of the elderly male who has simplified his code of living, watched Effie Templeton as she started to gather the dishes with the deftness of long practice, looking for plain evidence in support of his belief that no woman was capable of acting except in her own mysterious and usually tortuous interests.

There was really not a great deal to do in the garden but much to talk about : such as the encouragement of early peas checked by late April frosts ; the best means of slaughtering slugs ; the wisdom of planting tomatoes out of doors in a northern latitude ; the advantages of a greenhouse. The evening gathered slowly about the old gentlemen, and as it came near half-past nine Sam said he ought to be getting along the road. John said there was no hurry, and one of the sudden showers of the western summer started to patter on the vegetation about them, and they agreed that it would be well to wait a while indoors over a last dram.

It was apt to happen like this, night after night ; it was almost a ritual. But on this one night John Rolland Cram felt uneasy and kept his guest in talk until he heard Effie's footsteps on the new gravel he had had laid thick up and down the twin paths before the house. She looked into the Big Room to make sure if they did not, after all, want anything before she went upstairs. Then Sam said jocularly that he ought to be off or he would be getting his books from the old wifie in Sunnyside, and John in his turn observed that there was just time for one for the road. He was

listening for the sounds of movement upstairs, for the final closing
of his housekeeper's door.

Sam had to go at length, and John went out on the terrace
with him. He lingered there until the heavy feet had crunched
down the path, the road-gate had clicked and a hollow roar from
his friend had reiterated his warmth of sentiment. He stood
awhile in the mild warmth of the June night and savoured the
superficially unpleasant but heady odours roused from the foliage
of flowering currant bushes by the passing shower.

It had been a good day. There were still the ghosts of golden
bars in the western sky. It was mighty queer to think that the
sun would rise and shine within six hours of man's sleep. They
had arranged to get the ten-thirty bus for Doon and have lunch
in the Ramshorn ; they were going fishing at night in the new
boat.

He shut the front door quietly, saw that all was well in the
Big Room, changed into his felt slippers, and went carefully
upstairs. A line of light still gleamed under the door of Effie's
room, but when he emerged from the bathroom it had disappeared. The house was going to sleep ; elderly folk needed a lot
of rest. He slipped into his own room and locked the door behind
him.

It had been a good day. They would get the wee boat going
to-morrow night again and have a shot at the mackerel and lythe
off the Brunts. John undressed and said his prayer. The new
sheets of his bed were crisp and cool. He was tired, but he
remained restless. He kept turning over and over in his mind the
question of why he had locked his door ever since Effie Templeton
had come to be his housekeeper. He wondered if it wasn't simply
silly, an awareness of sinfulness in himself. It was that damned old
fool, Sam, bringing it up somehow. And Beth had been queer
about it, too.

2

Donald MacGilchrist Kiddie, Master of Arts of the University of Aberdeen and parish minister of Killadam, made his way homewards after a round of pastoral visitations. His step along the shore road was jaunty ; the umbrella, which he carried rather as a staff of office than as a necessity on a June afternoon of singular brilliance, swung at the trail with such a swagger as an ambitious subaltern of the Rifle Brigade might bring to the management of his cane on parade.

Mr. Kiddie's spirit was filled with the sense of success. He had had a good day in his reckoning of such matters. The Misses Butters at " Kilveen " had provided an excellent tea and an eagerly flattering audience for his bright talk of parochial affairs. Colonel Christie Macbain in the White Lodge had received him brusquely enough, being at the moment of the minister's arrival explosively engaged with the black fly in his broad beans, but had sent him off with two cigars in his breast pocket and the promise of a middle-cut of salmon, to be brought to the manse in the evening by the chauffeur of the big Humber that would wait for the Hon. Mrs. Christie Macbain's return by the five-forty boat. In Woodbine Cottage the recently-widowed Mrs. Sam Peterkin—Peterkin of Peterkin's Kempock and District Laundries —had provided another afternoon tea (not quite so *recherché* as that of the Misses Butters, the little minister phrased it to himself), listened piously to his comforting words on her loss, wept with discretion, and wrote a cheque for £25 towards the cost of the new vestry : adding that she would deliver to the manse on the morrow, in person, some blooms from her late husband's cherished conservatory.

This little man who strutted along the shore road of his remote and negligible parish might well have stood for the pattern of nonentity in the eyes of the larger world, but the completeness and perfection of his nonentity made him unique. His cheerfulness, as of a bluetit, came of a complete absence from his make-up of any mysticism that might trouble another man's performance of the pastoral duties ; and the Church of Scotland had no austere bishops to trouble his blithe spirit. The collection of gifts in kind he took as, firstly, extremely desirable additions to what could be bought in the open market on the minimum stipend of £300 and a manse, and, secondly, as proper tributes to his personality and influence. The little fellow thought it quite remarkable that he, a country blacksmith's son, should be such a respected figure and welcome guest, such an obvious recipient of gifts, in a community which included so many persons of position and wealth. He greatly enjoyed a sense of power within his obscure dominion.

He took to whistling as he marched along, happy as a sandboy. The air was that of *The Boys of the Old Brigade*, a measure which delightfully suited his lightsome step. He had no great interest in the quite splendid beauty of the scene about him. If he had cared to pause for a moment and peer through the clump of ash-trees on the eastern side of the Strone point he might have glimpsed what an artist would have yearned to paint—the bright, rippled waters of the loch, rich in blue and silver and deep purples, and the greens and golds and cerulean blues of land masses and mountains beyond : the vision given the proportion of remoteness by the grey boles of the trees, framing the fabulous scene.

Mr. Kiddie's eye, however, had little truck with the external. It was nearly always turned inwards on personal and social concerns. It was watchful in its possessor's interests ; and as the minister came round a bend of the road it spotted for him the significance of the new-washed front of Penang Lodge, the steep front garden with the twin paths and the great araucaria in between. Ah ! Mr. Kiddie's self said to itself : Mr. Cram, a wealthy newcomer, home from the East ! He has always been cordial. Let us see what a surprise visit may bring forth.

Mr. Cram was in that moment in his bedroom, changing into old clothes for a night's fishing, and at the sight of the minister approaching up the path he uttered an irritable " Damnation ! " As a rule, the little jack-in-the-box in a dog collar amused him sardonically. It diverted him to be a victim of the trick with the empty pipe and the missing pouch, and he had once written, out of a considered sense of his obligation to the community, a cheque for ten guineas towards the cost of the new Vestry. But he had made it very clear to the Reverend Mr. Kiddie that he had never been a church-goer, having had too much of it in his childhood, and wasn't going to start again in his old age ; and now, when the late Superintendent Engineer of the K. & S. looked forward to an outing with his friend Mr. Lightbody, and was due to meet him at the pier in exactly thirty minutes' time, he decided that the priest was a confounded little pest.

He heard Effie invite him in with glad cries of welcome. The conversation continued in the Big Room. His housekeeper had the proper native respect for the ministry and its social standing. She was still clinging to the handle of the Big Room door when John came down, heavy and inhospitable.

"Here he is, Mr. Kiddie!" cried Effie as John's solid foot landed on the lobby waxcloth behind her. As he passed her into the room she added gaily : "Will I get you and the Minister a nice cup of tea, John?"

"No, thank you, Effie," said John. "I'm going out immediately. Well, Mr. Kiddie, what can I do for you?"

"Nothing, nothing!" the little man protested eagerly, his eyes bright under the thatch of hair that looked so like a wig. "Just called in in passing. A friendly word."

He waved a hand to indicate in arch mime the blameless cordiality of his intentions.

"It's not very convenient, if you don't mind me saying it, Mr. Kiddie," the host went on severely. "I've an appointment to keep. I've got to be at the pier "—he drew out his watch—" in just about twenty minutes."

"Ah, then! Let us walk along together and talk."

"Sorry. I've one letter to write."

"In that case——"

Mr. Kiddie retired. His movement down the path was quite as jaunty as his approach had been, but the complacency induced by his earlier successes was gone from his mind and spirit, leaving them ruffled and resentful. He was aware that he had been dismissed from Penang Lodge, and the slight on his importance was hard for him to bear. John's obvious unwillingness even to walk with him to the pier hurt the sentient man within the clerical garb. His vanity was touched, his sense of power shaken ; and he felt, what he could least easily bear to ponder—not merely that he had been made a fool of but might, in fact, be the fool this downright stranger seemed to think him.

Mr. Kiddie made for the hotel. The umbrella confessed his inner disturbance by digging into the path at every step instead of swinging happily at the trail. The minister could not, of course, be seen entering licensed premises. His good parishioners could be watchful and foolish in their talk. He therefore strode up the brae behind the building, ostensibly to have a kindly word with old Calum Bain who, he knew, would be out in a chair at his cottage door, enjoying the sunlight of such a fine afternoon. The little chat completed, what more natural than that the minister should take the short cut through the hotel grounds to the manse? Round the blind corner of an outhouse he dodged featly through a discreet door that led to the private apartments of the innkeeper and his wife.

Captain and Mrs. J. Birnie Hoy (for the licensee clung tenaciously to the temporaty rank granted him in the Royal Army Service Corps during the war of 1914-18) were at tea in their dark sitting-room between the bar and the office. Their greeting of Mr. Kiddie was at once friendly and casual, such as would naturally be extended to a regular visitor. The innkeeper heaved himself from his chair.

" Come in, Padre," he said in a voice singularly hoarse and breathless in one not yet old. " I suppose you're up to the back teeth in tea. What about a drop of the Old Kirk? "

" That would be very nice ! Just a thimbleful, Captain," Mr. Kiddie completed the piece of empty, familiar ritual, " just a thimbleful."

The Captain lurched into the bar and returned with a glass of whisky three fingers deep. He added to this a small dash of water, as according to a familiar recipe, and laid it to Mr. Kiddie's hand.

" I thank you," the latter said. He turned with a courteous little bow to the Captain's lady and said : " Your continued health and success, madam ! "

" Thanks a lot," said the blonde lady flatly.

Mr. Kiddie was no alcoholic. His weekly tot at the expense of Captain J. Birnie Hoy was one of those parochial perquisites he could not bear to forgo, for it cost nothing and introduced him into such a clandestine and influential circle as ministered sweetly to his inclinations towards intrigue and power. He was even too simple to perceive that his host, as the only retail merchant of liquor in an extensive district, wielded an even greater power than was his own and, mankind being incorrigibly sinful, as well as inveterately furtive in its drinking, much more effective.

"And what's the buzz along the shore to-day?" asked the innkeeper roughly.

He was a rough man. Born the son of a decent baker in the Glasgow suburbs, he had been in the middle of a reasonably industrious apprenticeship to that trade when conscription took him in 1916. When it was all over, and after Jimmie Hoy, as his friends knew him, had enjoyed a profitable year on the catering side of the Army of Occupation, it did not seem right to him, nor to the proud father of Captain J. B. Hoy, that he should return to slavery and the social obscurity of the retail.

The hotel at Killadam was bought for him. He was to be Captain J. Birnie Hoy, the gentleman-innkeeper, the ex-officer host. He had been beaten, however, by the allure and strength of his own wares and, twenty years after the opening of the glad adventure, he had little left to him but his nominal rank (with permission to wear the prescribed uniform, it said in the paper Scottish Command had sent him), his power as licence-holder, and the inflamed, resentful mind of one who has succumbed to the bottle and hates himself for having been so seductively defeated.

"A strange state of affairs at Penang Lodge," said Mr. Kiddie in answer to the question. "A very strange state of affairs, if you ask me."

He pursed his lips and indicated generally that the facts were painful, the revelation to follow of an extremely disagreeable character.

"Give us the dope," commanded the innkeeper's wife, brightening a little.

Mr. Kiddie raised a warning forefinger. He smiled ruefully at his hostess as if she had put upon him such an obligation as no gentleman could be expected to discharge.

"Come on and spill the beans," the lady urged him, chuckling in her great bosom. "I know you've got a right dirty story up your sleeve."

"But it is really rather shocking," protested poor Mr. Kiddie honestly.

He could well have saved his breath. One chapter from the private reminiscences of Mrs. Birnie Hoy, as she now liked to

be called, would have opened to the little minister such a realm
of adventure in the erotic as he had never entered, as he had not
even dreamed of in the worst moments of a timid celibacy.

She had been picked up by her husband on the front at
Douglas, Isle of Man, both being romantically impressed by the
fact that, meeting so casually in that arena of easy mating, she
was also of a Glasgow shopkeeping family, in fish. The circumstance allowed her to bind the Captain to her with stronger bands
than he might have chosen ; and now in middle-age—bleached
and dyed in the hair, marvellously plastered with cosmetics,
but too lazy and greedy to check her ever increasing weight—
she was well content to be the lady wife of a superior licensed
victualler.

" Christian names, Effie and John. That's how it is at
Penang Lodge," the minister told the worst. " Quite offhand
with each other. Obviously a very intimate relationship, *very*
intimate."

" Christian names don't make much of a scandal," observed
Mrs. Birnie Hoy, disappointed, and with a woman's realism.

" No, no ! Of course not. But the atmosphere . . ."

" And I can tell you something about the same good lady,"
announced the Captain hoarsely.

He had not forgotten his brush with John over the letters
weeks before. That had rankled, flaming up as a rancid grievance
when, frequently, his system was soaked in alcohol and the sour
acids. Then, one day lately, driving back from Doon in his
flashy little M.G., flushed, inflamed and defiant after what he
called " a few wee hoots " with his brother-tradesman in the
Imperial there, he had seen the discreet van of Messrs Faill &
Forfar delivering supplies to Penang Lodge—a case of whisky and
six cases of bottled beer.

He had been at pains to explain to his wife when reporting
this insult that he did not mind a fellow choosing his own whisky
—and he, J. Birnie Hoy, would be the first to allow that Faill &
Forfar's " Laird's Choice " was a good dram, if you didn't mind
an awful lot of malt—but he was damned if he could see why the
obvious local supplier should be passed over in the matter of
bottled beer. Did Bass or Younger or anybody else supply F. & F's.
with better beer than they 'supplied to the Killadam Hotel ?
Obviously they did not. Therefore F. & F's. were a bunch of

ruddy interlopers with their smooth, maroon delivery vans and always ready to rub their hands and say " Yes, sir ! " " No, sir ! " to the County and the shooting tenants ; and as for that old bustard in Penang Lodge, who was no class at all, the Captain would like to kick his ruddy face in.

Now his wife and the minister awaited his revelation. In response to their mute inquiry he raised his elbow and went through the motion of draining a glass.

" Dear me ! " cried Mr. Kiddie, shocked.

" Like a ruddy fish," the innkeeper assured him.

" Buys it in gills," his wife added. " The kind that buries her dead men in the garden.

" This is very shocking," said the minister.

They had woven a plot that satisfied them. They had created among themselves the illusion of a scandal and, within themselves, the conviction of righteousness. The power of the nonentity, which is the power of evil, had been set to work.

Even as the minister pranced away towards the manse, the umbrella swinging jauntily again, the public bar of the hotel was opened and the Captain was working on his first batch of customers to create the chinks through which, with a nice affectation of amused indifference, he would insinuate the news. The story was enriched as the night wore on and whisky broke down his inhibitions : a cloud gathering about the head of John Rolland Cram, who more than a mile offshore, sat on the middle thwart of the *Golden Girl* and blissfully awaited the next tug of a mackerel at his penny fly.

3

Beth Bryden, born Elizabeth Cram, sat on the garden seat in front of her brother's new house at the Coast, turning the heel of a winter sock for her husband.

The Bryden's were at Penang Lodge for the Fair, and this was how Beth most fully enjoyed her holiday. It was just nice to sit and knit in the sun and watch the steamers pass and, best of all, know that the work of the house was being done by a hired woman. Simply to realise that she had no fires to lay, no cooking to do, no dishes to wash up after, was a refined species of bliss for a woman who had been working with her hands and plotting domestically with her brains for thirty-five years on end.

John had insisted that it should be so. He had been really angry, for him, on the very first morning when he had come on Beth and Addie washing up the breakfast things in the scullery. "That's not your job," he had lectured them. "You're here for a holiday. You can make up your own beds or give the Big Room a dust over, for that helps the housekeeper to get on, but you're not going to start skivvying and skittling here. I pay a woman good money to do that for me and my guests."

Thus spoke the late Superintendent Engineer of the K. & S., and his sister greatly admired him for his firmness. It was in these matters of discipline that John could always take a strong line which rather frightened a working man's wife, soft as he was about things like lending Davie all that money for this silly caper to turn Curly into a boxer.

That fear had left her now ; the aggravation and shame had lost their edge. She knew her Davie, and she knew her Curly, and with Addie's help she had created within the tight, loyal circle of the family the tacit understanding that, while Curly might train with that coarse big lump Macluskie—and the discipline of training made for clean living in a boy, she admitted to herself—there was going to be no question of putting Curly into any professional Ring (which was a daft-like way to describe what Beth had seen from the Pictures to be a square) before she had her say. She had now little doubt but that it would be decisive.

But this was no time to worry about wee things like that. The sun was warm, and it was nice to hear the bees bumbling from flower to flower in John's garden. He had made a nice garden of it. It must be grand to have the means to create so much loveliness. John had worked for it, worked hard and done well. It must be most wonderful of all to create comfort and leisure and peace about oneself. Beth thought that she could live here for ever, knitting a sock and listening idly to the bumbling of bees and the kindred beat of paddle-wheels while the afternoon sun blessed the garden.

And Curly was coming on Friday for the last week-end of the Fair. The thought of it was her deepest joy. Like the daft boy he was, Curly was away with the hikers—and a rare cod some of these lassies managed to make of themselves, with their great big red haunches like plum puddings and shorts that were a disgrace : near stark naked the lot of them—but Curly was all right. Curly was a good boy ; and this she knew for a certainty. He was like the father who had begotten him on her own willing body : simple, clean, active, cheerful. He was not wise like Addie, but few men were as wise as most women, and if she ever heard anybody say that Curly Bryden had done a mean thing, there would be murder somewhere. He was coming on Friday, her son : Curly with his grin . . .

She started to at a shout from the back garden behind her. Her eyelids blinked in the sunlight.

" Beth ! Come here a minute. Here and look at this."

She must have dozed. She laid down her knitting and turned to see Davie at the gable-end of the house, his brown boiler-suit contrasting oddly with a rich fall of purple clematis above his bare head.

" Were ye sleepin', lass ? " he asked kindly, his brown eyes taking hers with quizzical affection.

" I must have dovered over," she agreed.

" Well, come and see what I've been doing while ye were in bye-byes. What do you think of that, now ? "

" O that's wonderful, Davie ! John will be pleased."

" Aye, I think it's no' a bad wee job," he said, cocking his boyish head sideways to consider his handiwork.

This was her Davie, the simple man who rejoiced in a bit of sport, even if it meant hard manual labour in the creation of a pond in a friend's garden. Put a tool near that man's hand, and you couldn't stop him. This was Davie enjoying his holiday to the top of his bent. From the very beginning, when he should have been loafing—or when, as now, he should have been away with John and Addie and old Sam Lightbody in the motor-boat— you couldn't stop his talking about the Dam and working on it. He had found in the Post a willing labourer to give him a hand in the evenings, and now he had wrought in the heat of the afternoon to finish the job. He was therefore very happy, this decent man of hers.

" You see how it'll work now, Beth ? " he anxiously inquired.

Mr. Lightbody's first bold plan had been modified after much discussion. The embankment of the pond—though it was invariably called the Dam—had been built up to a level of only some six feet above the scullery door, at a point where the burn from the hill made the second of three marked leaps over the rocky outcrops of the upper garden. It had been built out to the side of the stream, and Davie was at pains to show his wife how two simple cuttings with the spade would, when the cement-work he had been so lovingly fashioning throughout this hot day had dried out, allow a steady flow of water to come in at one end and pass out at the other through a sluice he had cunningly fashioned out of a sheet of perforated metal.

"That's to catch twigs and rubbish," he explained earnestly, like any little boy demonstrating the workings of his clockwork toy, "and it'll keep in any goldfish or the like John might have a fancy for."

"It's beautiful, Davie."

"Aye, it's a right wee topper o' a dam, though I say it myself," he repeated, cocking his head sideways once more to get a true vision of its excellence. "But if we've got to go to this show in Doon to-night, I'd best get inside and have a wash and a change."

Beth returned to her garden seat and her knitting and willingly gave herself over again to the mild torpor of contentment with the moment. She saw the tiny shape of the *Golden Girl* standing off Blairletter Point and heading across the loch towards her moorings. She heard Davie whistling like any lintie as he splashed in the bathroom upstairs. At length she started into a state of vigilance as somebody came out of the house and crunched across the gravel of the terrace.

"I think you'll find everything all right, Mrs. Bryden," said Effie Templeton. She was dressed for her evening out. "You'll just need to infuse the tea. Leave the dishes and I'll see to them when I come back."

"Thanks, Mrs. Rolland. Addie and I'll clear up a bit if we have time before the bus."

"O, don't put yourself out for me, Mrs. Bryden!"

"It won't be any trouble, Mrs. Rolland. I hope you have a nice evening. It looks as if it will keep fair."

Beth watched this other woman move down the path. She was quite unconscious of any complexity in the relationship which had kept herself and Effie Templeton on the correct, distant terms of that small snatch of domestic conversation. This was the woman who had once jilted John and then wheedled her way back into his life. Beth could give her little more mercy than she would have shown to a woman she suspected of seducing young Curly. Nor had she been in Penang Lodge for a week without picking up small bits of village gossip with a sour taste to them, without catching some undertones of caution in old Sam Lightbody's blundering but shrewd observations on the nature of parochial life.

She rose and went indoors to the Big Room and from the sideboard took the bottle of whisky from which, before lunch, John and Davie and old Sam had had a drink apiece. On the edge of the austere label of Messrs Faill & Forfar the nick she had made with her thumbnail was now fully an inch above the level of the liquor left in the bottle. So Addie was right—downright Addie, fiercely loyal to her Uncle John, who had come running up to their bedroom one afternoon and, biting the words, said : " That woman drinks like a fish. The scullery is stinking with it." And she had scolded Addie for rashness.

Beth passed out of doors again, thoughtful. She was keenly aware of the blessedness of the afternoon, of the warmth now being thrown back from the solid stone walls of Penang Lodge, and of that air of easeful peace about her which was belied by the shabbiness of her suspicions, now in part confirmed. She did not in her mind triumph over that other woman. She was sorry that it should have happened at all ; and even in the intensity of her care for John's interests she knew that a problem of responsibility faced her alone. Davie was too simple to help, Addie too brusque.

John and Addie returned, halooing and waving to her from the road. Davie came out in his best suit, shaved and washed, eager to greet the sailors and still more eager to demonstrate to John the beauty of the completed Dam. When all the reunions and inspections were over, John said fervently :

" I wish I hadn't to go to that confounded show to-night. It would please me a dashed sight better to stay here and have a quiet night, the lot of us with the house and the garden to ourselves."

" Mebbe," said Beth in one of her tart moods, " but you promised Lily, and that's that."

" Seeing you paid for their training," observed Addie, " it would be a slap in the face to Beryl and Sibyl."

" I wouldny like to miss the show," said Davie tolerantly.
" These two lassies of Lily's can punish the ivories a treat, or my
name's McGinty. D'ye ever hear them in thon fantasia thing
about *Sweet Chiming Bells* ? "

" All right, all right ! " John laughed the scoldings aside.
" I suppose I'd better get changed and go ahead. You three'll
get the six o'clock bus. I suppose Effie left everything in order ? "

" Away inside and get ready," said Beth, sticking to the
present point.

The faint sense of irritation with Lily and her family lingered
with John as the five o'clock bus for Doon rocked gaily round the
sharp and numerous bends of the shore road. He drew her letter
from his pocket and considered once more its ecstatic terms and
the ebullience of the handwriting that matched them in a riot of
n's that looked like *u's* and tall decorative capitals, so that any
word might rival the record of a distant earthquake on a seismo-
graph. The woman had good enough reason to be excited, he
allowed. The Rolland Rhythmic Twins had secured their first
professional appointment—with Ben Chorley's " Cheery Chums "
Concert Party at the Beach Pavilion in Doon ; Cha had been
accepted for the tea plantations by Ballingall's and had been
instructed to assemble his kit in anticipation of an eastward
passage by P. & O., probably in September.

Very good, thought John to himself a trifle sourly, for he was
not at all sure, though willing to be convinced, that six months
of training was just what he would have thought the Twins
needed, or that an engagement with a seaside concert party was a
right beginning to their professional career. He himself, without
making any pretensions to knowledge of these matters, had
innocently thought that the concert platform was more the sort
of thing. As for Cha, the thought of that boy had a lamentable
power to irritate him. John did not grudge the money. Perhaps
it had been his own fault to give the lad so much cash in his hand.
But there had never been any reckoning by our Cha for the twenty
pounds advanced to cover his interview in London. There had
been no squaring up ; and John did not like people who did not
square up.

There it was, however. What was done could not be undone.
There was no stopping Lily where the interests of her children
were concerned, and John would allow to himself that he was

just a bit unreasonably irritated because he was now jolting in a country bus to have high tea in an hotel and then go on to a pierrot show he didn't particularly want to see when he might be having a nice supper with Beth and her folk at home, and then going out for a night's fishing with Davie and Addie and old Sam Lightbody. So now to get it over and done with—see about getting Cha fixed up finally, hear the Twins perform on a stage, and get back to Penang Lodge by the nine o'clock bus at the latest.

He did not consciously perceive the importance of this almost urgent sense of finality that had come into his attitude to Lily and her young people ; and if he had been aware of it he might not have been able to compass an analysis of it. When the bus had jolted to its oily stance on the sea front at Doon he had only this vague feeling of being a somewhat unwilling guest at the feast in prospect : an emotion unhappily complicated by nausea, induced by the rolling of the bus and the fumes of petroleum that filled its interior.

Lily was bearing down on him even as the swing doors, operated by an excessively vigorous pageboy, propelled him into the lounge of the Imperial. Her greeting seemed to him in his given mood a thought on the effusive side, and he saw with annoyance that the heads of many sitting round the tables turned to regard their encounter. He noted with particularity that Lily was, with her obviously best clothes, wearing a fancy hat that just did not suit her at all. If he had known the fashions of the day and the appropriate terminology, he would have recognised it as a halo hat worn off the face in the manner popularized by Her Majesty, Queen Elizabeth.

When he had disposed of his hat and stick, John urged Lily into the drawing-room which, dating from nearly two decades before the creation of the lounge in leather and chromium and glass that made the money for the modern hotel, he knew would be occupied, if at all, by only a few aged ladies capable of subduing by the mere exhalation of disapproval the most ebullient intruder.

" It was wonderful of you to come round, John ! " she started off. " I suppose Beth and her husband will be coming on for the show. I don't know how on earth I'm going to bear the excitement. Fancy seeing Beryl and Sibyl on the stage ! They've got to thank you for that, John, and that's what I keep telling them."

"There's not much to thank me for, Lily. The girls have their own talents," John sought to by-pass the embarrassments. "There's one thing first, Lily . . . We've not much more than an hour before the show starts, and I'll have to get away immediately for the last bus . . . I just wanted to have a quick word with you about Cha. There's a lot of wee things about his kit and so on we've got to get fixed."

"And isn't it wonderful about our Cha ! That's you again, John. Where we would have been without you I can't think, upon my soul."

"Yes, yes ! But now we've got to get the boy safely on the road. I don't know what Ballingalls will do about his kit allowance, but Cha's got a long way to go to India and there'll be a good many expenses, so I'm going to give him as my present just what I always planned to give all the young folk in the family to help them on ; I'm going to give him a hundred pounds, and I want him to have the handling of it. The first thing a young chap going East has to learn is how to use money sensibly."

"John ! A hundred pounds ! It's too much."

"It isn't," said John curtly and with a wry, brief smile. "Now that's settled, and not another word, Lily. About the Twins, now . . ."

But he had to listen to Lily's expressions of thanks, and they were so sincere he could almost forgive the loudness of them that caused elderly heads and gold-rimmed spectacles to be turned towards their corner with owlish looks in which disapproval and curiosity were comically mingled. He wondered for an unhappy moment if he was not himself an old fraud : an old hypocrite accepting gratitude and praise for what was but a paying-off of Charles, a squaring of his last account with Lily and her children.

The awkward passage was happily ended by the appearance of the Twins, with Cha and a short man John took to be this Ben Chorley fellow who, Lily had told him, was to join them at the high-tea table.

He was truly pleased to see Lily's two tall girls again, striking in identical summer dresses of a boldly-striped material, and he observed with sympathy the bright eyes and nervously exaggerated gestures of most young females who chance to take, however fleetingly, the fickle limelight of prominence. Somewhere in the background of the group, as John saw it, was our Cha with his wholly personal air of aloofness, uneasiness, sophistication, vaguely good intentions and mystery in the modern blend beyond John's comprehension. Beside this complicated product of the new civilisation the personality of Mr. Ben Chorley had a pleasing solidity.

He was so obviously, as he kept repeating, nowt but an old trouper and showman. His broad comedian's face was pink, and above this a thin thatch of sandy hair helped to create the illusion of a solid, jannock geniality. He puzzled John by speaking much in puns and quick turns of phrase—which he himself lumped under the heading of " gags "—and John noted that, while the broad and apparently jolly face could grimace elastically and send Lily and her children off into spasms of adoring laughter, the steadiness of the small, black eyes in the man's face, like the eyes of the cruel and pugnacious robin redbreast, belied the wrinkles of mirth about them. There was no smile at all in Mr. Chorley's eyes, no mercy for any save himself.

" Well, now that we all know each other," Lily at length commanded the gathering gladly, confident in a pride not unreasonable in her own scheme of things, " we'd better go in to tea. I booked a nice table near the window."

" Aye," agreed Ben Chorley, " I could do with some grub after that rehearsal. Come on, girls ! " he archly commanded the Twins. " Lead me into the took-in I mean, took me into the . . . Ah, but where's me manners ? You're too young to know what it means to be tooked in, nice and cosy."

He raised his elbows invitingly, and the Twins each seized one with cries of joy ; and so, the grey faces and the gold-rimmed spectacles following them to the door, the party left the drawing-room with something of the rough gaiety of a students' revel or a Scandinavian bridal procession.

There was no lingering over the meal. Mr. Chorley was a trencherman of parts ; a large plate of fish and chips disappeared quickly into his mouth, washed down with several cups of tea, while he still maintained the flow of gags that, as John came slowly to perceive, was part and parcel of his professional equipment. The Twins also ate quickly, fidgeting the while and eyeing each other in their secret mutual confession of nervousness. (It must be queer to be a twin, thought John for the first

time in his life.) All Lily's exuberance and passion to make
it a gay feast could not save it from being a scrambled, nervous
affair.

" Got to get back and see those chaps haven't made a moock
of the lighting," Mr. Chorley said frequently, turning over his
left wrist to look at the face of a highly ornamental watch. " And
these girls have got to get their make-oop on. I'll make oop to
them, Ma," he assured Lily to her intense delight, " by making
them oop myself. Ready, chickabiddies ? "

John took the opportunity of following Mr. Chorley to the
toilet. As they bent together over the wash-basins he asked what
he hoped would seem a casual question.

" What do you think of the chances of these two girls, Mr.
Chorley ? "

The lad from Lancashire, the wary survivor of many a battle of
wits, was not to be deceived by John's device. He raised the hard,
small eyes from his wet hands and with the latter made certain
cabalistic signs.

" On the level, choom ? "

" On the level."

" Then I'll tell thee, lad," said this strange person with an
almost Elizabethan simplicity. " They'll do—they'll do well
enough in the Number Two 'alls and that. But if you was
thinkin' of the top o' the bill at the Palladium or a big date with
Moss's Empires, forget it."

" Anything for them on the concert platform ? "

" Choom, the concert platform's lousy with better pianists
than these two girls will ever be," said Mr. Chorley earnestly,
rubbing his pink face with the damp towel. " It's the small 'alls
or nothing. What they want is to work up a proper act—a bit o'
comedy patter, fancy lightin' effects, or goin' on as the Manchurian Mystery Musicians or summat. They'll be all right,
laad, but they'll never be the top o' the bill ; and that's the dope
on the level."

" Thank you, Mr. Chorley. That's exactly what I wanted to
know."

" Welcome, Uncle. Now I'll skeddadle and see about them
roody lights. Come round after the show."

John waited in the hotel with Lily and Cha, oppressed by the
thought that the former's brittle high spirits were based on such

shaky assumptions. The Scots engineer was unhappy. It was instinctive in him to understand that for a job worth doing there should be careful, patient preparation ; and now he had to believe that the Twins were indifferently prepared for an obscure career. It did not comfort him to realise that this was what he had feared would happen ; it could not relieve him to say to himself that, if Lily must rush her girls into the prominence she coveted for them, the responsibility was hers. He had upon his own spirit the sense of a personal failure, of a cherished and benevolent plan failing to mature through some fault in himself. Something of the fabric of his own life was shaken by the false start he feared the Twins were making.

The Brydens were waiting in the vestibule of the theatre. The meeting between the two branches of the clan was awkward, even Lily's proud excitement giving place for a moment to her feelings towards this other woman who had such stronger claims on John than she. For a lengthened moment the six assorted men and women stood in a condition of near-paralysis, all caught up in the social awkwardness of people not used to anything but plain speaking, not tutored in the art of polite falsity.

"Let's go in, then," said John irritably. "You and Cha are up in the balcony, aren't you, Lily ? We're downstairs, row D. We'll see you later."

He tried to force his mind into the mood for gala, but he found everything conspiring to thrust upon him a sad sense of the shabby third-rate about the proceedings—the garish little seaside theatre in lath and plaster, the crude local advertisements on the screen, the scrapings of a seven-piece orchestra, and the crowd of chattering holiday-makers about him : carefree, uncritical, greedy and noisy with their caramels and bananas, indifferent to the howling of an occasional infant in arms. When the performance started he wistfully remembered the sad little concert parties of English artists who would turn up to wander precariously round the European settlements of the China Coast and the Straits.

How sad they were, how cheap their degraded women, letting down the Flag wherever they went, but that under the ardent patronage of the sex-starved men who lived by Empire ! Take almost any woman out East and she became a tart of some sort ; her body commanded the price of rubies. What with that and

inevitable miscegenation, thought John as the leading comedian
sang a dirty little song about the joys of mixed bathing, the world
of conquest and development and wealth he had known in the
great days was sick of what you could almost call an occupational
disease.

He was startled out of his morose reflections by a quite
singularly filthy *double entendre* in the comedian's patter that raised
a roar from the women in the cheap seats and a nervous titter from
the stalls. A sideways glance at his own party told him that only
Davie was amused, and he wished that he had Davie's simplicity
of enjoyment. It was a relief to see the funny man disappear, to
be replaced by an abundant contralto whose repertoire included
My Ain Folk. To the emetic strains of this ballad John turned an
ear as receptive as Davie's and was awkwardly aware, when the
curtain fell again and the number 5 appeared in the frame, that
his eyes were wet.

"This is the Twins," said Addie, taut with private concern
by his side.

From opposite sides they swept on to the platform with the
aplomb of amazons, dwarfing the audience's memory of the smutty
small comedian. Their mere height and similarity roused that
primitive audience to a welcoming storm of clapping and cheers.
They had been provided now with two baby grand pianos, so
arranged side-by-side that the girls faced each other and, each
half-turning on her stool, also appeared to be confiding in the
spectators. They ostentatiously dropped their bangles on their
instruments ; and each pulled a ring off the engagement finger.
The four hands hung high above the keyboards for a moment
and then fell in a crashing, precise chord.

John almost lost himself again in admiration and pleasure.
The Twins had chosen, or been told, to open with a medley of
those old popular songs that by some mystery of melodic appeal
survive their season, even their generation, and take on the
immemorial character of folksong. He did not ask himself what
special magic resided in the swinging air of *A Bicycle Built for Two*
or in the subtler phrases of *The Lily of Laguna*. He only knew it
was pleasant to hear them, and he innocently admired the garish
little flourishes and the tricks of false emphasis Lily's girls had been
taught to put into their renderings. There would not leave him,
however, his feeling of pity for those two young women who were

chasing after false gods, a fond and foolish mother at their backs, and were looking for sparkling success in the near-slums of their profession. The billowing of the backcloth to the draughts set up by the rising night wind without spoke to John of vagrancy and the makeshift.

It seemed to him that the applause which swept towards the Twins as they took their final bow was voluminous. He was amused and touched to see Davie Bryden, enthusiastic, sentimental and loyal, almost on his feet, shouting " 'Core ! 'Core ! 'Core ! " and then turning his fine face as if to ask Beth and Addie to share his delight ; and Addie, to be sure, was clapping vigorously.

But the applause died away, as applause must always do, and shortly the audience was absorbed in a sketch by all the remaining members of the company ; and John bleakly knew that the Rolland Rhythmic Twins had competently and fairly given about twopence-in-the-shilling's worth of value to a friendly, careless audience of holidaymakers : that and no more. Only in the private records of one or two unimportant people had history been written that night.

The lamentable orchestra of cynics in dirty white shirts was scraping its way through the first few bars of the National Anthem when Ben Chorley appeared in the gangway at the end of row D where John was gathering his gear. Professional exuberance lapped the impresario in a miasma of self-contentment as false as the lighting scheme that had played on his puppets. The pinkness of the carnation in the lapel of his dinner jacket was matched by the smooth pinkness of his face. The beady eyes, however, were still unsmiling.

" Come round behind and see the girls," he invited the company. " They went over big, didn't they ? "

John turned to the Brydens and said curtly :

" I'll see you outside in five minutes."

He wondered afterwards precisely why he had debarred the Brydens from this unusual experience : especially Davie, whom it would have surely enchanted. At the same time, he felt that his instinct had been sound. There were squalor and falsity behind those scenes : stinks of cosmetics, a congestion of vulgar people, including the comedian, racing along narrow corridors, bare red bricks and draughts.

He found the Twins, with Lily and Cha, in a tiny dressing-room tiled white like a police cell or a public lavatory.

" Well done, girls ! " he contrived to congratulate them heartily. " Well done, Beryl ! Well done, Sibyl ! " And he shook hands with both.

" I do think they did awfully well ! " cried Lily, really appealing to the patron.

" Walked away with the show, if you ask me," said Cha more professionally.

John then found himself in the physical grip of the Twins. Their four long muscular arms were about his neck, and he caught through his condition of near-strangulation their ecstatic yelps of gratitude for their brilliant introduction to glory.

" O, Uncle John, thanks a million ! . . . We couldn't ever have made it if it hadn't been for you ! . . . Was it you sent us up those bunches of roses ? I'm sure it was. Don't try to kid me ! . . . It's an awful pity you can't wait for the second house."

John was glad to escape and rejoin the quiet Brydens. As he settled down in the bus beside Addie they heard him say with feeling :

" Well, that's that."

It was bliss to be back in the sacred, protected peace of Penang Lodge and its garden. The night held fine and warm and calm, and even between nine and ten the light was clear and strong with a golden radiance that would not indeed wholly die out of the summer sky all night. Davie eagerly proposed to Addie that they should go climbing the hill behind and chase the sunset across the peaks to the North and West ; and off went father and daughter, lithe and tireless. Beth got herself a shawl and went out to the garden seat with her knitting. There she was joined by John after he had taken his ritual stroll among his plants and vegetables and noted their subtle progress since the morning.

" I'll go and get myself a dram and bring it out here with my pipe," he said, announcing a matter of importance within the recaptured scale of the quiet life, and turning indoors.

The lightness of the bottle in his hand interested him. He held it up to the light of the window and reflected that there had surely been a good deal more in it when he had last put it back. But perhaps Davie had quite rightly helped himself to a good jorum after his labours on the Dam, and he was not greatly interested. He went out of doors again, laid the glass gingerly on the seat, sat down beside his sister and set himself to the important business of filling his pipe.

" I wonder," he said at length, his mind unable to rid itself wholly of a doubt, " if Lily is wise to let the Twins go in for the sort of show business we saw over there," and the stem of his pipe pointed across the water to Doon.

" It's not what I would allow any girl of mine to do if I could stop it," said Beth, " but it's Lily's choice. I wouldn't try to interfere, if I were you, John. You gave them the chance ; what they make of it is their own affair."

" Perhaps you're right," grunted John, for he was now lighting his pipe.

He puffed calmly for a while, enjoying to the full the fragrance of an excellent tobacco. He sipped his grog and reflected again that Faill & Forfar put out a rare good tipple, and that it was a wonderful satisfaction to be able to afford these little luxuries in old age and have peace in which to enjoy them.

" It's a beautiful evening," he remarked.

" A beautiful evening," Beth repeated. " This is my idea of a holiday and a rest. I'll be heart-sorry to go back to Garvel on Monday."

" You can wait till the Tuesday morning surely."

" Not me ! I must get my shopping done and the house aired properly before I get these men of mine back to their work." She hesitated a little. " There's one favour, John, I wanted to ask you."

" Favour ! " laughed John. " Fire ahead."

" Addie. She's had a hard winter at school, working for her Highers. She'll have a hard winter in the hospital. I'd like her to get a real rest—if you could keep her with you for a week or two more . . ."

" Keep Addie ? " her brother cried. " Nothing would please me more, Beth, nothing. Addie's my best girl, the best of the whole jing-bang, and I don't care who knows it. But do you think the lass would be happy with a couple of old sticks like Effie Templeton and me ? "

" She will. She's a queer, quiet girl, and she never says much, but I can tell you this, John," and she dropped into the sentimental doric of their childhood, " she's fell fond of her Uncle John."

" That's settled then. Grand. Splendid. We'll have a great time, the lass and I."

He was well content indeed. It satisfied a profound need of his spirit to think that his house was to have the grace of its daughter by all the rights of blood and sentiment. On her part, Beth was glad that the solution of her problem had been simple after all and so easily applied.

4

John tapped the barometer in the lobby of Penang Lodge and saw with satisfaction that it appeared to be steady, but he made a mental note at the same time to buy himself a barograph at some suitable opportunity. The little aneroid with the clock-face was a good wee job in its way, but in a fickle climate like that of West Scotland you wanted something which would display in graphic form the subtlest fluctuations of atmospheric pressure.

His anxiety in this matter came of a wholly masculine, even boyish, passion to know if it would be reasonably safe that evening of August to go fishing off the Brunts with old Sam Lightbody in the *Golden Girl*. It was more than a week now since they had dared to risk more than an afternoon turn round the loch in one of the few bright breaks in a long spell of wet and stormy weather. Since mid-July the expanses of the Firth and the mountain ramparts about it had been almost continuously shrouded in mist and drenched in rain and, in the absence of mist, lashed by half-gales from the South-West.

John felt the effects of this visitation in both his body and his mind. For the first time in his life he had become conscious of the incessant dampness of sheets and hangings, even in his own well-heated house—" It's that hill just behind us," said Addie in her impatient way—and of muscular twinges and crepitations in his own person.

More than that, much more, a spirit accustomed to the long sunshine of the East was depressed by this incessant dripping and blowing and lowering among the hills of home. A chap wanted to let out a shout of protest that would split the pall of

cloud and let the sunlight through. The fallible man—John
Rolland Cram, late Superintendent Engineer of the K. & S., and
accustomed to have his own way—grieved that his first summer at
home was being stolen from him, day by day and even week by
week, at the instance of these damned depressions from the
Atlantic the announcer chap on the wireless kept talking about
in his smooth voice.

On this particular day, in the morning, the pall had promised
to lift a little. The solidity of the cloud-mass over the Firth was
broken. There still straggled along the hillsides, obscuring their
bold peaks, those trailing scarves of what the romantic English
tourists loved to call " Scotch Mist " ; and what they could see
in it to rejoice in Mr. Cram would have liked to know. But
behind these flocculent streamers there gleamed now and again
a shaft of authentic sunlight, strangely lighting up in its natural
greens and bronzes a segment of mountainside. The Piermaster,
being gravely consulted about noon, had allowed : " She'll mebbe
be lifting a bit, but I wouldn't like to be sure," and that, from a
Highland piermaster, was an expression of optimism.

Having tapped the barometer and found it steady, therefore,
John went out of his house and round the gable to call in a loud
voice :

" Sam ! Are you never finished yet ? It's about time for tea."

" I'm near through," returned the wheezing voice from the
back of the house.

" Well, hurry up ! I think we could have a try at the fishing
to-night. The glass is steady."

" Good enough," came the distant voice.

John chuckled, thinking again how that silly Dam of theirs
fascinated Sam and Davie Bryden equally. It had never meant
much to himself, but these two good lads just couldn't let it be—
as if they were desperate to present him with a decoration of his
garden.

Old Sam, of course, had had holes to pick in Davie's final
scheme ; that was not as he would himself have finished the job.
Now the Lammas rains had given him the opportunity of
demonstrating beyond any discussion that, while Davie had
undoubtedly meant well and laboured hard, his conception was
faulty. With a good deal of justice on his side Sam pointed out
that Davie's device of a perforated sheet of metal to screen the

outlet of the Dam would not serve in a flood ; it was already cluttered with stuff brought down from the hill. He had therefore gone out in a drizzle during the afternoon to clear the obstruction and reconstruct the outlet according to his own nice ideas of engineering propriety.

John went indoors to the Big Room and casually put out a bottle, glasses and a carafe of water. The old chap would need a dram after his exercise and as a proper sharpener of the appetite for the meal—ham and egg it smelt like—now cooking in the back premises. Then it occurred to him that Sam was taking a long time, and John was always a stickler for ritual and promptitude. He went out on the gravelled terrace and again shouted round the gable of the house, but there was no reply.

He hurried round to the back and saw his friend seated on the edge of the Dam, almost crouching with his head in his hands.

" Sam ! In God's name ! "

The old man dizzily raised a grey face to smile to his friend, but bleakly.

" A wee bit of a turn, John. Mebbe I was bendin' overmuch for my build. Kind o' short o' breath, like. A bit giddy . . . It's here."

He laid his hand protectively over his left breast. John put his arm firmly round the great body and helped Sam to his feet.

" Try and walk into the house," he urged. " That's the boy. Take it easy. Canny, Sam, canny ! You're going fine. What you want's a drop of spirits."

When he had steered his friend's slow walk to a seat in an armchair in the Big Room John darted to the sideboard and seized a bottle of brandy.

" Take that, Sam," he urged. " My, but you're a damned old fool to be bashing yourself to bits out there, at your age ! I'm just about fed up with you and Davie Bryden and your Dam."

He watched Sam's recovery with a curiously detached interest, as of one who studies the calculable effect of one chemical upon another in the test-tube. The big, confident man recovered his physical balance palpably at the touch of the liquor on his metabolism and, with it, regained his spiritual aplomb.

" That's that," he announced at length. " That's me as right's rain, now. It's a rare drop of brandy, that—none o' your grocer's muck, but the real thing. I think, John," he announced with clinical gravity, " it was mebbe just the wind. That's the curse with big fat chaps like me—fair fu' o' wind till you're ashamed to go inty another body's house for fear it comes back on ye when ye're no' expecting it. Me bendin' at the job back there—that would force the wind inty the heart like. I'm fine now, though."

" Perhaps you are, Sam," said John dubiously, " but I think you should take it easy for a bit. We'll leave the fishing till to-morrow."

" Nonsense, man, nonsense ! D'ye think I'd miss a night's fishing for a bit rift o' the wind ? Nonsense ! "

Effie Templeton put her head round the edge of the door to announce that their meal was on the table.

" Aye, and I'm ready for it," said big Sam defiantly.

He ate heartily as usual, and John forgot the little alarm, while Sam embroidered the theme of the Dam, making it clear once more that while Davie Bryden was a first-class tradesman and a real worker—witness the excellence of his labour on the concrete parapet—he had failed to touch absolute perfection in his arrangement of the outlet. It was not quite good enough, Sam suggested, to take a sheet of zinc and punch it full of holes ; one who had thoroughly studied the hydraulic possibilities of the stream running down from the hill would have quickly perceived the limitations of this device and substituted such a length of stout wire netting as he, Mr. Lightbody, had just been at some pains to instal. John agreed that Sam was probably about right there ; the thing was to maintain the flow through the Dam, especially since there was no sluice arrangement at the infall ; and Sam declared that, if he was spared, he'd get a sluice put in quick enough.

Little more than an hour later the *Golden Girl* was at anchor over the bank behind the Brunts and the friends were absorbed in the quiet joys of fishing for whiting, with an occasional wry-mouthed flounder for luck. John's absorption was not, however, complete.

There haunted the rearward chambers of his mind a feeling of truancy. There would not go from his memory the quizzing look in the Piermaster's grey eyes and his careless but dismissive phrase as they set off : " O, you can risk it if it's your will, but don't blame me if it blows up a snorter from the sou'-west." So he could not keep his eye from the sky and its weather-signs, could not lose himself in the familiar feel of the line with the drag of the tide vibrating through it.

The ceiling of cloud was still low over the estuary, but there was an opening all round and under its edges, so to speak, and through this there poured the hard, cold light that had encouraged him to take the risk of sailing. It was cold upon the water for the time of year, but he and his companion were well happed against it in oilskins and sweaters. What chiefly troubled John was the loneliness of the inland sea ; they were so alone upon it in their little boat, as if two ageing men must be foolhardier than all the longshoremen and the thousands of eager holidaymakers on the coasts about them. These shores seemed distant and desolate although seamarks much farther away by map or chart appeared ominously near at hand in the damp-laden atmosphere of the August evening.

The breezes came and went fitfully through the meteorological paralysis that hung over the sea. There was no steadiness of wind ; only a vicious, spasmodic arrowing of airs that came at the *Golden Girl* from a variety of acute angles around the fixed point of the constant South-West. One would bring a scud of rain, through which the nearest shore could be seen to be illuminated by a shaft of late sunlight ; another would bring off the top of the water that angry sheet of spindrift the prudent user of coastal waters regards with apprehension. One such came at them so roughly that the fishermen were constrained to turn their heads away from its fury and the *Golden Girl* swirled round her anchor like a foolish animal that has lost its head. When it had passed, John said :

" I think that's about enough, Sam. There's no fun in the fishing to-night."

" You're about right," Sam surprised him by agreeing. " It's my bed I could be doing with."

They wound in their lines and threw overside the mussels they had gathered from the pier at low tide for bait. Sam heaved himself up from the middle thwart and moved forward.

" I'll get the pick up if you'll swing the engine. She'll be cold. God knows," he added, shivering, " she's not the only one ! "

The *Golden Girl* was considerably down by the head while Sam in the bows hauled in the dripping cable and the weeded grapnel at the end of it, and John primed his engine amidships and breathed heavily over the starting-handle. The engine fired promptly enough, but spluttered.

" Get you back to the tiller," said Sam, " and I'll watch her. Cold—that's the trouble. Did ye remember the choke ? "

The engine laboured against its great difficulties of circulation and respiration, and then it stopped again on a cough and a sigh.

" I'll sort this bitch ! " cried Sam with rough venom. " Stay where ye are, John, and mind the helm."

The large, fat man stooped low to swing the handle. The engine roared into life again, as if cowed to obedience by a superior mind backed by relentless physical superiority. John cried :

" Throttle her back a bit, Sam, for the Lord's sake ! "

Then he saw the great body of his friend fall forward over the wooden box that covered the engine, lie there for a moment, wobbling, and then roll off to tumble on the floorboards beside it, the enormous head ludicrously twisted by its collision with the midships thwart. In the same moment, irrelevantly, he observed that the shell of the *Golden Girl*, untethered, was being carried by the tide towards the rocks.

" Sam ! " he shouted.

But Sam could only snore now, his mouth wide open and slack. Without thinking what he was doing, John peeled off his own oilskin and threw it over his friend. The collar covered Sam's face, but no matter. He knew that his business was to make for the shore as fast as might be. He left the engine to its racing and, with a roughness repugnant to his engineering scruples, threw in the clutch. Then he leapt aft to seize the tiller and bring the little boat round in a sharp turn that no more than saved her from having her port side ripped open on an outlying skerry.

When he had conned the boat round the Brunts and clear of danger for the time being he left the tiller and jumped forward to open the throttle to the full. He bent down and pulled the oilskin from his friend's face. The drooping moustache looked silly, somehow.

" Sam ! " he appealed again, without much hope.

There was no reply. There was not even a snore. Another squall came down on the small craft, with lashing rain and short waves that had the *Golden Girl* bouncing and slashing her stem into

short seas. John jumped back to the tiller and steered for the
pier at Killadam, on which there had suddenly appeared, an hour
at least before its due time, a steady green light.

The wind increased in force, and the sky lightened in the
West. This was the wind that came with a rising glass to sweep
away the mists, but John knew that it would come with strength,
driving great, grey-green seas up from the outer Firth. Coolly
mastering the nature of his dilemma, he saw that he might escape
the worst of it by steering close inshore and following the indenta-
tions of the loch round to shelter at Killadam, but his infinitely
greater concern was to get his friend ashore as soon as might be,
if Sam was indeed still within the range of human aid. So he
drove straight for the green light on the pier, knowing well that he
was taking risks with such a small and primitive craft in the steep,
rising seas that ever and again licked over the port bow. It was
terrible to see a cruel lash of salt water occasionally slash on the
oilskin that covered Sam Lightbody, their fall unnoticed by
whatsoever indifferent thing lay beneath it, but he must keep
driving on.

He was most oppressed by the sense of time, by the slowness
of the *Golden Girl* to force herself through the short seas. His ear
was alert to the beat of the engine, and for a moment or two
he thought proudly that if the little ship did succeed in crossing
the mouth of the loch that night she would have earned her own
patent of nobility and justified the good craftsmen who had
laboured to build and engine her.

For a space, again, his mind swung foolishly like a compass in
an unstable magnetic field and played verbal tricks with the name
of his friend . . . Sam Lightbody, but not by any means a light
body . . . How to lift it overside seemed a daunting problem ;
how to pack it into a coffin was a puzzle of the most grotesque
and fascinating character . . . He did not observe that he was
soaked by the flying spume ; he did not feel the cold that was
creeping into his body. The only thing was to hold the swinging
nose of the boat on the green light.

He came at length under the lee of the Strone to where the
water, though still disturbed, was unbroken by the rising wind,
and it surprised him that the *Golden Girl* now seemed to race over
those smoother seas. He saw that a little knot of men had gathered
on the beach by the pier and guessed that something of his plight

had been observed by the wary longshoremen who were his friends and mentors. A cable's length offshore he jumped forward and throttled the engine back, but the *Golden Girl* was still under power when he drove her aground at the feet of the waiting men. Four of them jumped forward and practically lifted the little boat out of the water even as he switched the engine off.

He became aware that the Piermaster was addressing him angrily.

" Where have you been on a night like this ? I was watching you through the glass. Could you not see the wind coming up ? Where's the old man ? "

Dumb under the scolding, John pointed. The Piermaster bent over the gunwale and lifted the oilskin from off Sam's face. He dropped it quickly and turned on the men with him.

" Away up the road as fast as you can and fetch the doctor, Roddie. Post, take you Mr. Cram up to the hotel and get him to a fire with a hot drink, then on to your bicycle and fetch Miss Addie from the Lodge. Come now, Mr. Cram."

John felt himself almost lifted out of the boat by immensely strong arms, and he swayed when his feet were on the shingle. In spite of the postman's firm hold on his body he felt that he could hardly master the slope of the beach in the half-light. He suddenly realised that he was old and feeble and foolish, especially foolish. It was this sense of childish guilt that held him silent even when they got him to the fire in the hotel kitchen and Captain J. Birnie Hoy had prepared a hot punch of rum, strong and odorous. He was just a foolish old man with a shaking hand and every shred of confidence gone out of him : so feeble now that the innkeeper's wife had to scold him into changing into dry socks and warm slippers at least.

He was scolded again when little Dr. Cameron at length arrived.

" What about old Sam ? " John contrived to ask, raising his head with an effort.

" Gone. Probably went out in a second or two. What on earth were you two old idiots up to ? "

He was an impatient little man with a small, comic face like a comedian's and, the gas of Loos still nagging at his lungs, impatient with those who defied the obvious rules of health.

" He was swinging the engine," reported John dully. " The

wind came up. I thought he had a bit of a turn this afternoon
. . . We shouldn't have gone out. I shouldn't have let him
go out."

" My holy stars ! " cried the doctor with a vehemence that
would have been comic in another setting. " When in Heaven's
name will chaps like you begin to understand that sixty years of
life is sixty years of wear and tear. Can't you get it into your heads,
dammit ! that stooping to swing an engine is about the heaviest
sort of strain you can put on the heart, especially in a flabby, big
man like poor old Mr. Lightbody ? Thank God we haven't got
any nosey coroners in Scotland ! "

From these heights of indignation he quickly dropped into
the tenderness of which they were only the defensive ramparts.

" Come on now, Mr. Cram, and keep the mind easy," he said,
patting John's shoulder. " I've got the car outside, and that
bonnie niece of yours is waiting for you. I want to see you into
your bed with something to make you sleep. Come, man ! "

He was being driven home. He was out of his own control.
He had been scolded, and he had indeed done very wrong to
take poor old Sam out fishing on such a night and after such a
clear warning. His Grannie would have called it a Judgment.
Addie by his side in the back seat of the doctor's car was silent.

" This is a terrible business, Addie," he said.

" That's a silly thing to say," immediately returned the voice
of the doctor at the wheel, but calmly. " The old man was
bound to go at any moment, anywhere. It might have been in his
bed ; it just happened to be in your boat. You did very well
getting her back through this storm. That's more than I could
have done."

John felt Addie's hand move silently to cover his and squeeze
it confidentially. That was much from Addie. If Addie was still
with him, there was something left of worth. The doctor also
seemed to be a sensible, kind man after all.

5

The people of Garvel bury their dead on a hill high above the
sea. Even from the upper streets of a town built on a series of
steep slopes the tall Victorian tombstones are seen to be uplifted
on a crest, making against a winter sunset such a solemn gothic
pattern as is liable to frighten children and haunt their dreams.

The cemetery itself has thus, however, a breezy, open air.
It takes every gleam of sunlight that breaks through the northern
skies, and even where conventional piety has planted yews and
other funereal shrubs, the spirit of grief does not linger. The place
has rather the atmosphere of an old garden, for it is joyously
bird-haunted ; and when John Rolland Cram stood in one of
its narrower paths to witness the burial of Sam Lightbody among
his obscure kindred, he thought sentimentally that this was
indeed a pleasant place to lie, for such as himself a prospect that
seemed to rob death a little of its terror.

The Co-operative Funeral Department had brought the
body of old Sam in style from his son's house in a motor-hearse,
followed by two gleaming Austin 20's, the latter containing the
ten male mourners who were all of Sam's relationship and
acquaintance that could be mustered. In spite of his grief and
the lingering symptoms of the shock he had suffered, John was
interested to study the new technique of burial in the 30's of the
Twentieth Century.

He remembered across the years the long processions of
silk-hatted men that used to follow on foot the hearse drawn by
shining Belgian stallions, and he was almost amused by the smooth
rapidity of the new procedure. It even seemed to him that the
minister was in no mood to waste time unduly over the committal
service, as if he feared that another August shower would come to
drench the party before they were safe again in the cars. He was
positively astonished when, the religious ceremony over, there was
no solemn shovelling of the earth on the coffin lid but, instead, a
sort of conjuring trick whereby evergreen branches were drawn
over the opening of the grave and a smooth official, with almost
the air of a theatrical manager, bowed to the party and said
" Thank you, gentlemen," as if they had just pulled off with his
collaboration a feat of some dexterity.

"I think the Co-p. made a nice job of old Father's funeral," murmured Alec Lightbody in John's ear, inviting his approbation.

"Very nice, Alec," John agreed. "Quiet and respectful."

"You'll come back to the house and have a cup of tea with Peg?"

"Thanks Alec, but no. Please give my best respects to Peg, but I think I'll just walk out the West gate and down the hill to the pier. I've half-an-hour before the boat."

Davie Bryden was at his elbow.

"I'll go with you, John," he suggested, and as they moved away after a formal shaking of hands with their fellow-mourners, added : "I want to have a word with you about something."

They passed out of the dell in which the Lightbody lair had been established for a century, holding now the bones of a galaxy of honest tradesmen and their wives and those numerous children who fell victim to the Victorian ignorance of elementary hygiene by dying in infancy. Their way to the West gate lay across a small plateau, pleasantly intersected by the wider avenues along which the more substantial citizens of Garvel had been more expensively buried and more elaborately memorialized in an array of white crosses, broken columns, dolorous angels and draped urns : some of the great, plain tombstones of the older familes looking, with their columns and rows of careful lettering and figures, like the documents of a half-forgotten civilization.

As they went along, John would pause here and there to recall a character or, with wistful particularity, to tell some family story out of the community's past which, a searing affair in its day, was now but a pathetic echo of human folly, faintly overheard in this plot where all were equal in the last silence.

His talkativeness contrasted with the unaccustomed glumness of David Bryden. John knew all the signs of uneasiness in his brother-in-law, and he thought little enough of this visitation, assuming it to come partly of the good man's racial respect for the very idea of death and for the formalities of sepulture. It was always best to leave Davie to blurt out at some surprising moment what was on his mind.

Thus they came to the small West gate that gives on a steep path running downhill to mingle with the residential streets of the upper town, and John paused there to consider the view of the anchorage that, in a burst of afternoon sunshine, was spread out under their feet, as it seemed.

"Aye, Davie!" he announced heavily. "It's a grand view; and I tell ye, man. I'll be glad to get home this night across that bit of water and see Addie and have a bit of peace for a change. When you think of it, man—that blackguard nearly blew the head off me down at Corsewellhill, and then I had that business with poor old Sam! You'd think," he appealed to his friend, "you'd think an old retired sort of chap like me might have been spared all that upset."

"You're about right, John," agreed Davie, but morosely.

"Ah, well! Let's get down the hill now."

John had not commented on his own misfortunes with either drama or self-pity. From that splendid viewpoint on the hilltop he had merely been moved to see the vagaries of one human lot, which happened to be his own, against its spacious physical background. The little fragments of barbituric solace which Dr. Cameron had given him to take regularly had smoothed most of the urgency out of his worries, and though wholly aware of the cause of his present calm, he was for the time being a curiously interested spectator of the scene in which he was a leading actor. He was almost amused to wonder what species of primitive worry burdened the simple soul of Davie Bryden.

They marched down the steep, tree-lined streets, past the villas and terraces in yellow sandstone : the suburban world drowsily moribund at this mid-hour of the summer afternoon ; and hardly a word was said. But when they came to the Marine Station and were walking along one of its airy platforms Davie surprisingly suggested that they should have a cup of tea, and in the buffet, over mugs of the wan fluid provided by the railway company through the hands of an insolently listless girl, he came to the point of his business.

Digging into a picket of the overcoat he wore out of respect for the dead, he produced a creased but bulky envelope and thrust it into John's hand.

"That's yours, John. And not a word, please. I'm ashamed."

"But what in Heaven's name, Davie——?"

John turned up the flap of the envelope and saw that it contained a wad of notes.

"That's the cash you lent me for Curly's training," explained

Davie in a tone of unwonted harshness. " Macluskie's packed up and bolted. We weren't going to see you out of pocket for that."

" Davie, Davie ! Do you need to——? " He was going to say ' insult me ' but pulled himself up with a harshness which matched that of his brother-in-law and said instead : " All right. I'd sooner you had shoved the rubbish into the fire. Now we'll forget about it. When are you and Beth coming across to see me again ? "

He was angry and sad at once, and when the little steamer pulled out from the pier he stood behind the paddle-box, looking at his native town in its sprawl over the foothills and wondered what sort of curse there was on money that made so many decent people go half-mad over its acquisition or its loss.

He perfectly understood why Davie had forced the packet back upon him. That was Beth and her prickly pride : Beth, who had raided her own savings and made her man do penance by returning the loan in person. These miserable notes would go back into a savings bank account in Curly's name. All that was simple enough ; but what held John fuming and sorrowful at the same time was the feeling that his sister's pride of money was as silly and sinful as—well, Lily's greed for it.

They had, all of them, a consciousness of money that (he suddenly realized) was beginning to weary him. He bitterly supposed they all had the notion that he was a rich man instead of an ordinary sort of chap who had gathered some decent savings and wished to give everybody a nice present by way of a share in his good fortune, and no silly wrangling and bickering and attitudinizing afterwards. He had come a long way to find peace, and it seemed to be eluding him, all because of this money business.

On her way across the Firth the steamer passed under the stern of a Holt liner ready to sail, the Blue Peter drooping from the foremast. The spectacle of the great ship interested John absolutely. He wondered again why the Holt's stuck to this oddly antique and highly individual design for their vessels—the long hull low in the water, the slanting bow, and the high, straight funnel with the relatively fat exhaust-pipe at a distinct interval behind it. There must be some idea behind it all ; the Holt's had known their business in the East for many a long day.

She would be sailing, this one, for Liverpool for another load and perhaps a small complement of deck passengers, and then, drumming along at a steady fourteen or thereabouts, through the Med. and the Canal, through the torment of the Red Sea, across the Indian Ocean and, still sturdy and purposeful, make her landfalls where the multi-eaved temples and the green-bronze roofs of the pagodas stood above low-lying coasts far away.

6

Miss Adelaide Bryden regularly performed her ablutions according to a ritual all her own. Even when she was a little girl not all her mother's impatience nor the satirical laughter of her father and brother could move her to abandon the system of washing that was a completely spontaneous expression of her temperament, even if it was of a fastidiousness beyond the ordinary.

She was not one to wash face, neck and ears in a frenzied mass-attack with soap and water. It was her custom to set about her upper parts with something of the deliberation of the cat. Thus she would first wash the mask of her face to a line below chin and jawbone and then dry it with a funny little dabbing, as distinct from a sweeping movement of the towel. That done, she turned to her ears, using sponge or face-cloth with precision lest the ends of her glowing hair be wetted and thus bedraggled. The ears dried by dexterous twirlings of towelling over her forefinger, Addie turned to her neck, shoulders and bosom, now using on the wider expanses of the torso a relatively free technique.

She had always been an odd girl about this sort of thing, to the extent that she had saved as a schoolgirl to buy herself a toilet case in leather, oilskin-lined, to hold the bits and pieces of cleansing material she felt herself to require. At an early age she had decided that only Knight's Castile Soap had the right properties of plain goodness to satisfy her, and not all the stringencies of working-class economy nor the proffering by retailers of more widely advertised and more highly scented solvents could shake her from that allegiance. More than once her patient and fond father, denied the use of the bathroom while Addie occupied it beyond the normal term, would cry :

" Lord, lass ! Ye're shaping to be a right old maid."

"Just you wait and see," was the girl's invariable response.

Her strength of inner balance was never to be broken down ; and now, as she stood in her dressing-gown in the bathroom at Penang Lodge and heard the angry turning of the door-handle, she called up that reserve : all the more promptly since the attack on her privacy was not unexpected.

"Are you never finished in there ? " demanded the irritable voice of Effie Templeton.

"No, I've hardly started, and I've still to take my bath," Addie replied distantly.

"If you've been in there a minute, you've been an hour," snapped the voice outside, then it dwindled away in a grumble. "Always washing, tittivating, and never a hand's turn of work. If I had my way in this house . . ."

It was about four o'clock of a late August afternoon. The day had been windless and heavy with a moist heat, and Addie, her head throbbing to the thunder in the air, had characteristically decided that she would escape the oppression with a wash, a bath and a complete change of garments, and then have a walk along the shore road to meet Uncle John off the evening boat. So she remained coolly in possession of the bathroom, her title to it secure. She had heard the housekeeper use it according to fixed custom after the midday meal, when she changed from her working clothes into the good black dress of afternoon formality ; this was not the woman's night out. She was only making trouble in Uncle John's absence, as she had been trying to do ever since he went away after breakfast. It was necessary, as Addie saw it, to remain apart and assert, calmly, her right to use the bathroom as she pleased, as the daughter adopted of the house. She knew that Effie Templeton had been drinking.

There was thunder in the air indeed : the thunder that had been gathering for weeks between two women under the same roof : one the favourite of the master of the house, the other thwarted by being a servant, correctly if generously treated.

Enjoying her bath, considering her pink toes emergent from the flood at the other end under the taps, Addie thought deeply of the complex responsibility that had been put upon her by her mother. She understood perfectly why she had been left behind to stay with Uncle John, and in fact accepted it as a perfectly natural duty. She was of the skilled working folk whose women take it for granted that most men are credulous and compromising, and that the maintenance of decency and dignity is a part of the housekeeping duties. What troubled her was that the state of affairs behind the white walls of Penang Lodge was more sordidly complex than even her mother had guessed.

She could have gone to her mother with the whole story, and her mother would have stepped in to help her. She could have taken one way of the female and made a scene with Uncle John, demanding with sobs and cries that he choose between her and Effie Templeton, since they could not live under the same roof together. But Beth's daughter had no inclination towards either course. It was simply her own problem. Her task, as it was her will of sentiment, was to stand between Uncle John and the sordid, petty factions, which in his simplicity he did not know to exist, in the small world he had built for himself round Penang Lodge.

As she slipped her best silk vest over her glowing body Addie worried about that particular point. Herself reticent but watchful, she had seen him irritated of late when he should have been calmly happy in his possession of a house of his own by the sea. She knew, with a subtlety more acute than her mother's, that the affair of the Rolland Twins had deeply disappointed, as it had ruefully annoyed him. She had had the best of reasons to realize how, the doctor's little tablets notwithstanding, the death of Sam Lightbody had induced in him a haunting sense of guilt, foolish but real, beyond his grief for the loss of a friend. If she was too young to know what it is in age to fear death and the loss of the world's brightness, she was sufficiently frightened by the change in Uncle John and his new habit of staying up late in the Big Room alone, to watch with early morning intentness the level of the whisky bottle. This very day he had departed for Garvel—and perhaps Glasgow, he said—on a sudden impulse, as it seemed, and without the usual ponderous warnings of his longer adventures.

That was largely why she deliberately lingered in the bathroom, holding Effie Templeton at arm's length, as it were, while she thought out a line of action in the crisis she felt impending as certainly as the thunder in the air. All day she had known by instinct that the housekeeper, inflamed in the mind by jealousy and drink, was spoiling for a fight; she had this day realized in certain brief, sharp clashes that Effie Templeton had come to know that her own secrets, such as could be hidden from a man like John Rolland Cram, were in the possession of the girl in the house.

It was a sordid load of knowledge Addie carried at eighteen. From the first she had guessed, wildly and unhappily, at the stories nailed by the curious and feeble on the gate of Penang Lodge : gathering her impressions from arch, sly things said to her by people about the pier and in the few small shops ; from the subtle-sly Highland jokes in the cruel vein of a defeated people ; even once, horribly, from the catcalls of children who followed her along the road. If they thought, however—or rather, wanted to think—that her Uncle John lived in sin with his housekeeper, then she knew it was not true and the gossips were only fools, almost pitiful in the emptiness of lives that must have this colouring of lies to make it interesting. She could have wept for the cruel unfairness of it all, but the sense of Beth Bryden in her held her steady in the belief that it would all die down and be forgotten.

But there came the day, less than a fortnight past, when the District Nurse opened her mouth in a flood of self-righteous confidence and thrust the bewildered girl into a mess of com-plexities that puzzled and frightened her.

Addie had sought the acquaintance of Nurse Chrystal, who was a fresh-complexioned, vigorous and able person in the mid-thirties. The older woman had, on her part, been much flattered by the approaches of the young lady from Penang Lodge and by her own position of adviser to a girl about to enter her profession. She lived by herself in a tiny white cottage of one room and kitchen ; and though her long day's work was with sickness and poverty, with the curt imperatives of birth and death, she was still a lonely woman who, though thus intimately and even bitterly acquainted with the interplay of human passions among others, had no passionate satisfaction for herself as an individual. It was nice—as she phrased it to herself—to go walking of an evening with Miss Bryden, telling her stories of her own pro-bationer days under a legendary Matron and of her doings among the wives and children of the shepherd-folk in the glens behind the Strone. It was a really wonderful afternoon when she had been to tea at Penang Lodge and Miss Bryden's Uncle John had been the soul of courtesy and hospitality and had shown himself most interested in her work, asking questions and saying that he must give a good subscription to the Fund. He even went so far as to suggest that the District Nurse ought to have a car instead of a bike and hinted that he might get something started in that direction.

" I'd never believe a single word they say about such a nice old gentleman ! " Nurse Chrystal was heard to declare more than once thereafter.

That was really the beginning of it, thought Addie miserably as she started to do up her hair. Too many women of the lonely kind went too fast in their enthusiasms and their wonderful new-found friendships, spilling the privacies about the place in a fashion that embarrassed the reticence of Beth Bryden's daughter. Addie had felt awkward when, within only a few days of their first meeting, Nurse Chrystal had suggested the confidence of Christian names, confessing that she was known in her own home as Mousie, sort of short for Margaret. Soon after the wonderful visit to Penang Lodge—and it was, in fact, the first time the poor woman had been invited into a private house of standing in the parish— there burst upon Addie the storm of belligerent confidence that had held her alarmed and bewildered ever since.

" I was never one for gossip," the District Nurse announced stoutly, as if somebody had just accused her of the weakness. " I wouldn't listen to a single word the people in this place say about each other. The spitefulness, Addie, you wouldn't believe ! But when I think of some of the things they're saying about your Uncle John . . ."

It puzzled the girl that this should be put upon her in the name of friendship. She had been familiar all her life in the tenement houses of Garvel with the virtuous scandalmonger, but now she wondered what strange blindness to the delicacy of all female relationships should move this otherwise sensible woman to tell her so much that must wound. Charitably, and shrewdly, she put it down to loneliness, to the oddly-named Mousie's pitiful claim to knowledge and power.

Frightful, distorted, sneaking garbage it was, but the Minister's sister whispered it at the Guild, according to the District Nurse, and every man who used the hotel bar took the tale back to his wife. The scandalous relationship between her Uncle John and Effie Templeton was only a theme with infinite variations. There was a story of orgies of drinking in Penang Lodge. The circumstances of old Sam Lightbody's death were well remembered and darkly debated. There was the report, apparently well-founded, that Effie Templeton frequented the hotel and drank furtively, placing herself thus in the power of Captain J. Birnie Hoy and telling him in her alcoholic confidences of hectic ongoings in which she herself figured romantically.

As it seemed to Addie, this woman was the prime source of the poison, treacherous through and through ; an evil creature who had spun about the innocent person of Uncle John an indestructible web of scandal.

She left the bathroom and crossed the landing softly in her bedroom slippers, all her senses taut to avoid the clash with the housekeeper which must come sooner or later, but for which she was not yet ready. In her own room, sitting at the dressing-table, she tried again to understand the sort of woman she believed Effie Templeton to be but could not get beyond her youthful hatred and contempt and fear.

Perhaps she was too young, she was certainly too loyal to have any conception of the tortuous complications an ageing woman, both weak and unfortunate, can bring into her own life and that of those about her. Being herself strong to the point of asceticism, Addie—if it could have been explained to her—might still have dismissed as unimportant in terms of a woman's self-respect the long strain of a mistaken marriage and lonely widowhood on a poor mountainy farm. She could not know the dark power of the claim on John Rolland Cram this woman's secret soul believed her to possess.

Wearing a light raincoat over her summer frock, Addie at length moved quickly down the stairs and out through the front door. It was heavily on her mind that she must get to her Uncle John's side as soon as possible and stand by him : if possible, stand between him and shock.

This sense of crisis would not leave her. The tense heaviness of the afternoon air was no more than an appropriate condition, as if nature nicely adjusted itself to an isolated domestic mood. The Firth was grey and motionless. Across the main estuary the tower of the Riccar Light was distinctly white against a smear of remote land. The dip of the *Duchess of Buccleuch's* paddles, audible while they were still a league away, had a metallic ring, as if they were turning in an enclosed and hollow chamber. The tides slapped on the beach with a sort of indolent disdain.

When he came down the gangway Addie knew at once that her Uncle John was preoccupied, if not in a bad temper. Exquisitely sensitive to moods like any fond woman, she caught in his greeting and in his casual question as to how she had spent the day the overtones of aloofness. Her heart sank at that, and she unhappily wondered how, if trouble must come upon them, she could fight with him on a right basis of unity. He was thinking. He was even beyond his wonted concern for the contentment of those he loved. As they marched along the shore road he broke the silence between them only once, asking :

" When exactly is it you go into the hospital, Addie ? "

" September twentieth."

" Not much more than three weeks. We'll have to be thinking about our arrangements. Perhaps we'll close the house. However, we'll see."

The implication that he was already approaching conclusions, on what grounds she had no means of guessing, was only another trouble for Addie. Now she feared more than ever that some explosion on the part of Effie Templeton would bring the storm upon their little group. As they approached Penang Lodge she became all the more oppressed in spirit, all the warier in outlook. She made one dispirited effort to engage her companion in talk.

" Did you see my mother and father to-day ? " she asked.

" No." The reply seemed abrupt and final, but shortly he relented. " No, I hadn't the time, dear. The fact is," he added bitterly, " I had to spend my time and temper sorting out a mess in another branch of our precious family."

It was still all very confusing and alarming for Addie, but she breathed a little more freely when, entering the house, she smelt the good smells of cooking from the kitchen and knew that Effie Templeton was keeping to the domestic programme. When her Uncle John went upstairs to wash she slipped to the sideboard in the Big Room and, hating the necessity to spy, saw that the whisky bottle at least had not apparently been touched since she had gone up to her bath two hours before.

Uncle John greeted the housekeeper kindly when she served the evening meal in the little dining-room. He seemed to have relaxed a little, Addie felt hopefully. He asked her again what she had been doing through the day and suggested in a vague sort of way that they might go round to the Pictures in Doon one of these evenings. Ah ! thought Addie bitterly, only three weeks ago it would have been a night's fishing in the *Golden Girl* or a picnic up Finlas way on a fine afternoon. But Uncle John had left the motor-boat on the beach with the body of old Sam Lightbody inside it, and the Piermaster had towed it out to its moorings, where now it lay forlorn.

"Is this Mrs. Rolland's night out ? " her uncle suddenly surprised her.

"No."

"Well, tell her to go out if she wants to. I'd like it quiet in the house to-night," he explained in a distant sort of way. "I've a lot of letters to write. I'm going up to my own room, and then I think I'll get to bed early."

"Very well, Uncle John."

Thus he wrapped himself in a troubled mystery from the view of his niece, and she wished that he would release himself and her from tension in a burst of confidence, however forthright. But he left her with a faint smile of apology and went upstairs, and she went dutifully to the kitchen and, her hand trembling on the door-knob, looked in to where Effie Templeton was busy about the stove.

"We're finished in the dining-room, Mrs. Rolland," said Addie as calmly as she could contrive. "My uncle is tired and is going to bed early. He said that you might like to go out for the evening. There's nothing more we'll need."

"Nothing more ! Nothing more ! " Effie Templeton repeated in a sullen mutter, as if she were addressing herself on the topic of a monstrous intrusion on her personal dignity. " ' Nothing more we'll need.' " She turned to the door to snarl : "There's dam' all more ye'll get ! "

Then a frying pan was smacked on the top of the patent stove with emphasis.

It seemed to Addie all very hopeless. She wandered out of the house, down the path and across the shore road to the beach. The tide was full, and, propping her body against a boulder, she considered with morbid interest the play among the stones of the salt water which, unruffled by the faintest breath of wind, nevertheless moved with mysterious dynamic force among the stones, its surface mottled with blobs of sand and clots of obscure marine life.

She concluded that she had never been more unhappy in all her life. She was a female, only eighteen years old, and she cried a little to herself for fear and loneliness. The confession brought some relief, however, and by reflex action aroused the hard pride in her. Crying was the most useless thing. All her instincts and her training told her that there could be no running away from a battle. That was the last shame, even if the battle held no promise of glory whatsoever.

Nevertheless, she lingered on the shore like any forlorn mermaid until she heard the clatter of the Penang Lodge gate. At least that woman was going out, not waiting to make mischief. Addie heard the footsteps pass away in the direction of the pier, and then at length she stood up and made her way back to the house. It seemed that a very long, anxious empty evening lay before her, for she must be vigilant until the woman was home again and in her bed. She thought of the mending bag under the wireless cabinet in the Big Room.

She was startled to find her uncle there, standing by the sideboard, a bottle in his hand.

" Somebody's been at my whisky," he said.

" It certainly wasn't me," said Addie for want of something wiser to say.

" I know it wasn't you, my dear," laughed Uncle John emptily. " I suppose it's that confounded woman. I've been wondering lately . . ."

He appeared to be communing with himself, when suddenly he banged the bottle down on the sideboard and cried :

" Damnation ! Am I to be rooked right and left by my precious relatives ? "

He turned to Addie, his face dark with anger, and thrust into her hand a folded sheet of paper he had drawn from his jacket pocket.

" Just have a look at that," he said angrily, " and then, for God's sake, shove it into the fire ! "

He stumped out of the room, and Addie, trembling with fright and anxiety, unfolded the sheet. It was of business notepaper of the first quality, and it was headed in black embossed letters AMOY & SINGAPORE BANKING CORPORATION, Ltd.

" My dear John," the letter began, " unless there has been

some misunderstanding, I fear that what I have to tell you may cause you a good deal of concern, just as the circumstances have been extremely embarrassing to me personally . . ." and as she read on Addie was overwhelmed by anger, pity and shame in an engulfing wave. It was too much! They were all being false and cruel and selfish beyond belief. Poor, poor Uncle John!

When, automatically, she sat down to the mending ; for one must do something since there was nothing else to do ; she found herself sobbing, quietly but harshly and painfully, over the toe of a grey sock.

7

The letter, arriving with the morning post, had sent John Rolland Cram across the water in the forenoon boat. The honour and pride of the late Superintendent Engineer of the K. & S. had been wounded to the point of indignation : an emotion he had hoped to escape for ever in his decent retirement.

From the pier at Garvel he walked stoutly to the ironmonger's shop in the main street and threaded his way through a miraculous assortment of hardware to where, in a tiny cubicle at the back, attired for business in a black lustre jacket, Dan Rolland sat lugubriously over his account books. He welcomed John without much show of interest.

" Well, John. And what brings you over the water this day ? "

" Can you not guess, man ? " asked John impatiently. " Is there any word of that boy of yours, Charles ? "

" Our Cha ? He's at home. He's in his bed. He was taken kind of ill in London."

" Kind of ill ! But he didn't keep his appointment with Ballingall's."

" That's right, I suppose," Dan agreed, but apparently without any passion of interest. He scratched his hairy cheek. " To tell you the truth, John, I'm not right sure what did happen. You'd have to ask Lily."

The feebleness of the man, implying a fundamental indifference to what, for John, was the almost regal importance of an appointment with Ballingall's, sped the latter up the steep streets to the upper town, so that he arrived on the doorstep of "The Neuk" as short of breath as he was of temper.

He rang twice before Lily came to the door. He saw the trouble written on her face, but he was still too angry to think of sparing her.

"You know what I've come about," he said.

"Yes. You'd better come in."

She showed him into the dining-room with its stiff chairs and air of staleness. She waited for him to speak again.

"This is a serious business, Lily," he said, trying to be reasonable. "Your boy can't play fast and loose with a firm like Ballingall's, and I can't have my business reputation fooled about with and my friendships abused. Where is the boy now? Has he told you what happened?"

"But he fell ill, John," Lily tried to assert stoutly, but it was with a quaver. "He's in bed upstairs. I've had to get the doctor in. And," she added on a little scream, "I'm not going to let you or anybody else bully him."

"I don't want to see him. I don't want to see him again."

"You won't listen . . ."

"Because there's nothing to hear," John was relentless. "What's the good of trying to bluff me, Lily? The lad went on the skite in London and made a damned fool of himself. Isn't that it?"

Lily started to sob.

"And this was on the money I gave to help him in his career! Well, never mind about that; perhaps I was the fool to begin with. But I'm angry, Lily, I'm heart-broken, I'm sick; and I've just come here to tell you straight that that's the end of Charles as far as I am concerned. That's absolutely the end."

"John!" she wailed.

"Yes, it's a hard thing to say, but I came over here to say it, plump and plain. I hate this shuffling and lying. And let me tell you, Lily, before I go, that you had better start thinking of your own responsibilities to your children."

"O, John! John!"

She was kneeling at his feet as he rose from the chair, her arms tight round his legs in supplication; and if she had held herself there as a penitent she would assuredly had worn through the armour of his anger to his abounding kindness and pity. Instead, a demon in her frivolous soul prompted her to rise to her feet, and throw her arms about his neck, while her body, still desirable, pressed closely against his. She whispered in his ear.

He raised his arms to her shoulders and threw her away from him.

" For God's sake, Lily ! Are you mad ? What do you think I am ? Let me get out of here, and . . ."

He walked eastwards, blindly. If there was any purpose in his direction it came of an instinctive desire to be in the calm company of his sister, Beth Bryden, but when he came at length to the familiar street of tenement houses in a staggered huddle on its slope he crossed the intersection and went on eastwards.

As the heat in his mind died down and his pulse steadied after shock he wondered why Lily should have so insulted him. He thought at first that she must have acted in panic. Then he more cynically considered the possibility that, by a tortuous working of the female mind, she had desperately sought, by compromising him, to have him in her power : the dark weapon of blackmail always to her hand thereafter. At length he was disposed to think more charitably that she had foolishly and pitifully thought thus to discharge the debt of her feckless and beloved son.

John found himself at length passing behind the shabby buildings and confused sidings of the Main Station, heading down the long slope to the Five Arches. The thought quickened his step. Hereabouts he had been a boy, long ago.

He stood at the corner of the street that ran steeply downhill, outside a public house that fancifully called itself Ye Olde Stannersgate Taverne, though it had once been simply and quite adequately known as MacGuigan's. He sensibly reflected that he ought to be moving westwards for a bite of food and then making for the afternoon boat. But he saw the bow of a ship fitting out in the Regent Harbour, and drawn by the professional curiosity that is strangely as strong in elderly persons as the more human passions, headed downhill again to have a look at her.

His way took him under the Five Arches, and he deliberately chose to pass through the fourth, counting from the left or western end. On this dull, clotted day of imminent thunder it was darkly shadowed ; and he moved with all the more eagerness towards Miss Macarthur's eating-house and his way of escape across the Firth to Addie and Penang Lodge.

8

The house was very quiet, the minutes seemed to drag. By nine o'clock Addie had finished her mending, and the light was going out of the overcast sky. She lit the lamp and took up the morning paper. The burden of its news was of German troops on the march and of the rantings of Adolf Hitler, and she dimly but unhappily discerned that the tidings were of import to herself and her generation. She dropped the paper and tried the battered crime story she had got out of the miserable little library in the post office—general store, but its machine-made sensations seemed to her pitifully absurd. She was beyond distraction.

She went out of doors, but the garden was without life and colour in the burdened gloaming ; even the cloud of perfume from the night-scented stocks seemed cloying. She went indoors again, thinking that she would go into the kitchen and make some of that lemon curd, of which her Uncle John was so inordinately fond. That thought she quickly dismissed ; she must still avoid an encounter with that woman who could be unpleasant enough when sober about her rights in " my kitchen." There was nothing for it but to return to the Big Room and wait. From her uncle's room came no sound at all. Even at ten he had not come down for his accustomed toddy.

Addie started out of a doze to the banging of the gate. Here she came, that woman, her walk up the path apparently steady enough. Please God she would keep quiet and go to bed ! The woman crossed the terrace and reached the door ; her footsteps sounded hard on the tiles of the porch. But she seemed to hesitate there. Her hands clasped in an agony of apprehension. Addie sat waiting for the next sound.

It came on a crash and a clattering, followed by a wailing cry of terror and then by shrieks. Addie jumped and ran out and in her turn cried aloud at what she saw. The woman lay under the weight of the old-fashioned hallstand she had brought down upon herself in a clutch for balance at one of its curved pegs ; she was pinned and humiliated under a mass of coats, walking-sticks, umbrellas, mirror, oak and clothes-brushes. Addie always remembered afterwards the crescents of tiny brass nails in the upturned heels of her shoes.

She was straining to lift the stand from off the woman's body when John came upon them, roaring angrily.

" What in God's name is this, now ? Are you trying to wreck the blasted place ? . . . Get a good grip, Addie ; now lift."

They put the stand back upon its base, and they raised Effie Templeton to her feet. She contrived to stand upright, with Addie's hand under one elbow, but she swayed. She raised a slack hand to a lump that was ludicrously waxing above her right eye.

" That's only a bruise," said John, angry. " The trouble is that you're drunk. Get up to your bed and get out of my sight."

" Can she manage ? " asked Addie more tolerantly. " I'll make a cup of coffee."

" Manage is it ! " cried Effie Templeton with what she pitifully believed to be enormous dignity. " I'll go to my bed when I'm ready. I'll make my own cup of tea—and be damned to the both of ye ! "

" Your bed, woman ! " ordered John, pointing the Superintendent Engineer's finger towards the lobby.

The woman lurched from Addie's support and propped herself against the jamb of the inner door.

" My bed ! " she started to shriek again. " Aye ! And your bed if you were a real man. Bring me over here, and never a move to make an honest woman of me ! Think ye're a big man ! Think ye can make a lady out of that wee bitch from the slums ! "

John stepped forward, and Addie thought he was going to strike the woman. She put out her hand.

" You will go out of this house first thing to-morrow morning," her uncle was saying in a vicious but controlled voice she had never heard from him before. " Out of my sight before . . . before I slap your dirty mouth for you."

Effie Templeton started to cry with a rich self-pity, but John's pointing finger was merciless, and she set off across the lobby towards the kitchen with a terribly pitiful reassumption of her grand manner. The door slammed behind her.

Addie was alarmed for her Uncle John. He was breathing heavily ; his face was white and strained.

" You'd better have a glass of whisky, Uncle John," she said.

" I'm sorry you heard all that, lass," he returned, panting. " Yes, I'll have a tot, I think. God help us all with a targe like that in the house ! No, I think I'll have a thimbleful of brandy."

They were back in the Big Room. John drank his cordial and seemed to breathe more easily.

" Now, Addie," he said, " will you be a good lass and run along the road to the telephone box and tell Bain to have his taxi here at seven in the morning. That woman's going by the first boat if I have to kick her out. Here are some coppers."

Addie moved to the eastern window.

" I'll have to put on a coat. I think that's the rain started."

She felt her Uncle John's hands on her shoulders and, turning, she was surprisingly kissed on the forehead and closely embraced.

" You're a good lass, Addie," he said to her great surprise and secret delight. " You're the best friend I've got."

9

The thunderstorm broke about midnight, and its cracks and rumblings reverberated among the hills for more than an hour on end. When the rain came, the thresh of it was loud on the garden and among the young larches in the plantation behind Penang Lodge.

Addie had little sleep throughout that night. The noises of the storm were only exasperations of her inner qualms of alarm and anxiety ; she was tortured by disgust and pity together. Across the landing, until the early hours of the morning, the housekeeper bumped about her room, slamming drawers and drawing her boxes over the floor.

It was something that she prepared to go, but Addie felt that she must be up early to see her off the place, and she could not imagine that the departure of the housekeeper could be anything but tempestuous and unpleasant. When she tried hard to compose herself and shut her mind to worry, her ear would be caught by the brawling noises of the burn, now swollen with the rains and rushing down past the house to the sea.

The dawn was a dismal one. The rain was still heavy, and now the mists had come down to smear all colour and shape out of the landscape. It seemed a shame to send even such a woman as Effie Templeton off on such a miserable morning ; and that event, when it came to pass, had only the shabbiness of a triviality in the setting of the storm's aftermath. Addie heard the woman rise early and go downstairs to the kitchen. For her own part, she jumped out of bed and dressed promptly, but waited in her room until she heard the old taxi grind past the gate, turn at the point and come back to stop with a screeching of brakes. She went downstairs only when the driver came up the path for the housekeeper's cases.

Effie Templeton seemed but a bundle of dark and subdued nonentity, the bruise on her forehead the pitiful brand of her folly. She would not face Addie's look but snatched at the envelope John had left out for her.

"You can tell that uncle of yours it's a lawyer's letter he'll be getting next," she muttered as she passed through the door of Penang Lodge for the last time, but even Addie knew that the threat was utterly empty ; and as, from the front window of the Big Room, she watched the dumpy figure move down the path and climb into the car, she saw naught but the negligible, though pathetic, figure of a weak woman in defeat and disgrace.

Then, suddenly, she felt almost happy. The evil was gone from the house ; she had it to herself in the willing service of her Uncle John. She went into the kitchen and symbolically threw up the window in spite of the rain.

That woman had left a litter on the deal table—a cup half-filled with tea and a piece of thickly-buttered bread with a semi-circular mouthful bitten out of it. But it was a pleasure to clear this away and dump the dirty dishes into a basin of hot water always ready from the boiler fired by that wonderful slow-combustion stove. Addie thought it strange enough that the woman, drunk or sober, had automatically tended to this most precious of the household gods before staggering upstairs to her room the night before.

She attended again to the fire, raking out the ashes and the bits of stone that will come with the best anthracite, stoking up from the hopper beside the stove, nicely adjusting the slides and grids that would best serve the machine on this almost windless morning. She laid the breakfast table and, while doing so, considered what it would best please her uncle to eat. It gave her pleasure to remember one of his favourites, French toast and bacon ; and she recalled with satisfaction that in Doon two days before, when she was paying Faill & Forfar's account, that excellent firm had sold her a pound of Belfast ham of superb leanness and flavour. Uncle John would enjoy that. She returned to the kitchen and laid out her equipment for battle.

And there he was, moving about upstairs as usual, even to the morning cough, as he crossed the landing to the bathroom. Addie found herself singing as she worked : softly and to a slow, romantic air, but still singing. She took time to go into the Big Room and, after a brief tussle and tugging with and at the cushions in there, studied the barograph John had lately installed on the sideboard and saw that the steep downward curve of the graph was beginning —as the late Engineer Superintendent of the K. & S. had sternly instructed her—to flatten out. There might be sunshine by the afternoon, and happiness again.

She called upstairs to say that breakfast was ready, something like a lilt in her voice, and his rumbling acknowledgment was soon enough followed by the padded thump of his carpet slippers on the stairs.

" Good morning, Addie," he said. " This is nice—just you and me together."

" Yes, that was a good riddance," agreed Addie, fitting the knitted cosy over the teapot in soft Chinese silver. " I've made you some French toast."

" Good lass ! Yes, I heard her go away, but I didn't come down. There would only have been another scene."

" Well, she's gone."

" Yes."

The monosyllable was flat, however, and she perceived that he was still looking inwards, contemplating morosely his private worries and disappointments. His occasional sentences during the meal were those of one who has to shake himself out of preoccupation for the sake of convention.

" There'll be a lot of work for you to-day, Addie," he suddenly observed over his second cup of tea. " Can I do anything to help you ? "

" Goodness, no, Uncle John ! " she protested. " This is an easy house to run. I'll enjoy every minute of it . . . even if I have to make up that woman's bed after her."

"Good. Well, I'll use the dining-room here once you've cleared away. I've still a lot of letters to write."

He rose from the table to take his pipe, pouch and matches from the mantelpiece and stood for a few moments, looking out of the window over the dripping trees and the shrouded loch.

"I'm afraid it's a poor holiday for you, Addie. When did we last see the sun? You would think this confounded rain will never stop."

The noise of the rain was not to be escaped. It seemed to establish a tyranny over mere human beings beleaguered within narrow walls and under frail roofs. Now and again, as she worked in the bedrooms and then in the more resonant kitchen, Addie got it into her head that it was like the incessant drumming of some dark tribal rite : the fall of the drops, the chattering of water in rones and pipes, the hissing and mumbling and shouts of the burn all mingling in deliberate and mocking menace.

It must have been an hour before noon that the storm ceased to be a spectacle and became a surging reality within the house.

Addie always remembered afterwards that she was peeling potatoes in the scullery when it happened ; the succession of sounds was imprinted on her memory for ever. It started with a sort of muffled explosion, followed by a growl ; then there was a slapping of heavy waters outside, with a clattering of gravel, and finally a heavy thud against the back wall of the house. Even as, quickly recovering from fright, the girl jumped to the back window to see what had happened, she paused to stare at the muddied waters of the mountain stream come pouring over the sill of the back door and spread out swiftly towards the kitchen.

She ran indoors through the flood, crying :

"Uncle John ! Uncle John ! The Dam's burst."

He was out of the dining-room in a flash, only to meet the water coming through the lobby and feeling outwards like something indecently alive for every way of escape. It washed against the door of the Big Room and swirled back to seep under the front door. John jumped to open the latter wide.

"Quick, Addie !" he commanded. "Your coat and gum boots. We'll have to try something. Out of the front door and up the side of the house."

Some of the water was flowing that way to join the stream

again lower down the garden, taking a wilful and ruinous course across a bed of antirrhinums, but behind the house it was as if they had come upon a shambles. Gravel, peaty soil and small boulders were piled against the wall, forming around the back door another dam in which the escape waters eddied and boiled to burst into the scullery and through the house. The volume still pouring from above was such that separate streams fanned out to run past both gables of the building.

Angered and distressed, John was still able to consider the problem with an engineer's eye. Tested by emergencies in the engine-rooms of ships at sea, he disciplined himself to take time to see exactly what had happened. Poor old Sam's patent sluice had given way under pressure, tearing with its collapse a jagged rent in the lower parapet of the Dam. Through this gap there still poured some of the burn's swollen flood, but the mass of water in the pond had thunderously escaped. It now clamoured at the back door as if ravening to force a way inside and despoil the house.

" We can stop this," John pronounced curtly. " Start rolling these stones down from that old rockery. I'll build them up as they come."

Addie worked with all the energy and strength she possessed, and John laboriously built the foundations of still another dam across the path of the flood. He built it so stoutly and carefully that, after nearly an hour of labour, the running water tended to turn towards and even round the corner of the eastern gable.

" Now," he commanded, " get a spade or something and help me to shovel soil on to the stones. Or cut chunks of turf. Anything to send this confounded water away from the back door."

They bent once more to racking labour with sodden earth, turves and gravel ; but as they worked the water started subtly to assist them as, meeting the obstruction, it bit a new course for itself through the gravelled space behind the house and finally flowed cheerfully in a bee-line for the bed of antirrhinums and the parent stream.

Only when Addie and her Uncle John were finished and leaning on their spades and considering their handiwork did they notice that the rain had stopped at length.

Slowly they dared to enter the house again by the front door, and Addie at least thought she would have to cry. The wilful, hooligan water still lay puddled in hollows all over the ground floor, and some of it was still flowing in lazy fingers into the rooms. The embrasure of the dining-room window contained a pool, and the fine Indian carpet in the Big Room was sodden and muddy up to the fireplace. A thick deposit of sand and slime gave greasily under the rubber soles of their boots. The smell of the peaty hillside filled the house.

"Must sit down, dear . . . Not very well . . . Out of breath ; feeling a bit seedy."

Addie was startled out of her housewifely woe to see that John was ill. His face had gone grey and small, his eyes troubled ; his breath was short and difficult. She got him on to the chester-field in the Big Room and poured him a glass of brandy. She had to steady his trembling hand while he swallowed it.

"Better now," he said, but still panting. "A bit too much violent exercise at my age. What the doctor said when old Sam went. But let me rest a little, and I'll be all right—soon. Don't worry, lass."

Of all the hopeless things to say in that moment ; as if the conventional phrases could cover even the edges of this catas-trophe ! Addie stood at the window and looked out to sea, observing, but without any enthusiasm, that there was a patch of blue in the eastern sky above Garvel, that winds were beginning to stir the surface of the loch. Nothing like that could ease the load of anger and concern she carried ; or so she felt. At the same time, her inherited habit of orderly industry turned to concern itself with the given problem, and she began to speak again, though in a subdued voice.

"I'd better get started. All these rooms will have to be aired. I'll lift the carpets this afternoon. If it's fair this evening I could get some of them out on the line. It'll be a job getting that muck out of the place. I think I'd better go and open a can of soup at least. I hope the fire isn't out."

This was a jerky monologue delivered to the window-pane. It was just Addie Bryden trying to square up to a set of facts.

"It's no use, Addie," said her uncle's voice behind her, weakly. "We'll send for Macfarlane to come and clear the place up."

"To-morrow's Saturday. We could wire my father to come and give us a hand."

"No, lass. We're packing this afternoon. We're going back to Garvel by the evening boat. We're beaten."

"But, Uncle John!"

She turned to challenge him, and he turned to smile at her weakly.

"No, Addie. I think I've had enough. Quite enough. It's a pity, but . . ."

He shook his head over an insoluble problem.

CHAPTER SIX

THE PRISONERS OF WAR

I

"I WONDER what poor John would think of the place if he could see it now."

"I wonder if he isn't past caring altogether."

Davie Bryden spoke to Beth gloomily, and her response was equally dispirited, nearly bitter. She sat on the garden seat on the terrace before Penang Lodge ; he leaned on the back of it, having just completed an inspection of the garden and the premises behind the house. The amber sunlight of an afternoon in the autumn of 1945 lay kindly enough on the hillside, but for this man and woman there was no cheer in it. Their thoughts were directed inwards and backwards in time, and the wistful quality of the autumnal glow had, if anything at all, only the power to evoke the nostalgic sense of time past and old assumptions riddled.

"I believe it's worse than after the Evacuees," said Davie, adding hopelessly, "and I suppose it'll be long enough before we get a penny of compensation out of them. Just the same, Beth," he tried to interest his wife in a pleasant possibility, "I'd like fine to have the place in trim for John coming home again."

"If John ever comes home again," added Beth bitterly.

"O, there'll be word from Addie soon, don't you worry ! "

The Evacuees had been first in Penang Lodge, leaving behind them, in broken windows, battered paint, greasy floorboards and a garden despoiled, the stigmata of the unhappy slums. When Davie had crossed the water as John's appointed custodian to reassume possession after the first few weeks of panic he could see from the shore road that the old sanctions of private property had been flouted crudely. The branches of fruit trees hung in withered fracture. Flower-pots had been trampled into beaten paths by the feet of unhappy children who never had had a chance to know what a garden is. He was particularly grieved by the fact that the steep, grassy embankment before the house was as bald and ugly as a slag-heap, worn by the boots of infants who had made of it a glorious mud-slide.

Then the Navy had requisitioned John's house, used it for nearly four years, and only lately, the fleets concentrating in the Pacific, surrendered it. Now Davie and Beth had just seen what celibate men under the discipline of a system can make of a modest home. They had counted themselves, and John, lucky in that Penang Lodge was reserved for a few specialist officers of a secret training establishment, but Beth could have wept to see what the brutal carelessness of temporary power without responsibility had made of a decent home.

It was not the dirt, the mud and the general untidiness abhorrent to any housekeeping woman ; it was the crudeness of alterations : of big nails hammered into thin lath-and-plaster to carry garments, of shelves and lengths of boarding harshly rigged up where somebody had happened to want a temporary accommodation, of fittings stripped without regard for appearance and decency. Even in the Big Room, which as a species of wardroom had escaped the worst, a crude stove had been set up at one end to reinforce the fireplace, its fumes carried into the outer air through a stove-pipe which, in a series of eccentrically-angled pieces, finally passed though the window and a segment of sheet metal in place of a pane of glass. On the rear wall there still hung a dartboard, the wallpaper about it pitted with shots that had gone astray in the abandon of after-dinner gaiety.

Seeing all this, Beth had unhappily retired to the old garden seat, its paint now thin and grey through weathering and neglect —and she remembered how brightly white it had been in John's time. Meanwhile, Davie had continued to look round the house with a tradesman's eye and seen what the years and their exigencies had done to a pleasant cottage by the sea.

Behind the scullery door he found that the Royal Navy had deemed it necessary to put up an extra cookhouse ; and he also noticed that rats had come to feast on the shards of bread and fat left behind by the mariners. The passage round the eastern gable had been blocked by a store in which he counted twelve jerricans full of petrol. Where the fated Dam had been the Navy had excavated a bomb-proof shelter, and now the hill-burn ran through a conduit of fireclay piping from the very top of the garden almost to the garden gate. The late tenants had casually left behind a dump of coal, which Davie estimated to contain some four tons, on what had once been what old John had loved to call the Rose Garden.

Davie had thus sauntered round the house, noting where rones and gutters stood in need of repair. He made jottings on his mental map of the roof where slates had worked loose or fallen off. He marked down for immediate attention a drain at the back of the house which was loathsomely regurgitating a decaying surplus of naval rations.

Now he stood behind the bench on which his wife rested and looked back at the fabric of Penang Lodge : this time to see that the original whitewash had been sadly thinned by a succession of winter storms, and that a great section of the harling on the southern gable, like the map of a continent, had fallen out, leaving the naked, vulnerable sandstone exposed.

When he turned to look at the garden it was to behold a dump in which the native weeds, the grass and the skinny survivors of horticulture were mingled in shaggy confusion. The lower part of the garden had been used for the dumping of anything from cans to motor tyres worn down to the cotton. The rusted frame of a motor-cycle topped a heap of half-burnt official papers, and a lavatory seat had been hung on the broken bough of a tree down there : whether in the spirit of rough humour or in sheer brutal indifference to order, one could not guess. Even the Royal Navy's one serious pass at honest housekeeping—a vegetable plot on a terrace hard by the araucaria—was now but a thicket of runts, despoiled by the wood pigeons, like rows of bad teeth in an old man's head.

" Aye, it's a terrible thing is a war, when you come to think of it," said Davie sententiously. " It puts years on everything."

He might have seen that his wife, Beth Cram that was, had gone grey in the hair since they last lived in Penang Lodge ; that her mouth tended to sink inwards, as it were, between deep furrows in her fair skin, and that her eyes, on the other hand, often seemed soft and distant, as if she communed with ghosts. If he could have seen himself compared with the man he was in 1939 he might have wondered ruefully that long hours of work to speed the ships, shock, lack of the food a blacksmith needs and the long-drawn agony of waiting, which is the lot of all who give hostages to fortune in war, had whitened his hair and given to his fine face the pinched, sallow quality of a death-mask.

He noticed then that Beth was crying, softly and hopelessly. That was often the way with her nowadays, and Davie suffered with her in every one of her surrenders to grief, fearing that he too must break down and weep with the mother of their children. He turned round the edge of the seat and, taking both her hands in his, raised her to her feet.

"Come on, lass," he said kindly, "I know it's hard seeing John's house again. It reminds ye . . . But come, and we'll have a quiet walk along the road and a cup of tea in the hotel before the boat comes in."

He put his arm round her waist, and Beth was comforted by the loverly, protective gesture.

"I wish I didn't have to cry, Davie," she confided as he supported her down to the gate, "but it's just when you feel that it'll never be the same again. Working and hoping and doing your best all these years, and then just waste!"

"I don't know about waste," said Davie sharply, taking the metaphysical point with racial gravity. He dropped it quickly in favour of tenderness. "But come on and we'll step it out. I could do fine with a cup of tea. I wouldn't wonder, Beth," he added with clumsy optimism, "if there was a letter from Addie waiting for us at home."

So they passed along the shore road under the shadow of the Strone, two harmless survivors of the storm that had swept across half the world. They could have seen, if their thoughts had not been turned so darkly inwards, that even the innocent beaches of the Firth bore stains of pollution in a black and rancid film of oil over all the weed and the stones up to high-water mark, and that even seabirds had died by the hundred because men must carry on their squabbles as fiercely and unreasonably as the parent birds fighting to the death for nesting-ground on the bald skerries of the western seas.

2

Out on the Stanley Peninsula the Defence Force still held its lines, hopelessly but with the ferocity of desperation. Every movement of the yellow men could still draw a fierce crackling of fire, a thudding of machine-guns. The December afternoon wore on, the sunlight blinding, but the Nips were still held. No European in the trenches hoped to repel the attack or dared to dream that relief might still miraculously come. So they fought all the more bitterly, staving off to the last second the unthinkable horrors of capture. Some of them hoped for the merciful bullet ; more clung all the more desperately to life, thinking of the women and children huddled in the schools and hospitals of the settlement behind.

John Rolland Cram thought that his eyes must close with weariness and sun-glare. He despaired of being able to bear the gleam of his rifle barrel and the dancing of the foresight should the yellow monkeys come on again. His head drooped, and his forehead came to rest against the parapet. His body was beginning slowly to sag when his neighbour caught him under the armpits and eased his fall to the floor of the trench.

" You're too old for this game, Dad," said the young man sternly but with admiration. " You should be back on the Peak. Think you could make a shot at it ? "

John liked this boy, a bank clerk from Aberdeen, now a brave soldier with a bearded and blackened face and a corporal's stripes on his shirt sleeves. John wanted to stay with such a good comrade.

" No, no ! " he said, adding with a wan smile, " It doesn't matter a damn what happens to me now, does it ? "

" Well, get into the dug-out and have a spot of shut-eye. Here, Dad, better have a sip before you lie down."

He uncorked his water-bottle and put it to John's lips. The latter took just enough to wash out his gritty mouth.

" Thank you, lad, thank you ! " he breathed, knowing the value of that spoonful of water freely given by a brave and generous youngster.

It was good to be out of the pitiless glare of the sun, and it was so fantastic he should be in the fighting against the Japanese on

Hongkong that the fact could not trouble him. This was the last of it now, the black shadow in the fifth arch ; and with the mental abandon of a man who has resigned himself to death John let his mind range freely and with detachment over the set of circumstances that had brought him here. A damned old fool, and always had been for all his success in business ! Couldn't get his roots down anywhere.

Who was it had put it that way ? Ah, yes ! the skipper of the Blue Funnel liner that had brought him back to the East almost exactly three years before. He was in his stateroom, packing the last suitcase, when an apprentice lad had knocked and commanded.

"Cap'n's compliments, sir, and he would like to see you in his room."

The ship was safe at anchor in the Canton River, and this was the agreeable gesture of the shipmaster towards an old-timer, the last drink and yarn before their ways must part again.

"What I can't fathom, Mr. Cram," the big man from Wallasey had said, "is why you want to come out to this stink-hole again when you could be sitting pretty at home with a nice house and a garden of your own."

"I tried it, Captain, and it didn't work," John had replied with a little, uneasy laugh. "Perhaps if I had been a married man . . . Anyhow, the old bug got me and here I am."

"Yes," the sailor agreed thoughtfully. "That's the hell of giving the best of your life to the foreign trade ; you seem to belong nowhere. I reckon that when I swallow the anchor, which I'd give my shirt to be able to do here and now, after a year I'll find it hard to get my roots down anywhere. But your good health again, Mr. Cram, good health ! "

And that same evening, so long ago, when he had entered the Club in high spirits to meet the Boys again, they had greeted him with a cheer that set the glasses in the bar a-tremble, but one lone, sardonic American voice had said in the ensuing pause :

"But why come back, you old sinner ? Is the booze too dear at home, or are you hell-bent on having a close-up of the horrors of the next war ? "

Everybody had laughed again at that ; and now, in the trenches on the Stanley Peninsula, John found the echo of the laughter bitter to hear. Sore and weary in a body now growing really old, he blamed himself for wandering and wasting his substance—from Canton to Shanghai, back again to his old haunts among the K. & S. folk, and then to Japan itself with the daft idea of summering there in '39. It had ended miserably, that trip, in a scuttle back to Hongkong when any man could see the balloon starting to go up in Europe.

He might still have got home, he reflected, and he pondered philosophically what forces had kept him hanging round the East just a little too long. Some queer feeling of loyalty to the expatriates, his brothers in uneasy exile from Home, the lads who held the fort overseas ? Had he been timid about facing again the queer complexities of the life he had tried to establish in Penang Lodge, with the ghost of old Sam Lighbody hanging about the place ? Had he, in fact, fled from the smears of greed and sex Lily Rolland and Effie Templeton had laid across his dream ?

Perhaps it was just that he had failed as a real man, and it did not matter now. There disturbed him as he rested, waiting for death, one sweet picture out of that brief adventure in settling down. It was on one of the lovely nights of the Fair week. Beth was on the garden seat, knitting calmly, Davie on a ladder against the house to fix a wire trellis for the clematis that flourished so bravely by the front window of the Big Room. Addie moved slowly among the roses, a creature apart in a light summer frock.

It was nothing, yet it was everything. The memory of peace and kindness was unbearable ; an old man was not to be allowed to die without regret and pangs after all. One sob was wrung from him as he thought how sad it was not for him to have the joy of seeing Addie grow up, of having Addie near him in his old age. That was something lost from the life that might have been. Queer that it was on Addie he had fastened his love, not on young Curly, the heir male, the bearer of his name.

Cries of warning along the trench and an outburst of firing roused him, and wearily enough he felt for his rifle and crawled from the dugout. He was just rising to his feet when a bugle-call surprisingly rang out over the battlefield. There was a confused shouting down to the right, and John saw the heads of all his comrades turn that way, forgetting the foe in front. A rumour rustled up the line, and men looked puzzled. In its wake came an officer of the Staff, hurrying and curtly ordering.

" Lay down your arms, everybody. Throw them over the parapet towards the enemy. The Cease Fire is ordered."

As he passed the point where John stood dazed, the lad with the corporal's stripes dared to ask with the edge of incredulous indignation in his voice :

" Does this mean surrender, sir ? "

" I told you to throw away your arms, didn't I ? " the officer replied out of the ferocity of his own shame.

" Christ Jesus Almighty ! " the young man shrieked, all control going from him now. He sobbed : " Surrender to those ruddy wee yellow rats ! But we *can't* . . ."

He went on sobbing dryly, and now it was John's turn to pat his shoulder, and the boy calmed down a bit. At length he took his rifle by the barrel near the muzzle and heaved it over the parapet towards the enemy.

" And there goes the bloody British Empire for all I care ! " he yelled. Then he slumped down on the firestep and hung his head between his knees.

They waited, dull in reaction from strain. Their little snatches of talk were elaborately careless but carefully formal. They exchanged priceless smokes, and they were only brought to sense when Jensen of the Swedish Salvage shouted the warning :

" Do not touch the water-bottles, boys ! We will need every drop."

At length the Japanese came up the slope, a bow-legged monkey of a boy-officer trailing a long scabbard at the head of those who approached John's section. This homuncule paced the parapet shouting orders, in Nipponese English, in a voice that foolishly reminded John of the clack of typewriters in an office.

" Plisoners, obey ! Listen ! " he clattered in falsetto. " I give message from Impel' Majesty, our Emplow Hirohito . . ."

Somebody laughed, and Jensen shouted angrily :

" Shut up, fool ! They have the bullets and the bayonets now."

While the foolish little officer ranted, non-commissioned officers posted sentries along the line, and a working-party of Chinese prisoners collected the abandoned arms.

It was all a sort of pantomime to John, something seen on one of those newsreel strips. He was weary, and he saw it all as the unimportant prologue to death. Jensen was right ; these little devils would massacre the lot out of hand and never turn a hair. John had no will to fight any more, and he believed that he was being marshalled with the others for the firing squad when the British line was ordered to turn right and file along the trench. The sun was down in the sky now, yellow as its beams approached the atmosphere of a troubled earth, but still hot.

They were marshalled in a hollow behind the old lines, shepherded by small, cruel men who used the points of their bayonets on the bodies of those on the outskirts of the mass. Some men lay down and slept. John found himself sitting cross-legged like a tailor, the bank clerk from Aberdeen asleep by his side. Time passed over them. They were without food, as they had been all the day. They tried to abide by the wisdom of Jensen and touched their water-bottles as the chain-smoker feels for the packet of cigarettes, withdrawing guiltily their wilful hands.

It might have been two hours, three, four—who knew or cared ?—before a paunchy major of the Imperial Army came squealing orders at them. The host of the defeated rose stiffly to their feet. John thought that he could not stand and was lief to lie down and be shot or bayoneted out of weariness for ever. He found himself, however, taken under one arm by the boy from Aberdeen and, under the other, by a fair Canadian lad with a smear of dried blood down his forehead.

They helped him along through the darkness that was falling so quickly over the island, but John's mind toyed with the secret knowledge that they were wasting their time. They were all the defeated, the lost, the abandoned, footing it within the ring of ready bayonets to the place of torture and execution. He felt in the night wind from the sea the chill of darkness within the fifth arch. It was a queer thing that, away back in Garvel under the Scottish hills, they would never know in what circumstances of humiliation he had departed this life.

3

It was twenty to one by the alarum clock on the mantelpiece under the print of Fujiyama. Beth Bryden crossed her kitchen to the dresser and, with extreme caution, turned a knob of the wireless set so that the programme started to come through in a murmur, as from a place far away. Her fingers lingered on the milled edge until she was perfectly satisfied that the sounds so miraculously produced through this box of tricks would not waken Davie—though she had often said, in another mood, that that man of hers could sleep through an earthquake.

Her mood at the moment was of great tenderness and concern for her husband. She loved him ; and she had thought to see lately that he was ageing and weakening after two years of night-work and overtime. Half the trouble was that he got short-tempered when she mentioned his state of health.

"What's bitin' ye, woman?" he would ask quite sharply when she might meekly ask if he was feeling quite right. "Of course I'm all right ; never been better in my life. We've got to get on with the job, haven't we?"

That sharpness was itself a sympton of the thing that worried her. She saw Davie's hair go grey, his skin yellow with too much work by night in the blacksmith's shop that was so hot from bright fires under the black-out shutters. Beth, a child of the Presbyterian tradition, implicitly believed it wrong for a man to work so long and hard at the wrong time, turning night into day. Davie's wife, the keeper of the hearth, she feared for their ultimate security, for the big wages of these bad days were surely sinful and wrong. But at this moment he was just Davie Bryden, her sweetheart and lover of thirty years ago, and she cared for his comfort and security with that passion of concern which is the cross every faithful wife and mother must bear.

He had slept in Addie's old room ever since the nightwork started, and that was something by itself. It was a queer business when a decent wedded couple hardly ever bedded together nowadays : not for what of passion might be in the situation, just for the kindliness of the old companionship, the talks about their warm, small affairs in that sweetest of confessionals. But it was all past now. Men were fair daft when it came to a war. It was just like them and their football teams ; they had to take sides and shout their heads off about the rights of this and that, and work themselves to the death. Any woman could tell them that it was a folly and a madness and a waste from first to last. And the craziest thing about a crazy world was that any woman in love with a man would fight like a cat to defend him and his follies and work herself to the bone to preserve him in his illusions.

Her attention returned to the wireless set as a dance band thumped and trumpeted to the end of a piece of the feral new music she could never make heads or tails of and a voice, elaborately familiar in an acquired American accent, announced to a factory audience, somewhere in distant England, that the Rolland Rhythmic Twins, Two Girls at Two Pianos—" and how ! "— would now tickle the ivories in a selection of old-time melodies.

" Boys and girls, the Rolland Rhythmic Twins ! Swing it sisters ! " The voice rose in a nasal frenzy. " *And let the people sing !* "

The sounds that followed pleasantly contradicted the *ersatz* passion of the announcer. The notes of the pianos came agreeably over the air, and now the playing of Lily's girls, its volume reduced to the limit of audibility, had a faraway charm, such as might please the ears of a serf who hearkens at a distance to the music from the mansion of the great among the trees. They played the old, sweet tunes Beth loved for memory's sake—*The Chorister's Waltz*, *The Old Bull and Bush*, *The Lily of Laguna*. She found herself humming, happy to be listening ; and then she was dabbing her eyes to hear how the girl-workers in that distant factory, the innocent automata of the great war-machine, sang out the choruses in the brief moment of escape from their boredom.

The Twins crashed into *Daisy, Daisy*, and the female children far away sang as if their hearts must break. The B.B.C.'s experts in Effects superimposed on the noise their reliable record of crowd enthusiasm, with its ever-so-slightly excessive impression of mass-hysteria and its dubious whistlings. The announcer plunged into a corybantic gabble. Then it all quite suddenly ceased on the air, and six pips intimated the inexorable passing of time. A sauve voice spoke for a calmer civilisation, if one in rapid decay :

" Our bombers were over Germany again last night."

Beth switched off and started to think a little sourly about the Twins. She wondered if two strong young girls should not have been at the lathes with the other lasses instead of just playing the piano to them. But that was the way of it with these Rollands, always the easiest and flashiest way out. Beth had listened just because she had encountered Lily in the main street that morning, both at their shopping.

"You simply must listen-in to-day about ten to one," Lily had babbled when they were together in the queue at Tennant the fishmonger's. "The Twins are on. Yes, ENSA, you know. One of these concerts for the factory workers. Down in England somewhere—they couldn't tell me. They say the censorship's terribly strict. It's all hush-hush really. I shouldn't be talking myself. But I hope you'll manage to hear them. It's a great success for the Twins, isn't it, being taken up by ENSA and all that and then going on the air? They say the announcer's a lovely chap. No airs about him at all."

Beth had politely asked about Lily's son, Charles.

"O, our Cha! Just the same old sixpence!" his mother laughed happily. "Still at that big aerodrome at . . . But there it is; I just daren't mention names. And the poor boy! Wants to get a commission and go flying with the other boys, but the Group-Captain just won't hear of it. Says Cha on the ground is worth ten pilots in the air. It's awful for Cha, but I suppose everybody's got to obey orders and do his best."

Beth happened to know a good deal about that, perhaps more than Lily knew. Curly had come home on one of his leaves with a laughing story of having encountered our Cha on an aerodrome in Lincolnshire: our Cha with a small moustache, a corporal's stripes and a cushy job in the flying officers' mess.

"A piece of cake," Curly had described Charles's function in the argot that baffled and annoyed Beth. "The rackets that lad's in! Sugar, butter, cigs, booze—nobody's business! Our Cha doesn't want any commission," Curly had grinned. "Too dangerous, no future in it. Quite content to sport the brylcreem on the flat."

The silly way these boys talked! The glimpse of Service life had distressed Beth, and she had been even more worried by the fact that Curly took it all for granted and rather admired Charles for being a highly successful smooth type.

Trust a Rolland ! thought Beth sourly again, considering how her own Curly had cheerfully elected for dangerous service. That a man must fight in this war, she understood perfectly, but that any sensible lad should leave the Argylls for the Airborne, getting off the feet God gave him to go flying through the air and jumping about the place, was more than she could understand. And his father, of course, was as proud as a child with his first watch, telling all their friends about Curly in the Airborne and, when the boy was at home on leave, never leaving him alone with his questions. Men were daft. Just bairns, the whole lot of them !

But so dangerous ! As she sat by the kitchen table, thinking, Beth was startled to hear a great aircraft come roaring above the chimneys in its swoop down to the anchorage. She had been hearing the roar of the Catalinas for two years now, but it always took her back to the fearful night of the bombs. She could glance across the street and see the gap where one had sliced through a tall tenement of stout sandstone and carried nearly a hundred souls into the unknown with it. She had been almost hurt in her own bed by the shock of the explosion ; she remembered the clamour of ambulances and fire engines in the night and the cries of outraged people. But she had stayed in bed as she had started, in spite of the warden's angry orders, and it was queer that she had been most terribly frightened for Davie down in T. & B.'s, under all that glass.

Now she thought of the careless boy at the controls of the great amphibian, loving at once the sense of power and the danger; and that brought her to thinking again of Curly, who had been taken from her long ago and was now a travelled and highly-trained stranger who came to lodge for a few days about twice a year, throwing off casual remarks in a queer slang, describing the work of the Airborne to his enchanted father, protesting that he was weary of the English camps and burning for action. And one day there would come the letter that must surely break her heart, telling her that he was coming home for the few brief, brittle days of embarkation leave.

It was the emptiness of the years of waiting that corroded the spirit. Even the night of the bombs belonged now to another life ; it was almost enjoyable in retrospect ; it was at least something happening. War had taken her husband and her children from her altogether, for Addie also was lost to the

fireside now, lost in her work and fretful study for these over-
weening exams. She came for an occasional week-end with the
blue rings round her eyes and that air of thinking of something
else : just another pre-occupied lodger. Beth saw herself miserably
deserted under influences she could neither define nor combat.
She had so lost herself that she had almost forgotten her housewifely routine and fiddled about with cups of tea most of the day.

Silly old fool ! she suddenly laughed at herself and rose to
put on the kettle. Another cup of tea ; and there was Davie's
dinner to get ready for four. He always wakened at the back of
three, had a great time washing and shaving, read the morning
paper, ate a good meal and took a turn up by the bowling-green
before going down to the shop and the timeless nightshift. And
this was one of her nights at the canteen by the docks. They were
a rough lot down there—Free French and Norwegians and
Dutch and Poles as well as our own boys, and they would fight
with their shadows. But Beth Bryden saw them simply as so
many mothers' foolish sons astray in the darkness of the war,
and she loved to serve them with firm affection as she prayed and
believed a few decent women in foreign parts might one day serve
her own Curly.

As she selected potatoes from a basket below the sink and
placed them in a colander for peeling she felt through the open
window the heat of the June afternoon rise from the street below,
the stink of tar in it. That set her thinking of her brother John,
and she was unhappy again.

She had lost her hope for him. A letter of his from Hongkong
in mid-1941 had struggled through, but there had been nothing
since then. Other people in Garvel had got letters from remote
prison-camps. Mrs. Gavin Taylor of The Whins, a nice ladylike
person whose husband was with the high-up prisoners in Manchuria and who was president of the Aid Committee, had taken
the trouble to climb all these stairs and tell Beth that they had
done their best but she was sorry there was no word anywhere,
through the Red Cross or the Colonial Office, of John Rolland
Cram. It was a bad time for relatives, Mrs. Gavin Taylor had
agreed ; and she would be very glad indeed to have a cup of tea.

Beth thought with some detachment of the strangeness of her
brother's fate. She reckoned that, his age taken into account,
he could hardly have survived those forced marches and clubbings

the papers told you about. On the whole, she took it that he must have gone under bombardment or bombing, probably while the older folk and the women and children were sheltering in a building, just as the people in the tenement across the street had gone in a flash.

It was a queer way to die, a queer end to an honourable and useful career. It was a pity that all that nonsense about Effie Templeton and old Sam Lightbody had driven him away from the cottage. If he had only had a bit of patience, or come to her . . . But he was her brother, and she sobbed a little as she infused her little brown pot of tea and turned to peel the potatoes.

She was left far too much to herself. That was the whole truth about it. She found it pleasant to think of having a bath before going down to the canteen in the evening.

4

He turned the edge of his spade in the gravelly earth and lazily threw about one pound's weight of soil on the parapet of the drain they were supposed to be digging. He wondered how many million times he had gone through the motions in all these years. These ugly little yellow brutes were fools. He despised them even more, now that he was their prisoner, than he had done in nearly thirty years of contact with them in the way of business. They strutted and leered and bullied, but this endless navvying to which they had set their prisoners in Sam-Shui was futile, and they had not the wit to see how many of the defeated had won a secret victory by cultivating the art of appearing to work. The little apes were content with their swaggering pantomime of conquest.

God knew it had been bad enough in the first year or so—beatings with the buckle-ends of belts for the recalcitrant, the moans of men under torture, the agonies of pellagra mouth and electric feet, the incessant hunger, the slowness, the awful slowness of time ! But what John Rolland Cram had seen in these years was the triumph of adaptation within the power of European man at least. You learned not to go to hospital when sick, for the Nips automatically reduced the rations of those who could not work, and good friends in the huts could cover up your weakness. You learned the kindness of man to man in adversity and were proud to see how few would kowtow to the Japanese or be bribed into any sort of truck with them. The young chaps invented games and jokes the Nips could never see. You shared everything and received your share. Even an elderly man could work out a regimen and make the miserable food serve to meet an output of physical effort just sufficient to avoid prominence in either direction.

John feared only that his years would beat him, that he would crack under their weight and be eliminated as redundant by a Japanese sort of accident. Thus, though he was free from passions that intolerably racked the younger men, he suffered perhaps more terribly from the sense of the slowness of time. The slow hours of time one must spend contemplating the nature of time! The long evenings when, feeling out of sorts, one sat cross-legged on the floor of the hut, head in hands, despairing utterly, seeing all sorts of intolerably sweet pictures out of the past, believing that if freedom were to come to-morrow one would only laugh bitterly and go on waiting for the shouts of the guards.

For himself John saw no escape; here in Sam-Shui was his end; his grave was already dug, as it were, in the camp cemetery. Often enough he was in the low mood to run and get the bullet through his back and be done with it, but there was in fact no line of real escape that way. A chap could never surrender to the yellow monkeys; a chap could never abuse the trust of the loyalty about him.

Now, in the drizzling twilight of the Chinese winter, he leaned on his spade, for the nearest guard was a hundred yards away, chatting to his mate in the corner where two sides of the compound met.

"That's right, Dad, take it easy," said the young man from Aberdeen, still his best friend in the camp, his mentor and bodyguard. " I'll give you the tip when Banana Legs is coming back."

The valley of the Canton River was dismal in the mirk. Surely they would soon be blowing their silly whistles and marching them all back to the huts in their parties. John's head suddenly jerked towards the electrified wire.

" Mis' Clam !" he heard. " Mis' Clam !"

But it was impossible! Nobody could be out there to talk

to him. This must be the madness of imprisonment. But still it was the voice of Hop Li, his Number One boy in the old days with the K. & S. He stared from the drain towards the low bushes in the gloaming outside the wire.

" Yes," he said.

"Shut up !" muttered the lad from Aberdeen behind him abruptly. He spoke to the other men about them in the strangulated voice they used for their secret communications. " Go on working like hell. Don't look towards the wire."

" Mis' Clam ! "

It seemed a whisper, but mysteriously, ventriloquially projected as along a speaking tube from the wilderness outside. John did not see any arm rise above the brushwood. The parcel was coming at him through the twilight, so unexpected that he ducked ; so perfectly aimed that it landed on the parapet exactly before where the boy from Aberdeen was working. With a swift move of his spade the latter raked it into the trench and thrust it inside the blouse of his worn battledress.

" Bullseye, by God ! " he muttered admiringly. " Go on working, boys ! The ruddy whistle will be going soon."

But their guard was still engaged in the corner, and once more the ventriloquial voice from the free world came towards them.

" Mis' Clam ! Hop Li come back soon, same piece time."

John waved vaguely, hoping that the signal would be seen and understood. Jock Drynie from Aberdeen whispered :

" There's guts for you ! "

The whistle shrilled across the dismal paddy. Their guard came stumping up from his chat, calling on the defeated to clamber out of their drain and be marched back to their barracks.

" Hope the wee beggar doesn't notice the bulge under my oxter," muttered Jock Drynie to John in the vernacular. " Wonder what's in it. Sugar ? "

The sentry squealed out against this disregard of the wise ordinances of the Son of Heaven for the treatment of his captives. A paunchy N.C.O. was behind him to see the sorry parties fallen in and marched off in their ragged humiliation to the hutments. The guard, Sasaki, was a peasant from Hokkaido and as easygoing as any Japanese could be. Nakamoto, the pot-bellied sergeant, was a rat from the outskirts of Nakasaki, the professional soldier of Nippon, and the prisoners marched circumspectly under his eye, chary even of the witticisms that serve the British folks as heroics. The power of life and death was, ironically and intolerably, his.

Exulting in their secret, they opened the parcel in a corner of the hut. The little canvas bag, stoutly stitched, contained a powdered material, grey-brown in colour so far as they could see in the dim light, and with a faintly rancid smell.

" In Heaven's name ! " exclaimed John, disappointed.

" It is a trick," whispered Jensen the Swede vehemently. " It is a substance to make one ill, and thus they find who breaks the rules."

" Let's see," said Jock Drynie.

He moistened the tip of a finger, dipped it into the bag and tasted.

" Queer stuff," he pronounced thoughtfully. " Tastes a bit like peasemeal . . . Say, Jen, hop across and ask Doc Mulligan to come and have a look-see."

The Irishman arrived and put his nose into the mouth of the bag, looked up towards the roof, then did as Jock Drynie had done and tasted the stuff. A big smile spread over his face.

" Boys-a-boys, this is the answer to the maiden's prayer ! The man that sent this stuff in has his head screwed on the right way. It's yeast, lads. Vitamins. The very stuff we need for the chaps with beri-beri."

The group exchanged delighted grins. This was one up on the dirty little Nips.

" This goes into my medical stores," said the doctor. " That okay by youse boys ? "

" Okay. Okay. Okay."

" Now I'll start dosing poor Charlie Keene right away."

They were delighted. Charlie's legs were swollen and bleached like white bolsters, and it was one of their queer occasional entertainments to poke a finger into the dropsical swellings, make a deep hole and watch it fill out again. This was, indeed, one up on the ruddy little monkeys with their miserable rations of polished rice.

John lay down happily for the night. The arrival of the parcel gave him a great deal of face in the camp. It had on them all, he reflected, something of the effect of a wedding in a happy family. He wondered who had sent the strange gift. Hop Li was brave, loyal, cunning, but he would never have known the properties of yeast. This came out of the subtle wisdom of the educated Chinese, and he liked to think that his old friend, Mr. T. K. Chuang the Canton merchant, had remembered him and, what was so much more, taken the trouble to trace him and think out how best he might help. The loyalty of a Chinese to the bond of friendship and trust was a lovely thing indeed. And John could have hugged himself under the thin blankets, thinking again how the British and Chinese folk could diddle the Nips under the very points of their victorious bayonets.

Three times in five weeks the parcel of yeast came over the barbed wire. In the sixth week the peasant guard, Sasaki, was replaced by a more fearsome type : a little sharp, nervous doll of a thing with thick spectacles, Nagami by name—and Hop Li's fifth throw was short.

No witness could have told afterwards what was exactly the sequence of events. The little sack dropped three yards short of the trench, just beyond the reach of hand or tool. Although Jock Drynie shouted and clutched to stop him, John moved to reclaim it. Whether Nagami had seen the parcel hurtle through the mirk or had been attracted by the movement of a prisoner in his squad, he was quick to send the bullet whistling a foot above John's bent head. Then there was the great blowing of whistles and the rushing of guards.

They jerked John from the drain as if he were a bag of coals and threw him to the ground. Nagami, the dutiful and anxious apology for a soldier, stood over him, the point of the bayonet trembling over his throat. John's companions looked on, dumb and paralysed in their helplessness. With bayonet-point and rifle-butt the guards hustled him across the rough ground to the administrative block, and they threw him into a cell.

And this, said John Rolland Cram to himself, is truly the end at last, the last black segment of the fifth arch. He was afraid. Neither philosophy nor faith could sustain him now. All the reactions of his body were lowering—the pulse of excitement in his head, the excess of saliva in his mouth, the cramping misery of visceral contractions. He wanted to vomit, to cry, to lash out against these, his villainous gaolers. But all that kept him to the point of sanity was the fear of showing that he was afraid, the fear of betraying his comrades into a hell even worse than that they now endured, the fear of letting the late Superintendent Engineer of the K. & S. collapse before the yellow rats he had always despised.

They came for him when it was dark, after an hour, it might have been, and marched him into a place so brightly lit within whitewashed walls that his eyes watered. Through the blur he recognised, seated behind a bare table, the commandant and the interpreter, with the senior warrant officer of the camp at attention behind them. This was it, the appointed end, but the very act of abandoning his human hopes brought him a strange sense of contemptuous detachment.

The commandant barked a question, and the interpreter put it to the prisoner with the hissing, leering superiority of his kind.

" You have received over the wire more than one bag of yeast ? "

" Yes."

" How many bags ? "

" Four."

This being translated back to the commandant, he banged the table with his fist and gabbled. Again the interpreter smoothly translated, his teeth gleaming in a horrible parody of the gesture of ingratiation.

" Major Inawe say that for this breaking of rule you must be punished, also those of your party. He now wish to know who sent the parcel ? "

" I do not know who sent the parcel. I have many good friends in China."

" There was no message with same, no ? I ask you once more—who sent the parcel ? "

" I do not know."

The translation of this passage brought a scowl to the face of the commandant. He barked an order, and the interpreter, grinning at John, said :

" Strip."

There was nothing for it. They had every power of humiliation they could desire. Rather than have the guards tear the clothes off his back, he promptly started to divest himself of his poor garments. It occurred to him (so strange is the working of the human mind) that at least the revelation of his elderly corpulence would not seem in the least ludicrous to the small sadists of a paunchy race.

The guards forced him by coarse pressure on his head and neck to bend forward. The warrant officer raised the buckle end of a belt and swung it at the bare back of him who had once been Superintendent Engineer of the K. & S., the hero of a considerable family group in remote Scotland. The leather and the pointed metal seared and stung the white skin and thin flesh of his back. One, two, three, four . . . He began to lose count as it went on. The Japanese laughed as he tottered about in the effort to keep his balance when they were done with him. They threw him his clothes and told him to get back to his allotted place.

"The swine ! O, the bloody little swine ! " cried Jock Drynie as he and Jensen the Swede sought to comfort the body of John Rolland Cram with stuff borrowed from Doc Mulligan.

"This," said the earnest Swede, " is a degradation of the accepted laws of humanity. What we consider now is the collapse of all morality. Here we have nothing but brute force in triumph over the good."

"And I'll tell the world, Jen," said Jock with bitterness. " Give me a hand to get Dad over on his stomach . . . You'll have to try and lie that way, Dad ; they've made such a mess of your old back . . . And the Lord alone knows how I'll keep my hands off the first of these wee bustards that shows his face into the hut in the morning. Hold me down, Jen, if I look like going berserk."

"To this situation we have to bring philosophy," the Swede insisted.

Then he bent over John and stroked his hair with a nearly feminine tenderness.

"You will try to rest, my friend," he suggested softly. " I am here, also Yock. We shall be with you through this night."

The Nips made him parade for work on the following day, and in the evening they dragged him off again to the white-washed room and its bright, merciless lighting. The interpreter showed his teeth and hissed.

"You have received over the wire four bags of yeast. Major Inawe wish to know who sent the parcel."

"I do not know."

"Major Inawe say you must know."

"I do not know."

This was translated to the commandant. He rose with a clattering of a sword and scabbard nearly as tall as himself and struck John on the nose with his clenched fist. Then he shouted an order, and John saw the warrant officer come at him with a wooden chisel and a mallet in his hands. The ape was grinning. One of his guards nearly throttled him while the other forced his jaws apart.

The blow hurt cruelly, and the shock of it sent darkness and dumbness through his brain. When the light returned, he was on the floor, trying to vomit, but his tongue could only expel a few remaining teeth from his lower jaw in a welter of blood and saliva. The Japanese were laughing heartily.

"You will tell us the truth to-morrow, no?" the interpreter suggested genially.

They did it again on the third night, smashing away the last of the natural teeth left to him, and laughing. When the guards brought him back to the hut and threw him down, he let out a terrifying howl of agony and distress, the anguished cry of an animal trapped and lost, and Jock Drynie jumped up and flew at the guards in a splendid, futile folly of anger. He sent one spinning with a blow on the jaw, and then, the next second, he squealed as the other brought a cosh down on the back of his neck. They carried Jock away, while the sergeant of their party stormed and strutted and kicked at any limb in his tempestuous path.

They did not trouble John again, having had their way with him. He relapsed into the awful anonymity of the expendable defeated. Jensen the Swede looked after him, and Doc Mulligan worked with his spare resources to heal his wounds and reduce the degree of shock he had sustained. Both saw that the old man had been aged and sadly set back in the mind by his ordeal. He kept asking after Jock Drynie like a senile grandmother asking after a favourite child among her brood, and one night Jensen the Swede, having been pummelled that day by the rifle-butts in a brush with the guards, spoke impatiently.

"Yock has gone up to the Railway," he said, "and that means death."

"Dear me!" said John mildly. "He was a fine boy."

It came about in the long run that most of the guards came to be tolerant with John, as even the savage may be with an old and genial dog, and so the days and the weeks and the months went on turning slowly over those who languished in the camp at Sam-Shui.

5

Her naked body covered only by a dressing-gown of frail shantung, Sister Adelaide Bryden, Q.A.I.M.N.S., lay on her bed and tried to rest. She had hoped to sleep through the Indian afternoon. The jalousies kept out the intolerable brightness of the sunlight, but not the noises, the queer chatterings, whinings, bleatings and screamings of a Hindu community; nor could they abate the moist heat of the upper Bay of Bengal in the last days of a monsoon period. So it was all the more important, her training told her, to lie still and relax, and if her mind would not halt from its workings and let her roll down the slopes of unconsciousness, to grant the physical tissues surcease from the fret of work in a military hospital.

It troubled Addie Bryden on this sweltering afternoon that she was so restless in the mind. There were all the private troubles of her private self; and then this clinical consciousness of the existence of the troubles, and then the consciousness of this particular consciousness, and then again the consciousness of the consciousness of the consciousness . . . You got like the squirrel in the cage, revolving endlessly but without any prospect of a conclusion.

Beth Cram's daughter was not, however, one to surrender to the complexities of the inner life. As she understood the business of living, the thing was to find one or two reasonably clear lines through the muddle of thought and emotion and follow them steadfastly. She had found that the discipline of the Nursing Service, so stupid and stiff in many of its aspects, had at least this virtue of simplification and purpose. The terrible thing about it was that a girl got her foolish emotions all tangled up with the clear line of duty. Every nurse in the Far Eastern theatre of war (though Sister Bryden in the twenty-third year of her age) must be—except for just a few old sticks and inveterate virgins—in the same emotional mess as herself, created by this fantastic collision between the lean, lonely, long-suffering men of a far-

flung legion of brave men and quite a few clean, efficient and
still-desirable women : both parties thrown together by the
accident of violence in a strange setting.

They had put her into a surgical ward for officers. This was
to the clear annoyance of Matron, but Colonel Strang, the
specialist surgeon, had insisted.

" I feel strongly that young girls just out should do their bit
in the men's wards first," Matron had suggested in her righteous
way. " Besides, the girl is attractive, admittedly, and after that
business with the Tomlinson woman . . ."

" Look here, Mrs. Grundy," the surgeon had wheedled Matron
in the way that so delightfully made her feel quite young again,
" the Bryden kid's going to be so damned hard worked she won't
have time to squeeze a hand. She was with me in the Royal,
and she's the answer to a surgeon's prayer : the hands and the
brains and the know-how. Now, have I got to fight you up to
old Bonker, or will you cave in like a good lass and come out
dancing at the Club to-morrow night ? "

It was wonderful to be working with the legendary Strang,
his silent and infallible aid in the theatre, ready always with the
right instrument to his sure hand, his sheet-anchor in the nursing
of the difficult cases, in which he delighted as other men do in
battle or games. And thus the sardonic gods had put her to the
nursing of the Brigadier, the most difficult and interesting of all
Strang's cases. He had been out on a mission with the Chindits,
and the sniper's bullet had taken him in the nape of the neck so
that he was blind. Now Strang swore by all his fiery Caledonian
gods that he would bridge the lesion somehow and give the
Brigadier back his sight or throw himself into the docks.

He was a brigadier, an exalted person, and that made it no
easier for a simple Scots girl with the two pips of a Nursing Sister
on the epaulettes of her tunic. Yet the card at the end of his
bed in the little room of the main C Ward said that his Christian
names were Phineas John Sackville, his age 31, C. of E. by way
of formal religious attachment, with a mole on his left buttock.
Also, he was badly hurt and most gravely threatened in his
enjoyment of life, a case in which she felt her own professional
honour bound up with that of the great, the wonder-working
Strang. And what a damnable thing that her foolish, feminine
heart must threaten to betray her strong sense of integrity !

It was his patience, his courtesy—and O, a lot of other things besides ! You saw him lying so still and quiet on his back and, below the bandages over his eyes, the bold, lean nose, the little black moustache, the tight mouth and the neat chin—the physical pattern of the Regular Officer, so recurrent in the process of English evolution that you were tempted into the error of thinking that they had bred for looks to the sacrifice of brains. You had washed his lean body from top to toe and given him, for nothing is spared the woman who has devoted her life to nursing, such intimate services as a mother must give her uninhibited child. Lord, to think of it ! She had cut his toe-nails. And still he had always been something more than a case, an individual with the power to pull her off the pedestal of professional rigour.

There were his patience and courtesy—and so much more. The quietness with which he bore his pains, the calm with which he faced the near-certainty of darkness for the rest of his days. He loved to experiment with his sense of touch ; he made her test his powers of subtle hearing.

" May be useful some day, you know, Sister," he would explain, " and I apologise for being such a bore. And," he once added wryly, " I wish I could see you."

" There's not much to see," she had replied off-handedly.

" That orderly chap, Sam Muggridge, assures me there is," the bandaged man chuckled. " I asked him, and he says you're ' a ruddy smasher.' "

" Muggridge's taste is for blowsy barmaids, and I suppose I'm his type."

" Not at all. You have reddish-fair hair, grey eyes, and a slightly pale, remote face. Muggridge had it all pat, except that he didn't use the word ' remote.' He said you looked like ' a bleedin' aristocrat or something.' "

" Muggridge is just a blether."

" There it goes again ! " the Brigadier had laughed. " That lovely Scotch voice . . . Sorry, Sister, I mean ' Scots ' . . . But those clear, crisp consonants. They are enchanting."

" Never mind consonants," Addie remembered herself to have said. " I'm more interested in dressings at the moment."

To keep her head and her position she always had to be roughish against his charm. But that was only another word for his quality. She liked to think of him as reticent and steadfast—

those qualities that were in her own humble folk with quite a different history : those that were in her own mother, those she had learned to be the right equipment of a traveller through life.

Addie heaved her body off the pallet, wincing to the feel of sweat through her thin dressing-gown. She threw it off and started to powder her body all over. With ice-cold water from the porous jar by the wash-stand she dabbed her temples. She pulled on the few, flimsy garments that could be worn in the Indian heat, but took great care in tying and setting the splendid headdress of her trade.

She was not due on duty until seven, but Sister Jones, the dark and garrulous Welshwoman, was free from the professional jealousies, and Addie passed through the main ward as she made for the common room. As she went along, the streamers of her cap flowing behind her, all her patients—the foolish, charming, naughty maimed boys of half-a-dozen nations—chaffed and chirruped happily.

" Hi-ya, Sister ! How's tricks ? "

" Sister ! I'm feeling faint. Kiss me or I'll die."

" I love a lassie, a bonnie Hielan' lassie. She's as fair . . ."

At the door she turned and grinned.

" You're just a lot of impudent blethers," she cried, exaggerating the Scots accent.

A howl of delight greeted the observation. This was her daily performance which they rejoiced to provoke, so small are the pleasures of hospital life. In contrast to the rough cheerfulness of the ward, the little room off it seemed to be filled with the strained silence of anxiety.

" Sleeping ? " she whispered, closing the door behind her softly.

" No," returned the bandaged figure on the bed. " These beastly shooting stars inside my head were worrying me a bit, so I soothed myself by thinking of you."

" Dear me ! " she evaded the personality. " Now I'm going to switch on the light. Tell me if you don't notice any difference."

The switch clicked, and the man said " No difference."

" It'll come all right," she insisted professionally and turned to glance at the chart at the foot of his bed, then to lift the cloth from a tray of instruments and dressings on a side-table.

" Tell me, Sister," said the voice behind her, " are you really serious about wanting to get up the line when the big push starts ? "

" Yes," she said tensely.

" I suppose life in a big base hospital is boring," he went on quietly, " and then there's your brother up there and the uncle beyond. What I was thinking about was this. I'd hate it if you were to go, and Doc Strang would be furiously sick, but if you are determined, there's a friend of mine at GHQ who can push you along if anybody can. Shall I give you a chit ? "

" Yes," she faltered, suddenly wanting to cry.

" Right, there's a pad among my things there. You've got your own pen." He started to dictate. " Dear Bill . . ."

When it was done she watched the little smile about his tight mouth.

" I hope I can sign the thing now," he said. " Prop me up a little, Sister, then you'll have to guide my hand."

Thus her face had to be close to his, and she did not know that her hair lightly brushed his cheek, the scent of it in his nostrils. She held her small hand over his and watched the long, sinewy fingers work finely as he wrote his name. Then his left hand came over suddenly to fall on hers.

" Stay there just one moment, Sister," he whispered. " I am a little lonely to-night. May I touch your face ? After all, I have no eyes to see it."

The blood flushing her cheeks, she held her head beside his and felt the gentle, subtle fingers of the blind run over her forehead, explore the sockets of her eyes, trace the line of her nose, brush across her lips and pass over the soft skin below chin and jaw.

" Thank you, Sister," he said. " Now I'll know you even if the old eyes never get better."

She rose hurriedly from his side, shocked at her own breach of the professional code, and tried to speak sensibly.

" I simply must run for supper. We'll leave the dressing till I come on again at eight. Is there anything you want before I go ? "

" Nothing, except one promise. That, if you do get up the line, you write me a note now and again, and come back when it's all over."

"Goodness, you'll be better by then and home in England," she contrived to laugh.

"I'll find you," he laughed in turn, "even if I have to put the whole of M.I.5 on the job. Blind men need their props."

"I wish you wouldn't talk so much about being blind!" she said with a sudden and tearful petulance and went quickly from the room.

She could not face the dining-hall and supper and the brittle, edgey chatter of her colleagues. She went back to her own room by a devious route and cried a little; so hard was it to throw away love. She wondered miserably if he guessed that she was really seeking to escape the charm he held for her. Probably he did; the delicacy of his apperceptions had often surprised and enchanted her. And then she wondered if he, in his turn and according to his code, was sending her away before it was too late for both of them, the eager young and the maimed.

6

No. 14452763 Corporal Bryden, J. C., drew up his section by the glider on the field at Kilaghat and bade them stand at ease. Six of the great kites stood in line, each with its complement of Airborne troops beside it, and behind that again were ranged row upon row of machines and their attendant groups of soldiers. The engines of the six great bomber-tugs that were to lift the first wave were warming up, their exhausts creating small mirages in the heated evening air. The coolies were running out the light, frail-seeming towing lines. The glider-pilot, with a shock of fair hair and a coloured scarf about his throat, fretted up and down beside his machine, smoking endlessly.

It was coming now, the moment for which all these Airborne men had been elaborately and expensively trained. The most stolid among them felt the screw of tension within : that feeling of one's mind hardly belonging to one's body, coupled with a cramping of the belly muscles, a tightening at the throat. And this was going to be a strike in force, no mere sally of a disruptive party. The mighty bombers and the serried gliders gave the air of majesty to the undertaking. This was the moment when, as they had so long dreamed and so often boasted over pints of beer in East Anglian pubs, the Airborne were going in to turn the fortunes of a war. But it was a nasty moment, waiting. Curly Bryden was surprised at the sharpness with which he reproved one of his men for fumbling at the last moment with his equipment.

He brought his section to attention as his company commander came hurrying up, biting at the corner of his own upper lip.

" All set, Corporal Bryden ? "

" All okay, sir."

" You remember your orders, exactly what to do when you touch down ? "

" Yes, sir."

" Good. Pile in now. We're lifting immediately. The best of luck to you, boys ! And remember, every one of you, that you'll find me or some sort of Command Post at Ack fourteen on the special map."

" Good luck, sir ! "

Soon the glider was rolling over the field, the tug gaining height above and beyond its nose. Then the powerless kite started to lift from the ground and, with just a bump or two, took the air sweetly. The silence of their passage eased a little the minds of the men packed tight in the fuselage with so much hard and lumpy equipment about their persons. Looking forward through the shield of perspex before the pilot, Curly Bryden was fascinated to see how deeply the towrope sagged between the bomber and the kite. You would wonder how any pull could be exerted over that lax bond. He saw also that they were climbing steeply.

" Going high to-night," he remarked to the pilot.

" Gotta get over the hills, son," drawled the American boy, now chewing gum with intentness. " We've quite a way to go this night."

Some time later the pilot pointed downwards and said :

" Jungle. It eats you if it gets you. But you'll be landing on clear paddy."

Jungle. It looked from the air for all the world like a rug of dyed lambskin or one of those knotted mats elderly persons like to fashion. It was all crinkly, in several shades of green, and matted over hundreds of square miles, so that the thought of being lost in it with a wound and without water was like thinking seriously of suicide. The expanse, however, was threaded in the near-darkness by streaks of silver.

" Rivers ! " exclaimed Curly.

" The ruddy old Chindwin is the squiggly one," said the pilot carelessly; " and that's saying a mouthful. As for the straight line to port there, that's no river, brother. That's the Ledo Road."

The tropical night came down upon them. The flight continued on its way, now swinging and again bumping in the thin air at more than a mile above the earth's level. Within the glider the only light came from a few fluorescent tubes on the panel before the pilot. Curly Bryden thanked his Maker that he hadn't this Yankee chap's job.

His head nodded. He slept uneasily, dreaming a bad dream about going into the boxing ring with a paralyzed left arm against a Japanese champion who, he had been warned by sinister seconds, would use every foul trick without hindrance from the referee. In the twelfth round, it must have been, the Nip caught him by the left shoulder with the open glove and shook him ; and when Curly looked round, the referee was grinning at him.

But it was really only the glider-pilot who had wakened him, saying :

" Say, Corp, get your boys alerted. We're casting off pronto. And if you can pray, Scottie, this is the time right now."

Curly waited for the sag that, however slight, followed the cast off. They were going in at last. A few anti-aircraft guns on the ground below started to bark, the spits of flames from their muzzles like the cheap fireworks of small children. He was in the mood to disdain the wild ack-ack fire of the Nips, but the pilot started to bawl, and the bawl rose to a scream.

" Out of control ! Christ, I'm out of control ! Swinging . . . Come back on your keel, you bitch ! " he cursed his machine, kicking wildly at the bar. Then he made a noise like a jungle animal on the point of death. It was a high-pitched, nasal wail of terror in failure.

Those on the strip who listened to the whistle of the falling glider heard a rasping thud from the jungle trees on its edge and grimly said to each other that that unlucky kite and its crew had had it and could be written off. Others were still coming in, and there was a battle to be fought.

The war machine turned in its deliberate way to deal with the deaths of Curly Bryden and his comrades, dead in action without having fired a shot in action, small elements in the fantastic wastage of war. A chaplain read a service over so many still forms wrapped in brown blankets, laid by so many shallow graves, and then made a note for the form to be filled in for the benefit of the War Graves department. A soldier-clerk in the Q Branch at divisional Rear Headquarters altered a figure in his Strength Returns and, noting a name for once in a while, remembered briefly how little Corp Bryden, away back in a crowded Corn Exchange in an East Anglian town, had knocked hell out of the Paratroops' champion at the same weight. He had ended by knocking the beggar through the ropes into his own C.O.'s lap. That had been a ruddy good laugh ! A great little boxer. A pity.

The forms passed through Third Echelon back in India and so through the vast machine of SEAC. They were carried by air to London and scanned by a man working in a room that overlooked Eaton Square and the gardens that had gone so shabby under the bombardment and the collapse of the sanctions. A warrant officer took a file of names and addresses of Next-of-Kin from the Out tray before this diligent official and returned to his own table, piled high with prepared telegraph forms. The teleprinters started to click and shudder in the Post Office, and within an hour or so the arrows of grief were speeding towards the hearts of women in cottages, farms, mansionhouses, urban back rows, tenement dwellings and suburban villas all over the island, from the cliffy edges of the Pentland Firth to the warm and leafy valleys of Devon, from the craggy headlands of Pembroke across the smoky Midlands to the wide flats of the Fens.

The last antenna of this long line of communication, a boy in Post Office uniform, rather dolefully whistling *Lili Marlene*, climbed a steep street in Garvel and looked for the close in which dwelt a family called Bryden.

Next day, those readers of the *Garvel Courier* with a taste for the savage ironies so lavishly provided by the Gods of War, might have observed in close juxtaposition the curt, stunned announcement of Curly Bryden's death in the Far East under the heading IN ACTION and a report of a social occasion in the town. This, under the headline in 18-point Old Face, LOCAL TWINS PLAY FOR WAR CHARITY, said :—

A successful musical in aid of the R.A.F. Benevolent Fund was held yesterday afternoon in the spacious ballroom of Blackwood's Hotel. The organiser was our fellow-residenter, Mrs. Dan Rolland, and a large company assembled to share a feast of song and instrumentation.

Messrs. Dickie and Blythe, Mrs. McCourt and the Misses Hoy, Bonella, and Hetherington gave of their best in songs and pieces, Mrs. McCourt's rendering of You Are My Heart's Desire *being particularly appreciated.*

It is no reflection on the brilliance of these local artists to say, however, that the honours of the day lay with the twin daughters of the organiser, the Misses Beryl and Sybil Rolland. Nationally famous now as the " Rolland Rhythmic Twins," these two gifted young ladies delighted the audience with their skilful and delicate renderings of tunes, both classical and popular. It was a " big break " for Garvel that these young ladies of genius could spare a day from their exhausting duties with ENSA, of which they are now leading lights, heading for ultimate stardom.

Deputising for Provost Crombie, who is indisposed, Bailie Tanna-hill, thanking Mrs. Rolland and her coadjutors, said it was a peculiar pleasure to have among them that day Corporal Charles Rolland, R.A.F., on leave from his duties at one of the largest bomber stations in England, " one of the few to whom so many owe so much." (Applause.) He made bold to say that the Rolland family had truly " done its bit."

Acknowledging the compliments in a happy speech, Mrs. Rolland announced that the drawings would be in the region of £47.

Cutting this report from her copy of the *Courier* next day, Lily was vexed to see the clash between its gaiety and the few sombre lines in small type which intimated the death of Curly Bryden. She could all too easily imagine, and actually phrase, the cruel things people would say ; and she worked up within herself a private indignation against the difficulties of living nicely with your neighbours when you meant so well, really and truly.

She went downstairs to look out a sheet of the marbly, deckle-edged notepaper she favoured (with " The Neuk " and the rest embossed in bright red) and considered how she would phrase her note of sympathy to Beth Bryden. She was quite sure it was not her fault at all, and in that she was quite right, but she could not hear the sardonic chuckles of the Gods.

7

The world turned over and over. The unwise, fretful, little men who peopled its surface proceeded with their task of self-destruction in war, each party capable of producing on demand proof of Divine sanction for its attitude. In a culminating frenzy of drunkenness through power two Japanese cities were reduced to middens of ashes and putrefying flesh, and at length most men sickened of the slaughter, but not before a large proportion of their little world's resources had been blown away.

In the near-vacuum created by the bombs there was immediately a swirling of masses of humans over wide areas of the world's surface, such as takes place when the complex structure of an antheap is destroyed by a giant foot or riddled by a boy's cudgel. Some sought to rebuild where their homes had been shattered about them ; some were too stunned to do aught but hang about in stupor and await a miracle ; most strove passionately and without mercy with others in the blind desire to get back whence they had started—the armies, the prisoners, the uncountable displaced of a war merciless beyond the imagination of the most gifted of the species.

One of these eddies halted and froze at length, remotely, in and about the house called Penang Lodge at Killadam in the sub-Highland parish of Finlas, whence John Rolland Cram had departed nearly eight years before. Now his sister, Beth Bryden, sat again with her knitting on the garden seat, repaired and repainted white, on the terrace before the cottage and considered the perplexing, heartbreaking but always fascinating nature of life after two major wars.

She was proud and happy that her own Davie, with the help of some of his mates in the yard, had made such a rare job of getting the place into order after Addie's cable had reached them from Singapore. He had got the big men at T. & B.'s to assist him in getting compensation out of the Admiralty ; he and she had crossed the water nearly every week-end, and her Davie had wrought himself to the bone, painting, mending, plastering, to get what he called "the old place just right for John."

It had been the saving of his mind, perhaps. Poor Davie had taken an awful blow in Curly's death : more than she, the woman who had contemplated it hourly for years, had done. She had almost prepared the empty place in her heart. His hair was white now, his face gaunt. It was a blessing to see him interested in something, working out of the pride and goodness of his honest soul to do something useful and interesting for somebody else.

He was somewhere behind the house on this warm forenoon of a Sabbath in June. Never had he been able to get that silly old Dam out of his head. It had almost come that he believed in the foolish way of a man that his failure to build it soundly had been the means of sending John into captivity. Now he was busy fortifying the banks of the original stream, the Navy's rubbish all cleared away, as if by securing the flow of water he performed a necessary act of private expiation.

He had Phin up there with him : Phin stretched out on the warm bank above the stream, patient in his blindness but as eager as a child to know how Davie's work proceeded, gentle, intelligent. Next to Addie, nobody was so good with Phin as Davie, who saw in his son-in-law another fascinating job to be tackled, another challenge to his sense of craftsmanship. He developed notions for the education and liberation of the blind.

That was a queer turn-up, if you pleased, the return of Addie with a tall, blind husband. Her cables from the Far East after V-J Day had nearly driven Beth out of her mind, with their revelation of the way in which her familiar world was changing. The one about her finding her Uncle John in Singapore and bringing him home soon was all right ; Beth would trust Addie to get to Tokyo when her mind was made up to it. But it was the one that said she was getting married, and they were to wait for the letter by air-mail.

Beth admitted to herself that she had been unreasonably angry, and that Davie on the other hand had been the wiser for once in a while.

" It's a kind of a facer, right enough," he had admitted, " but I'll back our Addie all the way. She's young enough, but I've never seen that lass behave like a fool in all her born days."

His fairness had impressed Addie's mother, and she had come

to perceive that she was just like any mother, vain in the assumption that she must have a say in her daughter's choice of a man, the manner of her wedding, and the appointment of her first home.

When the long letter came, however, it had been she, Beth Cram, who understood better than Davie the passionate, pitiful, painful implications of Addie's decision. Davie had been nearly ribald in his incredulity.

"A brigadier, begod!" he had cackled. "It's a good thing this chap Mountbatten is married, or our Addie would have him by the scruff of the neck by this time. A brigadier—three up a dirty old close in Garvel! Will we have to bed them in the kitchen?"

"Will it matter, Davie?" she had retorted gently. "It's not that he'll see anything. It's what we are ourselves, better or worse."

"There's something in that," he had agreed, adding thoughtfully: "Poor lad! Blindness must be an awful business . . . But our wee Addie married to a brigadier!" he had laughed again. "Upon my Sam, Beth, it's a real pantomime when you come to think of it!"

And it had all been so much easier than they had imagined in their social apprehensions. Phin's father and mother were dead long ago in a tragic episode of Indian rioting, and a sister wrote kindly enough from a manor house in Somerset. Addie brought home her lines, duly certified by the Presbyterian minister of a St. Andrews Church in one of those funny Indian places. On his own part, Phin pointed out that the War Office had prudently reduced him to his substantive rank of lieutenant-colonel, and that he preferred to be plain Mister from then on; but that he thought his pension would keep Addie and himself in fair comfort.

It was a queer mix-up one way and another, as Beth saw it, but a sensible body had to take this new world as she found it. Phin was quiet and gentle in his blindness. Beth perceived clearly that his love for Addie and his trust in her were complete, and that Addie loved her husband; and if there was a bit of pity thrown in, no woman was the worse of having someone who must utterly depend upon her. All the small matters of money and manners and accent she and Davie had worried about were suddenly found to have no relevance in that relationship. It would be a long time, thought Beth, before she would get used to having a born gentleman for her son-in-law, but she liked him and admired him ; because he had made Addie happy she secretly loved him. As a sensible Scots mother she reckoned her daughter had conducted her adult life with good sense towards a reasonable prospect of happiness.

Beth stirred out of her absorption to the sound of footsteps coming slowly across the gravel round the gable of Penang Lodge. She did not need to turn to know that this was Phin, walking alone. He insisted in learning in his own way, to the point that he objected to belonging to what he called " the Order of the White Stick." He was firm in the thesis that a blind man could so sharpen his remaining faculties by practice, he could reasonably succeed in getting about his necessarily small world without aid. Davie had found this an enchanting idea.

"Ye're about right, Phin !" he had cried. "It's juist like this new Radar business."

"That's the very idea, Davie !"

"We'll have to think about this," Davie had said, speculating deeply on the properties of batteries, mine-detectors and other fascinating objects.

They were all in the conspiracy now. Beth, who was apt to be foolish about these things and always wanted to rush in the female fashion to the aid of those in distress, had learned that her proper function was to sit still and let Phin do it for himself, instead of trying to do it for him.

She called to him calmly.

"Here I am, Phin. On the garden seat."

"Thank you, Mother !" returned the blinded soldier. "Now I've got my bearing. Just watch me make a happy landing. Give me a word now and again."

He always called her Mother but addressed his father-in-law as Davie. The distinction was understood by all parties concerned. Now he moved towards the seat, slowly, with something of the wary air of a thrush listening for worms.

"About six steps now," said Beth quietly.

"Yes, I'm dead on the beam. You're at the right end of the seat, aren't you ? I'm making towards the left end."

She did not say anything more until he hesitated just short of the bench and put out a hand gingerly.

"Just about it, Phin."

"Got it!" he cried triumphantly, his hand falling on the back rest. "That was a pretty good shot, I think. Some day I must have a go along the shore road."

"You'd better ask Addie about that," Beth warned him.

"No, I'll tell her afterwards you said I could try it," he teased her. "But tell me, Mother, tell me how the Firth is looking to-day?"

This was about the queerest thing of all in Beth's experience with her daughter's husband. Since Addie was now in full, bustling, contented charge of Penang Lodge, she had leisure to sit much out of doors, and Phineas came to her often on the garden seat, asking her to describe what she saw with her living eyes; and Beth, a town-bred woman, found herself discovering the world for the first time through the eyes of the blind!

His humble eagerness had urged her to see for herself and put her vision into words, just as he had taught her to listen for the first time in her life consciously to the morning and evening songs of the birds : tutoring her to identify the glittering cascade of the blackbird's solo and to distinguish it from the subtly less lyrical vaunt of the mavis, with its recurrent "Did he do it? Did he do it?" to learn with innocent surprise that the red-breast has a sweet song of his own, and to be able to delight, in the early mornings when she lay awake by Davie's side, in the tinkling on a silvern anvil that is the chaffinch's call.

Now she had to catalogue all the aspects of the scene for him : whether the shore on the other side of the loch loomed near or was mistily remote, what manner of ships lay at anchor in the Deeps off Garvel, and was the smoke hanging over that town in the cleft of the hills or were the slate roofs shining? He had to have some account of the Highland peaks away up to the North. Did the summer sun gleam on the pillar of the Riccar Light? What could she tell of the outer reaches of the Firth and the aspect of the islands?

A river steamer crossed the line of her vision making from Hamilton's Quay round the Strone to Killadam, and Phin said, his strong profile uplifted :

"That's the ten-forty from Kempock, and it ought to be the *Duchess of Buccleuch*, but it isn't. The beat of the paddles is quite different."

T.F.A.   U

"I couldn't for the life of me tell you, Phin," she confessed, marvelling at his subtlety of male apprehension. "Davie will know."

She was about to rise and move round the gable to call to her husband when Phin casually remarked, long before she saw the movement with her own eyes :

"Don't trouble, Mother. Here come Uncle John and Addie."

And there they were, moving from the porch towards the garden seat. Beth had a sudden access of vision, in which she saw the ghostly streamers of the nursing sister's headdress floating about and behind the bright hair of her daughter. The lass had been upstairs with John for nearly an hour past : carrying his breakfast and seeing that he ate it, washing him, helping him to the lavatory, helping him to dress, tying his tie, and always persuading him that he must learn to do all these things for himself.

It was a blessing, when you thought of it, that Addie had the qualifications and status of a professional nurse to get her over the awkwardnesses. Beth knew that, while she would herself have given John the most humble service within her power, he was best managed by one who, having his love and trust, had the brisk way of the skilled with him. Addie was a good girl ; she had always been a good, sensible girl—and worth looking at, too, even if it was her own mother who said so—but Beth sometimes wondered a thought glumly if her Addie had not fated herself to be a nurse for the rest of her life.

This had once come up between them in the way of confidential talk between adult women.

"I don't see the point, Mother," Addie had said in her direct way, her grey eyes wide. "I'm trained to look after sick people, and Uncle John and Phin are both good men, aren't they ? There aren't many girls nearly as lucky as I am."

In the Scots way she had avoided the use of the word "love," and Beth in her turn had been careful not to say anything about bairns and bringing up a family.

Phin rose and greeted the newcomer.

"Good morning, Uncle John ! Feeling better to-day ? Come and sit between Mother and me."

"Thank you, Phin," replied John mildly. "I'm pretty well

to-day. Good morning, Beth. It's a nice day, isn't it ? Sit down, Phin."

Several hands reached out to help the late Superintendent Engineer of the K. & S. into his place. It was significant that he was set down between the other two. He was not yet strong. His hands and limbs trembled a little all the time, and he was prone to a working of the sunken lips, for Addie had judged that he was not yet fit to submit to the dentist. His face was by now full enough, but it still had the ivory pallor brought on by under-nourishment over the years and then by the mecrapine with which the Army doctors had robustly dosed him on his release. John Rolland Cram was an old man now, and frail.

As Beth watched him out of the corner of her eye, however, she was concerned again, as they all were always, with what the Japanese had done to his mind.

That smiling, nodding mildness of his was frightening to those who cared for him. He was never excited, angry, even irritable ; he just smiled mildly, and nodded. His interests, if a word so strong could be used of his acquiescences, were in the small immediate things. What of horror he had known, what of spectacular and dramatic value he had experienced, could not be known. Under the smooth shell of his gratitude for kindness, behind the smile and the dim, long-sighted eyes, the personality of the man remained a mystery. It was as Phin had wisely summed it up for them one night when, John safely bedded after supper, the family frankly discussed his condition.

" My feeling is that poor old Uncle John is still in Sam-Shui. And I think the drill should be," Phin went on, " never to jolly him, or be hearty, or force him to see what he can't see ; just let him feel the family about him, and get the feeling of safety again. We might get him going on the garden, for instance."

This was all a bit beyond Davie, who would have had John round to the Pictures in Doon twice a week, but Addie had laid it down that her husband was in the rights of the matter ; and now they were all in the kind conspiracy to rebuild round Uncle John the palisades of security. Phin started to tell him how he was getting on with his own efforts to move without aid and how he had, in fact, only a few minutes past, contrived the passage from behind the house to the garden seat ; and John was visibly pleased, nodding vigorously and saying :

"Good lad! Good lad! You keep at it, Phin. Chaps like you and me have a bit of leeway to make up."

They heard Addie calling round the gable of the house.

"Father! Father! Come and sit with Uncle John and Phin. Mother and I have a lot to do before these people come."

"Just a tick, Addie."

"No tick about it. Come you at once when you're told. And don't you forget to put on your good suit and wash yourself before these folk come."

Uncle John and Beth and Phin all smiled to overhear this familiar passage. Addie joined them again.

"That man would break your heart," she observed. "Can you come now, Mother? We'd better get started."

Davie arrived heartily.

"Hear me being bossed about?" he asked genially. "And how's yourself to-day, John? That's fine, man! Did ye see the big carrier that came up this morning? That's her up by the Patch thonder . . . You know about the launching of that one. Fairfield built her; but this was in 1943, I think it was; everything hush-hush and Bob's yer uncle; and the Queen was to do the job; and it was the most hellish day of rain I ever seen . . ."

Davie had lately discovered for himself the few and simple virtues and rewards of the art of narrative. In his own honest way he had been delighted to find that his stories of shipbuilding achievements, adventures and misadventures of launching, and all sorts of oddments from the lore of a century of craftsmanship, had the power to entertain Phin as he himself could be entertained by tales of adventure in distant parts; and that they had, above all, the occasional virtue of rousing John out of his bland apathy and telling of his own great days with T. & B. and in the engine-rooms of ships.

The tale of the launching of the carrier was a long and technical one; and within the house, meanwhile, the womenfolk ran between kitchen and dining-room in anxious preparation for guests. Any other woman could have seen that they expected guests out of the ordinary. Beth, who was not schooled to grandeur in catering, had continually to run and ask Addie how this and that and the other unfamiliar object should be set on the table. In the kitchen Addie played exquisitely with the preparation of

a salad that was to go with a beautiful cold tongue (extorted by
guile and cajolery from a butcher in Doon who remembered old
Mr. Cram and was glad to hear of his safe return) and with a
confection of rhubarb to be served in ramekin moulds.

" If they have that," she announced a thought viciously,
" with a plate of good soup to start with and our cheese ration
to follow, they'll do jolly well."

" If it's a fishing holiday they're having," added Beth tartly,
" they might have sent down a cut of salmon. I suppose these
rich folk never think about the rations."

" I suppose not," said Addie absently. " Now, Mother, away
into the Big Room and lay out those glasses I washed this
morning and the decanter with the curly top. Set them out
nicely on the sideboard, and don't forget to put down the
Japanese tea-cloth with the peacock thingummyjigs on it. And
remember that it's sherry and won't agree with you a bit."

" Such a lot of nonsense I never saw in all my born days ! "
declared Beth, but without sincerity, for she was in fact very proud
to be entertaining swells and to see how competently her daughter
could cope with such an important occasion. " I'll be glad when
I'm back in my own wee kitchen in Garvel. Four courses to
your dinner ! "

" And give that father of mine a shout to come inside at once
and get himself washed and properly dressed. O Lord ! I forgot
the coffee cups. Hurry, now ! "

Mr. and Mrs. Tertius Troquair Bannerman were coming to
lunch. When the news of John's return had been published in
the local papers with some account of the romantic circumstances
of his niece's part in the affair, old Tertius had written a very
decent letter, welcoming an old acquaintance home and expressing
the hope that they might soon meet. Later came a letter in the
large triumphant hand of Mrs. Bannerman, to the effect that she
had secured a passage to the Far East where family interests
required her prompt attention, and that she would be glad to
have quite the latest information from Mr. Cram and the
Brigadier as to conditions out there. They were fishing at Uglas,
only a few miles away, and could run down the glen at any
convenient moment. Mrs. Bannerman added that she was sure
she had known the Brigadier's people in Bangalore in '24 or
thereabouts.

The three Brydens had taken this problem into anxious family conference, and Addie had almost fiercely insisted that it be luncheon and not afternoon tea. Beth failed to understand wholly this determination, such a lot of bother with it, too, but she guessed shrewdly enough that Addie's several prides were involved, and if it was the right thing to provide lunch to keep your end up with big folk like the Bannermans, then she would not fail her daughter. It sort of explained to her one of Phin's odd, affectionate sayings about his wife :

" Addie has the makings of an absolutely first-class tactician. She never advances until her base and lines are perfectly secure."

So Beth was now laying out the polished glasses on the exquisite tea-cloth from Japan, and a car came along the road, passed the house slowly, with that curious air of indecision transmitted to his vehicle by a driver in doubt, stopped some fifty yards beyond the gate, and then backed slowly. Addie came through from the kitchen and joined her mother at the window of the Big Room.

" That's them, and don't ask questions about petrol," she said tartly. Suddenly she started to giggle a little hysterically, crying : " O Lord ! Look at the woman's hat. How on earth will I keep from laughing ? "

" Addie ! " her mother severely reprimanded. " That's no way to behave, and your guests at the door ! "

" It's a scream just the same," Addie insisted, dabbing at her eyes. " Now for high society."

She was out on the terrace, her mother with her, to greet the guests and head them off from the men of the household on the garden seat.

The approach of the Bannermans up the eastern path was a sight for sore eyes, indeed. Tall, untidy, her great feet encased in brogues with goffered tongues as usual, her wild hair now nearly white, the lady sported a hat that would have tempted more urbane persons than Addie to laugh. With a dyed plume on the front, it was such a large, floppy affair as might have graced an Edwardian garden party, and quite probably had, and it went very strangely with the quasi-sporting note of the rest of her attire. Mr. Bannerman's hat was equally eccentric, being a stained and shabby green felt too small for him and cocked high on his distinguished head. His gold-rimmed pince-nez were awry on his nose. He carried in his hand a fishmonger's bag with the tail of a sizable fish sticking out of one end.

The guests were ushered into the house, and Beth led Mrs. Bannerman upstairs, while Addie saw to the removal of Mr. Bannerman's coat and deplorable hat prior to inviting him into the Big Room.

" But I say, Florence, what do I do with this object ? " he cried piteously after his wife, holding up the straw bag.

" Leave it with the cook, of course," commanded Mrs. Bannerman.

" Let me take it," suggested Addie, perceiving in Tertius one of these confused old gentlemen who have to be looked after. She liked him on sight.

" Ah, yes, my dear ! Very good of you, I'm sure," said Tertius with the relief of one who has had a dangerous reptile taken off his hands. " Caught it last night myself. You'll find it an uncommon nice grilse. Myself, I like my salmon plain boiled with a touch of vinegar and new potatoes. A matter of taste, to be sure."

" Now, if you'll take a seat for one moment, Mr. Bannerman, I'll get the others in from the garden. I think you know," she faced him deliberately, " that my husband is blind, but perhaps I ought to warn you that poor Uncle John is still very frail and not quite used to company, even to being safe at home."

" Yes, yes ! Dear me ! Tragic ! "

Shortly the party was assembled in the Big Room, and Addie watched its progress as she might the fluctuations of a patient in high fever. She saw her mother sitting a little apart from the rest, but that was as it must be. Her father—and what a fine face he had ! she irrelevantly realized—was dumb in the presence of one of whom, as the last of the Bannermans, he had an almost feudal awe, but he was being quietly useful with the decanter and empty glasses. Inevitably, Mrs. Bannerman had seized on Phin and in a voice you might have heard in Doon was seeking to establish her supposition that she had known his people at Bangalore away back in '24. The fact that her supposition was ill-founded had no power to daunt one of the Birch-Pitkeathlys ; she went on sounding robustly for the mutual acquaintances they must surely have.

Before she went through to serve the soup, Addie heard Uncle John explain with surprising liveliness to Mr. Bannerman how his house had been recovered from the Admiralty and restored promptly, thanks to Davie's industry.

"If it had been the War Office, now," she heard old Tertius complaining. "You remember Killogie Old House, Mr. Cram? And what must they make of it but the headquarters of a tank school? Wantons and despoilers! I hang my head when I must go back. My library was apparently a species of cocktail-bar. But outside! My trees cut down! My grass churned to mud! Concrete blocks where we once watched the sun on the old sycamores, you remember? The age is to the barbarian. Power corrupts."

John shook his head in sympathy and sorrow, and Addie heard Mr. Bannerman add vehemently and, as she thought, wisely:

"Desolation! Waste!" and again: "What word is there for it but Waste?"

Mrs. Bannerman's plumed hat (to the puzzled consternation of Beth, who did not know the ways of the gentry) dominated the luncheon table. The Brydens were all somewhat astonished to remark that she could eat as swiftly and noisily as she talked, and Beth wondered where good manners came in. The woman seemed to dominate, if not bully them all. No matter what ordinary bit of conversation might be passing between, say, old Tertius and Addie, she could come crashing in like a horse with a loud "Now tell me, Brigadier. See much of In-jah on your way home?"

"I was naturally in India for quite a long time, one way and another, but only on the military side," Phin would fence. "It was one way of escaping the rocket bombs. Had you any experience of them, Mrs. Bannerman?"

It would all be manageable for a time thereafter, and then, at one painful point, she turned on John and said:

"Now, tell me, Mr. Cram, just how many of our people died on the Railway? One hears so much about every sleeper representing one body. Seems a bit out to me."

Addie cut in quickly: "My uncle wasn't sent up there."

Phin added swiftly: "Nobody knows the truth about the Railway yet. I'd rather let it wait a bit."

"History, my dear," said Mr. Bannerman patiently but, as the others understood his statement, apologetically, "can't quite be taken in terms of hearsay . . . You were saying, Mrs. Bryden," he turned courteously to Beth, "that you remember Killogie forty years ago. Did you ever encounter old Dan Dinwiddie, the head gamekeeper ? Now, there was a character."

The fantastic thing about Mrs. Bannerman, as Addie saw it, was that she was without the slightest desire to hurt, without the faintest notion that she was hurting. She was some sort of primitive survival into the new world of loss and penury, the world wasted, as old Tertius's phrase suggested. She was like a spirited hunter out of an Edwardian stable which had failed to realise that its familiar paddock was long ago turned into a graveyard. Soon, in a pause in the conversation that Addie could not quickly enough bridge, she was back to her single subject.

"Tell me, Brigadier," she belled, "about this General Slim. Never heard of him before. I must say the Burma campaign was a jolly good show."

"Slim is a very fine leader of men," said Phin quietly. Without appearing rude he turned to old Tertius and their interrupted talk. "About those yachts, Mr. Bannerman : I suppose that was the great sport on the Firth in those days ? "

"Ah yes, indeed ! " cried Tertius, thus happily returned to one of his own subjects. "Money was plentiful then. We were on the top of the wave of industrial expansion. Labour was still cheap. A topsy-turvy economy, if you please, but a great deal of beauty was created. The great yachts of yesterday . . . *Valkyrie*, *Thistle*, *Bona*. Dear, dear ! And all gone, like my trees and my grass. Tanks, concrete, my library a species of public house ! The apes in command . . . "

Addie's nervous eyes swept round the table in an embracing glance. She saw her father staring at the flowers in the middle of it, and perceived that her mother, her face grey and stony, had been struck a grievous blow, so that for her the rest of the day must be haunted by the ghost of Curly. Only Uncle John behind his mask of dazed indifference seemed secure.

"Phin," she attracted her husband's attention quickly. "Will you help me please ? "

He rose at once, and she led him out into the hall, carefully closing the door behind her.

"After lunch," she whispered intensely, " promise me to take that old bitch and keep her beside you till we get her away. She'll have Uncle John out of his mind, and she's broken my mother's heart already."

" I've got all that, dearest," he whispered back. " Just park her with me on the garden seat and say that I mustn't be left alone."

He suddenly took her in his arms and held her tight within them, whispering in the ear he kissed :

" It's all right, dear soldier. We'll get through."

" Phin ! " she protested, at once alarmed, scandalized and enchanted. " Quick now for the coffee. Pretend you were helping me."

Their contrivance was successful, absurd as it might have seemed to more alert observers that a blind man should be entrusted with a scalding coffee-kettle when his mother or father-in-law might have more securely discharged the task. The absurdity passed unnoticed, for Uncle John, by some quirk of delayed action in his mind, had remembered a great steam yacht built for an American banker by T. & B., and Tertius had remembered it also, and Davie had recovered from the shock of grief renewed to insist that he remembered in his turn of her being lost in the Med in the last war. Their eager male discussion of mere dates had fortunately occulted the rising sun that glowed so brightly through Mrs. Bannerman's mind, and she was discussing with Beth, and with force and sincerity, the disparity between the sugar ration and the fruits available for jam.

Addie broke up the party as soon as she decently could and carefully disposed her forces. Rather elaborately she led Phin out to the garden seat and suggested to Mrs. Bannerman that there were the time and place for a good talk. She was pleased that Tertius protested he would like nothing better than a stroll round the garden with his old friend, your excellent Uncle John, my dear young lady. She saw her father range uneasily round the gable of Penang Lodge, his mind happily returned to the problems presented by the stream from the hills. She knew that her mother, with that ghostly, bright, boyish face smiling to her, and mocking her in its smiling, would be best employed clearing the table and washing up.

She ran upstairs to her room for a cooling dab of powder and to satisfy that desperate longing, which every hostess that ever lived has known, to escape from the strain of a difficult party. She sat on the brocaded chair before her dressing-table, stared at her reflection in the mirror and wondered a little anxiously what the couples in the garden were saying to each other.

She had no need to concern herself as to how Uncle John was faring with Tertius Troquair Bannerman, for John was feeling tired and dazed after so much sociability, perhaps a thought battered by the loud insistency of Mrs. Bannerman's conversational style, and old Tertius quickly perceived the degree of decay inflicted on his friend's faculties by the years of captivity and the shock of maltreatment. Provoking only an occasional " Yes, indeed," or a vague " Is that so ? " from his companion with the nearly fixed bland smile on his face, he took the burden of conversation on himself and prattled on mildly about matters small enough. The experience gave him a subtly painful sense of his own age, of years wasted by the locust, of interests once warm and vital now bleached by time and the unreasoning angers of mankind. Though the June afternoon was bright enough, the garden flourishing again, he had the feeling that he and his mild companion walked in the hooded light of the autumn sun.

" Some day," he found himself saying, " I trust we may have a fine reunion at Killogie. No doubt I can get my house restored to decency. No doubt I can get compensation from these vandals. Perhaps even the parklands may recover quickly once we have cleared away the shards of their brutal exercises. But my trees ! I shall never see them in their glory again."

" No," agreed John with surprising sharpness. " There's a terrible lot old chaps like you and me will never see again."

" A lot humanity will never see again . . . There was one matter of some historical interest . . ."

Then Tertius checked himself abruptly and fell silent. He had come to Penang Lodge that day with the somewhat indeterminate idea that he might, given a suitable opportunity, reveal to John Rolland Cram the fact of their consanguinity. In the light of events which had torn their world apart, it had seemed to him historically just to reveal and establish the claim of brotherhood. He had also thought, not unsubtly, that the revelation of his identity with a great family would please the prisoner of war and do something to restore the pride and self-respect the Japanese had knocked out of him with his teeth.

Now he thought to see that it was too late. The man was but the mild ghost of the successful Superintendent Engineer ; the fact was irrelevant. Atomic bombs wiped out tradition as well as the flesh. Tertius wondered if he should one day show Addie the Watson Gordon portrait of her grandfather and let her see whence she had derived much of the dignity of her features. No, he would leave it to her by will. A mere codicil . . . A charming girl. It was a sore emptiness in a man not to have an heir.

" But there are my wife and that gallant, blind soldier on the seat up there. I fancy," Tertius chuckled, " that the Brigadier has had his work cut out to explain the Far East as it is to-day. And there is your delightful niece coming out to sit with them. Shall we join them, Mr. Cram ? "

Addie had looked into the kitchen on her way downstairs.

" How are you getting on, Mother ? " she asked.

" Fine ! " Beth replied. She looked up and smiled ruefully. " I doubt I was born to be happier in a kitchen than in high society."

" Well, leave it all till these people go, and Phin and I'll wash up afterwards."

She reached the garden seat in time to hear the end of a discourse by Phin. His voice was taut, his sentences clipped, as always when he was exasperated ; and his wife looked for the tell-tale widening of his nostrils.

" I can only assure you, Madam, that the East has completely changed since you last saw it. The Raj is in rags now, I'm afraid. To keep these people on our side—even the Karens and the Shan folk—we made promises. We keep our promises, I hope. That gave them the sense of power. We abdicated in the East in order to save our skins. You may make business arrangements with the Asiatics. We'll never boss them around again, never. The punkah-wallah isn't frightened any more. That may be a pity. It remains a fact."

" Extraordinary ! " exclaimed Mrs. Bannerman, clearly unconvinced.

The tremor of the dyed plume in her hat suggested a profound and perfectly honest suspicion of Bolshevism in unexpected places. She turned at the sound of Addie's footsteps on the gravel.

"Ah, there you are! Your dear husband has been *most* interesting on Burma and In-jah, most interesting. Not that I agree with every word he says by any means : not by any means. But it has been most interesting. Now I think we must be going. Where . . . ? Ah, Tertius, there you are! Can you find Susan ? "

" Susan ? My darling ! I am at a loss completely . . ."

" The bag. The straw thing we brought the fish in. Most precious these days."

" I've got it ready," lied Addie, swiftly apprehending the lady's anxiety.

She ran indoors to get it, also to bring her mother out and, through the back door, hurriedly warn her father that a last formal appearance was expected of him.

There were two minutes of confusion on the terrace as thanks and farewells were exchanged.

" So good of you . . . A delightful meeting . . . It has been a pleasure. Thank you, my dear child, thank you ! And you will remember that reunion at Killogie, Mr. Cram . . . I hope you will have a pleasant voyage, Madam, but shipping is terribly scarce, I'm afraid."

The conventional tags clattered in the air, and then they were away down the path. Davie Bryden went with them to do the honours for Penang Lodge, but Addie and Phin watched the remarkable progress downhill of the Bannermans ; the gallant, pathetic and elderly *memsahib* still flying the brave plume of Edwardian security, old Tertius lurching short-sightedly behind her, the silly little green hat on his head, the empty bag of straw dangling at the end of one of his long arms.

" That's that," said Addie with finality, adding sourly : " And did we fight the Burma Campaign for Mrs. B.? "

" The old lady is an ass, but still a person," observed Phin mildly.

Davie came back up the path, grinning, and remarked :

" That's a rare old battleaxe for ye, eh ? "

John Rolland Cram, late Superintendent Engineer of the K. & S., alone remained aloof. He sat down on the white-painted bench and was smiling blandly towards the sunlit eyebrows of the hills above his native town.

"Your rest now, Uncle John," Addie turned to him. "Father, will you see Uncle John laid down properly? . . . Yes, I'll sing you *The Lea Rig* after supper to-night . . . You get your knitting, Mother, and have a nice rest in the sun. I'll finish the dishes and Phin'll dry for me. He's getting really good now."

As she washed the dishes and piled them on the drying-board, while her tall, sightless husband stood beside her and dried and stacked them with greater certainty than most healthy servant-girls could compass, Addie was troubled by the thought that something important had happened that day, if only she could determine what it was.

"Well, that's that!" she idly said again.

"That is indeed that," Phin replied with surprising decision.

"What do you mean, Phin?" she asked quickly. "Why do you agree so thoroughly with what I didn't put into words?"

He laughed gently. "The blind really see a good deal. You feel other people's feelings vibrating about you. Surely it wasn't difficult to know that your father and mother were under a terrible strain with these Bannermans to-day. I suppose the association with Burma did it, then that old horse blundering all over the shop. And, of course, it was in my very bones that you had the double worry, the responsibility over and above the grief. You could never bluff me about yourself, Addie darling."

"And you're right, Phin, you're right."

"Another funny thing. I got it—not terribly clearly, but clear enough—that there's some queer affinity between Uncle John and old Tertius. I can't explain it, but there it was. It may be, of course, simply because they belong to the same generation."

"I couldn't say anything about that," said Addie vaguely.

"No. And it's all finished now; that's the point. As soon as these people went away my own mind started to clear. I knew that your father and mother were relieved, as if something difficult was over and done with. I can't explain it . . . As if their war was finished at last."

"Yes, Phin, yes! I wonder . . . I hope so."

She lifted the heavy tray and started to carry it into the kitchen.

"What about a walk along the shore road?" she asked over her shoulder.

"You bet!" he replied, following her slowly. "I left my cigarettes in the Big Room. Now, don't you start running to get them for me. Just watch this."

As she wiped the kitchen table with a wet cloth Addie felt glad beyond the ordinary that the task was done. She hated the reek that hangs about any kitchen and scullery after the cooking of a meal ; the stink of drying dish-cloths alone was revolting. Well, it was done now. But what a queer turn-up it was that the Bannermans and the dishes they had used should symbolize for the Brydens the real end for them of the Burma campaign! All her life long she was to remember that moment of inner illumination in the kitchen of Penang Lodge when she had perceived, through the apperceptions of a blind man, how an episode of family history had been closed in an awkward meeting of near-strangers in a remote corner of Scotland.

"Ready now, Phin!" she called happily.

"All set with me," his cheerful voice replied.

Beth watched them emerge from the porch arm in arm and halt on the edge of the terrace, and she knew that Phin would be asking how the Firth looked in this afternoon hour, what of clouds and sunlight were about, and were the hills to the North standing out clear or remote in haze? Herself, she had returned to her favourite place on the garden seat with her knitting. In the warmth and peace of the garden she found such solace as she could reasonably expect of life now. In her mind was much the same sense of the autumnal as had floated about the persons of Tertius Troquair Bannerman and John Rolland Cram while they had wandered the paths an hour before ; unwittingly she shared Addie's feeling of a phase having ended.

Even so, her feminine interest in the married lovers near at hand stirred as she watched them, unobserved. These two were fully pledged to each other beyond the most cynical question. That man must have that woman near him always, and that woman, even if it was her own daughter of whom she said it, would never betray the trust of her stricken husband.

Beth considered with a matronly eye the outline of Addie's figure, revealed by the play of the breeze with her light frock. Not a sign to be seen, and never a word would you get out of

Addie until she was three months gone and certain on every physiological ground ! But it would be nice if there was a baby to come. It would be like starting afresh. He would come of rare stock ; a boy, of course. Then Davie, her poor Davie, would have to be prevented from spoiling him . . .

Beth's eyes closed in a doze, and she was only vaguely aware of the noises of the young people's feet on the path. In his upstairs room of the comfortable home he had made for himself slept her brother, John Rolland Cram, the successful Superintendent Engineer of the K. & S., for a brief space of time the fabulous uncle home from the East, but now slipping gently into the shadows of the last of the Five Arches.

THE END